I0772344

PEREGRINATION SERIES

BOOK 2

WIND

S.G. BOUDREAUX

Peregrination Series Book 2 Wind

S.G. Boudreaux

Peregrination Series Book 2

Wind

S.G. Boudreaux

ISBN 978-1-9600919-1-8 (Hardback Special Editon)
ISBN 978-1-7339636-0-2 (paperback)
ISBN 978-1-7339636-1-9 (digital)

www.zanchierpublications.com

sgb@sgboudreaux.com
www.sgboudreaux.com

This book is dedicated to my three children, Samantha, Adam, and Jasmine. May you always strive to achieve your dreams, but may your dreams align with God's plan for your present and future. All my love and prayers.

-Mama

Peregrinate : To leave one's homeland and wander for the
love of God; to travel especially on foot;
(v.)   to travel over or through something.

GLOSSARY

Capped letters are the annunciated parts of the word, while **bold** letters receive the long sound.

Bakrashan (Ba kru SHAN) Fictional city in a fifth-dimension plane on Zanchier.

big six A 1930's slang term used to describe a strong man, comparing him to the six-cylinder engines that were new at the time.

Carpasmere (Kar pas **MEE**r) Another region or city in Zanchier.

Catamount (CA ta mount) *Gorge:* Fictional river and cliff area in the Xantifal Mountains.

compass rose A symbol located on a map detailing how to determine direction such as north, south, east, or west.

Kabihanxu (ka bi HAN j**u**) The firebird's scientific name.

Pagorinx (PA gor inx) Mythical large wildcat residing in the Xantifal Mountain range in Zanchier.

Scaithers (SK**A** ther) A band of cutthroat outlaws that reside on Zanchier.

spindrifts spray blown from waves during a storm a sea.

Tarphamor Horn (TAR fa moor) horn of an animal resembling a ram native to Zanchier.

Xantifal Mountains (ZAN ti fal) Where Oz's treehouse is located on Zanchier.

Zanchier (Zan **KEER**) Fictional country in a fifth-dimension plane somewhere in the universe.

This book series is a work of fiction. Although it is based upon some biblical truths, all characters are fictional and in no way represent any living or deceased persons. Any similarity is purely coincidental.

AUTHOR'S NOTE

First let me start by saying that book 2 in the Peregrination Series will begin with the introduction of several new characters with whom we will take spectacular journeys. However, do not fear, for we haven't forgotten about our old friends from book 1. Heavens no! We open our next story with a few new Peregrines and Dragoman and their stories of life and travels before and during peregrinations. It won't be long before we return to our favorite heroes and heroines from book 1. So sit back, relax, and prepare yourself to take another grand journey through time with friends new and old. I hope you enjoy this second book, *Wind,* in the five-book series entitled the Peregrination Series.

PROLOGUE

The whole of the earth is being plagued by more and more violent storms. Man's greed and sinful nature are causing dishevelment upon the earth. Violence, rage, intolerance, hatred, and murder are just a few of the things that are happening at an alarming rate. The more evil that plagues the world, the more violent and frequent the storms become.

There are those called by God to battle the great evil taking place. These chosen are called Peregrines, and they travel the worlds through portals generated at the peak of the strongest storms. There are also those known as the Dragoman, who lead and guide the Peregrines on these missions from God.

It is the job of the Peregrines to complete these missions and stop the destruction of all mankind. Not only do they traverse space and time through storm portals, but along the way they must also battle demons that will do anything to stop the progression to save the worlds.

Seth Jager, Jason Marshal, Alec Chevalier, and Odessa Megalos, led by Simon Lane, are just a few of the brave men and women whom God has picked to do just that. Their stories and adventures started with book 1 and continue into book 2.

Seth was torn apart from his wife of only seven hours during the great San Francisco earthquake of 1906. He was transported into the year 1500 BC to Simon Lane's safe house on the border of Garganthera at Barrier's Edge. Unknown to him, Caroline, also chosen by God, was transported into the year 1580 AD to Dover, England.

Told by his Dragoman leader that God had never before chosen two people from the same era, let alone a husband and wife, Seth is encouraged to accept that he will never see Caroline again. Seth is told that, given the magnitude of the storm that hit California in 1906, Caroline was most likely dead. Caroline has no one other than a sixteen-year-old girl and an old book to guide her and must figure out on her own how to function in this new world of hers. Adjusting to their new lives with no choice either way, they have made new friends as close as any family and now peregrinate to save the world.

Book 2 picks up where we left Seth, Jason, and Alec searching for the eleventh Peregrine in Dover, England. They found her but then missed her and her unknown traveling companion by just a few minutes as the two women peregrinated through a time portal to an unknown land. Both Seth and Caroline were unaware that those few minutes could have reunited them.

Their stories continue here with many new Peregrines, Dragoman, and villains whom I hope you will enjoy reading about. I know I have my favorite characters, and I hope that if you don't already, you will very soon.

Before I formed you in the womb I knew you, and before you were born I consecrated you; I appointed you a prophet to the nations.

Jeremiah 1:5 NRSV

Chapter 1

Grenoble, France, Maritime Alps, 2018

Nicholas Turner and Sean Doran did their best to instruct Wade Connolly in the art of swordplay, but the young man, although athletic, just could not seem to master wielding a sword—or a bow, for that matter. Both Nicholas and Sean had been peregrinating for years and had experience training new Peregrines in the skills needed to survive this way of life. But the newcomer just couldn't seem to grasp the skills needed to fight. Wade had been with them for a total of four months and still had not picked up the necessary skill sets. Nicholas was beginning to wonder if he was really meant to be a Peregrine. Perhaps the young man was meant to be a Dragoman instead? He would have to speak with his mentor, Prisca, about it when they returned to the river camp at Barrier's Edge where her safe house was located.

Prisca Delacroix was a Dragoman and very French. She had been Nicholas's mentor since he first peregrinated eleven years ago. When Sean Doran joined them six years later, Prisca paired them together for time-jumping since Peregrines weren't allowed to go on missions alone anymore. Many years ago several Peregrines went missing, never to be seen or heard from again. Since that time everyone had to have at least one partner. Now, thanks to Ryan Halloran's new chip technology, they had a way to track the Peregrines and Dragoman alike.

Wade sighed heavily. "I'm sorry, Nick, I just don't understand why I can't get what you're trying to teach me." Frustration laced his words and body language. "In high school I was a football player, good enough that my parents had hoped I'd be accepted into college football. You'd think I could do this stuff!" The young man ran his hands through his thick, short, sandy brown hair in aggravation.

"Don't concern yourself about it, Wade. We'll get it figured out. I'll speak with Prisca when we get back to camp. She'll know what to do." Nick patted the young man on the back to reassure him and decided to call training done for the day. They had been at it since midmorning, and it was now three in the afternoon. Wade was a strong young man of nineteen, but his coordination was lacking. He seemed to be a very simple-minded fellow, with a heart as big as anyone Nick had ever known, and he had been around a lot of different people in his lifetime.

Nicholas had been a high school teacher before his peregrination years, so he knew that Wade's intelligence wasn't up to the normal standards. He wasn't ignorant, just simple, perhaps having had one too many concussions due to his, or his parents, sport of choice.

Nick noticed the young man's sensitivity to the pain and suffering of animals shortly after Wade arrived. He and Sean had taken Wade hunting for food when they spotted a deer. Upon Sean shooting the animal, Wade's eyes filled with tears when he saw the dead doe. He tried to play it off as dirt blowing into his face, but Nick knew better. Being a teacher he had spent most of his time around kids of all ages. He knew how to spot emotions that most people tended to overlook. Especially since he had suffered more than his fair share of heartaches.

Yes, Nick's personal demons went way back. He was drafted into the Vietnam War as a young man fresh out of high school. He had been overseas only a year when he lost his right leg above the knee. After a lengthy hospital stay, Nick lived with his parents until he could learn to handle getting around with one leg. He then decided to go to the local community college close to his parents' home to earn his teaching degree. While there, he met and fell in love with Jenny Owens. They dated for a year and then married. After only a few short months, Jenny became pregnant, but Cassie, their only child, passed away at the age of eight.

Cassie had been diagnosed with a very rare disease that was a result of a genetic disorder caused by a deformity on the father's side. There was no cure at the time, and Cassie's death left Nicholas hollow and angry. He withdrew from everyone, including his wife, and she eventually left him. He then threw himself into his work as a high school science teacher, drank too much, and wanted nothing at all to do with God. But God called him into peregrination and marked him with the symbol for Gad as one of "The Twelve." With everything he had witnessed while time-jumping, Nicholas couldn't deny the existence of God. He may not be happy about it yet, still angry over the cards he had been dealt all his life, but this existence was much better than the one he had left behind. Plus, he had a state-of-the-art prosthetic made specifically for him by Ryan Halloran, which was almost as good as his real leg. Ryan was an amazing designer when it came to technology, and Nick was very grateful for it.

When he first peregrinated no one could really understand why God would call a one-legged man into battle. But Prisca had told him that they must trust God. He knew what He was doing; He was God after all. Fortunately, when Prisca found Nick, she had had the good sense to call on Ryan immediately for help. By the time Nick came out of PS and had the time to absorb what had happened to him and the strength to begin training, Ryan had a prosthetic made and delivered. The first prosthetic wasn't perfect, but after a few tries, Ryan was able to develop one that was comfortable and would allow Nick to train like anyone else. The finished product was far superior to anything that Nick had ever seen or could ever imagine.

Nick and Sean, being the two oldest Peregrines under Prisca's mentorship, travel with others due to the status and untrained abilities of the other Peregrines. They are also the only two from Prisca's group that have a mark of "The Twelve." Wade is the newest addition to the group, but Dinah Adams, who is Nick's new partner, and Kristen Wright, who is Sean's, have both been peregrinating about a year. Prisca paired them based on age, stating that they would probably have an easier time getting along with someone closer to their own age. Dinah, who is thirty-four, is closer to Nick's age of forty-three. Sean and Kristen are both in their early twenties. Wade hasn't been allowed to peregrinate on missions yet due to his lack of skills.

All the Peregrines had recently returned from an all-out manhunt through Dover, England, in the years 1540-1590, looking for a new Peregrine who the Dragoman believed to be one of the final Twelve. The unknown person was dubbed "Eleven" by the Peregrines since no one knew of her existence at that time, only her peregrination order.

Prisca had just received word from Simon Lane that one of his groups had located a young woman they thought was Eleven but she had disappeared through a portal during a storm. They had been successful only in finding out her name, which was Bridget Burke, and that she traveled with another woman, whom the locals in Dover had identified as the girl's aunt. They had no description of the woman or information about her other than her relationship to Eleven.

Now the Peregrines awaited new information from Safra Driscoll to tell them where Eleven and her aunt may have time-jumped to. So until then, with no other missions to go on or artifacts to find, the Peregrines would spend their time close to the Dragoman safe house, training and gathering food and supplies to see them through the winter.

Prisca's safe house, like the safe houses of most Dragoman, sits on Barrier's Edge. Hers happened to be in the mountains surrounded by nature. Prisca was a true nature buff and loved the seasons that living in the mountains brought with it. Her home, like the others, was in the fourth dimension, just outside a third-dimension location where supplies could be easily accessed when the need arose. Prisca enjoyed the technology that came with living in a later time period, and so her place was just outside the modern city of Grenoble, in the Maritime Alps, where France and Italy border, in the year 2018. Her home stood at an elevation of approximately seven hundred feet and bordered the Isere River, allowing her all the amenities that nature had to offer.

"You're back from training already?" Prisca asked in her thick French accent as the five Peregrines walked into camp. She had been outside tending to her flowers.

"Yes, we decided to call it a day." Nicholas stopped in front of Prisca and, keeping his voice low so the others wouldn't hear him said, "When you get time there is a matter that I wish to discuss with you in private." He didn't want to give poor Wade a bigger complex than he already had, and there was no reason for him—or anyone else for that matter—to know that he would be the topic of their discussion.

"All right, how about after dinner? Meet me on the fourth-floor conservatory deck, say around seven?" Prisca replied.

"That will be fine. Right now I think I'll hit the shower and wash off some of this sweat and grime." Nick gave a slight grin, then turned and went into the four story, six-thousand-square-foot home that was Prisca's safe house.

Prisca's home was a combination of a log cabin and a modern style dwelling with a glass conservatory serving as the fourth floor. A large stone fireplace ran the height of the house and sat in the direct center of the home, with special duct work to carry warmth between each floor and into every room of the large dwelling.

Each floor was set apart for certain things and consisted of fifteen hundred square feet of living space.

On the bottom floor were the living and dining rooms, the kitchen, an office, two full bathrooms, and rooms for archives, artifacts, mapping, and bedrooms to accommodate the help.

The second floor was a recreation area with a pool table, a foosball table, an air hockey table, board games, a chess board, darts, a theater, and a bar. Since no one really drank alcohol here, the bar held water, juices, and sodas, with a few bottles of wine that Prisca enjoyed on occasion. This floor also had two bathrooms.

The third floor had eight bedrooms with their own bathrooms and, in the center, a commons room, which offered several couches and comfortable, roomy chairs, a coffee table, a few end tables, and several bookcases loaded with all manner of books for leisure reading or learning. The bedrooms were on the outside perimeter of the floor, and in each, one wall served as a huge window with a sliding glass door opening to the third-floor balcony. Each bedroom also had a skylight with a staircase that extended upward to the fourth-floor conservatory's open deck, also surrounded by a balcony with a handrail.

The conservatory was where Prisca grew her own organic vegetables and fruits, as well as some of her favorite flowers and herbs for medicinal purposes. She also had two telescopes, one on each of two corners of the deck, for viewing and recording the stars and any unusual activity in space. Because her home was so large, a few retired Peregrines and Dragoman also stayed on to help her with the chores. There was a housekeeper, a cook, and a groundskeeper, all people Prisca once mentored or who had themselves mentored others years before.

Nick showered, changed, and headed up the staircase through the glass skylight door onto the conservatory deck to meet with Prisca. She held a bottle of her favorite, Italian, burgundy-blend, wine and poured them both a glass.

"So, what is this important conversation about that we needed to have in private?" Prisca handed Nicholas the glass of wine and took a seat in one of the Adirondack chairs scattered about the conservatory deck.

"Thanks." Taking the glass and then a sip of the wine he continued, "It concerns Wade. We have been diligent in his training since he arrived four months back, unless we were out on missions. But the kid just can't seem to get it. Maybe he was meant to be a Dragoman instead?"

"Yes, I have noticed his struggles with the training. I've never encountered this problem before. Usually when people first peregrinate, they don't have issues learning what God called them to. He has always equipped them with the abilities and training that they need. I would think if he were to be a Dragoman, he would have some gift or skill set in that area, but I have not seen anything that would lead me to believe that either. I have noticed his propensity toward nature and that when he is out in the woods, the forest creatures do not fear him. They just stand and watch him as if he belongs there. Perhaps I need to search the archives to see if they say anything about the untrainable." Prisca paused; her brow furrowed in concentration.

"I will send a grid message to the other Dragoman and inquire of them about the subject as well. Simon and Nuncio have been at this a bit longer than I have, so if anyone knows anything about it, they would. You know, come to think of it, he didn't seem to be affected by Peregrine Sickness like the rest of you either. That struck me as strange then, but I just brushed it off as his being fortunate. Now, with further thought, there could be something to it."

"Perhaps? It does seem strange that he wasn't afflicted with PS at all. Like you, I just assumed he was lucky as well. I'm really curious to hear what Simon and Nuncio have to say on the matter myself. What do you say we send them a grid message soon?" Nick said, leaning against the railing. He watched Prisca as he took a sip from the glass of wine.

"I agree. The sooner we get some information on this the better. He has already been here for four months and has not taken to training of any kind. We need to know what we are supposed to train this kid for." Prisca stood and drained her glass of wine. "I think I will go write that inquiry right now. I'll speak with you about it more once I have a reply."

Prisca and Nick walked to the main stairwell that wove its way through the top three floors from the balconies, which allowed easy access to the levels without the necessity of using a doorway to enter and exit them. There were separate, offset entries to the main house with steps to every level, but the balcony stairwell made access and navigating quick and easy.

Entering the second story, Prisca continued down to her office; using an interior staircase; on the first level to compose the message, while Nick stayed on the second floor where the rest of the group were hanging out, currently enthralled by one of Sean's far-fetched stories while playing a game of pool.

"Sean, what tall tale are you telling this time?" Nick asked, a sly smile gracing his lips as he approached the group.

"I'm sure I have no idea what you mean, sir," Sean protested, smiling broadly as he leaned over the table to take a shot into a corner pocket.

"Right, I'm sure you've been completely truthful about all of our adventures so far." Nick grinned knowingly at his young friend as he took a seat in one of the overly large chairs. Sean was a great kid who just liked to embellish their peregrination adventure stories for fun. He was a gifted storyteller, very well spoken and very charismatic. People just seemed to be drawn to him. The addition of his Scottish accent tended to help as well. Not to mention he was a very good-looking young man and he knew it, which seemed to get him into trouble with young women a little too often. Sometimes it was a chore keeping him on this side of the barrier.

Nick had noticed that there was one young woman in particular, however, who seemed to see through all of Sean's charms quite well right from the beginning. Kristen appeared to be put off by Sean almost as soon as she arrived. She was always agitated by him and his unique personality, which made their paired status a bit tough for both of them. Sean's cockiness and her attitude toward him made for some rough missions in the past. For one thing, Kristen had a hard time following orders from Sean, which had caused quite a few mishaps on missions. *It's as though she barely tolerates him.* He tried to keep a close eye on their relationship to make sure things didn't get out of hand. But he could only do so much since he wasn't on missions with them. *Besides, they are both adults and need to learn to work out their differences on their own. Maybe that's why Prisca paired them together,* Nick speculated. *She must have sensed the tension right from the start and decided to make them work it out from the get-go.*

Nick watched Kristen's facial expressions as she sat and read a book, trying to ignore Sean as he continued telling the others the rest of his story. Kristen's body was rigid, and she looked uncomfortable. No one could mistake the look of irritation on her face as she rolled her eyes at his exuberant anecdotes of peregrinations past.

Nick also noticed that Sean would glance over at Kristen and smile ever so slightly at her obvious discomfort. Nick believed that Sean truly enjoyed ruffling her feathers. These two hardheaded kids were in for a rude awakening one day. If they didn't learn to get along soon, there was no telling what kind of trouble their attitudes were going to get them into.

He and Dinah on the other hand got along fine and worked together very well. They had quickly bonded as partners and anticipated each other's actions well when on missions. Nick looked on her as a sister. He had a feeling that she was interested in more than a friendship with him, but Nick wasn't looking for a relationship; not to mention he just didn't feel that way about her. His last relationship hadn't worked out so well, and he had no intention of ever falling in love or marrying again. Besides, he was too broken mentally and emotionally to be of any use to anyone. His failed marriage had taught him that.

No, he didn't need any more heartache. He still thought of, and missed, his little Cassie more than words could say. She would have been nineteen years old by now. He would not allow himself to feel that much again.

"You look serious. What's on your mind?" Dinah asked. She had strolled across the room and perched in one of the large chairs next to him.

Lost in his memories, he hadn't heard or seen her sit down.

"Nothing." He shook off the dark thoughts. "Just lost in the past."

"Yeah, I know what you mean. I've only been at this for a year compared to your eleven, and I still have trouble. I guess that means the past still haunts you no matter how long you do this peregrinating thing." Dinah sank back into the chair and tucked her feet up underneath her.

Nick didn't correct her thinking when it came to what haunted his past. He had never shared his life story with anyone. Everyone of course asked about his leg; that was unavoidable. But he offered nothing about his past other than that he had been a high school science teacher before peregrinating. He wasn't ready to talk about his divorce or daughter with anyone.

"Hey, Nick, you want to play the next round?" Sean yelled across the room to his friend.

Nick looked up at him. "No thanks, Sean. It's been a long day, and I think I'm going to retire to my room." He stood and stretched a bit. "Good night, everyone. I'll see you all tomorrow morning."

Everyone chimed in with a "good night," and Nick headed to his room. His prosthetic provided an amazing and comfortable fit, but his leg needed a breather every once in a while, and he was ready to take the thing off for the night. He had spent so many years just using a crutch or wheelchair that it had taken his leg a while to get used to the prosthetic. He couldn't afford one when he returned home from the war and made do with what was available to him. When he was on missions, he had to leave it on all the time. Here at Prisca's safe house, he was able to relax and could remove it without fear of attack. It slid on easily, but it did take a minute or so to get it into the correct position.

Nick sat on his bed and removed the prosthetic, then put it against the wall next to the pair of forearm crutches he kept available for when he wasn't wearing it so he could still get around if needed. After changing into his night clothes, he leaned back into the thick, soft feather pillows that each room contained and gazed out the large glass window that formed the wall along the right side of his bed. As he lay there looking up into the night sky, watching the stars twinkle in the heavens, Nick thought about creation and God. He knew God was real, but he just didn't feel like talking to him. God never seemed to care about him much in his earlier years, and since God hadn't had time for him then, Nick didn't much feel like giving God his time now. The way Nick saw it, he was doing plenty for God as it was. Lying there quietly, he soon drifted off into a troubled sleep.

For, "Everyone who calls on the name
of the Lord will be saved."

Romans 10:13 NIV

Chapter 2

Barrier's Edge, Garganthera, Simon Lane's safe house

Simon sat at his desk looking through archives once again in search of information he wasn't sure existed. It seemed that God had dropped all manner of new and perplexing problems into their laps and left them to figure things out. First was the manner in which Seth had arrived, appearing in a portal with Jason from a completely different dimension and time era. Then came finding number Eleven, who was identified as Bridget Burke, traveling with an unknown figure who could quite possibly be a new Dragoman or Peregrine as well. The Peregrines needed to find them once again and bring them on board with all the others to prepare for the final battle.

Then he received a message just last night from Prisca that they have a young man who is untrainable as a Peregrine or a Dragoman and has also shown some peculiar traits. So far none of the Dragoman had found any answers to the questions. Perhaps he should call another Dragoman council meeting to discuss the current problems in person. Maybe the extensive archival library at Reader's Island still held the answers. They just hadn't found them yet.

There was a knock at Simon's door. "Yes, come in." Simon answered without taking his eyes from the book in his hands.

Odessa stood at the door of the office. "Simon, do you have a minute?"

"Certainly, Odessa, come in." He looked up from the book.

"I need your help with something. I had a dream last night. It was quite unusual, and I'm not sure what it means. I'm hoping God has given you the answer." She entered the room, and at Simon's gesture of invitation, she sat across from him at his desk.

"Well, it has been awhile since God has communicated with me through a dream. Tell me about it, and we will see if it is from God." Simon closed the book after inserting a page marker and then turned his full attention to Odessa.

"Well, in the dream, I was standing on the edge of a cliff. I couldn't see what was below me, but I could hear what sounded like the pounding of the ocean's waves against the rock cliff. Suddenly the view changed, and I was inside, in something like an ancient temple. Inside the temple were five beautifully decorated books sitting atop pedestals. Each book had a lock, but I had no keys. However, I had the feeling that each one was extremely important and held a vast amount of information that was imperative to something. Then suddenly, I was in a dense forest and I was surrounded by five beautiful waterfalls. At the bottom of the waterfalls where they connected with the river was something that shone brightly up from the bottom. What is even more interesting is that the waterfalls, even though they were encircling me, seemed to all be in a different location. What I mean to say is, the vegetation and landscape around each one was different. I remember everything very vividly, as though I had actually seen it all before. I could draw the waterfalls for you, but I'm not much of an artist."

"Hmm, that's all very interesting. You know, you may not be much of an artist, but Safra is. Perhaps we should get with her, and you could instruct her in the drawings." Simon sat quietly a minute and thought as he leaned back in his chair, silently praying to God for an answer.

"Odessa, I do believe that God has given you this dream. And I believe it could be the answer to all the strange things that have been happening lately. We seem to have a series of unanswerable riddles and problems, and I believe this dream is God's answer to them. I believe that the things you saw in your dream are either representative of, or actual places and things that God wants us to locate. The books may be other archives that were lost or instruction manuals from God Himself. The waterfalls may be the locations of the books, or perhaps the keys that unlock the books. The cliff and the sound of the waves; I'm not quite sure. It could be that you were standing at the top of the waterfalls for some reason, above where we may find either the books or the keys. I'm also not sure about the shining below the surface of the water at the base of the falls. We need to go over this dream carefully again, and I'll record everything you've said in this year's archive book. We don't want to leave out even the smallest of details."

Simon and Odessa spent the better part of an hour going over the dream again and recording everything Odessa saw, heard, and felt in the dream. Simon had also called for Safra, who sat and listened as she sketched with her colored pencils what Odessa described about the waterfalls, the appearance of the books, the inside of the temple, and what she could see when she was standing upon the cliff's edge.

Simon truly believed that God had given them the location of something, perhaps more artifacts that were essential for the final battle. He would certainly need to call another Dragoman council meeting now to discuss this dream of Odessa's. He spent the remainder of the morning writing and sending out the grid messages to all the Dragoman, calling a meeting at Reader's Island for the very same evening. He felt an urgency about it that he couldn't explain. The time was actually perfect for him to be gone anyhow since there were no Peregrines out on missions. They were all waiting on God to give Safra the new location for finding Bridget Burke and her companion. He believed that all the other Dragoman were waiting as well.

Having finished sending the grid message, Simon joined the others for lunch. As they ate, he discussed his findings with them and the need for calling a Dragoman council meeting, citing the unknown woman with Eleven, an unusual situation with a new Peregrine at Prisca's, and Odessa's dream. He still did not mention Seth's unusual arrival. No need to make the man wonder over something he himself wasn't sure held any strange circumstances.

"I'll head to the cave and be off for Reader's Island after lunch," he concluded. "Odessa, Seth, I wish for the two of you to join me on the trip to the island. I have a very strong feeling that I am to bring you along with me. We'll also take along the pictures Safra drew and the notes that I made in the archive book to distribute to the others. We need all members working on this information."

Odessa relished the thought of the beautiful tropical island. "Sure thing, Simon, I'm in. It's been years since I've been to the island. I certainly wouldn't mind visiting there again."

"I've heard Jason briefly mention it the last time you went. I have no other plans," Seth said a bit jokingly.

Simon smiled at the two of them. "Wonderful, now go and get packed, and we'll head out shortly. We'll only be there for a day or two at the most, so pack lightly. Oh and Seth, there's no need for weapons where we will be going, so you don't have to pack anything of the sort."

Simon stood. "I'm headed off to gather some needed materials. I'll meet the two of you in about an hour in the living room." With that, he left the room, headed in the direction of his office.

"This ought to be an interesting trip for you, Seth," Jason said, still sitting at the table and sipping from his glass of lemonade.

"Why is that?"

"Can I speak to you in private for just a minute?"

"Sure, let's go into the living room," Seth answered as the two of them walked out of the kitchen.

"I just need to explain some things to you, Seth, before you leave. Reader's Island is different from most other places. You'll see what I mean when you get there. Being a sailor, you've surely heard of the Bermuda Triangle?"

"Yes, who hasn't?"

"Reader's Island is located directly in the middle of the Bermuda Triangle and surrounded by the barrier. It is different there, though. The barrier allows quick access to any place and any time period at the wave of a hand. It can be a very tempting prospect, so just make sure your heart doesn't overrule your head while you're there. It is easy travel one way only. Getting back to the island, or anywhere for that matter, works the same as it does here. With no coordinates you can get lost in time forever, traveling from place to place, never really knowing where or when you are in time." Jason watched Seth's face carefully. Then he leaned forward and his voice took on an added urgency. "Seth, the reason I'm saying this is because I know you still think of Caroline, and I'm pretty sure you've been trying to devise a plan to get back to her. But you don't even know if she survived the quake. Things may not work out the way you think they will, and God could just yank you right back here anyway. Or you could have all the consequences from rash decisions to deal with and never be seen or heard from again. The island has a lot of temptations. Just remember why God brought you here in the first place and keep your focus. The world needs you, man. *We* need you. You're crucial to these missions. The fact that Simon is willing and ready to take you there shows great trust and respect for you on his part. Don't blow it."

Seth stared at Jason for a moment, noting the sincerity in his eyes and voice.

"I understand what you're saying. Thanks for the heads up. I appreciate what you're telling me." Seth shook his friend's hand. "Promise, I'll stay focused."

"Oh, and if you see Ryan Halloran, ask him if he's made any progress with that device we asked him to make."

"Sure thing, Jason."

Seth left the room to pack for the trip ahead. He had to admit he was anxious about the island and what it was all about. And even though he thought about Caroline with almost every free moment he had, Jason's words echoed through his head. His friend had read him correctly. Jason apparently sensed how much Seth loved and missed Caroline. This could be the opportunity he had been waiting for, but according to what Jason said, it could very well end in disaster. Not just for him but for everyone he had grown to care about as if they were family.

On the walk to the hidden cave and the Tesla coils, Simon spoke to Seth as Odessa followed quietly behind.

"I'm not sure if you've heard much about Reader's Island, Seth, but I need to clarify a few things before we get there." Simon navigated the well-known forest path with ease.

"If you mean to tell me about the barrier and the ease of travel, you don't have to worry. Jason already gave me a pep talk."

"I see that Jason has as much foresight as any of the Dragoman. I often wonder about his calling to peregrination instead." Simon smiled at Seth. "I've sensed that you still struggle deeply with the loss of Caroline. I was worried about taking you to the island, but I hope you understand that just because it is a possibility you could get back to her, it doesn't mean it would actually work. You couldn't go before the quake because your past self would already be there. And there's no way of knowing if she survived the earthquake to return to a later time. I'm afraid that if you attempt to travel back, Seth, you would be lost to us forever."

"I understand, Simon, and you're right. I have been trying to find a way to get back to her. I still hold out hope that somehow God will just bring her back into my life. I know you tell me that it is impossible or has never happened, but I just feel her presence so strongly still. I don't believe she died in that earthquake, and I don't feel like she's forever lost to me."

"Hope is a glorious thing, my boy. It's one of the few things that is hard to take from a man. It drives us on toward a particular goal, keeps us strong in the face of adversity, and lifts us up in times of struggle. Just don't confuse it with a strong will. That could land you in a heap of trouble." Simon's tight-lipped smile underscored his words as he peered at Seth over his spectacles, the way he often did.

"You have my word, Simon. I won't try anything stupid. Promise." Seth fully intended to stick true to his word. As much as he would like to try it, what his friends said to him made sense.

They walked the remainder of the way in silence, then time-jumped via the Tesla coils and walked out of another set of coils on the other end inside a round, stone, room. That wasn't something that Seth had experienced before. He had to admit that traveling by coil without all the weather effects was pretty nice. It certainly made for a much more pleasant trip.

Seth, Simon, and Odessa climbed the steps upward and exited just outside the bottom of a grand lighthouse, which appeared to be several hundred years old, although well kept. It sat on the edge of a cliff overlooking the sea. As Seth looked over the edge of the cliff, he saw waves crashing on the land. Large smooth and jagged rocks sat in the water quite a ways out. But nothing past that would be a danger to a ship other than the island itself, and the island appeared to be large enough for any sailor to spot without the need of a lighthouse to guide him.

Seth could also see the barrier and how different it appeared here. It seemed as though the whole world was visible through the many, little, opaque-looking, windows in the sky that surrounded the island. Seth stopped and stared in wonder.

Odessa also stopped and turned to Seth as he looked around at the odd appearance of the barrier. "Strange looking isn't it?"

"That's an understatement." He gave a half-smile, glancing down at her. Then he quickly lifted his face to look skyward once again.

Odessa chuckled. She explained how the barrier worked from the island. Then she repeated Jason's warning that a return would not work the same way.

Seth and Odessa followed Simon as he walked toward the interior of the island, and Seth was struck by the sheer beauty of the place. The temperature was perfect, the animals didn't seem frightened or bothered by them, there was a constant breeze off the ocean, and the sun felt warm and soothing upon his bare skin. The smell of tropical flowers filled the air, and the trees and bushes were all loaded with every kind of fruit and nut imaginable. *This must be what paradise is like!*

He gazed in admiration at the beauty of his surroundings, noting the boats docked out in the water, the Adirondack chairs and loungers that sat by the water's edge, the white sands of the beaches, and the hammocks swaying in the breeze among the palm trees. He felt a serene sort of peace that he had never felt before. No wonder it took a considerable amount of trust to bring people here, as Jason suggested. Seth could imagine that no one would ever want to leave.

"Tell me something." Seth turned to Odessa. "Is it very hard to get people to leave this place?"

"Oh yes!" she answered with a laugh. "The Dragoman have only brought the strongest Peregrines here so far for fear that many would refuse to do just that! This place was created for us Peregrines and Dragoman by God himself as a place of respite and contemplation. There are many other amenities that you have yet to see and discover. You can consider it a great honor that Simon believes in you enough to bring you here so early in your journey. Only the most trusted Peregrines have had this placed revealed to them. Not everyone knows of its existence."

Seth considered what she said about the amount of trust it took on Simon's part to bring him along. He looked at the older man who walked just ahead of them. He had never felt so much respect for another human being, or ever received as much as he did from these people; except, of course, Caroline.

He was beginning to understand how her faith had affected her life and how it affected those who came into contact with her. It was the same with his newfound family. That was the only way he could describe them. They treated him the way a family should. Unearned grace, respect, faith, and trust for things that he had not proven himself capable of yet. That was what Simon gave to him today. Complete faith and trust that he would do as was expected of him by God and his new family.

Seth finally understood what it meant to be a part of something bigger than just himself. None of these people chose this life, yet they served with all that was in them because of a love for a God that asked them to. Seth's head began to reel as he thought about the responsibility that his future held and about those he had become close to over the last few months. It was hard to believe that he had been a Peregrine for such a short time.

"Look there, Seth." Odessa pointed up the gentle, sloping, hill to a beautiful garden area surrounded on three sides by a narrow, c-shaped, building with wood-carved, lattice-panel, doors leading into multiple rooms. From what Seth could see from the c-shape, the backside of the building had large, wood-carved, lattice-panel, windows that graced the outer wall of the rooms allowing privacy, but also allowed the breeze and the elements inside the rooms as well.

"That is the prayer temple. On the other side of each one of the doors is a separate prayer room for privacy. You can also just sit on one of the several benches and chairs that you see staggered throughout the garden."

"Looks peaceful." He decided he would make a trip here later for a closer inspection while on the island.

Simon interjected, "The main house isn't far now, Seth, although it doesn't appear that you minded the three-and-a-half-mile walk inland."

"No, not at all. To say this place is beautiful is a blatant understatement. Thank you for bringing me along, Simon."

"Well, I must confess, it wasn't entirely my idea. I believe God wanted you here for some reason. He'll reveal why later, I am sure, to you, me, or Odessa."

Odessa and Seth looked at each other with raised eyebrows as they continued up the slope toward the main house that had just come into view when they rounded a stand of coconut palms and thick underbrush.

Seth was taken aback by the sheer size of the place. It looked almost like a two-story, rambling, mansion, although not quite as fancy as ones he had seen when he was younger and traveling the seas. Even so, it was spectacular in size and design.

An ornate wooden pergola covered in colorful flowers and vines provided shade for the patio area. Balconies on both of the building's two levels wrapped the entire perimeter of the Caribbean-style house. Seth thought it fit with the island so well he could almost believe it had grown on it like the foliage that surrounded it.

An older, kind-looking, woman met the group at the door.

"Simon, Odessa, good to see you." She smiled brightly. "And who might this one be?" She gestured to Seth but addressed Simon.

"This is Seth Jager, Shannon." Simon turned to introduce him. "Seth, this is Shannon. She is one of the retired Dragoman and Peregrines who stay and take care of Reader's Island."

"Nice to meet you, Shannon." Seth offered her his hand, which she took in her own.

"It's nice to meet you as well, Seth. So you're number Twelve are you? You're a big, strapping, handsome fellow, aren't you." Shannon's thick Irish accent stated rather than asked. "I haven't seen anyone your size since…well, for a very many years." She finished with a smile.

Feeling a little embarrassed about Shannon's compliment, Seth wondered what she was about to say before she changed her mind but decided to keep the thought to himself.

"Thank you, ma'am." Seth grinned at the kind woman.

"Well, come on in, you three. I'll show you two to your rooms, Simon knows where his is. We try to keep them the same for you, so that whenever you come you'll always have the same room if possible. Odessa, it's been a long while since you've been here, so I'll just show you to a new room. They've all been updated since you were last here anyway."

Shannon turned and led them up the massive staircase. Halfway up the stairs branched to either side, leading up another flight to the landing of the second floor. The stair-railing extended around the upper level of the landing allowing people to peer down to the main floor entryway. The hallway of the second floor was eight-feet wide from the railing to the outside wall, which housed three sets of patio doors perched over the main floor entryway. These doors opened onto the balcony that wrapped the second story.

As the group reached the second floor, Shannon explained that the bedrooms were all located on the outside wall, allowing for spectacular views of the island from any bedroom, as well as balcony access. She pointed to large rooms for sitting and visiting or playing a game of billiards and indicated a large reading library. She noted that six bathrooms were staggered in between the thirty bedrooms. The other four bathrooms, Shannon explained, were located on the first floor. The staff had their own quarters behind the house, accessed from the kitchen's side door entrance. Looking out one of the windows, Seth saw lovely little cottages that mimicked the main house but provided the staff with some privacy.

As she showed them to their rooms, Shannon informed them that dinner would be at six and went on her way. Seth looked around the large room and admired the beautiful, wicker-style furnishings upholstered with tropical colors. He noted that the bed was an oversized king to accommodate his height. After unpacking his one bag, which only took a minute, he opened the large French doors that led to the balcony and stepped outside. He leaned out, his hand on the heavy bamboo railing, and took a deep breath of the salty sea air. He had missed that smell and the feel of the breeze upon his skin. As he looked out over the landscape, his eyes settled on the prayer temple they had passed about fifteen minutes earlier. With almost four hours before dinner, he decided to take the opportunity to visit the temple.

Seth informed one of the housekeepers where he was headed and then walked the short distance up the hill toward the temple. He recalled a story from the Bible which he recently read, and that his grandmother once told him, about a garden where the first man and woman lived before they sinned and were cast out. She said the Bible described it as the most beautiful place on the earth and that it had been forever closed to man after he sinned against God. Seth glanced around at his surroundings, thinking that this place he was standing in must rival that garden. He had never before seen so many fruit-bearing trees, flowering shrubs and plants, and natural waterfalls all in the same place. He walked over to the oval building and peered inside several of the prayer rooms. They were all laid out the same inside, each having a small stone table against the back wall under the wood-carved latticed window, with a small mat that lay upon the floor. He supposed it was used for kneeling when praying, the way his Gran used to.

He turned to look at the garden around him as he walked among the fruit trees and soon noticed a beautiful rock waterfall in the garden's center. Running his hand underneath the clear, cool, fresh spring, he scooped a handful and sipped the sweet-tasting water. He decided to sit on a bench among the trees and flowers. A gentle breeze carried the scent of flowering trees and bushes to him, and he breathed deeply. Seth just closed his eyes and lifted his face toward the sky as warm sunlight sifted through the tree canopy above, casting light shadows behind his closed eyelids. He breathed deeply once again and realized he could sense God all around him. He thought back to earlier in the day when they were walking toward the main house and he had first realized his role here. It was at that moment that he had understood that God was as real as anyone. He knew then that he had to give up on the anger that he still felt from losing Caroline and their future together.

So, as Seth sat there, he began to truly pray as he never had. Before, Seth's prayers had been meager offerings, requests for what Seth wanted from God. He had never once asked what God wanted from him. As he sat praying, speaking to God, accepting Jesus as his Savior, he felt as though the weight of the world had been lifted off his chest. He felt a wonderfully calming peace about him, one he had never experienced before. From the time his father left them, Seth had always been aware of some sort of struggle going on inside him. Then, with all the tragedy and the rough life he led afterward, he had learned to live with daily stress, never giving God much thought until after he met Caroline.

But as he sat on the bench and absorbed the peace around him, he knew that God had sought after him his entire life, connecting him with people who would point him in the right direction. Seth sat talking to Him for the next several minutes.

"God, thank you for seeing something more in me than even I knew existed. Thank you for saving me from that earthquake and giving me another chance to truly live. I'm not exactly sure why you brought me here and chose me for this life, but I'm sure You know what You're doing. I just pray that Caroline is truly all right. I don't believe that we are done yet. I'm not sure how or when I will see her again, I just feel like I will. Thank you for that second chance as well. Thank you for dying and paying for my sins so that I don't have to."

He wasn't used to praying or talking to God, so he wasn't sure what else to say. All he knew was that things would definitely be different for him from now on. He now understood what Caroline was always telling him and what Alec experienced just a few weeks back. Seth had finally found where he belonged, and he mournfully realized it could mean a life without Caroline.

But now are they many members, yet but one body.

1 Corinthians 12:20 KJV

Chapter 3

Seth returned to the house around four with the feeling that he needed to find Odessa and explore the cliff with her. He walked through the front door of the house and was met by a woman who identified herself as Petra, one of the housekeepers. She informed him that Simon wished to meet with everyone after dinner. That left just a little over two hours to kill.

"Petra, could you tell me where I can find Odessa?"

"Yes, she's in the archival library with the others." She pointed in the direction he needed to go.

"Thank you." Seth smiled down at the woman. He walked down the hall and into the archival library. As he entered he saw quite a few people he hadn't met, all looking through archives in search of something. When Seth stepped forward, several people stopped and looked up; a few seemed taken aback. Perhaps they were overwhelmed by Seth's size. It certainly wouldn't be the first time. Seth was used to that reaction, but he still noticed it every time it happened.

"Seth lad, come, I want to introduce you to a few people. Nuncio you already know," Simon said as he pointed around the room. "This is Malachai Harel, Ryan Halloran, Vashti Mayer, and Prisca Delacroix. They are the other Dragoman who mentor other Peregrine teams."

"Hello, Seth." Malachai stretched his hand out to shake Seth's. "Sorry if our reaction when you came in seemed a bit shaken, but I don't believe any of us were prepared for what a large man you are."

"No problem. I'm used to that reaction," Seth answered with a half-smile.

Prisca stepped up to shake his hand. "My goodness, how you remind me of someone I once knew." A touch of sadness quivered in her voice and her eyes glistened with a wistful look.

"Is that a good thing or a bad thing?" Seth asked her, a little unsure how to reply.

"Oh my, I am so sorry. It is a very good thing," Prisca said with a sad smile.

"It's very nice to meet all of you, but would you all please excuse me? I need to speak with Odessa for a moment." Seth stepped away from the group.

"Odessa." Seth called to her as he crossed the room toward her. "I have a question. I keep getting the feeling that you and I should head down to the lighthouse. Do you mind taking a walk back there with me?"

"Sure thing." She laid down the book she had in her hands. "Any particular reason?" she questioned him as the two of them left the library.

"Not really. I just keep having the urge to go and take you with me." He was puzzled by the remark himself.

"Sounds like God leading you somewhere, if you ask me." A smile of excitement began to play across Odessa's face.

"Maybe." He smiled back at her.

As they walked toward the sea cliffs, they talked about the beauty of the island and the overall feeling of peace associated with it. When they reached the lighthouse, Seth, instead of walking up to the lighthouse, walked around it to the cliffs and stared over the edge. Odessa followed him to the cliff's edge and peered down. A dense fog had rolled in since their arrival earlier and blocked their view of the ocean but seemed to magnify the sound of the waves breaking against the cliffs below them.

Seth and Odessa stood still, watching, and listening.

Suddenly Odessa gasped, her eyes wide with a look of wonder. "Seth, it's just like in my dream!" She sounded almost breathless with excitement. "This is the cliff I was standing on. And the reason I could hear the waves and not see them was because of the fog. What do you think it means?"

"I'm not sure, Odessa. What happened next in your dream?" he asked as he leaned out over the cliff edge as far as he safely could.

She stood motionless with her eyes closed, obviously trying to concentrate on the dream she had just the night before. "I remember it suddenly changed to me standing inside a cave that was like a structure, almost like a temple. And I could still hear the waves breaking against the cliffs, but the sound was more muffled." She then opened her eyes to look at Seth.

"Odessa, you've been on this island before, correct?"

"Yes. Several times, but it was many years back. Why?"

"Are there any kind of caves or caverns here on Reader's Island?"

"Yes, there is!" Excitement shone in her eyes as she began to understand Seth's line of questioning. "Just a few hundred feet to the right there is a cliff spout. When the tide is high, it shoots water straight up into the air like a geyser every time a wave pounds the side of the cliff."

"Is the water level always high enough to produce the geyser?"

"No, only when the tide comes in at its highest."

"Do you know how often that happens?"

"Not really. I don't know that much about the island."

"We need to go back to the main house and talk to Simon. I think the caves below Reader's Island deserve a thorough examination. But to do that we need to find out about the tides to safely navigate the inside."

"This is so exciting! We've already figured out the first part of my dream!"

"Maybe by tomorrow morning we'll be able to get inside the caves and take a look." Seth smiled at the already exuberant Odessa.

"Oh, I hope so!" she breathed.

The look on her face made Seth think of a child on the brink of an exciting adventure. "Let's head back to the house. It's beginning to get dark, and we don't want to make everyone wait on us for dinner."

He and Odessa walked the distance back to the house in record time, partly jogging due to the excitement of the find. Odessa talked to

Seth about her dream the night before and what she saw in the cavern temple. They were eager to tell Simon and would hopefully get a chance to speak to him after dinner just before the council meeting.

They arrived back at the house just in time to wash up a bit before dinner was served, but with not nearly enough time to talk to Simon first. After dinner the entire group made their way to the council meeting room, where they could stroll around or sit and visit while they waited for Petra and Shannon to bring the coffee and cake.

Odessa and Seth pulled Simon to the side to fill him in on their earlier find. They told him how she recognized the cliff as the one from her dream and how Seth believed there could be something in the caves that ran through the cliff below the lighthouse.

"My word! I think you two have really stumbled onto something here. You know, I've always wanted to explore those caves, I've just never had the opportunity or a reason. It looks like God revealed His purpose for having me bring you along, Seth." Simon grinned, but his features soon turned thoughtful as he began to ponder what they might find.

"Simon, there is one problem. If we don't time the tides correctly, we could all drown down there." Seth's strong jawline tightened with the thought.

"Yes, I'm afraid you're right. Perhaps we can look through the reading library upstairs after the meeting and see what we can find about the local tides. I'll also ask Nuncio if he or anyone else knows about them. Perhaps the groundskeepers will know when they shift."

The housekeepers returned with the after-dinner coffee and cake, and Nuncio called the council meeting to come to order as everyone gathered around the table to sit down.

"We have several new things to discuss tonight." Nuncio took a seat at the head of the table. "First, we all know the young girl identified as Eleven we were looking for, disappeared again without any knowledge as to where. Second, we still have the matter that was on the table at the last meeting that we have yet to find an answer for."

Nuncio seemed to be deliberately vague about this matter, and Seth wondered why. Glancing around, he noticed several people looking at him and then hurriedly averting their eyes. He wondered briefly if *he* was the second issue to be discussed. He'd gathered before at Simon's shortly after his arrival, that there was something unusual about his appearance as a Peregrine. Then his attention was caught by Nuncio's words as he continued speaking.

"Third, we seem to have a new problem concerning a young man under Prisca's mentorship. He seems to be untrainable as a Peregrine or a Dragoman. This is baffling to say the least. We've never had a problem like this before, and we need to find out what it all means."

"Nuncio," Simon said standing, "I need to address the group for a moment."

"Certainly, Simon."

"Thank you." Simon cleared his throat and began. "Most of you know Odessa here." He gestured to her as he continued. "She had a dream last night. I believe that what she saw was not a figurative dream but one of actualities. She saw a cliff, five books in a sort of temple, and five waterfalls, each with a shining light at its base. Now, she and Seth have already located the cliff. It's here on the island, out where the lighthouse sits. Seth also believes that the caves that run below it through the cliff may hold another clue. I think it's a good place to start. I believe that God has provided, through Odessa's dream, the answer to some of these questions that Nuncio mentioned. We want to see if we can find an opening, if one exists, so we can explore the caverns. Our main concern, however, is the tides. Nuncio, do you know what time of day they rise and fall?"

"Yes, they rise about 12:00 a.m. and again about 12:00 p.m. The Spring tides which are what cause the geyser. At the current time we are experiencing neap tides which occur on the first and third quarter of the moon. When this is the case there is no great difference in the rise or fall of the tides. And if I'm not mistaken, we are in the third quarter stage of the moon right now. Which means, the caves do not fill up enough for the geyser to occur, and so there should be no serious flooding inside."

"Making it possible to explore the caves safely," Simon said excitedly, glad that Nuncio's lengthy explanation was over.

"It certainly should. However, I don't believe anyone has ever been down there before," Nuncio replied.

"Well, obviously someone was. If what I hope to find is down there, then someone had to place the items in their current resting place." Simon glanced at his friend with a mischievous smile. "I say we plan an excursion to explore them early in the morning tomorrow. As soon as the tides are almost out and we are sure it's safe to enter."

There was an excited buzz running around the table as almost everyone chimed in with a yes, exclaiming they would be up early and ready to go.

"Now about the other items still in question. We need to locate Bridget Burke again somehow."

Seth listened as Prisca replied, looking around the table in anticipation of answers, her words for some reason sounding as though they dripped with hatred.

"Is it just me or does her name ring a familiar bell with anyone else?"

Simon answered, responding to the tension beginning to build around the table as people fidgeted in their chairs. "Yes, the surname has not escaped my attention. However, it is unlikely. From what I understand, Dragoman or Peregrine traits do not pass from generation to generation, so let's not jump to conclusions, shall we?"

Seth couldn't help noticing the anger and tension obviously growing as whispered memories of the past trickled through the group, mainly from all the retired people working here on the island.

Simon continued. "Perhaps we'll find some answers to some of the questions tomorrow. I suggest we reconvene the meeting after we are able to explore the caves in the morning."

"Yes, I agree with Simon," Nuncio put forth, seeming anxious to end the proceedings before a verbal war could start.

Everyone agreed and the meeting was called complete until the following day.

Seth leaned over to Simon and asked, "What was with all the agitation I sensed brewing at the mention of Bridget's last name?"

"Well, now that is a long story. The abridged version is this. There was once a Dragoman named Hiram Burke who betrayed everyone years ago. Let's just say his name brings about bad memories for all of us who have been around for more than twelve years."

"I don't remember anything connected with that name, and I have been doing this for fifteen years," Odessa remarked, a bit confused.

"Yes, but if you remember, the first two years of your peregrination journey were spent at the monastery. You wouldn't have known anything about it. It happened months before I found you," Simon reminded her.

"Seth, do you remember when I told you that there were betrayers in our midst?"

Seth nodded his head yes.

"Well, we had one many years ago. Some very bad things happened. I pray this young woman is *not* related to Burke or she may have a very hard time of it once she is found. These people here are all Christians, but they are also human. And what transpired thirteen years ago is not something anyone will ever likely forget."

"Simon, I am sorry to interrupt, but may I speak with you privately?" Prisca was standing just behind them.

"Certainly Prisca." He stood and looked back at Seth and Odessa. "We'll have to finish this conversation later." He then turned and walked away with Prisca.

"Well, I don't know about you, Seth, but I sure would like to know the rest of that story."

"So would I. The name Burke seemed to rile quite a few tempers."

"Yes, it did. I kind of hope they don't find her now. If just the name can turn a room cold, what would the sight of her do if she *is* a relation?" she said shivering.

Ryan Halloran approached them, and they looked up at him.

"Seth, I'm Ryan Halloran. I didn't get to meet you earlier. May I speak with you a minute?"

"Sure. Odessa, would you excuse us?"

"Sure thing, Seth. Good to see you, Ryan. I'll talk to you both tomorrow when we go cave exploring." She smiled at them clapping her hands together in excitement and left the room.

Seth turned his attention to Ryan.

"I have that device with me that Jason asked me to develop," Ryan told him.

"Oh! I see. Let's go outside or somewhere more private to discuss this." Seth led Ryan out to the pergola covered patio where Ryan sat down at one of the tables and pulled something out of a backpack.

"Here it is. I-I call it a Portal Generator or-or a Portgen." He handed the device to Seth as he spoke. "I tested it to make sure it works. In theory i-it does, but there wasn't anyone to wa-walk through it, so I'm not pa-particularly certain that it works as it should. I was going to call it a Storm Generator or S-gen for short, but it doesn't generate a storm, j-just a portal. Which is actually more b-beneficial since you guys can stay dry now. I-it works by inputting exact coordinates, which means you'll need to know wh-where you're going ahead of time, or ca-carry a map with coordinates, kind of like the charging stations. But it's better th-than waiting around on a storm," Ryan stuttered a bit, apparently not used to explaining things in such detail. Seth assumed he seldom spoke this much.

Seth turned the device over in his hands as he listened to Ryan explain what all the buttons and screens were. The device was rectangular in shape with a small glass screen and several buttons with what appeared to be a type of compass rose for direction and a number pad. It also had a small woven screen on the bottom and some tiny switches on the sides.

"Ryan, this is amazing. Thank you. You'll have to show me how this thing works. I have to tell you, being from the 1900s, I'm sort of illiterate when it comes to this stuff." Seth smiled at the young man.

"I can do that. You want me to show you now?"

Seth hesitated. "How about we wait until tomorrow? Opening a portal now would likely draw a lot of attention since it's already dark. Maybe we can find a remote location tomorrow to test it."

"Okay," Ryan said simply.

"You hold onto this until then. I don't want to accidentally turn that thing on without knowing how to use it." Seth handed the Portgen back to Ryan. "I think—if you're all right with this—I'll ask Simon and Odessa to join us when we test it."

"I'm okay with that. I like Simon and Odessa." Ryan placed the Portgen in his pack. The two men made their way back toward the house.

"Will we see you in the morning?" Seth asked him.

"No. I'm just going to work in the computer room. I don't like caves."

"Then I will find you when we get back tomorrow. Goodnight, Ryan."

"Goodnight." They parted ways once inside the house.

Seth bounded up the steps headed to his bedroom. He was excited about the Portal Generator that Ryan had developed. It would certainly come in handy, and hopefully keep Simon from having to create any more storms. He grabbed his nightclothes and headed to one of the bathrooms located just a few doors down from his room to shower and brush his teeth.

After returning to his room, he picked up the Bible he had packed with his stuff from Simon's, stepped out onto the balcony, sat down in one of the chairs, and began reading where he last left off. Looking at the Bible he realized it held a greater meaning for him now that he was a believer. Something he would have to share with the others soon. He read for about an hour, praying as he went along that God would give him the understanding he needed while exploring His Word. He decided to call it an early night, stood, and then climbed into the large bed.

He was excited about the exploration of the caves the next morning. He could sense God leading him now, especially since they were so fortunate to find the cliffs from Odessa's dream so soon after she had it. And the fact that Simon had invited him to the island seemed to fit neatly into what was happening. He simply attributed all of it to God's design and orchestration. Seth was anxious to see where God would take him next. He closed his eyes, still praying for Caroline and hopes of finding her again as he slowly drifted off to sleep.

Surely the Sovereign Lord does nothing without
revealing his plan to his servants the prophets.

Amos 3:7 NIV

Chapter 4

A dozen people woke early and met in the kitchen for a hearty breakfast.
Then they headed down to the lighthouse and the cliffs. They split up
into teams to look for a safe and easy way into the caves below. Several
people ventured inside the basement of the lighthouse to check out the
rooms inside, especially where the charging station was located, in hopes
that there was a hidden corridor somewhere. Others walked the edge of
the cliffs in opposite directions looking for large cracks or openings in
the rock facing. Some went down to the beach below, and some into the
woods behind the lighthouse looking for a cave leading underground.
Since Odessa and Seth were the only two Peregrines there, and the most
in shape physically, they took the higher cliff edge, followed by Simon.
They walked around the opening where the water at certain times of the
year shot up like a geyser out of the large hole in the cliff's top.

Seth lay down on his stomach and peered into the hole but was
unable to see very far.

"Simon, can you hand me a flashlight?" Seth reached up in Simon's
direction.

"Here you are, Seth." Simon pulled the light from the small pack
he carried, switched it on and handed it down to him. "Can you see
anything?"

"Wait, I think so." Seth stood and walked to the other end of the
large hole to get a better look. He leaned over the edge, lay down again,

and shone the light down inside. "I think I found something. There is a large flat rock down here, and it looks like other large rocks that work like steps down to the floor of the cave. I'm pretty sure we can get in this way."

Seth stood, sat on the edge of the opening, and dropped into the hole. His head was just below the opening of the hole. He flashed the light toward the next lower level of rock, then hopped down and jumped from one rock to the next until he reached the cave floor, approximately twenty feet below the opening. As he shone the light back upward, he noticed Odessa and Simon following him into the cave, while Nuncio and Clancy, the cook, stood outside peering in.

"Simon, we'll stay up here in case something happens. I can't climb like I used to anyway with this bum leg. Just take some photographs should you find anything," Nuncio yelled down through the opening, his voice tinged with a bit of jealousy and aggravation that his body wouldn't allow him any further adventures.

"Absolutely, old friend; I won't forget!" Simon yelled, looking up and patting the camera that hung about his neck.

"Seth, this is so exciting!" Odessa exclaimed as she came to stand beside him and wait for Simon to make his descent.

Seth looked at her and chuckled at her excitement. Odessa seemed to get excited over every mission. Of course, he had to remember she had been on bed rest for the last six weeks since her last peregrination to Africa. She was probably thrilled to be back in action, whether it was mission oriented or not, especially since this was concerning something about which she had dreamt.

They could hear Nuncio and Clancy yelling to the others that an opening had been found. As Simon joined them they could hear and see others climbing down through the opening, no one willing to miss the adventure or seeing the treasures the island could be hiding.

Seth, Odessa, and Simon directed flashlights around the inside of the small cavern. It wasn't an extremely large area, only about four hundred square feet, barely big enough for all of them to stand on open ground between the rocks.

"So what are we looking for, Simon?" Seth asked, shining his light slowly and carefully over the rocks surrounding them.

"I'm not sure. This is my first undirected treasure hunt." He squinted into the dark, trying to focus on where the light beam shone. "But seeing as how I was an archaeologist in my past years, I'd say something out of the ordinary. I'm sure no one has been down here for at least thirty years, or if they did they certainly kept it from the rest of us."

Odessa crawled over the rocks to get closer to the wall of the cavern. She hoisted herself to the top of a rock and began stepping from one rock to another, shining the light's beam down at the ground at the edge of the cavern wall. "Surely there is something here." She slowly and carefully inspected everything the beam touched.

Simon, still searching the walls himself, replied. "Perhaps, but it could just be a coincidence that this cavern is here. It may have nothing at all to do with your dream."

The rest of the group had joined them inside the small cavern. Everyone went in different directions, all searching for something, but unsure what that something was.

"Wait!" Malachai yelled, "I think I've found something!"

Everyone turned to look where his light beam was shining. At the back wall of the cavern, almost at the top where the wall curved into the ceiling, a slight glint of something seemed to peek out of a hole in the rock. Every time Malachai moved his light beam in just the right direction, something would slightly shimmer in the light's movement.

"How in the world are we supposed to get up there? It's at least fifteen to twenty feet high," Vashti exclaimed.

"There must be something we're missing," Malachai said. "There has to be a way to get up there."

"Simon," Odessa asked, "Is there any way you can use your power to figure out what it is?"

Before Simon could answer her, Seth spoke. He had walked over to the cave's wall and noticed notches in the rock. Packed seaweed, sand, and shells made the notches almost invisible until he stood close to them.

"I think I found a way up." Seth dug the debris out of a few of the holes in the wall. "It looks like there are hand and foot holds in the rock. Here, someone take my flashlight, and everyone shine their lights on the wall so that as I climb I can find the next hold. If anyone sees it, direct me to where it is."

"Sure thing, Seth, we can manage that," Simon answered him as he took the light from Seth.

With Seth's height, size, and strength, he made easy work of the climbing; his arms and legs were long enough that the hand and footholds seemed closer than they would for an average man. On occasion someone had to call out the location of the next hold as everyone watched him climb. It took Seth only about ten minutes to scale the wall digging out the holes as he went. When he got to the top, he realized that the hole with the shining object was also packed with debris from the ocean, which apparently repacked the hole every time the cave filled with seawater. As he dug the debris out, he discovered the identity of the shining object.

"Seth, what do you see?" Odessa asked impatiently.

"It appears to be a lever made of gold." He yelled back.

He studied the design of the hole and decided the lever was meant to be turned counterclockwise. He tried to move it without success. *It has to move; why else would it be here?* he thought. Using his hip, he braced himself against a bulging rock in the adjacent wall and placed his head against the ceiling so he could use both arms. He was then able to take hold of the lever and twist it counterclockwise again with all his might. As he pulled he felt it give way ever so slightly. He put his back into it as much as he could, then held on as the lever suddenly turned. A loud rumbling sound filled the cavern as part of the wall just to the right of him slowly swung inward and small bits of dirt, sand, seaweed, and shells all fell to the cave floor with the release.

Odessa squealed with delight and stepped toward the opening.

"Wait!" Malachi cautioned, a hand on Odessa's arm. "We have no idea what's in there. We should go in slowly and stay together."

"Let's not leave Seth up there in the dark," Simon said. "Shine your lights on the wall again until he's down."

As soon as Seth's foot touched the floor, Odessa stepped forward again, with the others close behind and Seth and Simon at the rear. They entered the dark cavern, carefully watching for any unexpected surprises.

"You don't think there could be anything alive down here?" Vashti shivered with the question.

"I wouldn't think so, if this large, sealed door is the only entrance," Prisca replied.

"Yes, but we aren't sure that it *is* the only way in," Simon chimed in.

The large door opened to a smaller area that seemed to slant uphill slightly and narrow into a passageway approximately ten feet across from wall to wall. They had walked about fifty feet on ground that continued the slight upward slant, when the walls suddenly opened into what appeared to be a large empty space.

"Look! Torches," Vashti exclaimed as the group paused at the end of the passage. Someone had left a few torches leaning against the wall, the ends wrapped with rags that had been dipped in pungent oil that was still very recognizable after years of being sealed in the cavern.

Continuing on forward, Seth noticed a trench dug into the rock wall that seemed to run all the way around the cavern about five feet above the floor, an oily-looking substance filling the trench.

"Does anyone have a lighter or some matches?"

"Whatever for?" Simon asked curiously.

"I think we should light this trough here. I believe it runs all the way around the cavern wall and contains oil. I think it's meant to illuminate the cavern."

"I can take care of that, Seth."

Simon waved his hand over the trough, and suddenly flames chased along the oily substance all the way around the perimeter of the wall, lighting the area as it went. Soon the whole inside of the cavern was bathed in the soft, warm, glow of the fire on the burning oil.

Everyone stood transfixed, amazed at what was inside the cavern. It was much larger than the one that they just left. Carved into the back wall, was the shape of a temple's outer front wall, with an archway that appeared to lead deeper into the belly of the caves. The burning trough of oil running through the carved windows of the temple wall, lit the inside of the temple and beyond.

Odessa stood still, grinning from ear to ear.

"Simon, this is the temple entrance from my dream," she gasped with excitement.

"Yes, I recognize it from the drawings Safra did from your explanation. Good job remembering, by the way. It's almost spot on." Simon smiled at her. "Let's see where this leads and what else there is to discover."

Seth stepped in front of Simon to block his way through the archway into the carved temple wall.

"Hold on, Simon. You need to let me go first. Just in case there is anything dangerous in there. I may be a bit more capable of handling any surprises." Seth looked down at the man he had come to greatly admire.

"All right, if you insist. Just don't forget one thing," Simon said, looking up at the younger man. "I am the one with magical powers." He grinned, reminding Seth that he wasn't incapable of handling surprises.

"Yes, you're right, but I am much more fit." Seth grinned broadly at the older man.

They exchanged grins over the lighthearted banter and teasing, and then Seth ducked under the arch, which was about four inches too short. "Guess people were shorter back then."

"It could also be from settling and years of erosion. You know, dirt falling down from the cavern ceiling and settling around the edge of the walls. We have no idea how long this has been down here or how deep the edges of the wall's carving go down into the cavern floor," Simon offered up from his years of archaeological studies. "Wait a minute." He stopped suddenly. "I promised Nuncio some photographs." Stepping back he took a few photos of the entire area. He then instructed everyone to stand together for a group picture.

"That's an interesting Brownie." Seth looked over the handheld camera in Simon's hands.

"Actually, Seth, this isn't a Brownie. It is still a handheld camera like the Brownie was back in the early 1900s, but this particular camera is digital. You'll see what I mean by that when we get back to the main house and take a look at the pictures. All right everyone, give me a big smile." Simon snapped a few photos.

"All right, that's done. Now back to exploring!" He said with enthusiasm, this time keeping the camera in his hand so as not to forget and miss something.

As they walked through the low archway, they could see that the inside of the cavern began to narrow again into a pathway, still lit by the burning oil trough running through the cutout in the cavern walls. They saw nothing of interest until they walked another fifty feet and found themselves in another large open space like the inside of a temple. They all stared in wonder at large columns that rose from the floor to the ceiling of the cave. There were twelve columns in all, each one approximately three feet in diameter, running along both sides of the cavern and stopping at the bottom step of an elevated platform. The platform sat at the top of a twelve-step, stone, staircase. Upon closer inspection they noticed the columns were painted with layers of gold, jade, copper, amethyst, onyx, ruby, and then stone again. The pattern continued every six feet or so all the way up to the thirty-foot-high ceiling.

The steps leading up to the elevated platform had the same repeating pattern as the columns, painted the same color as one of the layers although covered with years of dirt. When Simon climbed the steps to the platform, he saw flat inlaid tiles that he realized resembled the breastplate of a high priest of ancient Israel. Embedded stones in that breastplate represented the twelve tribes of Israel. On each of the inlaid tiles, the colors, symbols, and inlaid stones identified a tribe. At the back of the platform near the wall, five pedestals held the five locked books.

Even though everything in the cavern was covered in layers of dust and dirt, the colors and details were still obvious. With a bit of cleaning, the cavern would be remarkably beautiful.

Everyone marveled at the unbelievable find. Odessa beamed, as did Simon. It seemed as though they had all lost their voices, unable to speak and unsure what to do next.

Seth and Odessa stepped up to the platform and stared down at the tiles that held the symbols God had marked their bodies with. The identity of the tribe they were to represent lay cemented in stone at their very feet. Seth could feel his destiny sink even further into his mind and soul as he and Odessa looked at each other with knowing.

Simon stepped up to the nearest book and, picking it up, said, "Looks like we found five of the items God showed us through Odessa's dream. Let's get these back to the house and cleaned up. We can't open them without keys so there's no use in trying. Besides, we don't wish to damage them in any way."

Malachai, Vashti, and Prisca, being the other Dragoman there, each picked up a book. Odessa picked up the last one, then brushed the dust from the cover and clutched it to her chest in awe and reverence.

"I suggest we close that rock door when we exit, Seth, just to make sure this place stays intact. We don't want the sea water rising inside and ruining everything here," Simon instructed.

"Sure thing, Simon. What about the burning oil?" Seth asked as they all made their way back the way they entered.

"Once the door is closed and the oxygen is used up by the fire, it should die out by itself. Either that or it will burn up all the oil and then die out. Either way there's nowhere for it to go and nothing to catch on fire."

By the time they made it back to the first cave where they entered, Seth made the climb back up to seal the heavy rock door once again, and everyone climbed back up to the opening of the geyser's hole, it was past lunchtime. The groundskeepers had returned with a ladder and had placed it inside the hole, making it easier for everyone to climb up and out.

Clancy, the main chef had already gone back up to the main house to begin preparing lunch, while the groundskeepers had stayed behind with Nuncio tending to his needs and making sure they could still hear and see those who had gone down into the cavern. Several of the staff members had followed the others into the hole, then stationed themselves in several places along the path to report back to Nuncio that the others were safe.

It was close to two by the time the group made it back to the main house. The head groundskeeper parked the battery-powered cart in the shed. They often used the cart to transport Nuncio around the island. With his old war injury, the man had a hard time walking and would not have been able to make the almost four-mile hike.

As they all sat around the large outdoor table enjoying the hearty lunch and beverages, they discussed what sort of information they thought the locked books held.

Simon gave his explanation as to what and why.

"I believe these books may hold the information we need to explain all the strange things that have been happening as of late. Also, I think they may give us some clues leading to the artifacts we need to find for the final battle. And, give us more information about what that battle will be, where it is to happen, and how it is to take place. However, we won't know any of that until we find the keys to open them."

Nuncio spoke next. "I suggest we have Ryan run a computer search for the falls, and each Dragoman group take one of the waterfalls, and strike out in search of whatever it is God wishes us to find there."

"That sounds like a very good plan, Nuncio," Simon replied. "Also, if we have teams not searching for one of the falls, then we need to assign them to search for Bridget. She still needs to be found."

Everyone agreed and after lunch went in different directions, most taking turns looking at the new antique books they had discovered that very morning, carefully cleaning them and wishing to find a way to look inside without the need of a key.

"Simon, Odessa," Seth caught his friends' attention, "I have something I would like to show both of you. I just need to grab Ryan, and we will meet you both on the other side of the hill just past the grove of mango trees."

"All right, we'll see you there in a bit," Simon answered.

After finding Ryan in the mapping/computer room running some kind of program, Seth walked with him to the mango grove, carrying the Portgen to show Simon and Odessa and to see if it actually worked.

"Simon, this is what Ryan here calls a Portgen. It's short for Portal Generator. It should allow us to open a portal to jump through without the need of a storm of any sort. We will just need precise coordinates."

"Is that so? Well good job, Ryan! Does it work?" Simon asked the timid young man anxiously.

"Well, I did test it and a p-portal did open; I'm just not sure if travel is okay by it. I didn't have anyone to t-test it."

"I wonder why we never thought of this before?" Simon said, pondering the question as he looked over the handheld device.

"It was just something Jason and I came up with when Odessa and Alec didn't return on their last trip. If they had had something like this it would have been easier to transport Odessa in her condition. Jason sent Ryan here a request for a design, and he came up with this." Seth tried not to say too much in case Odessa hadn't yet realized Simon's slight transformation.

"Ingenious plan, boys! If it works correctly it will certainly make travel much easier and a whole lot more pleasant as far as dryness and comfort goes. Let's test it, then, shall we? Ryan, will you do the honors and show us how this thing works? I'm sure Seth and Odessa will be happy to test it out for you."

"All right. First you fl-flip this side switch here to t-turn on the device, then put in your c-coordinates on the keypad and compass rose, flip the s-safety switch up, this keeps you from a-accidentally turning it on, then point the d-device straight ahead a-and hit the green button on the t-top center of the device." As Ryan performed these steps a portal opened in front of them, revealing a straight pathway to Simon's place back at Garganthera. "I p-programmed it with coordinates to y-your place, Simon, just in case they get through a-and couldn't return back through the p-portal. They can at least return by your ch-charging station."

"Amazing, Ryan! All right, you two, let's get on with it." Simon gestured Seth and Odessa through the portal.

Ryan handed the device to Seth, who carried it through with them to make sure it would travel through the portal and still continue to work and keep it open. They walked through to the other side, then simply turned around and walked back through to Reader's Island.

Odessa looked at Ryan. "Ryan, this is amazing! It is so much easier and faster than the storm portals, and you can control how long it is open. Storms only give us a certain window of opportunity."

"Yes, thank you, Ryan. You sure have saved us a lot of trouble by creating the Portgen," Seth chimed in.

"Well done, Ryan, my boy!" Simon exclaimed, "If there was an award for 'Inventor of the Decade,' you would certainly deserve it, as far as I'm concerned. I am amazed how you manipulated the space-time continuum to develop something that will allow us to time travel easier! God has certainly given you an amazing mind." Simon smiled at Ryan and slapped him on the shoulder.

"Thanks Simon. I…just like to invent useful things."

"And you're very good at it. We'll need quite a lot of those you know." Simon peered at the young inventor. "First you can start off by just supplying each team with one until you can get enough of them made for everyone. Let me know if you need any supplies to help you build them, or any manpower. There are several of us who can follow directions well enough to help with that also."

"I think I can manage Simon, thanks all the same. I d-don't have a lot else to do anyway. I can have three more for you b-by next week."

"That will be wonderful, Ryan. This one will suffice for my teams for now. You can send the others to the other Dragoman for their teams to use. We'll need to get the others out here and show them how it works so that when you send them over, they'll know how to use them, unless you plan to hand deliver them?"

"You kn-know I don't like to leave home m-much."

"Then we shall send Seth back to the house to retrieve everyone else and bring them out now to explain."

Seth went back to the main house to gather everyone and request they follow him outside to meet up with Simon, Ryan, and Odessa, who had started the walk back toward the house as well.

Seth and Odessa demonstrated how the Portgen worked, as Simon explained how the technology came to be. They all took turns using the device to make sure they understood how it worked, praising Ryan for the invention.

Eventually everyone went inside the main house to make plans for the upcoming week and to sort out the travel plans to be made for the hunt for the falls, the keys for the locked books, and Bridget Burke.

He performs wonders that cannot be fathomed,
miracles that cannot be counted.

Job 9:10 NIV

Chapter 5

Bakrashan, Zanchier, unidentified Dimensional Plane

Caroline and Bridget walked out of the portal to find themselves in the middle of an intense storm, worse than the one they had left. The wind was whipping wildly around them, and the rain was blowing sideways. They held onto each other so they wouldn't be separated and ran to the line of trees on the edge of the field where they landed. Once in the shelter of the trees, they discovered a cave at the edge of the hillside. Caroline hesitantly peeked inside to make sure there weren't any wild animals present.

"Goodness, what a storm!" Caroline entered the cave, followed closely by Bridget. They shook the rain from their cloaks as they peered into the darkness of the cave. "We need to build a fire to dry our clothes and warm ourselves." She moved about the small cave which was just large enough for them to lie down to rest.

"Yes, I agree," Bridget said in her always cheerful voice. "But wasn't that exciting, Caroline? I wonder where we are? I haven't yet found any information in the books on knowing where we end up. Do you suppose we just float around throughout time, just landing wherever God chooses?" She gathered some leaves and sticks lying about the edge of the cave floor.

"I'm not really sure, Bridget. Surely God has a hand in where we go since He is the one who chose us for such a life." Caroline bent forward using the flint and steel they had packed from Bridget's home to light the fire.

"What do you suppose we do after this?" Bridget found a place to sit by the fire after laying her cloak across a large rock to dry from the fire's heat.

"I suppose the books have no answers on that either."

"I'm not really sure. Perhaps when the storm lets up and we have more light to see by, we can look and see." Bridget tucked her legs sideways underneath her and leaned against an obliging rock.

"I wonder what time it is? It's hard to tell with the storm still raging." Caroline peered out of the cave into the lashing, windswept rain.

"I suppose there's no way of knowing."

Caroline returned to the fire and sat with Bridget to dry her soaked hair and clothing. In the relative quiet of the cave, Caroline felt tense muscles begin to relax.

Suddenly they heard something stirring just outside the cave opening. As they turned, startled, a large, burly man stepped into the cave.

He held up his hands in an attempt to show them he meant no harm. "Sorry, didn' mean to frighten ya none. Don't worry, I mean ya no harm. I noticed you two come out a' the storm there an' I came to warn ya of the dangers. There be people 'round here that search fer those like you two that *will* do ya harm. If you two wanna survive here, I suggest you be followin' me right now. Normally I wouldn' get involved, but you be looking awful young," he added, looking at Bridget.

"And who might you be?" Caroline asked suspiciously, glancing around the small cave for something to use as a weapon if the need arose.

"Most folks call me Oz. Let's just say I know what you two are, and there are quite a few others 'round here that if'n they saw ya, would know too. An' they won't be as friendly as I am. So, if'n ya want to live, I suggest ya put that there fire out an' folla me," Oz said, waiting for an answer.

Caroline looked at Bridget with raised eyebrows and a question in her eyes. Bridget, ever the optimist, shrugged her shoulders and smiled.

She stood and grabbed her bags and cloak as Caroline poured some of the water they had packed onto the fire to douse it.

Caroline stood and looked at the man. "All right, Oz, lead on."

With that, they all exited the cave into the bitter cold of the intense rain and headed up into the mountains. Their cloaks and hoods danced wildly about their bodies as they struggled to keep them closed about them. Where he was taking them they had no idea. Neither of them was any match for the huge man regardless, and if he had wanted to harm them, wouldn't he have already done so? Caroline could only hope and pray that God had sent this man to help them. If not, they would surely soon find out.

An hour later, as late afternoon began to fade into evening, the women peered into the gloom under the forest canopy, forcing weary legs to take one more step on the steep, rocky, root-smattered path. They could barely see Oz's outline in front of them as they struggled to keep up and not to lose sight of him in the gathering darkness. Caroline could feel Bridget shivering against her arm as the girl clung to her. Then the hurried, stumbling, journey up the mountainside was suddenly over. They stepped into a cavern-like structure, and Caroline noticed she could no-longer feel sparse drops of rain hitting her cloak.

Oz opened a heavy wooden door, ushered the women inside, and quickly made a fire so they could warm themselves. Bridget was shivering so hard that Oz made a pallet on the floor for her and gave her several heavy blankets to wrap around herself. Then he disappeared. Caroline removed Bridget's soaked cloak and tucked the blankets tightly around her as she curled up on the floor into a ball, waiting for the chills to ebb away. As her muscles began to respond to the heat, Bridget fell asleep, while Caroline sat listening to the thunder still pounding the sky outside as she rested her weary, drenched, body.

Caroline sat inside the uniquely disguised wood dwelling belonging to Oz, napping on and off while still drying herself by the fire he had built in the large stone fireplace. The intense thunderstorm had lasted the better part of the afternoon from the time they arrived in this strange new land until just a few moments ago, when it had finally decided to die down to a drizzle. Now it was completely dark outside and visibility was nonexistent. Meaning they would have to wait until tomorrow to get a good look at where they had peregrinated to and decide what came next.

Caroline tucked the blanket around the soundly sleeping Bridget, who was snuggled up tightly on the pile of animal skins just a few feet from the fire, exhausted from the hike and the chills her body had taken from being soaked through from the storm.

After picking up the now dry cloaks they had worn earlier, Caroline hung them on the hook by the huge, thick, oak-and-iron-hewn door. Then she decided to take stock of where they were. She had realized, after Oz had built the fire earlier, that they were actually in some kind of dwelling located beneath a huge tree. She could see the roots of the tree braided along the walls so thickly that there was no dirt on the inside. The floor was wooden planks, apparently placed there by someone, probably Oz. The chimney for the stone fireplace went straight up through the hollowed-out center of the tree. It was so huge and tall she couldn't tell where it vented. No rain fell inside, so she supposed it was sealed at the top and vented outside somewhere since the room didn't fill with smoke.

She glanced around the room at the meager furnishings which consisted of two stools, one larger wooden chair, a small round table to eat at and another table against one wall which held kitchen tools, and other useful items. It was obvious only one person lived here. There was what appeared to be another room on a separate level above the one where she stood. It turned to the right and disappeared behind some of the tree roots that acted as a wall. On the other side of the room was another flight of steps that went up into the tree, turning and twisting into the darkness.

As she looked around, Oz entered the room through the door, bolting it shut as he did. He looked at Caroline, took off his large animal-skin cloak, which gave him the appearance of a strange-looking large bear walking on its hind legs, and hung it on a post by the door. He then went and sat by the fire, where he began whittling shavings of wood into the flames as he sharpened a stick.

Caroline noted his disheveled appearance. He had a long, scraggly red and white beard and wild thick hair the same shade that obviously hadn't seen a pair of scissors in a very long time. His clothes appeared worn and patched so much she wondered how everything actually held together. He was a large man, and he reminded her of Seth because of his size. His hands were rough and scarred, probably due to the kind of life he lived here. She guessed his age to be around sixty, although he seemed in very good health and shape from what she had seen of him so far.

She didn't know what lay outside the large oak door, but the inside, although unusual, revealed a primitive way of life.

Caroline went and sat down beside the man.

"Oz, may I ask you a question?" Caroline waited on the man who had said next to nothing to them since they had followed him to his home. Of course he had busied himself building the roaring fire, then disappeared several times since they arrived, stating once that he had to "keep watch." For what she didn't know.

"S'ppose so," he said in his broken dialect and deep, raspy voice.

"Where exactly are we?"

"This here place is called Xantifal. It's the county you per'grinated to in the country, plane, or dimension a Zanchier," he offered, not looking at her much as he continued to whittle at the wood.

"I've never heard or read anything about either of those names or places. Where is it located? Is it on any map?"

"Well, I s'ppose it'd be on the local maps. It wouldn' be on anythin' you've likely ever seen. How many places you two gals jumped ta?"

"Honestly, this is our first time."

He looked at her oddly and then continued.

"Are ya both Per'grines'?"

"We aren't really sure. You see, I appeared, or apparently peregrinated, around six weeks ago to where Bridget lived, in the year 1580 AD. I am from the year 1906 AD in San Francisco, California, and I'm still not certain what all this is about or how it is even possible. From what Bridget and I gleaned from her father's books, I am a Peregrine and she may be a Dragoman. We really don't know how to tell the difference."

"What books ya talkin' about? Was her pa a Dragoman?"

"She believes that he was. He never really told her anything about his life or allowed her to learn about any of it. So we only have the books to go by. How do you tell what you are?"

"Well, she's fer sure one a' them things, or she wouldn' a been able to per'grinate. She'd a surely died. Only people I ever knew that could time-jump were Per'grines and Dragoman. It's a might unusual that she's one of 'em and her pa was too. That ain't the way things usu'lly work. It don't pass down the family line so ta speak. Course things might be differ'nt now. It's been a long time since I've come 'cross the likes a people like you two."

"You seem to know quite a bit about it all. Are you a Peregrine or a Dragoman?"

"Use ta be. A Per'grine that is. That life left me long ago. So'd God. You two are the first new Per'grines' I've seen in twelve years."

"Twelve years! Have you been living here alone for twelve years?"

"Perty much. There were others when we first came here, 'bout ten ta be exact. They all died navigatin' the mount'n, er were caught an' tortured by Scaithers. Last one died 'bout eight years back. I'm the only one ta survive that I know of."

"I'm sorry you've been alone all this time, Oz." Caroline placed her hand on the older man's hand as a gesture of kindness. Oz quickly changed positions to avoid the contact, and Caroline quickly retracted her hand.

"You said something about the others being captured and tortured by Scaithers. What is a Scaither?" Caroline was a bit afraid of the answer.

"Scaithers are those who traverse these here mount'ns in search a people like you, me, and her." He pointed at Bridget. "They're a group a' rogues an' bandits. Thievin' an' murderin' jus' 'bout anythin' that crosses their path. They ain't got a lick a respect fer life an' don't care what age a girl is neither. If you get my meanin'." He nodded toward Bridget.

Caroline looked at her young friend, fear suddenly gripping her. Dangerous places like this had never crossed her mind when they had decided to try and figure out what all this meant. Bridget probably would have been safer if they had stayed in Dover.

"They may be bandits, but they're smart. See, years back when we all ended up here, they saw all a' us jus' appear out a the port'l. Most people can't see the port'ls, but people here in Zanchier can. Back in the first dimension, people never paid much attention to that sort a' thing. But here, they knew we were differ'nt. They caught a few Per'grines right off, tried to torture 'em to find out where they came from an' why they were here. They got some information out a a few a' the weaker ones, not believin' 'em 'bout God callin' 'em to it. So they think we have some big secret 'bout how ta time travel an' they been huntin' us ever since. Well, at least those of us who didn't fall off the mount'n, er get eaten by the local wildlife." He finished his story and sat back looking at Caroline, sadness in his eyes as he remembered his fallen comrades.

"Why haven't you ever left here Oz? Surely there have been opportunities to leave by portal?"

"Sure, only problem is, ya gotta travel ta the Dustbowl. See the local storms 'round here just bring ya in, but ya can't jump inta the storms here to leave. Believe me, we tried. The Dustbowl always has tornados that constantly churn. Of'en times there's one big enough for a port'l. Nobody lives down that way cause a' the destruction the tornados cause. But ta get there, ya gotta get by the Scaithers, an' that is near impossible. The Scaithers, they done spent the last twelve years experimentin' with all this. Using the Per'grines they caught ta try an' make 'em open port'ls. If'n it didn' work, they'd kill one of 'em right there. Thought they were lyin' to 'em 'bout how ta do it. Especially after one time when they tried ta send one a' their guys through a port'l with a Per'grine. The Per'grine, Hannah, disappeared an' their guy fell dead. The Scaithers kept several of 'em alive fer years hopin' to figure it out. I tried rescuin' 'em an' almost got caught myself."

"Good grief, what a nightmare!" Caroline breathed in disbelief, staring into the fire. "I can't understand why God led us here. It just doesn't make any sense, unless it was to find you?" Caroline looked at Oz.

"Nah. God fergot 'bout me a long time ago. Don't see what He'd want with me now," Oz said, sharpening the stick again. "Not sure what you two are doin' here though; we ended up here 'cause someone back home betrayed us. We did fig're that much out."

Oz stopped whittling the stick for a moment, a memory from the past creeping into his mind. He looked at Bridget lying motionless on the floor as a look of recollection crossed his face. He quickly looked at Caroline and asked, "What'd you say that girl there's name is?" he eyed her as she answered.

"Bridget Burke. Why?" Caroline noticed that his back went stiff as he stood and looked at her. She stood as well, uncomfortable sitting now that he seemed agitated and found herself facing a man who towered over her by seven or more inches. Oz peered down at her as he spoke.

"You two can stay here fer' the night, but I want ya gone by mornin'," he almost spat at her as he turned his glower to Bridget's still-sleeping form on the floor. Then he glanced at Caroline and disappeared behind one of the root walls. She had no idea what had happened just now. Oz had been friendly enough, up until she had told him Bridget's last name. He had grown so cold that he was actually throwing them out of his home to face what he called Scaithers, man-eating animals, and the dangerous terrain of the mountain.

"Lord, I have no idea what You're doing, but I pray you keep us safe," Caroline prayed as she looked at the ascending staircase Oz had escaped to and the small sleeping frame of the girl whose very life she felt utterly responsible for. It had been Caroline who had talked Bridget into looking through the books and figuring out how to time-jump. All so she could find Seth. Not only had that not happened, but now they were in mortal danger. Perhaps she could make Oz see reason come morning. If it was as bad out there as he said, surely he wouldn't turn them out unprotected. Caroline prayed harder than she had in months, hoping that God would hear her plea and somehow change Oz's heart.

The night crept slowly by with Caroline unable to sleep well throughout, as fear of what was to come in the morning wrapped its ugly tentacles around her very soul. If it were only herself, she might be able to cope better, but she had Bridget to think about. Bridget had been taking care of herself for years, but that was in a much safer place than what Oz had described to her.

It wasn't only the Scaithers they had to fear. Falling off the mountain was another possibility, apparently. According to Oz some had perished that way. There also had to be some very large wild animals around judging by Oz's parka, which appeared to be made entirely of one skin. Caroline had never personally seen an animal that large or that color, but she had read enough about bears when she was growing up.

"Bridget, you need to wake up. We must be going soon." Caroline tried to rouse her young friend from her sleep.

"Goodness," Bridget said sleepily, "did I sleep all night?"

"I believe you did." Caroline smiled at the girl who sleepily smiled back.

Caroline was certain that if Oz only had the chance to talk with Bridget, she would steal his heart just as she had hers. Caroline wasn't sure what had caused Oz's reaction to Bridget's surname, but she had a feeling it had to do with whoever had betrayed them years ago. It was the only thing that made sense. Bridget would have been around two or three years old when it happened. And according to what Bridget had told her about remembering running through a portal at about that age, it would make sense that her father, or perhaps her mother, had been the betrayer. That would certainly explain why Oz was so angry. But Bridget didn't deserve his wrath, no matter who was responsible. At least not to the point of possible death, dismemberment, or a life of slavery and all that would entail for a girl like her.

Bridget sat up and stretched, then began picking up the things she had used as bedding. She folded them neatly and placed them in the corner of the room. Caroline sat and watched her buzz around the little room, doing whatever she could to be useful to the man who had taken them in the night before.

"Caroline, do you see a pot? I could make some tea and breakfast if I could only find the proper items." Bridget busied herself looking.

"Bridget, you need to stop and listen." Caroline watched Bridget halt what she was doing and look at her. "Oz has asked us to leave."

"Whatever for? Have we, or I, done something to upset him?" Bridget thought for a moment and offered another answer. "Perhaps we've just worn out our welcome. He was very kind to take us in, and give us a warm, safe place to sleep. But we can't ask anymore from him than that, can we?"

Caroline smiled at the sweetness and understanding that this girl constantly portrayed. She always seemed to take Caroline off guard with her grown-up attitude and deep understanding of people. "I'm not sure. All I know is he asked us to be gone by this morning. From what he told me last night, this place where we've landed seems to be a very treacherous place to navigate."

"We'll be all right, Caroline. God did send us here, after all. He'll watch over us and keep us safe. And if He chooses not to, then I suppose we'll see each other in heaven," Bridget said with a sweet, carefree smile. "This place is very interesting." Bridget looked around at her surroundings. "I've never been underneath a tree before. I wish I had a piece of paper and a quill and ink to write with. I would like to leave Mr. Oz a note to thank him for his kindness. Oh well, I suppose we just have to hope that he understands our regard. Are we ready to go, Caroline?"

"Yes, Bridget, I believe we are. Just grab your pack and cloak, and we'll head out. Just let me go out first, okay? And stay as close to me as possible," Caroline instructed her friend, hoping to be able to avoid any problems. Since Caroline knew of some of the treacherous things awaiting them outside, perhaps they could avoid them. "Also, if you see anyone, do not speak. Be as quiet as possible. I'll explain why later, just know there are some very bad men out there."

Caroline opened the door, and she and Bridget stepped out, pulling the door closed behind them. They found themselves not outside surrounded by green trees or sunlight, but deep beneath the roots of the tree, still inside the hollowed-out section. The circumference of the tree must be absolutely enormous to hide all of this underneath it. They could see a dim light filtering in through the side about sixty feet away, so they followed the narrow dirt path, trying to make sure they didn't trip over any roots or rocks as they navigated toward the slowly growing light source.

As they walked, Caroline was about to take another step when she noticed something move just before she put her foot down. Jumping backward she had to stop herself from shrieking.

"Umm…what was that?" She grimaced, half whispering in fear.

"Shh…Caroline, it is all right. It was only a little rat, I think. It is gone now, anyway," Bridget reassured her.

"How can you not be afraid of a rat, Bridget?" Caroline loudly and emphatically whispered, a little perturbed that nothing seemed to rile Bridget's nerves.

"Where I lived back in 1580, they roamed the packed and dirty streets of Dover quite often, usually finding refuge in my house during the cold winters. I am quite used to all manner of critters. They don't bother me, and I don't bother them."

"And here I was thinking I was going to take care of you," Caroline said wryly.

"Don't worry, Caroline. I am sure you will have ample opportunity to do just that. We all have different strengths that arise when we least expect them," Bridget offered, trying to boost her friend's morale.

"All right, Bridget, let's get out of here and see if we can make our way toward the Dustbowl and jump out of this crazy place." Caroline smirked at the consistently positive young woman.

As they emerged from the tree's massive root system and into the morning daylight, they found themselves in a thickly wooded forest, surrounded by massive trees, high atop the mountain. They began their journey downward, trying to gauge which direction they should go. Caroline wished she had asked Oz that rather important question last night, but he had taken her completely by surprise and then disappeared. And unfortunately this morning he was nowhere to be found. She would just have to rely on God's guidance to see them through to where they needed to go.

Oz stood at the top of the dark stairs leading up to the treetop's lookout station he had built years ago. He had started to descend into the main part of his home when he heard the two girls he found last night talking. As he listened, he heard the younger one saying how kind she thought he had been for taking them in and how she wished she could thank him. Her spirit and resolve to take whatever God handed them shamed him.

He had been downright horrid after he learned her last name, lending pain to his memory of her and her father. Because of that, he had treated the women badly and sent them out the door this morning to certain death, without so much as a "Good luck" or directions on which way to head. The Xantifal Mountain Range was deadly enough as it was with the constantly moving ground and changing scenery. They could get lost forever trying to navigate their way out of the mountains. Or die stepping off a cliff that suddenly disappeared beneath the dense heavy fog that was an almost constant companion this high up. If they did manage to safely make it down the mountainside, avoiding the landscape and the deadly animals that were always on the prowl for their next meal, then the Scaithers would surely find them.

Oz decided he had better follow the two young women just to make sure they managed to navigate the mountain successfully. After picking up his pack and grabbing his sword and bow, he stepped out onto the high branches that hung underneath the thick tree canopy that was his home. The lower limbs of the tree series so large he could lie down across the limb and still not touch the curved edges. Traveling by way of the large branches also made it safer to navigate the woods. Not all the trees were as large as this one, but most of them were close in size, making branch travel possible since one tree branch mostly intertwined with the next.

Most of the larger, more dangerous animals traveled via the ground as well, leaving him safe high above them. He just had to watch out for the big cats and overly large birds of prey that existed here in Zanchier. The species were about the same as on earth, but their appearance varied greatly. It had taken him several years to identify the animals and mark them as comparable species to the animals from back home.

For years, he followed high above in the trees as he listened to the Scaithers talking about what the animals were, and explaining to their prisoners what a specific animal was capable of should they decide to leave their uncooperative prisoner as a meal.

He had prayed and waited for God to give him the opportunity to set the other Peregrines free, but every time he thought he had a chance, something went wrong. He had watched most of his friends perish at the hands of the Scaithers over the years, unable to do anything about it.

He may not have been able to control the situation then, but he could with these two young women. He would not allow them to be taken alive by the Scaithers or become a meal for one of the dangerous animals that lived in the woods here in the Xantifal Mountains, even if Bridget's father had been the Dragoman who had betrayed them all years before.

After Caroline told him Bridget's last name, he realized he remembered her from when she was a baby. He couldn't hold her responsible for the evils of her father, but he also wasn't ready to let them know that. He would keep his distance unless he was needed. And since he had no intention of battling a wild animal or an equally dangerous Scaither, he hoped the young women's venture through the Xantifal Mountains and Bakrashan would be an uneventful one. Now he just needed to figure out a way to let them know which direction the Dustbowl was without letting them know he was following them.

Whoever gives heed to instruction prospers,
and blessed is the one who trusts in the Lord.

Proverbs 16:20 NIV

Chapter 6

Caroline and Bridget wove their way through the thick forest of giant trees, the like of which they had never seen before. Caroline had read about the giant redwoods and sequoias in Northern California and surrounding areas, but she never had the opportunity to see them. She imagined they were much like these trees here. Although she had a feeling the ones here in Zanchier were even larger than the famous giant trees of the Northwestern United States.

They climbed the mountain ridge as high as they could to get a bearing on where they might be and to see if they could spot which direction to travel. Caroline explained to Bridget all that Oz had told her as they walked, and every once in a while they could hear a faint rumble like a storm brewing. They walked the ridge until they came to a clearing that enabled them to see far enough over the giant trees to look for a building or town, anything that would show signs of human life or habitation.

As they gazed out over the expansive landscape, they were shocked at what they saw. The mountains were made up of individual smaller sections. Every so often, one of the sections would twist itself around in a completely different direction with only a little vibration and rumble, like thunder rolling in the far distance. Other sections would disappear only to reappear in a completely different spot somewhere else within the mountain range.

Staring in astonishment and confusion, Caroline asked, "How in the world are we supposed to navigate a place like this? We could get to a point only to be thrown back somewhere else without a minute's notice. The rumbling we heard earlier must have been from the land moving. I had assumed another thunderstorm was forming." She spoke almost breathlessly, partly from the walk through the forest for the last two hours and partly from the exasperation of their new discovery of the ever-changing mountainside.

"It is very odd," Bridget said bewildered. "I wonder how it happens and why? I've never heard of such a thing."

"Neither have I, Bridget. I just wish that Oz had been a bit more informative about all this before he sent us packing."

"Yes, I must agree." Bridget was unable to take her eyes from the scene in front of her. "It would have been ever so helpful if he had only told us how to traverse this strange place and how to find the place he called the Dustbowl. How are we ever to find our way down from this wretched mountainside? I fear we shall never leave Zanchier, much like Oz hasn't. Perhaps this is one of the reasons he is still here?" She turned to look at Caroline. "Perhaps he is unable to leave here because of the constantly changing landscape?"

"Maybe," Caroline answered her friend. "I do know one thing, though. Tornadoes do not form in areas such as this. We need to find a place that is flat and void of hills and trees. Tornadoes form in places that have little to no wind resistance—flat lands. We also need to find one large enough to peregrinate as Oz said when he told me about the Dustbowl. I do know that most tornadoes are brought on by thunderstorms as well, so maybe a place where warm, wet air meets cooler dry air. Like a dark spot in the sky signifying a storm brewing. That may be the direction in which we need to head. If nothing else, perhaps a thunderstorm will be strong enough for us to jump through. According to Oz though, the only way out of this place is the Dustbowl."

Caroline sighed heavily as the earth in front of them changed yet again in the short time she and Bridget were talking. "I wonder how many times the very mountain we're currently walking through has changed? I seriously doubt I could find my way back to Oz's house should the need arise."

"Well, I don't think we would be very welcome anyhow, so there's no point in even considering that. I suppose we shall just have to keep moving and hope that God leads us in the correct direction." Bridget turned and began walking down the steep hillside.

"Just watch where you step, Bridget. I have a feeling that the ground beneath your feet could literally disappear at any second. Just try and listen for any rumbling. Apparently the landscape changes right around the same time. Surely the louder the rumbling is, the closer we are to that happening." Caroline closely followed Bridget, staying only a few steps behind her.

They made their way down the steep incline without too much trouble until they came to the edge of a steep cliff that dropped off into a river approximately sixty feet below. They could hear the roar of the rushing river below them, which could prove to be problematic should the earth decide to suddenly adjust beneath them.

"What now?" Bridget asked, looking at Caroline.

"Well, I suppose we'll have to walk the cliff's edge until we find a way across. Hopefully we'll find a fallen tree that's lying across this gorge." Caroline pointed to the other side of the wide expanse.

They continued walking along the edge of the cliff, noting that it did indeed descend slightly every so often, bringing them ever closer to the cascading river. Caroline estimated that they had dropped in elevation by twenty-five to thirty feet over the last hour.

"Caroline, can we stop for a bit? I am slightly hungry and tired." Longing played on Bridget's features.

"I guess now is as good a time as any." Caroline offered Bridget a weak smile. "We need to make it a quick stop. We can't afford to wait too long. I don't wish to have to make camp on the edge of this gorge just in case this happens to be the border of the changing landscape."

"Agreed." Bridget removed her pack and then sat on a rock sticking up out of the ground.

They pulled some small packs of jerky and wafers along with their water bladders from the sling packs they carried. After eating and resting for about thirty minutes, they restarted their journey downstream, following the cliff edge as it took them closer to the swiftly flowing river beneath. They managed to get about fifteen feet above the water's surface when they did indeed come across a large tree that had fallen across the gorge. It was angled a bit precariously downward but still looked plenty solid enough to walk across. The landscape on the other side of the river seemed to continue downward, so crossing the river still seemed to be their best bet as long as the other side of the river didn't decide to vanish, taking the log bridge with it.

Caroline ventured out onto the fallen tree with Bridget hanging on to her cloak, and the two women began slowly crossing the river, trying not to look down past the log they were balancing on.

Oz watched the two women make their way through the woods, staying far enough away to not be seen but close enough to catch some of what they were saying as the breeze carried their voices up through the tree branches to where he stayed perched above them. When they reached the opening at the top of the ridge, he had to double back and watch from afar to learn which route they would take. So far they were doing pretty well gauging which direction to go. Following the river would take them down toward the Dustbowl, but it also took them ever closer to the Scaither camp. He would have to figure out soon how to make them steer clear of the area of the forest that the Scaithers frequented.

It hadn't taken the women long to reach Catamount Gorge, so named for the rushing river that cut through the mountains and the Pagorinx, the large wildcats that claimed this territory for their own. The Pagorinx wildcats of Zanchier were much bigger than any back on earth. Oz had already experienced a run-in with one of them. He had won that fight, but only barely, and he had a long scar down his left leg to prove it. The cat had ended up as a blanket for his bed and food for his table, and he had learned to stitch himself up in the process. It was a good thing that Oz had known how to live off the land before he peregrinated for the first time. That part of his life had served him well here on Zanchier.

He had to take to the ground for a bit as the women walked down the edge of the cliff toward the water and the fallen tree lying across the gorge. Hidden behind a large clump of bushes close to the side of the gorge, he could hear them discussing the possibility of crossing the river on the weathered log. Then he watched Caroline step out with Bridget holding on to her cloak.

Caroline kept her attention focused on the log. It was very large and at least fifteen feet above the surface of the cascading water, but it was covered in slippery moss. Caroline thought it quite possible that it was rotten in spots from years of lying across the gorge. Each time she placed her foot, she pushed down to make sure the log would support her weight. She also tried to avoid any visible algae. One careless step on the slippery surface could send them into the river.

Just as they reached the center of the log, they heard a low growling sound. They both froze in place and looked around at the thick woods on both sides of them, wondering where it had come from.

"Let's keep going, Bridget. We can't stop now. There isn't anywhere to go but into that river, and I don't fancy a swim right now." Caroline tugged gently on Bridget's arm.

"Agreed." Bridget nervously looked at Caroline wide eyed.

As they started to move again, the growling grew louder. They stopped again, frozen in fear, frantically searching for where the sound had emanated from.

Oz heard the growls and feared the worst for the two women. He would rather do battle against ten Scaithers than deal with a Pagorinx. Today might very well be the day they would all meet their maker, but he couldn't let the girls take on the animal by themselves. So he stood up and walked out into the small clearing at the edge of the log.

Caroline and Bridget jumped at the rustling sound coming from the bushes. Caroline clutched Bridget's hand and stared unblinking at the river's edge. When she saw Oz emerge from the bushes, Caroline almost dropped to the log's surface from sheer relief.

"Thank the Lord it's you!" she cried as Oz quickly approached, preparing to usher them across as swiftly as possible.

"We gotta move quick, ladies," he said anxiously, peering in every direction as though trying to see through the trees. "That growl ya heard was from a Pagorinx. Right hateful cat, so we need ta hurry an' find some shelter."

Caroline and Bridget took the hint and hurried across the log as quickly as they could. Questions could wait for later—if they survived. Forgetting about being careful, Caroline slipped and fell forward. Her knee disappeared into a large hole in the log, and she was pinned against it. Bridget tripped over her, and her full weight landed hard on Caroline, pushing her leg farther down. Caroline screamed in pain.

"Caroline, I'm so sorry! Are you all right?" Bridget frantically searched her friend's body for injuries until she pulled back Caroline's cloak and saw her knee buried deep in the log, her foot resting painfully stretched on top of it.

"My knee is stuck and I can't get it out." Caroline gritted her teeth, wincing in pain as she pushed against the log in an attempt to free herself.

The growling had continued to grow louder, and suddenly a huge catlike creature broke through the trees ahead of them. It slowly made its way toward them, its muscles tensed to pounce at any moment. Everyone stopped moving to stare at the cat. Caroline had never in her life seen a cat that size. It was almost the size of an adult elephant! It was so black that its fur shimmered with hues of purple and aqua as the powerful muscles rippled and the sunlight bounced off its hide. Its paws looked to be larger than Oz's head with large, sharp bluish-white claws that looked like curved knife blades. It had long, horizontal, bluish-white, braided-looking stripes in its fur, running from the tips of its ears and head all the way to the tip of its tail and over its hind quarters. The cat's head was huge, looking as though it could finish a man off in two bites. Its teeth included razor sharp canines that stuck out of its mouth, much like a Saber-tooth tiger's canines but not quite as long. Its eyes were an unusual color, the irises were the shade of clear, deep, aqua pools that seemed to mesmerize its prey. It was hard to look away from the animal. She wasn't sure if it was from fear or awe at its unusual beauty.

Suddenly Oz spoke in hushed tones. "Stay calm girls. That is a Pagorinx an' they be right mean creatures. Jus' don't make any sudden moves. I'm gonna' try ta make my way 'round you two. I've had dealin's before with these here beasts." Oz gingerly stepped over Caroline, careful not to put any weight on her already cramping leg and back. "Bridget, you try ta pull Caroline free from there. Jus' do it as quiet and quick as possible," he instructed, looking into the eyes of the frightened women.

Oz made his way toward the front of the group and pulled a large sword from a sheath across his back. The cat growled low, baring its large teeth, and halting its steps, leery of the large man. This struck Caroline as humorous, and she nervously giggled ever so slightly, unsure if it was nerves or the thought that the enormous animal might for some unknown reason fear Oz. Unable to tear her eyes from the large approaching beast, she pushed even harder against the log.

"Caroline, what could possibly be humorous at this moment?" Bridget nervously chided her friend as she struggled to free her stuck leg and at the same time keep an eye on Oz and the cat.

"I have no idea. Just nerves I guess. Bridget, hurry up. My leg is starting to lose feeling, and that cat is getting closer." Caroline did her best to help Bridget free her leg from its prison. Hardly able to stop staring at the scene unfolding in front of them, she and Bridget grew more anxious and nervous by the second.

Just as Oz made his way across the log, almost to the end, they all heard the deep growl of a Pagorinx on the other side of the gorge behind them. Looking back, they saw another fearsome cat, not quite as large as the first one, but still huge.

"Good Lord!!" Oz exclaimed. "We'll never survive this," he breathed, fear apparent in every tense muscle as he stood holding his large, curved, sword high, unsure which direction he should look for the attack to come from. "I'm afraid this might be it, girls."

"We could jump into the river?" Bridget offered.

"Yeah, we could, if'n ya could get Caroline's leg outa this here log."

"Oz, I'm not strong enough to lift her out. I need your help!" Bridget said, still trying to free Caroline's leg while watching the slowly approaching animals.

Oz rushed back to the center of the log, waving his sword threateningly.

"Here, hold this." He handed the sword to Bridget, who could barely lift the thing, much less use it. He placed one arm under Caroline's midsection as he used the other to try and work her leg out of the hole. All the while the cats were approaching them from both sides of the log.

Bridget stood watching the cats, the sword perched precariously in her small hands. As she watched them approach ever closer, a breeze blew softly across her face, and she heard a voice say to her, "Be still." She felt peace come over her and wash away her fear of the animals. She laid down the sword and turned toward the larger of the two cats, then began to walk slowly toward it.

"Bridget! What'n tarnation are ya doin', girl?" Oz growled at her, still working on Caroline's stuck leg as he watched her slowly approach the animal unarmed.

Bridget didn't answer and kept slowly walking toward the animal, with no fear at all.

Caroline's leg suddenly broke free, and Oz pulled her up to a standing position.

"Stay here," he told Caroline as he walked quickly toward Bridget, picking up the sword as he went. The larger cat, which had seemed to be a little calmer and less threatening, suddenly became agitated again as he did.

"Bridget, what are ya doin'? Stop! Yer gonna' get yerself killed!" he loudly whispered through clenched teeth.

She stopped walking and turned to him calmly, stating, "Oz, I'm not afraid."

"Well, I'm afraid fer ya.'" He reached her and grabbed her by the wrist, pulling her back toward him. "I've done battle with the likes a' these before an' I have the scars ta prove it!" He pushed her toward

Caroline, and the cat growled low, becoming more agitated by his actions.

"What do we do now?" Caroline asked, beginning to panic.

Oz looked from cat to cat as they both continued further out onto the log. "If we jump into the rapids, the river and rocks may kill us. But if we don't these things surely will."

"Caroline!" Bridget yelled, "I can't swim!"

Just then, as both Oz and Caroline looked at the slender girl between them, the log creaked and suddenly split. The girls grabbed for each other just as the log broke under the weight of the enormous cats and threw them all into the river beneath them. The rushing rapids carried them quickly downstream as they struggled to stay afloat. The unrelenting current forced them past large boulders and bounced them off others as they sped past. The cats, which were thrown farther ahead, yowled loudly in protest of the water and currents as they scratched at the edges of the bank, pawing to escape the torrential ride.

Oz tried to see where Caroline and Bridget had gone, fearful that Bridget may drown, but it was no use. He could barely keep his own head above water. He also needed to try to avoid running into the wild cats just ahead of him. They were nasty enough on dry ground. He didn't want to find out what a frightened, wet Pagorinx was like.

After a long, rough ride of about five exhausting minutes, the river seemed to slow and the rapids began to disperse. The waters calmed enough that the larger cat was able to crawl out of the river and onto the banks. Oz wasn't sure where the other cat had gotten too. It was nowhere to be seen. Oz managed to grab the branches of a fallen tree hanging out over the bank and held on, trying to catch his breath and muster enough energy to pull himself out of the water. As he hung onto the branch, he strained his neck hoping to catch a glimpse of the girls. He could make out Caroline, about seventy feet ahead of him, pulling herself out of the water onto the bank, sputtering and gagging on water. Bridget was nowhere to be seen. Oz began pulling himself along the tree branches to the bank. The sooner he got out, the faster they could find Bridget. He just hoped they would find her alive. He reached Caroline just as she began to scream Bridget's name across the river.

"Bridget!" Caroline called, desperately searching both sides of the shore for the girl.

"Caroline, pipe down, will ya. This here be Scaither territory. They'll find us fer sure with you a bellerin' like that!" Oz whispered loudly as he searched the trees for signs of the dreaded locals.

"I have to find her, Oz!"

"I understand that, but your gonna' have ta do it more quiet like."

"Bridget!" Caroline continued calling.

"Caroline, stop!" Oz said, grabbing her arm.

She yanked her arm free and spun to look at him.

"She's my responsibility, Oz, not yours! We didn't ask you to come help us, you know," Caroline said angrily.

"No, ya didn't, but I came anyway. I felt responsible fer sendin' the two a ya out without no protection."

"Too bad your conscience didn't stop you all together; we'd all be back at your place safe right now. We could have avoided all of this completely if you hadn't let your anger interfere with your good judgment. Seeing as how we're not, I have to find my friend!" Caroline spun around to walk along the river's edge, limping as she went, searching desperately for Bridget.

"I know, an' I'm sorry!" Oz said apologizing. "But ya need to listen now er we'll both be caught by Scaithers fer sure! Then there won't be no chance a findin' Bridget."

Caroline stopped walking as she realized Oz was right and turned to look at him.

"All right. What do we do?" She threw her hands in the air in defeat.

"We still search, but we do it quiet like, see? No bellerin', an' we need ta take ta the trees ta get a better view a' the area. Think ya can climb?" Oz pointed to her injured leg

"I won't know till I try." She followed Oz to the tree line.

Oz led her to a large tree that was about thirty feet back from the water's edge. He showed her where to place her feet to help her get into the tree's large, lower-hanging branches. Caroline stumbled a few times, wincing in pain until she could get her good leg underneath her and pull herself up with the aid of Oz's large hands. Once in the branches, she realized they were wide enough in diameter to walk across without having to worry about balancing too much. And the trees mostly stood close enough together to walk from one to another. They searched the shoreline for any signs of Bridget but found nothing.

"Perhaps she didn't get pushed this far down," Caroline offered.

"True. Let's double back an' head upstream. She could a made it out somewhere earlier 'an we did," Oz offered, as they turned in the tree branches and headed back the way they had walked.

"Oz, what if we don't find her?" Caroline asked, not sure what answer he could give that would help.

"'Course we'll find her. Like ya said, why would God drop ya here and then let ya die?" Knowing full well he didn't believe a word of what he said. He had lived the what ifs and whys.

"The others that came here with you didn't survive. I don't know what would make Bridget or me so special as to be any different." Realization that they could die settling in.

"Maybe, but that was a totally differn't set a' circumstances. We were all betrayed by one a God's own."

"Like Judas Iscariot." Caroline's agitation softened as she remembered Oz's story from last night.

"Yeah, suppose so. I know God's still in control a' the situation, no matter what. So, if'n He didn't save 'em, I reckon that means He was finished with us. He sure left us all here ta die."

"Maybe. But just maybe He left you here for such a time as this, Oz. You're still very much alive. And Bridget and I probably wouldn't have made it this far without you. I just hope *she* is still alive."

Oz glanced at Caroline over his shoulder and without saying another word continued to walk through the lower tree branches in search of the missing young woman. If they didn't find her soon, they would have to stop and find a safe place to make camp. He had hidden camps all over the mountainside, places where the Scaithers wouldn't find them. Oz knew these woods like the back of his hand, even though the mountainside had a tendency to change. He had figured out the pattern and knew what to do when it happened. He just prayed to God that the Scaithers or any of the unusual, treacherous wildlife wouldn't find Bridget before they could.

The Lord is good, a refuge in times of trouble.
He cares for those who trust in Him.

Nahum 1:7 NIV

Chapter 7

Oz and Caroline hadn't had any luck finding Bridget, and the sun was hanging low in the sky. Oz led Caroline to one of his hidden camps located in the top of a tall tree. The forest was heavily wooded in this area, and the trees so tightly packed together that they made easy work of moving about unseen.

Oz pushed on a piece of the tree's outer bark, and a door collapsed into it. Caroline followed him inside another hollowed-out area, high in the top of one of the large trees. She was amazed at how Oz knew to find these places. But she supposed since he had lived among these trees for over twelve years and traveled by the safety of their higher limbs, it gave him ample time to do so.

"There aren't any wild animals in here are there?" she asked, feeling a little skeptical about moving farther inside.

"Nope. Not anythin' large enough ta do ya any damage anyhoo. Most a the predatorial-type animals are too large ta climb this high, an' the predatory birds are too large fer a nest this small." He stowed his pack up against the side of the tree's trunk.

"Predatory birds?" Caroline asked, again afraid of the answer.

"Yeah, Kabihanxu. They're big red, orange, an' yella birds. The locals call 'em firebirds fer slang, 'cause they look like fire streakin' 'cross the sky, an' they breathe fire. Plus, it's a lot easier ta say than Kabihanxu." Oz brushed off a stump for Caroline to sit on, motioning for her to do so. When she was seated, he took the wooden, makeshift door he had removed from the side of the tree and replaced it, sealing them off from the rest of the forest. He then commenced to building a fire, so they could dry off, keep warm, and have a hot meal. The smoke rose through the center of the tree and out several smaller holes made by nesting animals at the top. The sealed door would conceal the fire's glow, and the smoke wouldn't be visible after dark among the thick trees. He had caught a few tree rodents as they searched for Bridget and set about cleaning and preparing them for dinner.

Once Caroline had found her voice again and Oz seemed to have a bit more time to talk, she began asking questions. "Do these firebirds attack humans?"

"Well, I suppose so, if'n they're hungry 'nough. They're 'bout the size a the large Pagorinx we met earlier today. Sometimes, them two will take ta battlin' but not often. Firebirds tend to hunt a bit smaller prey. Easier pickins that a way."

"What else is there out here that I should know about?" Caroline shivered from the thought.

"Lots a' things, missy. Plenty out here that wants ta kill ya. Some fer fun an' some fer food. Just stick with me an' you should be all right."

"Well, I wish I could say the same for Bridget. I hope that wherever she is, she's all right." Caroline stared at the soothing, mesmerizing, dance created by the flames of the fire.

Oz watched Caroline as he went back to cleaning their dinner, feeling quite responsible for the lost girl. Caroline had been right earlier. If he had just controlled his emotions, they would be safe at his place at the top of Xantifal Mountain, but he had let years of anger fuel his temper and mar his better judgment.

They spent the rest of the evening in relative silence, lost in their thoughts as they ate. Then they turned in for a good night's rest; planning to start as early as dawn would allow.

Bridget awoke unsure of where she was. Her head ached badly, and she lay shivering in the cold night air, trying to remember what happened. Oh yes, now she remembered. She, Oz, and Caroline had been on the log with the Pagorinxes, and it had broken with the weight, sending them all into the rapids below. She remembered struggling to stay above water but barely succeeding. Then she lost consciousness as the raging river churned her every which way. She vaguely remembered something grabbing her, like a large hand pulling her from underneath the water and depositing her on the bank at the river's edge. Perhaps it had been Oz or Caroline who had plucked her from the water. But if one of them pulled her out, then where were they now?

Bridget's head and body ached, and she shivered uncontrollably. She needed to try to stand up and find a warmer place to rest. She pushed her tired and achy body up from the cold, hard, ground and brushed at the dirt and pebbles stuck to her face and clothing. Peering into the darkness, she could barely make out the tree line about twenty feet away. The moon was only a sliver peeking out from behind the sparse clouds that hung in the night sky, illuminating very little of the area. As she put weight on her right foot, she felt a sharp pain course through her leg. She looked down at her foot and realized that she had somehow injured her right ankle. She tried hopping toward the tree line, making quite a bit of noise in the process as she kicked up the loose gravel beneath her feet.

Suddenly she stopped moving. *Is something stirring in the bushes?* The thought brought her heart to her throat as she squinted desperately into the darkness beneath the tree canopy.

Lord, please help me. I'm a bit frightened, and I seem to have lost my friends, Bridget prayed, pleading with God. *What do I do? Where do I go?* she asked, looking around in all directions for an answer.

Just at that moment the rustling under the trees grew louder, and she saw what was making the noise. Even in the darkness, she could definitely make out the smaller of the Pagorinxes as it stood at the forest edge, looking directly at her. Bridget froze and just stared at the animal. It stared back at her in return. Then it glanced around, looking up and down the river's edge, before slowly stepping out of the underbrush toward Bridget.

"Lord, what do I do?" she asked anxiously, unsure where to go. Surely the Pagorinx could outrun her even if she had two good legs. Then she heard it again, just as she had earlier in the day. *"Be still,"* the voice said. Bridget stood her ground and took a deep steadying breath. "All right, Lord, I understand. Whatever happens, happens. This is my David and Goliath moment." She took another deep breath and slowly exhaled.

The Pagorinx slowly and cautiously made its way toward Bridget, stopping every so often to sniff the air in all directions. It came closer and closer as Bridget stood and watched. The cat was obviously a little unsure of her, which Bridget found understandable because she was a little unsure of it as well. She could feel its hot breath ruffling her hair and the drier parts of her clothing. She looked up at the animal's large eyes that shone in the night like two bright candle flames. The aqua pools calmed her even more, pulling her closer as she clumsily took a small step in its direction. She held out her hand slowly, stretching her arm up toward the animal's nose. She stopped for a brief second, unsure if she should continue, but the Pagorinx didn't move. It almost seemed to be waiting to see what she would do. She reached her arm higher, and her hand made contact with the silky fur of the animal's coat. As she stroked the fur along its nose upward toward its head, the creature purred and gently pushed back against her hand, seeming to enjoy the movements Bridget made as she stroked it's coat, then she brought her other hand up and scratched under the large cat's chin.

"You're not such a grand hateful beasty after all, are you?" Bridget grinned and then giggled as the animal pushed against her arms and body with its head, leaning into her just a bit and almost knocking her over. She stumbled a bit and cried out in pain. The cat stopped moving, as if it realized its part in her discomfort. The cat growled a bit under its breath, not menacingly, Bridget thought, but almost apologetically.

"Oh, it's quite all right," she said, offering the animal words of comfort as she continued to pet it. "Now what do we do?" she asked it, knowing it couldn't answer her.

The Pagorinx took another small step closer to Bridget and knelt down on the ground in front of her. She wasn't quite sure she was reading its body language correctly, but she thought it wanted her to climb on its back. *It might not be able to answer me, but it certainly appears to understand me.*

"All right, here I go," she said, slinging her injured leg across the massive back of the beast. As she pulled herself up into a sitting position just at the base of its neck, the cat stood and slowly walked back into the cover of the forest.

Caroline awoke to the smell of the fire and something cooking on the small cooking surface that Oz had fashioned out of a piece of metal. It appeared he had already been up and outside since he was cooking eggs of some sort.

"Ya hungry?" Oz asked, still working at the task at hand.

"Yes, I believe I am. Thank you, Oz." Caroline stood to stretch and brush at the dirt on her clothing and hands. "Is there some place close I can maybe wash up and use the bathroom?"

"Yeah, there's a small stream a little ways out from the tree toward the north. It feeds the Catamount River. But yer gonna' have ta climb down ta the ground. Think ya can manage it alone with that knee a yers?" Oz looked at her as he spoke.

"Yes, I believe so. It feels quite well this morning." Caroline walked to the makeshift door and pulled it open.

"Watch fer Scaithers down there, ya hear? They be roamin' 'round down there fer sure. Keep ta the thick part a' the woods. Soon as I'm done here, I'll put things away n' meet ya at the base a' the tree, so's you won't have ta climb all the way back up."

"All right, Oz, I will try to be as quiet and inconspicuous as possible. By the time I reach the ground and clean up, it shouldn't take me but twenty minutes or so. If I'm not back in that amount of time, you may have to come looking for me as well." Caroline watched the big man cook their breakfast.

"Will do, missy, jus' don't get caught." Oz eyed her sideways with a harsh *Or else* look on his face.

"I promise to try not to. I'm not as familiar with this world as you are. This is only my second night here, remember?" Caroline stated firmly, not taking to being chided like a child.

Oz just looked at her again and then went back to cooking. Caroline stepped out onto the large limb and began making her way down the tree staying as close to the trunk as possible for the extra support. After about five minutes of climbing, her leg began to ache a bit, and she still had at least another five minutes before she was at ground level. As she worked her way down, she peered through the thick branches of the neighboring trees, trying to spot the stream Oz had mentioned. She had no idea which direction was north. She couldn't spot any moss growing on any of the trees, so she would just have to use her senses to find the stream.

She stood still for a minute to listen to the sounds of the forest, hoping to hear water running. She closed her eyes and stilled her breathing as best as she could and just listened. Far off in the distance she could make out the call of some birds. They sounded large, with deep, haunting squawks. Perhaps it was what Oz had called the firebird? She could hear animals rustling in the branches around the forest and could slightly make out the sound of running water. Turning her head to discern the direction it was coming from, she located the deepest sound, opened her eyes, and looked in the direction she believed it to be. She still couldn't see anything, so she continued her downward climb. She was finally at the lowest branch when she could better hear the stream flowing. She supposed it was safe to continue on since the forest creatures were still roaming about and making noise. If they weren't bothered by her, then perhaps no one else bothered them either. She surely did not want to get caught by Scaithers, so she made her way toward the tinkling sound of the stream by way of the thickest brush, trying not to rustle too many branches and draw any attention to herself. She didn't want to be mistaken for food by anyone out hunting either.

She made her way through the undergrowth and found a place to relieve herself, then she continued on toward the sound of the water. Soon she could make out the stream from her position in the bushes. After looking carefully around as best she could, she tried to plot a course that would get her as close as possible without requiring her to step into the full light of day. It was no use. She would have to give up her cover to wash up. Was it really worth it? Taking a deep breath and one last look around, she slowly stepped out of the bushes and up to the stream. She leaned down and took a drink of the clear, cold water, hoping she wouldn't get sick from doing so. She palmed the water and splashed it over her face and neck, scrubbing as best as she could. She took a relatively clean spot on her cloak and dried her face, neck, and hands and quickly slunk back into the bushes.

As she made her way back toward the tree, she could make out someone talking. She stopped moving, almost afraid to breathe. She couldn't tell from which direction the sound was coming. Whoever had been talking had stopped, as though they were listening as well. Caroline was so frightened she began to shake a bit. She had never been this scared, but she had never met people as horrid as what Oz had described to her.

The voices soon continued their conversation, possibly assuming that whatever they thought they had heard was only an animal. Caroline could make out at least three different voices, all males. *Lord, what do I do now?* she thought. It sounded as though they were making their way through the forest hunting for food, saying that if they didn't return with some meat, Riglan was gonna cook their hides instead.

Surely Oz was watching from high up in a tree somewhere. Could he see her from where he was? Caroline stretched her neck, trying to peer up through the trees for any signs of him to let him know she was okay. As she turned to look up, she saw a giant snake-like creature hanging right above her head, glaring down at her, its forked tongue flicking rapidly in and out of its mouth. Caroline squealed before she could think. She quickly threw her hands over her mouth in an effort to squelch the noise, but it was too late. The men had heard her muffled squeal and had suddenly fallen quiet, looking all around.

Attempting to be quiet and at the same time avoid the large snake that was slowly making its way in her direction, she tried to back out of the brush as silently as possible. She thought the people were probably more dangerous than the snake, but as she kept her eyes on the snake, watching for any sign that it was about to strike at her, she lost any sense of where the men were. She risked a look around and saw one of them slowly making his way in her direction. Slinking deeper into the brush, she backed into something solid. She felt an arm wrap around her waist and pull her from the brush.

"Well looky here, boys. I caught myself a live one!" The man who had grabbed Caroline was laughing at her attempt to get away. She tried pulling out of the man's arms, but he was too strong for her.

"Now where did you come from, gal?" one of the others asked her, but his question was interrupted by a third man.

"I got some meat for dinner, boys! Looks like Riglan will be mighty happy with us tonight. We got two for one!" the third man said as he walked up holding the snake that had frightened Caroline out of hiding, its limp headless body hanging from his raised arm as the length of it trailed along the ground behind him, its muscles still twitching in spasms.

"I might not turn her over to Riglan. I ain't seen anything this purty in a looong time," the man holding her said. She could feel his hot, stinky breath on her neck, his arm tightening about her waist as his free hand began to grope at her.

"Faigen, you best not damage the merchandise or else Riglan'll damage you. You know he gets first dibs at anything and anyone we find." Faigen's roaming hands stilled and his voice became agitated and violent.

"Man, I'm tired of Riglan getting' the best of everythin', Marnor! It's time we take over and run things ourselves!" Faigen said, anger and aggravation evident in his voice as he now held her at arm's length, clasping her wrist with his large, grubby, hand.

The man called Marnor stepped forth and pulled Caroline out of Faigen's grasp.

"You best hope Riglan don't hear you said that, or else you'll be done for." Marnor turned his attention to Caroline as he looked her over. "I ain't never seen clothes like you're wearing before. That usually means you ain't from around these parts. Surely she can't be one a' them Peregrines, huh fellas?" he asked, looking to his friends. "We ain't had a new one a' them since the last time they all came in together. If you are one a' them, Riglan's gonna' be *real* happy ta see *you*. Yes, he is! I might even get a bonus for this one." He smiled at her, sucking through grimy, stained teeth.

"If anybody gets a bonus, it'll be me! I'm the one that caught her!" Faigen growled at Marnor.

"Yeah. But *I'm* lead man in this here group! And I reap the benefits, Faigen! Besides, you don't want me tellin' Riglan about how you're wantin' what's his, now do ya?" Marnor stared down Faigen. The third man, not saying a word, watched the exchange. Still holding the snake, he grasped his sword with his other hand and planted his feet firmly on the ground. He looked very tense, as though he expected a fight to break out any minute.

Caroline watched the exchange, terrified out of her mind but trying to pay attention. Apparently these men were only working partners and not friends. No allegiance among thieves was apparently their motto. That might play to her advantage later.

The man called Faigen seemed to back down at Marnor's threat to tell Riglan about his plot to stage a mutiny.

Marnor, looking satisfied with himself, said, "We best be gettin' back to camp and hand this one over ta Riglan. He'll be wantin' to have a little talk with you," he said, grinning at her again.

Marnor took some rope he had tied at his waist and bound Caroline's hands together, noticing her wedding band in the process. "Well, looks like we got us a married woman. Riglan might just change your mind on that." He smiled nastily as he then tied the end of the rope to his waist, making a leash with which to drag her along behind him.

As they made their way through the woods, going in the opposite direction of the tree where she was to meet Oz, Faigen and the third unnamed man kept watching her. She could just imagine what was going through their heads. She shuddered at the thought and the looks that Faigen was giving her. Every once in a while, when she thought it wouldn't draw attention to what she was doing, she would dare a glance up into the trees, hoping that Oz was following them. He had to have heard the fight between the two men as they argued over who got her and the bonus they spoke of. She didn't think she had journeyed that far from the tree. Of course, he did tell her not to get caught. Maybe he wasn't up to battling three Scaithers, if that was who these men were, and was going to leave her to her fate? But seeing as how Oz was willing to take on two Pagorinxes to defend her and Bridget, she was pretty certain he would try to take her from these three. Besides, they didn't really seem all that competent.

Thinking of Bridget made her wonder if her young friend had also been caught by Scaithers. She certainly hoped not. From what Oz had told Caroline about these people, Bridget would be better off dead. What had ever possessed her to try this peregrination thing? She knew why; it was for Seth. Lord, how she missed him! If he were here now, she doubted that these men would have stood a chance. Then again, they might have killed him. Good grief! Where was her mind taking her? She had no idea whether Seth was even alive. Did he even survive the earthquake? She shook herself out of her reverie. She needed to pay attention to what was going on in the here and now. Her life may well depend on it.

As Oz was closing up the tree camp, he heard the Scaithers noisily making their way through the forest floor beneath him. Caroline had to be on the ground by now, but he hoped she had heard them and hid. He should never have sent her off by herself, he chided himself. Now she was in real danger. Scaithers were worse than any animal he'd ever encountered. They cared for no one, not even their own kind. They were all out for themselves only.

As he made his way in the trees just above them, he saw Caroline duck down into the bushes when she spotted the Scaithers. He also saw her get caught and the enormous mountain striker that had frightened her to give away her location. Blast! Now he was going to have to figure out a way to rescue her before they got to Riglan or else it would be impossible.

Riglan was a right nasty piece of work. Oz had seen him handle the other Peregrines and he feared for Caroline. She was a very attractive woman. Riglan would for sure try to make her his personal mistress, but he doubted that Caroline would allow that. In the short time he had known her, he had seen that she was a proud woman, and he had noticed the wedding band she wore. He also knew she was a believer and did not fear death.

"Lord, it's been years since you an' me spoke. I know I don't deserve yer time, but I'ma askin' fer these girls ya brought here ta me. Surely this ain't what ya had in mind fer 'em? If ya see fit ta helpin' me here, I sure wouldn't look down on it," Oz said by way of prayer, looking to the sky as he spoke.

Oz watched them bind her wrists and tie her to Marnor's waist before starting the long walk toward one of the outlying Scaither camps. Apparently Riglan was at this camp if it was where they were taking Caroline. That might be the break he needed. Most of the Scaithers would be at the main camp at the edge of the Dustbowl. Lord willing there were very few other Scaithers at this outpost.

The Pagorinx cub had taken Bridget into the woods and climbed into a tree with large branches in which to sleep. Bridget had held on to the cat's coat for dear life, trying not to tumble over its back and out of the tree.

The Pagorinx found an abandoned nest in the tree big enough for it and Bridget to curl up in. She was a little hesitant to sleep next to the cat for fear it may roll over on top of her, but if God had led them to find each other then surely He would protect her as they slept.

The next morning, she jumped onto the cat's back once again, and the two of them made their way through the sprawling tree canopy of the forest.

"We need to find my friends. I'm not sure what happened to them, but surely God has protected them as He protected me." Bridget patted the cat as they walked along. She was unsure of where it was taking her but unafraid at the same time. Wouldn't Oz and Caroline be surprised when they saw her riding the Pagorinx? She only hoped that the larger of the two cats would be as welcoming as the smaller one had been.

Suddenly the small cat grew nervous and still. It began to growl low in its throat at something it sensed somewhere in the forest. Bridget listened as the cat listened. She could hear what sounded like someone yelling far beneath them. Then there was another voice yelling as well. The Pagorinx slowly crawled across the branches until they could see far below them. Several men, probably Scaithers, were arguing, and it appeared there was someone they were arguing over. Bridget strained to see but needed to get closer.

"Come on, little fellow, a little lower, please?" Bridget coaxed the cat, surprised when it actually did as she asked. Was this her calling from God? She had always had a special connection with animals, and it seemed to progress as she got older. She had never thought that she would one day be able to speak to them and have them obey her.

As the cat moved lower, Bridget's breath caught in her throat. "Caroline. No," she breathed in fear. The men had Caroline. Where was Oz? Had he not survived the rapids, or had the men killed him? *Lord, what do I do now?* As if in answer a thought came to her mind. She leaned closer to the cat's ear and whispered.

"We need help, little fellow. Take me to find some help. Quickly now." With that, the Pagorinx turned west and quickly maneuvered through the trees, making growling noises and calls as it went.

The growling of the cat high above them in the trees caught everyone's attention. Oz looked over his shoulder, scanning the trees and taking stock of his surroundings, ready to disappear if needed.

The Scaithers and Caroline looked up, as the men pulled her quickly along the well-marked forest path. Everyone began moving faster, hoping to avoid a run-in with a Pagorinx.

Do not store up for yourselves treasures on earth,
where moths and vermin destroy, and where thieves
break in and steal. But store up for yourselves treasures
in heaven, where moths and vermin do not destroy,
and where thieves do not break in and steal.

Matthew 6:19–20 NIV

Chapter 8

Reader's Island

The Dragoman council meeting on Reader's Island reconvened with each Dragoman deciding to send out Peregrines in larger groups in search of the waterfalls and what treasures lay in wait beneath them. Since Safra had no new leads to indicate where Bridget Burke had disappeared to, they focused their attention on finding the items that Odessa had dreamt about. In order to find the waterfalls, they spent the remainder of the week and the majority of the next, running computer scans of historical maps and matched them with the pictures Safra created from Odessa's dream. They had located four of the five falls and were still searching for the last one. Nothing in the databases so far had matched the description of that one waterfall.

Odessa, refusing to stay confined to the house any longer, insisted on going on the peregrination. She, Alec, Jason, and Seth were sent to Waiahuakua Falls on the island of Kauai, Hawaii. Interestingly enough these falls happened to be located in a sea cave. Nicholas, Dinah, Sean, and Kristen from Prisca's group were sent to Jog Falls in India. Gabrielle Bailey, Zaccai Wekessa, Dominic Amando, and Uriah Mose, from the group mentored by Malachai Harel, were sent to Iguaza Falls, which lies on the Brazilian and Argentinian border. And lastly, Ezekial Davis, Nadia

Bonhomme, and Timothy Johnson from Vashti Mayer's group were sent to Ban Gioc-Detian Falls between Vietnam and China.

While the Peregrines were searching for the mysterious falls and trying to find whatever it was that God was sending them there for, the Dragoman and Safra would continue to search for the final unfound waterfall and pray that God would guide them to Bridget's whereabouts.

Once the Peregrines had found the items, they were all to meet back at Reader's Island. The Dragoman had decided that, with the new turn of events, the ever-increasing dangers, and the frequency and destructive power of the current storms taking place, it would be best to let all involved know the whereabouts and existence of the island. Not to mention that demon attacks and movements were increasing. They had seen more demon activity in the last few years than they had during the previous twelve years. They all felt that the demons were trying to stop their progress, leading the Dragoman and Peregrines to believe that they must be getting closer to something important and evil was trying hard to stop them. And, since the island was the only truly safe place, it was important that everyone knew about it.

The Dragoman decided that all the Peregrines would travel in the current time period to explore the falls. All the available modern technology would make travel and exploration easier. Sending them all through portals into the year 2018 would enable the groups to rent four-wheel-drive vehicles to make the journey to the falls, rent camping equipment and scuba gear to make searching beneath the falls a possibility, and avoid unwanted attention. They would just appear to be normal adrenaline junkies out for another excursion. Plus, they could carry their weapons without fear of having them seen. Open carry laws were in place in this time period, and a lot of people carried guns due to the rise in crime, so they should fit right in.

Seth had yet to see most of the technology of this particular time period, and he was anxious to get started. His team planned to take a brief scuba course so they would know how to use the equipment once they arrived in Hawaii. Jason was already a certified diver. It was something he did for a summer while in college to earn money for school. He decided a refresher course wasn't such a bad idea, seeing as how it had been many years since he had actually been diving.

Fortunately for everyone, Ryan Halloran developed three more Portgens, as he said he would, and each team now had one to make traveling easier. He still hoped to eventually make one for each Peregrine and Dragoman, but these three plus the first one would help tremendously.

Jason, being the most technologically savvy person in Simon's group, carried the Portgen. They could actually set the device to the exact location of the falls, but they still needed the training and equipment, so they set it instead for the most remote part of the jungle, on the edge of the nearest town. In Hawaii, dive shops could be found in every small town. Since Kauai had a relatively small population, the Peregrines hoped to exit the portal unseen. Not knowing how long it would take to find whatever they were searching for; they would also rent camping equipment and enough supplies to last at least a week. Having a rental vehicle also meant that if they ran out of supplies, town was only a short drive away.

Excited about their mini-vacation/treasure hunt, they all packed and prepared for their trip. Jason was interested to see Seth's reaction to modern day things, Odessa was ready for a mission, Alec was ready to spend some time with Odessa, and Seth was just ready to see where God would lead them to next. He was also waiting for an opportunity to let his friends know of his recent decision to become a believer. Seth still hadn't forgotten about Caroline, but his dreams and his days were more peaceful now that he had accepted God's plan for his life.

On the brighter side these modern clothes were quite comfortable. He liked the way the soft cotton T-shirts fit and felt, and the new style of blue jeans were a very comfortable fit with something stretchy called spandex woven into the material. There were also shoes called tennis shoes with a lot of cushion in them and grip on the bottom. He wasn't real crazy about flip-flops though; they reminded him of house shoes. He felt certain that running in them would be nearly impossible.

Simon always seemed to be prepared wardrobe-wise, for every mission. He told the Peregrines that he didn't want to draw any unnecessary attention to them because they were already impressive looking, being athletic and in excellent physical condition.

It never really mattered where Seth was or what he was wearing anyway. People always seemed to notice him, just because of his height and size. He couldn't be inconspicuous if he tried. Getting used to this type of life where sometimes they needed to lie low and try to blend in was a bit difficult for him. But he supposed that since God chose him for this life, He would give Seth whatever he needed to accomplish his duties.

Using the new handheld device known as the Portgen, they set their coordinates and time period for travel and pushed the button to open the portal. It was such a blessing to travel via the Portgen without the need for a storm, but easier travel brought its own set of problems. Simon had warned them they would have to be much more careful when traveling now to avoid being seen. They would have to find secure locations in which to open the portals, quite possibly indoors. Finding these secure locations meant searching records to pinpoint coordinates. The Dragoman, especially those who were technologically savvy, would have their work cut out for them as they searched for exact locations for safe portals, even with the valuable help of satellite imagery.

Clearly communication between all the Dragoman safe houses and the Peregrines would need to be improved. Ryan planned to start working on a communications device as soon as he had made a Portgen for each Peregrine. He planned to develop a device that Peregrines could carry and that would allow constant contact with anyone, anywhere, much like the cell phones of the most current time periods. But Ryan's devices would have to connect over time as well as space.

Safra had decided to stay at Garganthera with Simon to help him with tracking his Peregrines through the chip program Ryan created. So far they were working well and no problems had arisen as of yet.

Simon called his group together for a brief talk before they jumped. "All right, you four, be careful. Hopefully the area is remote enough so no one sees you. Keep your eyes open for anything unusual when exploring the falls. We have no idea what we are searching for. Good luck and God speed."

"Sure thing, Simon," Seth replied, as the rest of the group responded likewise, and the four of them disappeared into 2018 Hawaii.

Stepping out into the lush green paradise that was known as Kauai, they were indeed fortunate enough that the location was concealed by jungle underbrush. The Portgen, they quickly realized, worked well as a satellite mapping device, showing them how far the nearest town was. They would have to walk about three-and-a-half miles to rent needed equipment.

Alec was the first to speak, "I have to tell you all, traveling with that thing is awesome! I've been doing this wet for so long and staying dry is amazing. Why didn't we ever think of this before?"

"I suppose we never had the right motivation before," Jason muttered, trying not to say too much.

Odessa looked up at him, "You mean like Simon having to create another storm?" she said, catching everyone else's attention.

"We were hoping you wouldn't notice," Jason answered.

"Yeah. Besides, Simon made us promise not to tell you," Seth offered.

"I understand all that. And I have already spoken with Simon about it. It is kind of hard not to notice the added gray streaks in his hair and the fine lines it added to his face. I'm really grateful to all of you for saving me and to whoever came up with the idea for the Portgen." She looked at the men who were like brothers to her.

Jason spoke as they continued their walk toward town. "Well, Seth actually suggested making something like this after the last storm Simon had to create. He and I discussed the effects it had on him and contacted Ryan to see if he could do something about it. He quickly came up with this design and device. You know, it still amazes me—the things that exist and what God reveals to us and enables us to do. Like Ryan and his inventions."

"I know what you mean, my friend," Alec agreed. "I am still amazed at things we discover. You would think I would get used to it."

"Well, I have a long way to go then because I just started this peregrination stuff. I'm sure there is a lot I have yet to see." Seth questioningly looked at his friends

"That you do, my friend, and most of it will probably be on this trip." Jason smiled at Seth and he then looked at the others, who were also grinning at him.

"I'm not so sure I like the way you all are looking at me," Seth's stopped walking, his eyebrows rose questioningly. Everyone else passed him by, smiling widely at his expression.

Jason replied. "It's nothing that drastic, just a total culture shock. People act and dress a lot differently from 1906. And the tech advances are really major. Just try not to look like a total tourist, okay?" Odessa and Alec giggled at his comment.

"Thanks for the warning." Seth smiled sarcastically and followed the group as they came closer to town.

They broke through the edge of the forest close to the small seaport town of Waimea on the Nāpali coast, the closest town to the sea cave, which was located along the Kalalau Trail, in the Nāpali Coast State Wilderness Park, in the Waiahuakua Valley. They discovered from the locals that it would be quicker to rent a boat to explore the cavern than to acquire camping permits to hike the trail. When they inquired at a local dive shop about renting a boat to take them to the sea cave, they were informed that the closest port was located at Kikiaola Small Boat Harbor in Kekaha, a little more than one-and-a-half miles from Waimea Town.

They then found a small motel where they would stay that night and plan the next step in their journey.

"We'll need to find out when the tours run, then plan our dive around them," Jason noted.

"Maybe we'll need to make the dive at night," Odessa suggested. "That way we're sure to avoid any run-ins with tourists."

"Yes, especially since we don't know what we'll be pulling up from the ocean floor," Alec added.

Seth sat listening to his friends plan the mission, curious about what diving entailed. He had heard of men doing it in the early 1700s but had never seen it done.

They settled into their adjoining rooms, each with plans to call the local dive shops to map out the touring schedules. Also known as the

Sacred Water Cave and the Double Door Sea Cave, the underground waterfall on Kauai seemed to be a very popular attraction, with many daily tours by the local dive shops. They would have to plan carefully, if only for safety. The oceans current was rough in the small area where the falls emptied into the cave. Because it was early summer, the falls would be stronger than they would be later in the summer, and the divers would have to be careful of the rushing water.

After many phone calls to local touring companies and research on the cave, currents, and the marine life surrounding the area, they decided to rent a boat and three sets of diving equipment and plan for exploration early in the morning. Alec agreed to stay topside to keep an eye on the boat and watch for uninvited guests.

They called a dive shop to schedule a diving course for all of them that afternoon, including Alec for future possible needs, and a refresher course for Jason. This would also include an instructional course on swimming with sharks should they happen to run into one while diving off the coast. They did not inform the instructor that they would, in fact, be diving the sea cave. The less people knew the better. They hadn't found any information stating that diving the sea cave was prohibited, so they felt pretty certain that they shouldn't attract any unwarranted inquiries.

They went out to walk the town and get some lunch. Seth looked around at the small handheld phones that were smaller than a piece of bread. Everyone he saw seemed to have one, and they carried them everywhere they went. He also noticed that people didn't wear much in the way of clothing. Women and young girls walked around in swimsuits that seemed to cover less than underwear would, and guys wore only shorts. Some had on shirts with no sleeves at all, only small straps that went across their shoulders. Jason, Alec, and Odessa seemed to be explaining something to him every few minutes.

"What is that?" Seth pointed to the small oval-shapes that zipped through the sky carrying people out over the water. Then he saw a bigger one flying higher in the sky that looked like a cross.

Odessa grinned at him and explained. "That, Seth, is a helicopter. It flies with blades that rotate in a circular pattern atop it and on its tail wing. The one flying higher is a passenger airplane."

"I've heard of airplanes before, but they were only small, one-person devices owned by only a handful of people. You're telling me that they now carry passengers?"

"Yes. A lot of them actually. It's the fastest way to travel from country to country, much faster than traveling by boat like you're used to. Speaking of boats, the ships they have now, called cruise ships, are almost as big as the boats you saw back in Garganthera. They carry thousands of people at once from port to port. Usually just for a vacation though. If people want to travel to a foreign country, they generally fly. It's much faster."

"I'd like to see one of these cruise ships one day and a passenger airplane," Seth said hopefully.

"I can show you on the computer in the room tonight when we get back to the motel. You won't get the full effect, but you'll get the idea anyway. Matter of fact, the internet can answer just about any questions you have," Odessa replied, thinking of other things she could possibly show him that might explain his new world better.

They spent the rest of the day attending the scuba class, renting equipment and a boat for the next morning, and teaching Seth how to work a modern computer. They had dinner delivered to their rooms and then went to bed to get an early start.

The next morning, after gathering the necessary equipment, they boarded the rental boat. Seth being a sea captain took charge of driving, with a bit of help from Jason. It didn't take Seth long to learn the way the modern boats worked. The speed at which they could travel and the way they handled impressed him. It was fun to drive the small boat, and he realized how much he had missed being on the water. They left the docks before sunrise and arrived at the cave just as the sun began to peek over the horizon, flashing a bright yellow, orange, and green light across the ocean's bright blue surface. The boat was small enough to drive into the cave, so they could drop over the side of it close to the falls.

As they entered the cave, the light from the rising sun was barely bright enough to illuminate the colors of the cavern's interior. At the base of the cavern, where it dipped into the water, the walls glowed pinkish from the corals creeping up from below. The walls were also striped with white and gray from the oxidation of the saltwater meeting fresh water. The falls poured heavily into the sea cave from a hole in the top, splashing down over the rocks into the ocean water below. It was a beautiful sight to behold.

They dropped the dive flag into the water as they suited up in the wet suits. The water was warm, but not knowing what was below the falls, they chose to wear lightweight dive suits to protect their skin against unknown objects in the water.

With flashlights in hand and a quick group prayer for safety and guidance, they flipped over into the water below. Alec continued a steady watch on the horizon and a trained ear for any unusual sounds, which might be hard to detect due to the noise of the splashing falls. Fortunately, new technology gave them the option of renting masks that allowed communication with each other and the boat so that they were all able to talk to Alec topside.

Seth, Jason, and Odessa dove down into the waters below the falls, scanning the walls and sandy bottom below as fish swam by, some curious as to what was invading their home and some frightened by the intruders. As the sun rose and rays of sunlight penetrated their surroundings, the waters around them began to brighten. The deeper they went under the shadow of the overhead rock, however, the greater the need for their flashlights.

As they explored the ocean floor, they used the small vacuum-type device they had rented to scoop the sand away and began slowly moving it across the bottom as they searched. Odessa's light bounced off something shiny just beneath where the falls emptied into the ocean. She beckoned to Seth and Jason to follow her as she swam toward the cavern wall.

She was almost at the edge when something suddenly darted out in front of her, bleeding purplish-black ink that spread through the water. Odessa squealed and pushed back, dropping her flashlight.

"Odessa, are you all right?" Jason asked her through the diver communication masks.

"Yes, just frightened by an equally frightened octopus," she said sheepishly, feeling peeved at herself for being so jumpy.

When Jason swam down to retrieve her light, he noticed a large ring shape lying on the ocean floor, partially buried in the sand.

"Odessa is this ring down here what you saw?" She met him near the ocean floor and he picked up her light and handed it to her. Seth meeting them also.

"No, what I saw was up in the rock where the octopus swam out."

"Seth, what do you think it is? Should we pull on it and see?" Jason asked with a crooked smile.

"Isn't that what we're here for?" Seth smiled back. They all exchanged glances, then Jason sucked up the sand around the ring with the vacuum device while Seth pulled at it, trying to free it from its prison. Odessa watched in all directions, communicating with Alec about any other people arriving on site.

"No one visible yet, Dee. You just be careful down there. I'll keep you updated about what's up here." Alec perpetually worried about her now, no matter what she was doing. Ever since Africa he couldn't help himself. He liked it much better when she was confined to Simon's house. He knew he was being unreasonable, but he couldn't help it.

As Jason deposited the sand elsewhere and Seth pulled, Odessa swam the small distance back up the rocks to where she had seen the sparkle. Unfortunately there was nothing there. She swam back down to where the guys were working to free what appeared to be a chest.

"Is that what I think it is?" she asked excitedly.

"What? What did you find?" Alec questioned with excitement of his own.

Jason answered while Seth tugged the item free from the suction and weight of the sand and water. "It appears that we have found a small treasure chest of sorts." A smile evident in his voice.

Seth smiled as Jason grabbed the now freed other handle. Together they hauled the chest to the surface, followed closely by Odessa. When they reached the surface and the boat, they handed the chest to Alec. Water leeched out of every tiny crack and seam in the chest as Alec hauled the water laden chest onto the boat. He placed it on the deck and covered the small chest with some towels and equipment as the others climbed back into the boat. Seth steered them back to the harbor, all of them anxious to open the chest and look inside, but they didn't dare to open it until they were in the safety of their adjoining rooms.

Do to others as you would have them do to you.

Luke 6:31 NIV

Chapter 9

Jog Falls, India

Jog Falls was an almost two-hour drive from Shimoga, India, where Nick, Dinah, Sean, and Kristen picked up the Jeep and the other equipment needed to explore beneath the falls. By the time they located and secured what they would need and drove the two hours, they would reach their destination with just enough time to find a place to set up camp and possibly cook a half-decent meal before bedtime.

They could stay in a motel somewhere close, but they preferred to be away from prying eyes. Diving under Jog Falls would certainly raise some kind of suspicion, so they were trying to play it safe and keep the questions from forming in the first place. They would just have to drive the rented equipment back to Shimoga when finished with it. They thought they might even find a place locally that would accept it or possibly a transport company that would return it if they paid them.

Dinah drove the Jeep, Nick rode shotgun, and Sean and Kristen sat in the back seat. Kristen, as usual, had her nose in another book, hoping to avoid conversation with Sean. Nick would have to talk to her soon about her attitude toward him; Sean was her peregrination partner, after all. He realized Sean could be a bit difficult at times, but they had to learn to get along. Things could not continue on as they had so far. Nick wasn't sure why her feelings for him were so strongly antagonistic, but they both often acted like children or siblings, arguing over anything and everything.

The way things were escalating recently, Nick was sure the Dragoman were preparing for something big. Prisca had mentioned a final battle several times over the years, but it seemed like that same reference was coming up more often. If they were all preparing for some great battle, then everyone needed to be in accord with one another. Sean and Kristen would need to work out their problems soon, or they could endanger not only themselves but others as well.

The drive was an uneventful one so far and Nick hoped it stayed that way. This was the first peregrination they had taken in almost three weeks since they tried to find Bridget Burke, and he was ready for an adventure. What he didn't need was an encounter with any demons. He prayed for protection for his group, even though prayer wasn't his strong suit these days. He wouldn't ask anything for himself, but he would for the other teams and his friends.

Dinah found what looked to be an overgrown trail leading through the jungle in the direction of the falls. The Portgen was a great little device that they could use like a satellite map to navigate. So far it had been correct in everything it showed them. The fact that Ryan had added this little feature to it showed how brilliant he was; he knew how greatly they would benefit from its help. Nick, being a science teacher before peregrinating, realized that a feature like that doesn't just happen; it had to be created. He would have to try and remember to send the young man a thank-you when they returned to Prisca's.

The four-wheel-drive Jeep bobbed and wove its way around and over fallen trees, making little work of the whole ordeal. The only problem was that every once in a while Kristen and Sean would slam into each other in the back seat, sending Kristen off into a fit about Sean controlling his space. And of course he said the same thing to her, seeing as he wasn't the only one who lost the ability to hold on at times.

Nick and Dinah glanced at each other. She grinned as he rolled his eyes, shaking his head in defeat. *Lord,* he silently prayed, *You are really going to have to do something about those two. They sure aren't going to listen to anyone else I'm afraid.*

About thirty minutes into the trail ride, they reached the edge of the falls and a clearing on the edge of the river that would allow them plenty of room to pitch the tents and set up camp. The men set up the tents as the women set about unpacking the necessary items to start a fire and cook some dinner. Kristen and Dinah split up to walk the camp perimeter, gathering firewood and keeping an eye out for anything or anyone that might pose a problem. They seemed to be in a remote location, unused by anyone for a very long time.

By the time they returned to camp, Nick was trying to catch some fish for dinner as Sean set about sharpening some sticks to use as skewers for cooking the fish. If Nick didn't catch anything today, they could open up a can of beans and eat some cold tuna from the vacuum-sealed packages. They had plenty of provisions, but fresh fish was something they were all looking forward to.

Kristen entered the camp area carrying a load of firewood in her arms. Her foot got tangled in something on the ground and she tripped. She fell forward and landed on the wood she had been carrying, scraping her hands and arms.

"Ouch!" She yelped and pushed herself up off the ground into a sitting position.

Sean ran over to help her up, but she just pushed at his hands. "I'm fine," she said, agitated.

"Would you stop fighting me? I'm just trying to help you up!"

"I don't *need* any help; I can do it!"

The same ankle that had caught on something and caused her to fall gave out under her weight. She would have hit the ground had it not been for Sean's quick reaction.

"See. You do need help." He led her over to one of the chairs they had unpacked and sat her down upon it.

"Kristen, are you all right?" Nick yelled from the water's edge.

"Yes, I think I just twisted my ankle a bit!" she replied helplessly, clearly aggravated at herself for her clumsiness.

"Here, let me see your ankle," Sean stated.

"I'm fine! You don't have to pretend that you care. I'm a big girl." Kristen's voice dripped with sarcasm.

"Would you stop being so pigheaded and just let me check you out?" Frustrated, Sean knelt in front of her and looked at her square in the eyes.

"Fine," she reluctantly replied, crossing her arms across her chest in agitation, wincing at the pain it caused from the scrapes.

Sean assessed her ankle to check for any damage, then looked over the scrapes on her arms and hands. As he washed the cuts and scrapes with water, he noticed that Kristen looked even more uncomfortable than usual, and he tried to make quick work of it, feeling a bit uncomfortable himself. He had never been close enough to purposefully touch her before, and it somehow unnerved him a bit.

"Well, your ankle seems okay, although you're going to need to stay off it for the rest of the evening. Hopefully you can use it tomorrow on the dive. The equipment is pretty heavy, though." He quickly found the first-aid kit in their supplies, then wrapped her ankle in an Ace bandage and handed her some antibacterial cream to rub onto her scratches.

"I do know a little about medicine, Sean. I was a nurse before my first peregrination, even if it was for just a little while," she scolded huffily.

"Can you not just say thank you?" Irritation with her attitude obvious as he placed a cooler underneath her foot to keep it elevated. "You know, I'm not trying to be bossy. I'm just trying to help."

Kristen shifted uncomfortably in her chair, feeling a little put out by his chiding, but he was right. She was being very ungrateful. She had just never seen a caring side to Sean before and she wasn't sure how to take it. She sure wasn't going to expect it to happen very often.

"Sorry. And...thank you."

"You're welcome." He walked off to pick up her dropped pile of lumber and continue to work on the fire.

She stole glances in his direction as he finished her chore.

Dinah watched the interaction with keen interest. She had returned toward the end of their conversation and had quietly gone about unrolling her and Kristen's sleeping bags and getting their tent fixed up.

Then she walked over to the river's edge to check if Nick was having any luck with fishing.

"Hey, did you catch that little scene back there?" he asked her as she approached him, not taking his eyes off the bobber floating about twenty feet out in the water.

"I caught the end of it." She smiled as she came to stand beside him. "It kind of took me aback to walk out of the woods and see Sean kneeling in front of her checking her ankle. I don't think I've ever seen him concerned over anyone before, not even when we were training. He was pretty hard on her if I remember correctly."

"Yeah, he was. I asked him once why and his answer was 'a demon isn't going to be easy,' and of course he's right. But she'll have plenty of time to figure that out for herself."

Nick and Dinah glanced back over their shoulders at the two younger people now sitting quietly by the campfire.

"So, any fish for dinner yet?" Dinah looked around for signs of a stringer hanging in the water.

"As a matter of fact, yes." He pulled a line from the bank with at least four good-size fish attached. "I caught these pretty easily. I want to catch a few more. You have seen Sean eat, right?" He smirked at Dinah.

"Yes, I certainly have!" She giggled at his expression. Dinah looked at Nick out of the corner of her eye. He was a handsome man in a rugged sort of way, and even though he was nine years her senior, she cared for him deeply. This way of life was no place or time to start a relationship, but perhaps one day when things quieted down, they might be able to have a try at one. She hoped and prayed for it anyway. She admired him more than any man she had ever met. His quiet strength and ability to overcome any situation intrigued her. The fact that he had lost his leg in a war known as Vietnam made him even more attractive to her. It didn't seem to stop or slow him down at all. She had never really seen Nick in a major battle yet, but if the training field was any indication of what he was capable of, then she was sure he was a worthy opponent.

Prisca hadn't allowed them to start missions until they were properly trained, which had taken her almost all of three months. Dinah had been a widowed housewife as a result of World War II when she peregrinated in 1943. She had been a factory worker, taking the place of the men who shipped out to fight. She had no living relatives except her husband, whom she had been married to a total of one week when he left for war. When she received the letter telling her that her husband was killed in combat, the stress caused her to miscarry their only child. That was only six short months before her first peregrination.

Life as a factory worker had made her stronger than most women, but as a Peregrine she still had a lot to learn. Wielding a weapon and sparring with someone took its toll on her body at first, but she soon toughened up. She and Kristen had been peregrinating for about a year each. She had arrived a few months before Kristen's arrival, and neither of them had any battle skills whatsoever. Kristen was stronger than Dinah due to lifting wounded soldiers onto gurneys during World War I in Germany where she worked as a nurse near the battlefront. Kristen's nightmares awakened Dinah one night, and it was then that Kristen let Dinah see into her past, but it wasn't something she really wanted to talk about. She hadn't told anyone else these details except for Prisca and Dinah, and she asked them to keep it quiet.

When Prisca discovered Kristen after her first peregrination, she was fresh from the battlefield, her uniform covered with the blood of injured men. At first Prisca thought she had been injured herself somehow, which was unusual for a Peregrine, but once she cleaned her up, she couldn't find any marks on her body. The uniform she was wearing told Prisca all she needed to know after that. After Kristen came to, it took her awhile to recover from the mental stress of what she had experienced and seen, added to where she found herself and what was expected of her.

Sean saw her long recovery as a sign of weakness; he had no idea what the young woman had already seen and experienced in her young life. Dinah supposed that was why he had been so tough on her during training, which she bore like a trooper, never letting on about her past. But it had caused Kristen to greatly dislike the young, arrogant, man.

Kristen's past wasn't something Nick knew about either. He often confided in Dinah about his concern for Sean and Kristen's relationship and why it was so strained, but Dinah wasn't at liberty to tell him about Kristen's past. It was something Kristen would have to be willing to tell him on her own, in her own time.

Nick caught a few more fish, and he and Dinah carried them back to camp to clean them. When they reached the fire, Sean was handing Kristen some medicine for the pain and swelling she was experiencing in her ankle.

"Sean, come help me clean these fish up. Dinah can take care of Kristen should she need anything." Nick hoped to ease some of Kristen's obvious discomfort at the young man's sudden concern and attention toward her.

Sean looked up at his friend. "Sure thing, Nick." A bit relieved to be able to put some distance between himself and Kristen. For some reason she seemed to unnerve him more this evening than she usually did. He wasn't sure if it was because she was being a baby about her ankle or because she was so hardheaded and stubborn. She seemed to only behave that way toward him, and he wasn't sure why. Regardless, she needed to toughen up, and Lord knows he had tried during training.

He wasn't sure why God would call someone like Kristen to do this kind of stuff. He doubted she would be able to hold her own in a battle. She would probably run scared and hide, leaving the rest of them to deal with the fighting while trying to protect her at the same time. When they were at Prisca's, he had heard her wake screaming from a nightmare and then even cry herself to sleep. Probably upset about being pulled away from her life. She looked like she might have been a pampered princess before this. Sure she was pretty, beautiful even, which is why he figured her for a daddy's girl. Spoiled and privileged, probably never worked a day in her life.

Sean, Dinah, and Nick cleaned and cooked the fish, and while eating dinner the four of them discussed the details for the following morning.

"Kristen, I suggest you stay here in camp and make sure that ankle heals well," Nick offered.

"It'll be fine by tomorrow. It already feels a lot better. I should be good to go by morning."

"That's just the pain meds talking," Sean said, frustrated that she wouldn't listen.

"Actually, I didn't take them." She looked at him in aggravation. "I wanted to make sure it was really well enough to use by tomorrow. The ice pack worked well enough."

"All right then," Nick said, "if you're sure you're okay to use it, then we'll stick to the original plan. Dinah and I will explore the right side of the falls, and you and Sean can check under the left side. Just remember to keep an eye on your air supply and don't come up too quickly. We aren't really sure how deep it is down there or what we'll run into, so be aware of your surroundings. If we don't find anything tomorrow morning, we'll take a break until the coast is clear. The falls are a big tourist attraction, and we'll need to wait until people stop milling around. That means early and probably late dives."

"Can we look at the picture Safra drew again?" Sean asked. "I want to see if the light might be placed more in a certain area. I have no idea if she drew it exactly like Odessa saw it or not."

"That's a good idea, Sean," Nick complimented him. "I would have never thought to pay that kind of attention to the drawing. If I know Safra, she probably asked that question when she drew it. She has a habit of being very detail oriented, seeing as how she has to be. When God gives her visions, the details are usually pretty important."

They spent the rest of the evening looking over the drawing and comparing it to what they remembered seeing of the area of the river beneath the falls earlier. Now that it was dark they were unable to see the falls clearly, but in the morning they could compare Safra's drawing to what they could see before starting the search.

They rose early in the morning just before daybreak to gather the equipment and get ready for the dive. Fortunately, the trail that brought them to their campsite led them out very close to the base of the falls and they didn't have far to walk before they entered the water.

Sean noticed that Kristen was limping a bit. "Why don't you just stay at camp until your ankle gets better?"

"It's fine, just a bit sore. Other than that I can use it. I'm sure it won't hurt at all once I'm in the water. Besides, we need all the help we can get. Even with the drawing revealing what looked like a specific area, it's still a large area to search, and we need to stay in teams. If you have to go with Nick and Dinah, then that will cut the search time almost in half."

"It's not like we're pressed for time, but if you insist. Just try to keep up, will you?" Sean threw at her over his shoulder.

"Sure thing, boss man." Kristen saluted as she strode past him into the water.

Sean had to hurry up and fix his mask to his face while Kristen dove underneath the water's surface.

The water was surprisingly clear. It was early summer, so the falls weren't as strong as they were in early spring, but they still ran with quite a bit of force. They spent the next two hours searching the river bottom. With the dive tanks running low on air and no luck as yet in the search, they broke to eat brunch and wait for evening when the tourist crowds would have departed. Dinah, being artistic, sketched a map of the falls. They marked where they had already searched so they wouldn't search the same area on their next dive that night.

They had a lot of down time between dives, so they spent some of it exploring the jungle around them. Kristen decided to stay at camp, not wanting to overdo the walking with her ankle. It had been all right to dive with, but she doubted she could make a trek all over the jungle. She grabbed her book and went to lie down on her sleeping bag to read.

"Kristen, do you want me to stay behind with you?" Dinah asked her younger friend.

"No, you go ahead and enjoy the hike. I'm just going to catch up on some reading. The quiet time will actually be nice. We don't get to be alone very often."

"I understand that. All right, enjoy yourself. We'll see you in a few hours."

"Kristen," Nick called, "make sure and pay attention to your surroundings, okay? We still have to watch for strangers and demons. This isn't a pleasant vacation where we have nothing to worry about."

"I know, Nick. Thanks for the concern and the reminder," she replied, grateful for the older man. He was like a father to her. Her own father had been great, her mother too. It had just about broken their hearts when she told them she was joining the war effort and becoming a nurse. Her parents had worried over her something awful; her mother cried, swearing they'd never see her again. Her father was angry and frightened that she would choose such a life but proud of her decision and determination. She told them she would only be gone for a few years. Little did she know then that God had other plans for her life. She often prayed that her parents weren't too distraught over her disappearance and that God would give them comfort.

Kristen lay in her tent reading in the quiet of the camp. The others had been gone only about thirty minutes when she suddenly heard a noise outside the tent. It sounded as though someone or something was rummaging around in the food boxes. She sneaked a peek past the flap of her tent to see what was making the ruckus and spotted a bear cub with its head stuck in an empty pot.

Kristen then became very worried. Where there was a cub, there was a mother. Even though her ankle felt better and she was trained in combat, she didn't think she could handle an adult mother bear protecting her cub. She slowly peered around the perimeter of the camp, still within the cover of her tent. Surely the mother wasn't far.

What to do? she thought almost in a panic. Should she just stay hidden in the tent? The mother bear was bound to smell her scent. Should she risk leaving the tent and maybe hiding in the Jeep? That would be safer. Metal was much stronger than canvas. She peered out the flap again, eyeing the Jeep and wondering where the mother bear might be. She clutched the small rifle they had packed for protection and carefully looked outside. The cub was still curiously looking through the cooking equipment when Kristen slowly stepped outside the tent. She cautiously surveyed the campsite and quietly began to make her way toward the Jeep. When she reached the vehicle, she slowly opened the door, thankful it wasn't locked and quickly climbed inside. As she shut the door she heard the growl. The sound of the door had alerted the mother to the fact that someone was close by. The mother made an appearance from behind the tent Kristen had just vacated.

The adult bear wasn't huge, but if she stood on her hind legs, she would be bigger than Kristen. She growled and called to her cub as she looked at the Jeep, her nose sniffing the air. The cub seemed to ignore its mother, still interested in its current game of pawing at the pots and cups then chasing them as they rolled along the ground with each swat, clanking together as they did. The mother's growling and calls became increasingly agitated as it watched the vehicle and then the cub. She walked over to her cub, swatting at it as she coaxed it back into the safety of the woods.

Kristen sat as still as possible in the locked Jeep, hoping, and praying the cub would follow its mother back into the woods. It was very warm inside the vehicle with the windows up and no air flow, but she didn't dare move a muscle or chance even cracking a window.

The mother bear slowly ambled back into the forest still calling to the cub, who thankfully soon followed its mother. Even though they were both out of sight, Kristen still didn't dare move. She hunkered down in the seat propping her knees on the dashboard and trying to stay calm. She wasn't about to get out of the vehicle until the others returned. She only hoped they didn't run into the mother bear on their way back.

When Nick, Sean, and Dinah returned to camp several hours later, they immediately noticed the mess lying about the grounds. Worried about Kristen, they hurriedly searched for her in the tent, calling her name as they did.

"Kristen!" Nick yelled, looking about at the mess.

"Kristen, where are you?" Dinah called.

"Kristen!" Sean called, growing very worried. She might get on his nerves, but he would never wish harm to come to her. A thought suddenly occurred to him, and he ran to check the Jeep. When he did, he saw her lying in the front seat. He tried opening the door, realized it was locked, and started banging on the window.

Startled by the noise, Kristen sat up, soaked through with sweat from the heat inside the Jeep. She opened the door quickly, relieved to see them back. Then she nearly fell when she stepped out of the jeep; her left leg was asleep after being in the same position for the last few hours. If Sean hadn't caught her, she would have hit the ground once again.

"Kristen, what happened?" Nick asked her, as he hurried to the car.

"A mother bear and her cub wandered into the camp. I heard something outside the tent, and when I looked out, I saw the cub playing with our equipment. I knew the mother couldn't be far behind and decided I would be safer in the Jeep. I must have been in there awhile if I fell asleep."

"When did the bear and cub appear?" Sean asked.

"Maybe thirty minutes or so after you all left." He helped her sit in a chair Dinah set upright for her.

"That means you were in there for almost two and a half hours. No wonder you're so sweaty." Sean and the others continued to pick up the campsite while Kristen waited for the feeling to come back into her leg.

"I need to take a bath. I'm going to walk a little way down river and clean up."

"Not alone; Sean and Dinah can both go with you. Sean can keep watch in the woods while Dinah stays close to the shoreline with you. I doubt the bears will come back here. I will finish picking up and get us some lunch prepared." The look on Nick's face brooking no arguments.

Sean watched, as Kristen limped her way to her tent to grab some fresh clothing, and the trio set off about a quarter mile downstream. Sean, trying to give her privacy, stayed at the forest's edge, even though he had a strong urge to look back.

"What is going on with me?" he questioned himself out loud in aggravation. His thoughts began to run away with him as he paced the jungle floor. *It must just be from the stress of everything going on. Besides, most guys would sneak a peek if they could, wouldn't they? It's just overactive hormones. After all, I'm in my prime now, right? Most twenty-five-year-old guys spend their nights and weekends partying, not traipsing the world for God!*

Sometimes he felt cheated by this way of life that he had no say in. But then he remembered his upbringing and the life he led before he peregrinated. He had always felt like an outsider, in school and in his job. He never felt companionship with the people he worked with. Not that they were at odds or anything; he was simply not included in after-work gatherings or break-time conversations. He never had a best friend growing up, and the friendliness of the youth group at his local church had been a real draw. Though, even in the youth group, he wasn't able to find that someone special or even a close friend. He had stopped going for a while and had recently started attending the young adults class, when a major hurricane hit the coast where he lived and he peregrinated for the first time. He was a believer for sure, but sometimes he struggled with doing the right thing. Like now.

He shook his head to clear his thoughts and decided to walk a little farther into the woods to combat the urge. He had found true friendship here. Nick was more like family, like an older brother to him. He was actually old enough to be his father, but their relationship was more of a friendship, a close friendship. Sean had never had someone to confide in before or someone to tell him when he needed to step up or straighten up because he was behaving like an idiot. Nick did that and Sean respected him for it.

"Hey, Sean!" Dinah yelled from the bank. "We're finished and heading back to camp."

"All right, I'm coming!" He wound his way through the underbrush back to the river. He couldn't help but look at Kristen. Why did she irritate him so much? Oh well, it didn't matter. They were in no way compatible. They fought all the time. He wondered why that was. What was the reason?

As they got closer to camp, they could smell the smoke from the campfire. Nick was heating some beans and hot dogs on a wire-frame grill placed over the fire and already had the camp back to rights.

"Well, that didn't take you long." Dinah laid the rifle down on a small table. "Sorry we didn't make it back to help clean up."

"It wasn't as bad as it looked. It only took a few minutes. The cub was just curious. That was smart thinking on your part, Kristen, to get in the Jeep."

Kristen looked at Nick and grinned lopsidedly at him. "My parents and I used to go camping all the time when I was younger. My dad taught me all sorts of survivalist stuff. He said I might need it one day. If he had only known how right he was." Kristen hung her wet, freshly washed clothes over the wire makeshift clothesline they had attached between two trees.

"Smart man. I've always said a kid needs to be self-reliant, and they can't learn that from a book. Don't get me wrong; I'm not knockin' reading now. I was a science teacher, after all. But I firmly believe parents need to fully invest in their kid's lives."

"Did you ever have any kids, Nick?" Kristen asked, watching him intently, noticing he looked a bit uncomfortable but only for a brief moment.

"Sure, I had plenty of kids. Hundreds of them actually, ninth through twelfth grade," he smiled and chuckled.

They all laughed at his remark and grabbed a plate to eat lunch. As they ate they planned out where they would dive that evening. They could see several tour boats out on the water, with some of the people waving to them as they passed by.

Nick hoped that the tourists saw them as normal campers. They kept the diving gear out of the sight of prying eyes and the fishing equipment very visible. From all accounts they should appear to be an average happy family out on a vacation. Nick hoped that during tonight's dive they would find the item or items they were there for. He didn't relish too many days like this one; he preferred to keep busy. He didn't like down time; it allowed for too much thinking, and he had no wish to spend time reliving the past.

But blessed is the one who trusts in the LORD,
whose confidence is in him.

Jeremiah 17:7 NIV

Chapter 10

Bakrashan, Zanchier, Xantifal forest floor

Oz followed the three Scaithers from the treetops for as long as he could. Once they reached the open plains of the Xantifal grasslands, he had to change his strategy. He couldn't use the cover of the tree branches any longer and had to resort to following them at ground level.

After pulling Caroline along behind them for several hours, the Scaithers finally reached their camp with their prisoner. Fortunately, Oz knew it wasn't the main camp and hopefully wouldn't have but a small band of Scaithers stationed there. But apparently, from what he gathered in snatches of conversation he overheard in the forest, the leader of the Scaithers, Riglan, must be there. If true, that was definitely bad news.

Riglan was ruthless, cruel, powerful, and smart, and Oz would have a hard time getting Caroline out of there without his knowing. And once Riglan laid eyes on her, it was doubtful he would let her out of his sight. Oz just prayed the Scaither leader wouldn't do anything to harm her before he could devise a plan. Another concern was that all this extra trouble delayed the search for Bridget, whom he seriously doubted was even still alive.

It was just an hour before noon, and it would still be another six hours or so before it got dark enough to be able to attempt a rescue. Oz decided to find a place within earshot of the Scaither camp where he could rest. They would have to run and run hard if he was able to get Caroline out, and he would need his strength and energy. He wasn't a young fella anymore, and he was beginning to feel his sixty years of age. All things considered though; he did all right. God seemed to give the Peregrines strength and good health, and most Peregrines received supernatural abilities to use in battle against the demons. They didn't always find their gift right off. Oz hadn't used his in so long he doubted that it still existed. Maybe he could try it against the Scaithers. Usually, using a gift against another human being wasn't allowed, meaning it just didn't work. But maybe, since these men were as far from human as possible, God might make an exception this one time.

As Oz lay in wait in a cluster of trees, bushes, and rocks, just a quarter of a mile or so from the Scaither camp, he thought about the past. Thinking about his supernatural gift brought to mind all the friends he had left behind when transported to this world thirteen years ago. He thought about the gifts that had been given to all of them when this started, hundreds of years back. When God chose people to begin Peregrinating, different people were given different abilities, some greater than others, depending on what God wanted them to do. Other Peregrines and Dragoman came with their own sets of skills, which were enhanced supernaturally by God, allowing them great victory over the evil that plagued the dimensions.

Oz just didn't understand why those gifts had not served them all here in Zanchier, where they had been greatly needed. Sure they had put up a good fight and had taken out a lot of the Scaithers, but evil had won out. The bitterness he had felt toward God for the past thirteen years began to seep into his soul again, and he had to push it away. Surely there was a reason he was still alive and all his friends had perished.

He remembered that some of the Peregrines were using their gifts to benefit themselves and that they were turning from the missions that God had set before them. The lust for more power and gold began to eat at their very souls. Perhaps that is why they had perished in this horrid land. Maybe it had been punishment for their past sins against the Lord. However, not all who died here had turned, but he supposed that was how things had always worked in the world. The innocent often paid the price for the guilty. Add to that the betrayal of one of their very own, Hiram Burke, and you had a recipe for utter disaster. Even Jesus Christ had a betrayer. What would make them all so special to expect anything different?

God does have to work with human beings, and we are a fickle lot, Oz thought. He supposed he ought to feel fortunate enough that the good Lord saw fit to love people enough to care and to try to do something about the evil plaguing the world. He could have left humans to their own devices to perish forever.

Deciding he had better stop the wanderings of his mind and get some much-needed rest, he closed his eyes and leaned against the nearby tree and rock grouping. Hidden by the thick underbrush, and out of the heat of the afternoon sun, he got as comfortable as was possible and drifted off to sleep.

Caroline's legs were weary from being dragged through the forest and across the Xantifal plains. The sun was hot and she was thirsty and hungry. It was close to noon, and she had yet to eat anything today with her breakfast being interrupted by being caught. The Scaithers who captured her had all been chewing on some type of jerky-like substance, but they only teased her with the food, offering and then retracting the offer. She practically had to beg for a few sips of water, trying to avoid dehydration and them having to carry her to camp. Fortunately they agreed to the water, probably because they knew that if Riglan got word that they had another possible time traveler and they had let her die, he'd surely kill them all.

As they walked across the vast open plains at the base of the Xantifal Mountains, Caroline could make out a grouping of tents off in the distance. That must be where they were taking her. Even though the sun was high in the sky and there was no shade, making it unbelievably hot, there was a slight breeze that blew across her skin to cool her every so often. She looked out over the tall, waist-high grasses bending with the breeze, the tasseled tops loaded with seeds that occasionally fell to the ground or were carried off on a gust of wind to be deposited elsewhere. There were small groupings of trees and bushes planted on sparse areas of the plains that provided shade and homes for whatever animals might take up residency on the plains. It was really quite beautiful, if only she could enjoy it. At least the rumbling of the mountainside had stopped, leading her to believe that the changing terrain didn't come down this far.

As they drew closer to the camp she could hear a few people yelling that Faigen, Marnor, and Quenzie were approaching and that they had returned with a present for Riglan. Quenzie must be the name of the third man. Caroline hadn't heard anyone say his name yet, and she noticed that the other two seemed to push him around. She also noticed him watching her quite often on the trip here. Not in a creepy way, but kind of curious and naive. He was actually the one who had given her water but only after permission from the one called Marnor. Faigen, however, watched her closely as well, but in a very alarming way. She was certain that if she were ever left alone for very long, Faigen wouldn't waste any time taking advantage of her in a very cruel way.

Upon entering the camp, people began touching her cloak, hair, and clothing, making her very uncomfortable. Marnor turned and noticed all the attention she was getting.

"Hands off the merchandise, people! She belongs to Riglan! We think she might be one a' them Peregrines," he stated as the small crowd of people began to murmur and whisper amongst themselves. But they did at least heed Marnor's warning and left her alone. For that she was grateful. Apparently this Riglan had a lot of pull. It seemed as though everyone was afraid of him. She looked around the campsite as they walked along, noting the tents thrown up here and there, about fifteen in all. There was also an area where it looked as though they skinned animals for food. There was a line hung between two tall poles that had animal skins of various sorts drying in the sun. In the center of the makeshift village, a firepit was surrounded by logs split in half, which apparently were used as seating.

Marnor continued pulling her along until they came to a larger tent where they stopped. Just outside the tent flaps on either side, two scantily clothed women sat upon some sort of elevated platforms covered in large animal skins. One of them seemed to blanch when she looked at Caroline. She wasn't sure what the expression that flitted across the woman's face was, but it didn't seem to be a pleasant one. When the flaps parted, a man stepped out whom she assumed to be Riglan. He wasn't particularly tall or large, but his countenance and manner were very intimidating, and she could feel the tension in the air increase around her as people became a bit restless and nervous. She could feel Faigen looking at her, and when she glanced toward him, she could see the dislike, and perhaps even jealousy, on his face for the man they called Riglan.

"Well, well…what do we have here?" Riglan said as he looked over Caroline from his place between the two women.

"I found her hidin' in the Xantifal Mountains," Marnor said, looking at Faigen as if challenging him to correct him.

"And I caught dinner, Riglan!" Quenzie said quickly and excitedly, apparently attempting to please the man.

Riglan just looked at Quenzie, who quickly clamped his mouth shut, backed away, and looked at the ground in contrition.

Riglan slowly walked up to Caroline. He reached out and fingered her hair with his right hand as he walked around her, using his left hand to push her cloak back to look at the rest of her.

Caroline jerked her face away from him and looked away, not wishing to be manhandled but unable to do anything about it.

"Looks like you have a bit of spirit as well as beauty. That's all right, girlie, I like a little bit of fight in my women," Riglan breathed across her cheek.

Caroline didn't speak, knowing full well anything she said would only spur them on to hurt her sooner than later.

Riglan grinned a nasty, greasy smile at her and looked at Marnor.

"Put her in my tent for now and tie her to the center pole. I'll deal with you a bit later, girlie," he said, still fingering her hair between his blackened, dirty fingernails.

"Oh, and Marnor…get the branding iron ready. I want my *special* mark on this one. Do it quickly so there's no mistake that she belongs to me." He looked menacingly at Faigen.

Caroline stiffened in fear. Did she hear him correctly? Did he just say he was going to brand her with a hot iron? She began to beg, pulling against the ropes so that Marnor had to practically drag her into the tent as she fought against the restraints with all the strength she could muster.

"Please don't do this," she begged anxiously, looking at Marnor square in the face.

"You sure are a pretty one." Marnor looked closely at her. "Sorry, girlie, but when Riglan takes a liking to ya there ain't no stoppin' him. Besides, the iron is the least of your worries." Marnor bit his lip as he stroked the smooth skin of her cheek. Then he proceeded to tie her to the center post in the tent.

"It'll only hurt for a little while. I'll be back in about thirty minutes for you." He was lowly chuckling as he left.

Caroline sank to the floor of the tent, shocked at her situation.

"Good Lord," she sighed breathlessly, "what do I do now?" She looked toward the heavens, and closed her eyes, praying harder than she ever had in her life.

She was still praying when Marnor returned for her. He pulled her up off the floor and untied the rope from the tent pole. Caroline looked at him and he just smirked at her.

"Let's go, princess." He pulled her along behind him.

Caroline knew it was useless to resist; these men would only hurt her more, and they would still brand her, but she fought against the ropes all the same. She tried to think of a way to get away, but escape seemed hopeless. Everyone was watching her as Marnor led her to the firepit in the center of the camp. There were several people standing around watching as he pulled her over and almost threw her down on a log. Caroline righted herself to a sitting position, her hands still bound by ropes in front of her. Marnor picked up the branding iron and walked toward her with it. Caroline stared wide-eyed at the end of the hot, bright, red-and-orange iron rod as the heat from it distorted the air around it. She began to hyperventilate as he stepped closer and she jumped up to run not getting very far. She heard his cruel laughter ringing in her ears as two men grabbed her, put her back down on the log, and held her there.

Marnor walked over to her, pulled her cloak back off her shoulder, and ripped the sleeve of her dress down her arm, exposing her left shoulder. Caroline braced herself the best she knew how and began to breathe harder as fear gripped her body. She squirmed in her seat against the hands of her captors but to no avail. Marnor raised the iron, blew on the hot end, and then placed the iron against the skin of her exposed shoulder.

Caroline screamed in pain as the iron burned deeply into her skin and muscle and then passed out. When she came to, she found she had been placed back inside Riglan's tent, the unbranded arm and both feet tied to the side of the bed. The arm that Marnor branded had been bandaged haphazardly, and it hurt fiercely. She could smell the faint odor of burnt flesh emanating from beneath the makeshift bandage. As she lay still, trying to deal with the pain, one of the scantily clad women she saw earlier walked into the tent. She carried a tray filled with water, ointment, and some fresh bandages. She didn't look at Caroline, keeping her eyes on the tray in her hand. Caroline noticed a thin metal chain connected to metal cuffs placed around her ankles, linking them together. The chain must be stronger than it looked if it was meant to keep her from running away.

Caroline tried to sit up, but the woman stopped her and nudged her back down on the cot. She seemed to be kind although she appeared tough and broken. *She must be as much a prisoner as I am. How long has this woman been here?* Caroline wondered. The woman set about removing the bandages from Caroline's arm. Some of them had stuck to Caroline's skin in spots, and she moaned quietly. As the woman tugged the bandages away from the open sore, Caroline cried out in pain.

"You'll heal," the woman said as she pointed toward her own arm. "Yours is a bit different," she explained to Caroline. "Riglan marks only his most prized possessions with this particular brand." She motioned toward Caroline's arm. "It's a sailing vessel. Riglan longs to venture out to sea, but there isn't any place like that here on Zanchier. Just a few lakes and rivers."

Caroline lay still and listened as the woman administered pain and burn cream to her arm and redressed it. She seemed to be finished talking so Caroline decided to ask her a question.

"What's your name?" she asked, watching the woman's face. She still had not looked at Caroline.

"Riglan calls me Shraiva."

"But what is your real name?" Caroline heard the evasiveness in Shraiva's words.

"I haven't used it in a very long time," she said, swallowing hard, her eyes darting up to look at Caroline. "Riglan doesn't permit us to use our given names. Only the ones he gives us."

"I won't tell him, I promise," Caroline told her, hoping to gain a friend and ally.

Shraiva looked nervous and glanced over her shoulder toward the open tent flaps before turning to look at Caroline again. She swallowed hard again and whispered her name to Caroline.

"Sofia. But do not call me by that name. Riglan will punish me if he knows I told you." She stood to walk out of the tent and then spoke over her shoulder to Caroline once more. "I will be back at nightfall to prepare you for tonight."

"What does that mean?" Caroline asked her, paranoia lacing her voice.

"Riglan will take you tonight, ceremoniously. In front of the whole village." She looked at Caroline with understanding.

"Please, just untie my wrist. I'll slip away. No one will know it was you," Caroline pleaded with her. "I'm already married. See?" She held up her hand as best as she could.

"I can't. He'll know. No one ever escapes from Riglan. Besides, he won't care if you're married or not. He only cares about himself and what he can get. And tonight, that's you." Shraiva turned and left the tent quickly, leaving Caroline in despair as tears began to fill her eyes. She had kept herself pure until marriage, just as God's Word instructed, and she prayed again to God, begging Him to spare her the humiliation that was to befall her in just a few short hours. She also prayed that God would not allow the breaking of her marital vows to Seth, even though she doubted she would ever see him again. Regardless, she would forever remain true to him until God chose differently, and she knew this was not God's choosing for her now.

Lord, I trust you. Whatever happens, I trust you to take care of me. She lay still, waiting. Waiting on her God to come through for her just as His Word told her He would.

Oz jerked awake to the sounds of loud music and raucous laughter. Gunfire exploded into the air as party revelers screamed and bellowed, excited about the coming event.

"Good Lord! Not already!" Oz jumped to his feet as fear gripped his chest; his stomach churned as he thought about the ritual that was to take place. Riglan usually waited several days before taking a new girl. He must really be taken with Caroline, as Oz knew he would be. And that also meant that he had already branded her. Oz felt sick to his stomach.

"God, I need yer help, an' I need it now!" Angry words gritted out between clenched teeth. "Why would Ya lead these poor gals ta me if'n ya was gonna let this happen again?"

"Be still and know that I am God."

Oz shook his head to clear it. He thought he heard someone speak. Could God have actually spoken to him? *Nah.* It must have been a figment of his imagination, the stress of the situation making him crazy. He couldn't relive all of this. He had seen too much of it in the past and couldn't stomach it again. If he couldn't rescue Caroline, then he would put an arrow in her heart to save her from such a life. They would surely catch him, but he was tired of this half existence anyway. At least this time he would go out fighting and take as many of them with him as possible.

Oz quickly and as quietly as he could made his way through the tall grass of the plains. He figured the night watchmen were likely drunk in anticipation of the celebration to take place and wouldn't be paying as much attention as usual. Besides, the Scaithers feared no one and nothing. With all the noise they were making, they wouldn't hear his approach anyway. He decided to move faster; he accepted the likelihood that he would be caught, but the fact that he no longer cared smothered his fear. He was focused only on Caroline and saving her or setting her spirit free, whichever he needed to do. And this time he wouldn't hesitate.

Oz snuck almost silently to the edge of the camp, just behind one of the tents. He poked his head up to see over several barrels which were stacked to the side of the tent and scanned the area, looking for Caroline. He needed to get closer to Riglan's tent. That was where it would all take place, just outside the opened tent flaps. Oz worked his way toward the tent as the revelry continued. Scaithers stumbled over each other as they got drunker by the minute. That was good news for Oz. They wouldn't be as agile or able to shoot straight. He knew that Marnor, Riglan's second in command, would be sober, so he would definitely have to keep an eye out for him. Oz crept along in the darkness at the camp's edge until he came to where the majority of the Scaithers were gathering. The largest place usually marked Riglan's tent. As he approached, he tried to see over the heads of the people gathered in front of him. He found some stacked crates and climbed on top of them so he could get a clear shot at his target. He silently prayed the crates would hold his weight.

Steadying himself and readying his bow, he crouched and waited in the darkness. He had hoped that he could sneak into Riglan's tent from an unprotected side, but Riglan was smart and always placed his tent somewhere in the center of camp, securing all corners. However, no one would be behind the tent so maybe he could try it anyway. Just as he was about to jump down from his perch atop the crates, the flaps of Riglan's tent parted and he stepped out onto the platform. Oz was too late. Directly behind him, dressed in a skimpy golden dress, was Caroline being led to the platform behind him. The dress barely covered her chest and left her midriff exposed. The lower half sat low upon her hips and reached to the floor but was slit all the way up to the top of her thighs.

The top had no sleeves, only thin strips of material or what looked like thin chains that encircled her upper arm.

Oz could see a bandage, apparently where Riglan branded her. Her arms were spread wide open and tied to two poles that had been erected in front of Riglan's tent just for tonight. She looked surprisingly calm considering what was about to happen to her, but Oz shook with anger at what they were doing to her, memories of his former comrades and their similar situations invading his mind.

Oz raised his bow, his arrow trained on Riglan. This was his chance to kill the evil man. Perhaps it would cause enough chaos that he could free Caroline in the confusion. Just as he was ready to let his arrow fly and find its mark, a drunken Scaither stepped up on the platform and blocked his shot.

Oz noticed Riglan step toward Caroline. "You're going to make a wonderful addition to my collection. Now, I just need to think of a new name for you. Oh, and after tonight, you can take that ring off. You won't need it anymore. As a matter of fact, I'll take it as your dowry." He grinned slyly. "I must say, you seem rather calm. You must be looking forward to this."

"Actually, I'm calm because I believe that God will deliver me from your hand. I have no reason to fear you." She looked him square in the eyes.

Riglan roared with laughter as he turned to the rest of the camp. Knowing that his lackeys were unable to hear the exchange, he decided to regale them with her speech.

"Did you hear that?" he yelled to the crowd. "She ain't afraid of us! Her 'God' is gonna save her!" He laughed so hard that he was struggling to breathe. He was immediately joined by the loud raucous laughter of the crowd.

When Riglan finally righted himself, he stood in front of her again, mocking her with his words as he wrapped his hand around the back of her head and pulled her face toward his. "Your 'God' doesn't exist. I'm your god now! No one can save you from me!" he hissed, planting a wet, disgusting kiss on her lips, as she squirmed to get loose.

Oz saw his chance to take Riglan out of the picture, having a clear shot of Riglan's left side from behind. He only hoped his arrow would hit him hard enough to enter his heart and strike him dead. Oz pulled the bowstring taut and released it. The arrow struck Riglan under his raised left arm just beside his heart.

As Riglan screamed in pain, Oz heard a loud, fierce cry. A large Pagorinx jumped the tents and landed in the center of the Scaither camp. Several more Pagorinxes followed, and people ran for their lives. The cats swatted at the men and women, slinging them out into the night. The Pagorinxes were joined by several larger Kabihanxu, which swooped down from the night sky, plucking Scaithers from the ground and then tossing them out across the darkness of the plains, lighting the ground on fire behind them.

The entire camp erupted in panic. People ran in every direction or battled hopelessly against the animals. Nothing like this had ever happened before. Oz couldn't understand what would have provoked the animals to attack a Scaither camp, and that was when he saw her. Bridget sat atop a smaller Pagorinx cub that walked calmly to Riglan's tent. Bridget slid to the ground where she attempted to untie the ropes that bound Caroline to the poles. Oz rushed to help her, weaving his way through the chaos playing out around him. As he approached the girls, the Pagorinx cub growled at him. Bridget turned, startled.

"It's quite all right, little fellow. Oz is one of the good guys." Bridget smiled at the cub who quickly quieted, then moved aside to let Oz come closer to help.

Oz watched the exchange with unsure awe. He didn't know what to make of it. Apparently Caroline didn't either. She watched the animal cautiously, looking back and forth between Bridget and the cub.

"Bridget, I've never been so happy to see anyone in my life!" Caroline said as Bridget freed her wrist while Oz worked on the other one. "Same goes for you Oz!" Caroline smiled from ear to ear. God had come through for her and had not only showed up but seriously showed off.

As soon as Oz and Bridget got Caroline's hands free of the poles, Bridget called them to follow her to where the cub sat waiting for them.

"Come on, you two, follow me and climb up," she told them as the cub lay down and Bridget straddled its back. They looked at her uncertainly as the cat sat waiting. "Hurry up, you two! It will be just fine!" she reassured them. "Unless you would rather stay here?" She gestured at the chaos around them.

Oz let Caroline climb up first and then climbed aboard behind her. They clung to each other as the young cat jumped the tents and ran off into the dark grassland of the Xantifal plains. The other animals left the chaos in the camp and followed close behind them.

The Kabihanxu flew overhead, out of sight in the darkness of the night sky. Their piercing calls penetrating the cool, night, air in haunting fashion and echoed off the distant mountain range.

Oz and Caroline sat petrified and unable to move or speak, anxiously watching the pack of Pagorinxes surrounding them. They realized that the larger cat from yesterday and the cub were two of the ones that attacked tonight, apparently led somehow by Bridget. Caroline had no idea how or when she began communicating with animals.

The cats ran quietly back to the mountains, making short work of the distance. What had taken them half a day to navigate by foot, the cats ran in less than two hours, enabling them to make it back to the gorge before midnight.

"I've asked the Pagorinx to take us all the way back to Oz's place at the top of the mountain. He's agreed, but his mother will tag along as well. We should reach the top in just a few more hours. I think we might be more comfortable riding the rest of the way on the mother's back. I know it's sort of a tight squeeze with all of us riding this little guy, plus I think he's growing tired from the extra weight. He's already carried us ever so far. Shall we switch?" Bridget asked, as though it was normal conversation and absolutely not unusual that they were about to climb on the back of an adult Pagorinx.

"Bridget girl, how do ya know she won't mind us climbin' on her back?" Oz nervously watched the cats, afraid that they would turn on them any minute.

"Because she told me so of course." She replied with such surety and nonchalance that all Oz could do was shrug his shoulders and follow her lead.

The mother Pagorinx knelt down as they used her legs and joints to climb upon her back, pulling themselves up with her long soft hair. She never even growled as they tugged themselves into position and settled in. Once safe atop her back, Bridget patted the cats side. She stood and then climbed the mountainside quickly. All they could do was hold on tight, trying not to fall off her back as she ran, using the shortest route available. They were dead tired, but the rough, jerky ride on the back of the cat made sleep impossible and improbable. Riding a Pagorinx would take a lot of getting used to.

They reached Oz's place a few hours later. After bidding the cats farewell, they entered Oz's hidden tree house and found a place to sleep for as long as their bodies would allow. Sleep was all any of them were interested in. Caroline hadn't even thought about food or her burnt arm. She did drink several glasses of water before taking to the floor on top of the soft, skinned hides that she and Bridget had used before. Her body quickly succumbed to the extreme exhaustion and stress of the past few days.

Chapter 11

Waimea, Kauai, Hawaiian Islands

Seth steered the rented boat slowly into the docks, and all four Peregrines looked around, taking stock of how many people were milling about this morning. Since it was just past ten and not too many eager tourists were out yet, they had almost complete privacy. They would have to cautiously unload the small, twenty-by-sixteen-inch chest under heavy cover to make sure no one saw it. If anyone knew what they had on board the small boat, there would be trouble. Treasure hunters, as well as the local government, would be breathing down their necks, so being inconspicuous was of the utmost importance. Fortunately the chest was relatively small, and most of the water had already leeched out, making carrying it easy. They had wrapped the chest in a few of the dive suits they had removed earlier so Seth could just hoist the chest and pack it under his arm as though he were just carrying a bundle of wet suits. Odessa and Alec would keep in close proximity to him to make sure nothing was visible from any other angle as they carried some of the remaining equipment back to the rental car. Jason would deal with unloading what was left in the boat and returning the keys to the rental shed.

Once back at the car, Seth placed the chest in the trunk, removed the wet suits, and covered it with their towels. They would drop the chest off at the motel before returning the equipment. It wasn't due back for a few days anyhow. They had made sure they would have equipment for several days if they were unable to find what they searched for in one day and had to venture out again.

They returned to the motel by 10:30, after picking up breakfast on the way. When they unloaded everything, including the chest into their outside facing motel room, they pulled the window shades and laid out a few towels across the table to catch any residual water once they opened the chest.

They all looked down at the small waterlogged and sand-worn decorative box. Considering how long it may have been under the falls, it was in surprisingly good condition. It was built with thick wood and bronze. Brass was evident in some of the metal pieces, which were now green and brown from years of water exposure. The metal braces and hinges were still mostly intact and showing very little rust. The wood was a little swollen and splintered all over but still solid and strong. They could barely make out a few symbols that had been etched into the metal stays and braces, but between the encrustation of barnacles and the damage from the many years under the water, the symbols were not clear enough to tell them anything.

"Time to see what is inside this thing!" Alec anxiously rubbed his hands together as though excited for a treat.

"Yes, but try not to damage the chest," Odessa instructed him. "I wonder how old it is?" She fingered the wood and metal of the chest, curiosity eating at her.

"Maybe something inside will give us a clue," Jason offered.

"Hopefully there *is* something inside," Seth said with raised eyebrows.

"Surely this is what God intended for us to find. I saw something shining in the side of the cliff but there was nothing there. Then suddenly the chest handle appeared below me? That is not a coincidence fellas, *that* is God's leading." Odessa smiled a big toothy grin. She enjoyed seeing God's hands at work in her life and the lives of others.

"I agree." Jason stood with his arms across his big barrel chest and rubbed the stubble evident on his chin. "Now, how are we going to open this thing without breaking it? That may not be possible, Odessa. After all, whatever is inside is what we need, not the chest itself," he said, somewhat apologetically.

They stood around the table looking at the keyed lock that was dangling from the front of the chest. It was rather rusty and corroded and wouldn't likely open even if they did have a key.

Alec smiled. "I can try to pick the lock. It is fairly old and may not give me much trouble except for the corrosion. Besides, lock picking is one of the skills I have acquired over the years that I rarely get to use. If that doesn't work we can always purchase some bolt cutters from a nearby store." He walked into the adjoining room and returned with a small leather bag that held all the tools he used for just such an occasion. "I never leave home without them." He smiled again, holding up the small bag, then he sat in front of the chest and began to work at the lock.

It took him a bit longer than expected to dig out the sand and grit built up inside the keyhole. They had to take a few bottles of water and a toothbrush to clean away the sand and chip at a few barnacles that had taken up residence. Once the keyhole was cleared out enough, Alec went to work picking the lock. After a few minutes they heard a dull click and the heavy bottom of the lock fell away.

They all grinned, looking at each other in triumph and anticipation.

Jason slapped Alec on the back. "Good job, man."

"Why, thank you, my friend." Alec cockily smirked as he pulled the lock from its position and placed it on the towels. He then slowly lifted the lid, not wishing for any sea creature that had somehow found its way inside to leap out at him.

"Wow!" Odessa said breathlessly. "Look at this stuff!" She lifted a handful of precious jewels from the chest bottom. They were wet with sea water and did in fact contain a few very tiny sand crabs and seaweed. "We need to clean this stuff off with fresh water. I was reading books from Simon's extensive library while I was homebound, and I read in one of them that treasure plucked from the sea that had been there for a long time needed to stay in a freshwater bath for a little while to remove the salt water from every crack and crevice and to keep it from rusting once the air got to the treasure. Let's fill the tub with water and put the chest inside. We actually should have done this immediately. I was just so excited I didn't think about it."

"How long does it need to stay in the water?" Seth asked, hoisting the chest. He carried it into the bathroom behind Odessa, with Jason and Alec following close behind.

She put the stopper in the tub and turned on the cold-water tap.

"If I remember correctly it needs to stay for about a month, maybe longer since it's not a small item, and we need to change the water every few days or so. It allows for a gradual re-acclimation of the items to prevent rust of the metals and the splitting of the waterlogged wood."

"We only have one problem with this, Odessa. How are we going to sneak this chest out of town when we walk back out to the woods to generate a portal? It's going to be hard to hide. We can easily carry the stuff inside in our bags, but the chest is a different story," Seth asked, depositing the box in the bathwater.

"Now that we have the Portgen Simon did say that we should be able to generate a portal from inside. So why can't we just jump from right here in our rooms?" She looked at all the guys for an answer.

"I don't see why we couldn't," Jason replied. "It's definitely worth a shot. Once we see what all is inside the chest, specifically a key or set of keys, then we can return the rental equipment and car, check out of the motel, and just leave from here."

Suddenly, there was an unexpected knock at the front door. "Room service," they heard a man say.

"Did anyone here order room service?" Jason looked at the group. Odessa, Alec, and Seth shook their heads no, and Jason put his finger up to his lips to quiet everyone. Pulling his gun from his holster lying on a table, he walked toward the motel-room door. As the others left the bathroom, Odessa pulled the door closed, and they followed Jason into the room with their weapons ready. Jason pulled open the door, his gun pointing at whoever, or whatever, was on the other side.

The man on the other side of the door stood with his hands on a cleaning cart. He jumped and screamed when he saw the gun and the other three standing in the room with bows and swords trained on him. He threw his hands into the air, fear gripping his features.

"I-I-I'm just offering cleaning services! Sorry to intrude! I can come back later!" He backed away and hurried off as quickly as his cleaning cart would move, not even glancing back over his shoulder.

Jason stuck his head out the door and looked around. It didn't appear anyone else was around. He closed the door, then turned to everyone else with a look of aggravation.

"I'm sure he'll call the local authorities as soon as he can, so we will have to leave the rental stuff for the agencies to deal with. I could have sworn I sensed a de...."

Before he could finish his sentence, the door to the room burst open, and three men broke through. The Peregrines knew the authorities would soon be upon them; they had no time to deal with demons.

Jason fired off several shots as Alec's arrow flew and found its mark in the chest of one of the demons, killing it instantly. Seth swung his sword as one of the demons leaned back to avoid decapitation but Odessa was behind it and swung her katana, hitting the demon when it leaned back. It too fell dead. Jason had hit the third demon in the head several times with his pistol and finally had killed it. As they caught their breath, looking at the mess created by the demons' remains, all began to lift, then dissipated into the air and floated out the open door.

Jason quickly closed the door and turned to look at the group. "We need to leave now." They all quickly gathered their things, threw the treasure back into the chest, and opened a portal right there in the room, disappearing through to the other side right onto Reader's Island.

Jog Falls, India

When the tourist traffic had dwindled, Nick, Dinah, Sean, and Kristen donned their wet suits once more. With flashlights in hand they went back below the falls in search of whatever God had brought them here to find. Their only clue was that they believed they were looking for keys to open an ancient set of locked Dragoman archives. After searching for over an hour now with no luck, they surfaced to take a break and rethink their strategy.

"We must be missing something." Nick sat at the water's edge. "Are we certain these were the falls the computer matched Safra's sketch to?"

"Yes, according to what Prisca told us, this is the correct spot," Dinah answered.

"Can I look at the photo of the falls again? The one of Safra's drawing, not the computer match." Nick handed Sean the picture.

Sean sat and stared at the photo, glancing back and forth between it and the falls. Kristen peeked over his shoulder to peer at the picture. They both sat a moment studying the photo, then at the same time they both realized what was wrong. He and Kristen looked at each other when she pointed to the location of the glowing light that Safra had drawn near the bottom of the falls.

"I don't think we need to dive." Sean, realizing the light wasn't actually in the water but just at the base of the falls, looked at Nick.

"What do you mean?" Nick asked puzzled.

"I think there might be a hidden cave behind the falls. See here." He pointed to the area in the picture. "The light isn't sitting *in* the water, but just hovering over the surface, right here at the fall's base."

"Well then," Nick said standing, "let's go cave hunting, shall we?" He grinned at the others as they all excitedly stood and then followed him to the wall of rock located behind the falls.

They turned on their flashlights due to the lack of sunlight behind the water that gushed down beside them, wanting to make sure they found adequate footing on the slippery rocks. As they squeezed behind the falls, they had to walk through some of the cascading water to follow the rock wall. Soon they realized that there was indeed a large open area behind the rushing water. As they ventured farther in toward the center where the waterfall, which had divided above, came together again, they found a small cave entrance that seemed to lead farther back into the rock. Sean and Kristen looked at each other and actually grinned for the first time. Then they followed Nick and Dinah through the opening. It was a tight squeeze at first, but the entrance began to grow larger as they went until it opened into a small, squarish cavern about twenty feet by twenty feet. Ledges and rocks jutted out from almost every wall and at every height, with some large boulders jutting up from the rock floor.

"Well, if there is anything in here, we certainly won't be digging for it since the floor is literally rock hard," Nick said.

"Maybe we need to climb?" Kristen offered. "Some of those higher ledges are pretty large."

They all shone their flashlights up at the high ceiling of the small cavern.

"All right. Kristen and Dinah, you two look around down here. Sean and I will climb the rock and see if we can find anything up there."

They all set about poking around in the rock, looking for anything that stood out. Nick and Sean, taking opposite sides of the cavern walls, climbed upward while searching the areas around them and any available ledges as they went. After about twenty minutes of searching, Sean, who had climbed about fifteen feet up the wall and was standing on a larger ledge, suddenly bent over and then yelled to the others.

"Hey, I think I've found something! There is a hole in the wall up here, and there appears to be some sort of cloth tucked into it." He stuck his hand inside the hole and grabbed hold of the item. When he did, he felt something wriggle in his hand. Before he could see what it was, it bit his forearm just above his wrist. He yelled and yanked his hand out of the hole, pulling the cloth and whatever it was that bit him with it. His yelp of pain got everyone else's attention. Sean slung a snake to the floor below, dropping the bundled cloth in the process.

"A snake just bit me, and I think it was a coral snake."

They all shone their flashlights on the small snake, and Kristen and Nick both sighed in relief.

"You're fine, Sean," Kristen yelled up to him. "It's just a scarlet kingsnake."

"No, I'm pretty sure it was a coral snake. It had all the markings. I saw all of the red, yellow, and black rings. They are deadly. What am I going to do?" Panic laced his voice as he started to hyperventilate, sitting high above them on the cliff ledge.

"Sean…Sean, are you listening to me?" Nick called, trying to calm the young man.

"I can't believe it," Sean said, his voice growing higher in pitch with every word he spoke. "I'm gonna' die, right here in this cold, dark cave."

"Sean...you are *not* going to die!" Kristen yelled up at him, grabbing his attention and Sean stared down at her.

"How do you know?" he asked, still panicking, but at least he was paying attention.

He watched as Kristen walked over to the snake and picked it up. She held it high and directed her flashlight's beam on it so he could see it.

"This," she paused for effect, "is a scarlet kingsnake. It bears the markings similar to a coral snake, but it's harmless. See...if it were poisonous, I promise you I would not have picked it up." She gave him a look of reassurance as she showed him the snake dangling in her fist.

"Okay...okay. I'm climbing down now." Sean, praying that his still shaking body wouldn't make him miss a foot or handhold and cause him to fall, slowly climbed back down the wall.

When he reached the floor of the cave, Kristen had already walked out toward the sunlight and the falls, carefully carrying the snake with her to let it loose in the water. Nick had picked up the cloth wrapping that was bound with some sort of jute twine, and he and Dinah followed Kristen out of the cavern. Sean was the last to leave, his nerves still a little out of sorts. He felt a little foolish after being so paranoid about the bite, especially when he saw Princess Kristen actually holding the thing in her hand. He walked out of the cave just in time to see her deposit the snake in the water just behind the falls on the opposite side they had walked in from.

He cleared his throat and awkwardly waited for her to catch up with them.

"Uh, thanks," Sean said to her a bit hesitantly.

"For what? Showing you the snake wasn't poisonous?" she asked, unsure what he had to be thanking her for.

"Well...yeah. I was really panicking up there. I thought for sure that I was dead." They walked out of the opening behind the falls and along the slippery rocks back to the river's edge.

"Well then...you're welcome." She grinned. She stepped briskly ahead of him toward the campsite and caught up with Nick, who was pulling the cloth wrapping out of his pocket.

Sean watched her go, realizing he had a bit more respect for her than he had before. He would never have picked up a snake, poisonous or not. Not for anything or anybody. He could battle demons and do things he would never have thought he could, but when it came to snakes, he felt terrified. They were his greatest fear. He hurried to catch up with the others so he wouldn't miss the unveiling of whatever he had found.

Nick placed the item on the camp table as everyone anxiously gathered around it. He took out his pocketknife and cut the string, then unwrapped the dingy, discolored, once-white piece of thick cloth. Inside was another cloth, which they unwrapped to reveal a lone key, a note written on the inside cloth in a foreign language, and a small bag of gemstones.

"I think we found what we were looking for." Nick smiled.

Since the rental agencies were all closed by now, they decided to spend the night in the tents. While Nick and Dinah made a fire and some coffee, Kristen tended to Sean's wounded wrist.

"You don't have to worry about it, Kristen. I'm sure it will be fine." Sean again felt uncomfortable with her making a fuss over him, especially after the commotion he had caused earlier. Not to mention that her closeness was making his palms sweat.

"You need to clean it out, Sean. If you don't, it might still get infected. The snake may not have been poisonous, but it still put four holes in your skin. You need to put some antibacterial cream on the bite and keep it wrapped," she said, doing exactly that.

Sean cleared his throat again and looked over her head at the water. If he kept looking at her, he might end up doing something he would regret later.

"How did you know that snake wasn't poisonous?"

"Remember when I mentioned earlier about my dad taking me camping years back?" Sean nodded. "Well, he taught me all sorts of things, including how to tell the difference between poisonous and non-poisonous snakes. Here's a rhyme he taught me. Remember it. Red and yellow kill a fellow. Red and black, jump back Jack. See when the red and yellow touch, it means it's a coral snake. When red and black touch, it's harmless. The bite still hurts, but it won't kill you." Kristen grinned lopsidedly at him as she slightly peered up at him.

Sean grinned back at her briefly and watched her finish wrapping the gauze around the wound. When she finished she stood and said, "I think you'll live, but keep that clean, all right?"

"Thanks, Doc," he said jokingly. "How do you know about all this doctoring stuff?" he asked as they walked over toward Nick and Dinah by the campfire. "Something else your dad taught you?"

He noticed that her face grew more serious and her muscles along her jaw tensed a bit.

"I was a nurse before peregrinating." Kristen looked away.

Sean hesitated and then asked, "Where?" Clearly nursing must hold some sort of bad memory for her, but he was curious.

"World War I; the German front." She looked at him before walking over to the camp table placing the first-aid kit on top of it, then disappeared into her tent.

Sean just stood and watched her as she walked off. He had assumed she had served as a candy striper in a hospital somewhere. He would never have pegged her for being from that time era or for doing something so dangerous and hard. He imagined the things she must have seen and had to deal with. He was realizing he had her pegged wrong the entire time he had known her. He had been especially hard on her during training, thinking she had been sheltered her whole life and was weak. His opinion of Kristen had begun to change on this trip. He began to hope that their relationship would change a bit too. Maybe they wouldn't fight so much and perhaps get along better on their peregrinations. They had recently only tolerated each other enough to function. Maybe now that he understood her a little better, they could work on building a real friendship, or at least a decent working relationship. Sean pushed aside whatever feelings he thought he had felt earlier, relating those feelings to the situation at hand and the trauma of the snake bite.

He went to sit by the campfire with Nick and Dinah and enjoy a cup of hot coffee. The three Peregrines sat and chatted as dusk settled over the campsite. Before long Kristen appeared from her tent and joined in the conversations. They all sat and enjoyed each other's company and the quiet of the forest for the next several hours before turning in for the night.

Early the next morning they ate a quick breakfast, packed up the camp, loaded the Jeep, and were soon on the road for the two-hour trip back to Shimoga to return everything they had rented before they could return to Prisca's.

The drive to Shimoga was a quiet one with everyone lost in their own thoughts or sleeping from the boredom of the long car ride. Once they had returned all the equipment to the places they had rented from, the Jeep being the last, they found an out-of-the-way location inside an unused shed at the edge of town, walked inside, opened a portal, and walked out the other side onto an island.

Sean, Dinah, and Kristen all looked around in amazement at what lay before them. Nick turned back to look at his group. Realizing he had forgotten to tell them they weren't going back to Prisca's just yet, he smiled at his friends as he spoke.

"Welcome to Reader's Island. Follow me to the main house, and I'll explain what you see as we go." He had brought them out through the portal at the lighthouse because those were the coordinates that he already had from other journeys here. Nick talked and explained the barrier and everything else they saw before them as they walked the distance to the main house, where they would meet every other living Peregrine and Dragoman during this trip to the island.

To this you were called, because Christ suffered for you, leaving for you an example, that you should follow in his steps.

1 Peter 2:21 NIV

Chapter 12

Xantifal Mountains, Bakrashan, Zanchier, Oz's tree house

Caroline awoke later that morning, her stomach growling fiercely from hunger. The room was quiet, and she noticed she was the only one there. She went to push herself into a sitting position and winced in pain. Her arm was aching beneath the bandages, and she decided she had better take a look at it.

"Oz? Bridget?" she called. There was no answer. When she stood, she realized she was still wearing the rather provocative dress from the night before, so she grabbed her bag and decided to change into the clothes she was wearing when Bridget found her about six weeks ago. She had still been wearing the sixteenth century garb when she was captured by the Scaithers, so fortunately she still had her comfortable pants, shirt, and shoes from early twentieth-century California.

She looked around the tree house in search of a bathroom, finding one just on the other side of Oz's bedroom. It was a more of an outhouse on a landing outside his room. It had a makeshift toilet and a basin made out of some type of tortoise shell, that had a pull chain connected to a storage tank overhead. She removed the bandage from her arm and looked at the branded skin. It was still puffy and red, swollen from the irritation of the hot iron. The skin around it was peeling a bit and still oozing blood and liquid. Caroline found a clean cloth, filled the basin with water and cleaned the wound as best she could. She decided she had better leave it open for a while to dry out. She changed her clothing, ripping the sleeve of her shirt to allow the air to get to her arm, then finger combed her hair and went in search of something to eat.

Entering the kitchen once again, she found some bread and some pieces of dried meat. Grabbing the food and a cantina of water, she set out to explore the tree house. Oz had plenty of room on the branches beyond his home that still lay beneath the sheltering canopy of the massive tree. They would need to extend the tree house some and make another room or two for her and Bridget. They couldn't keep sleeping in his kitchen floor. Besides, they had no idea how long they would be here. Caroline still held out hope of getting to the Dustbowl, but she had no real plans for the present. Just being safely back at Oz's was a great relief.

She walked up the gradually twisting staircase that rose from the right side of his kitchen into the tree's branches. There were several windows that looked out over the land in all different directions as she ascended the staircase. One had a handheld telescope that was attached to a makeshift mount in the windowsill. She took the device in hand and leaned forward to scan the scenery before her. The telescope afforded her a view of approximately a mile, and as she scanned the mountainside she noticed the landscape changing again, this time very far off. She could also see a few of the native animals roaming the mountainside through the trees, as well as strange creatures in the skies. This brought back memories of the night before and their ride on the backs of the Pagorinxes.

She continued chewing on the bread and dried meat in her hands and guzzling the water as she climbed the staircase as far up as it would go and found herself on a flat platform area. It felt very sturdy but had no handrails. She had to be hundreds of feet into the air up the side of the tree. The platform actually extended across several branches, beginning at the tree trunk, and reaching outward on the large branches. Small sets of steps led up or down to other platforms. Moving from one platform to another, Caroline was able to see different spots throughout the forest all around Oz's tree house.

You could hide forever up here, she thought. There were so many platforms and different levels, all tucked nicely in the crooks of the tree's branches and hidden by its greenery. She wondered if it was all visible when the leaves vacated the tree? If that sort of thing happened here in this strange land.

She decided she had better head back down the tree and see if she could find Oz and Bridget. Surely they weren't far from the tree house. She made her way back down the stairway, through the kitchen, and out the large, heavy wood-and-iron slab that served as Oz's front door. She walked through the very dimly lit pathway underneath the tree's lower branches and roots, into the clearing just outside the opening leading away from the tree. When she had stepped into the clearing, she stopped and listened for any sounds that might tell her where Oz and Bridget might be. As Caroline walked the perimeter of the tree in search of them, she heard the faint, familiar rumble of the changing mountainside. She continued her path around the tree until she heard Oz's distinct voice carrying through the air. Now to gauge from which direction it was coming. Caroline followed the sounds until she came upon another clearing on the far side of the tree, almost below where she had been on the platform overhead just thirty minutes before. Oz and Bridget were standing in the field, and Bridget was holding a bow and quiver in her hand. Oz was apparently trying to train her to shoot.

"Hey, you two, what's going on?" Caroline asked, making herself known to her friends.

Oz and Bridget looked back over their shoulders as Caroline approached them. Oz zeroed in on Caroline's upper bicep near her shoulder.

"Is 'at there painful, girl?" Oz motioned to her arm.

"Yes, actually. Very painful. I figured I had best leave it unbandaged to heal."

"Smart. The air needs ta get to it." Oz walked over to examine her arm. "Aw, now I get it," he said, looking at Caroline with a strange look in his eyes.

"What do you mean, 'you get it'?"

"Well, unless I'm wrong an' this here just be a coincidence, that there mark is for the tribe of Zebulun."

"Zebulun? You mean as in the Bible? As in one of the twelve tribes of Israel?" Caroline asked surprised.

"Yep. I see ya know yer hist'ry," Oz gave her a brief, tight-lipped grin.

"Yes, but I'm still not sure why I would have the mark of Zebulun. I'm not Jewish." Caroline was feeling very confused by where this conversation was leading. "Besides, Marnor was the one to give me this"—she nodded her head toward her shoulder—"as a symbol of belonging to Riglan." She almost spat that last part.

"Yeah, you're right a course. But just like He did with me, God had ta mark ya as one a The Twelve somehow." Oz led the women to a large fallen tree trunk and they all sat.

"Why would God want to mark me? What do you mean by my being one of The Twelve?"

Oz then rolled up his sleeve to reveal a brand on the inside of his right forearm. It resembled a donkey or mule.

"I have one too. This here be the mark fer Issachar. Got this shortly after we landed here. I got caught by the local slave traders an' was forced ta work the Rhe Mines. This here also be the mark of a minin' slave. Worked it, oh, I'd say maybe a year, 'fore I escaped an ended up here."

"What is the Rhe Mines?" Bridget asked Oz, fascinated with his story.

"It's the name a' the mine where the precious metal crop is found, an' only in the deepest part a' the Xantifal and Carpasian Mountains. The mines lay several hundr'd er so miles east a' here. They're called the Rhe Mines fer the Ruthenium and the Rhenium that be found in 'em. They be precious metals used in weapons, armor, anythin' they don't want the firebirds, Pagorinxes er other wildlife ta get through. It makes fer better protection. 'Round here Ruthenium and Rhenium is as precious as any gold or diamonds we got back home. It could mean life er death to a body cause a their high meltin' point. Kabihanxu have a hard time burnin' through the stuff."

"But what does your mark and my mark have to do with the tribes of Israel?"

"Well, back in the day, when us Per'grines were all travelin' 'round takin' care a business fer God, the Dragoman told all of us a story they had come 'cross in the archive books 'bout The Twelve an' the final battle. Said the books stated that certain Per'grines would be selected by God ta fight in this here final battle. Not sure what against, but we'd have ta fight none the less. But only The Twelve would be able ta fight in the battle. Back in those days, none of us had marks. Some a the Per'grines thought maybe a birthmark, or somethin' like that they had, might a been one a' them marks, but the Dragoman all said no. Some a the Per'grine's decided since they had been workin' fer God an' He didn't think they were good enough fer the final battle, that they'd get what they could now, and kind a' turned on God an' their missions. Some amassed a small fortune, an' were in league with Hiram, but he betrayed them jus' like he had betrayed the rest a' us. So their money didn't do 'em any good. They all got killed here. Either captured by the Scaithers, fell off the movin' mountainside, eaten by the local wildlife, or withered away an' died by the poisonous fumes a' the mines. I think it was God's way a' cleanin' house. Preparin' room fer the next group a Per'grines. Thing is, I never thought I'd be one a The Twelve either. Didn't really mind neither. But once I saw yer mark there, the mark from the mines makes sense. I now realize that I'm one of 'em, too. I fig'red God forgot 'bout me here since I've been here so long. But here you two are, an' you just got marked yerself. So He must still be gatherin' his army."

"Oz, I noticed you mentioned someone named Hiram. Could that have been Hiram Burke, my father?" Bridget asked, worry obvious in her young eyes.

"Yes, Bridget, girl. Hiram Burke was the name a' the man who betrayed us all, leadin' us here." Oz carefully said as he watched the light in her eyes dim ever so slightly at the thought of her father being a betrayer.

"I never knew he was capable of something like that. He was always a good man and father to me. I never saw him take advantage of anyone. I do remember early on when I was about seven, my father had a few visitors, not together, they came separately over the course of a year or so. Each time one would show up, my father became very nervous and agitated and told me to stay out of sight. I'm ever so sorry, Oz, that all this has happened to you because of my father. I promise I would never do any such thing, to anybody. I see now why you asked us to leave that first night. I can't say that I blame you one bit."

"Well, I'm sorry 'bout makin' the two a ya leave. I ended up makin' a mess a' the whole situation. Can't blame ya fer yer father's actions. 'Sides, this must be where we were all meant ta end up. Many things happened here already that're impor'ant. We all found gifts we didn't know we had. You'll both likely find yers soon enough.

Now, time ta get the two a ya trained. We need ta make warriors outa the two a ya." Oz stood and had Bridget and Caroline both hold weapons and taught them to aim and shoot. Promising that tomorrow they would work on some stealth skills, tracking, and getting them into shape, citing the rigorous life of the Peregrines and the Dragoman. While they trained, Oz regaled them with stories of his past missions, the artifacts they had found, and the demons he had battled.

Reader's Island

Simon's peregrination group separated ways to put their bags in their rooms, agreeing to meet in the downstairs bathroom where the chest had been left with one of the groundskeepers. The groundskeepers ran water in the tub to submerge the chest once again.

Seth went down to the archival library where the books they found in the sea cave here on the island were placed. As Seth expected, Simon was there studying the cover of one of the books.

"Simon, come with me. We found a chest."

Simon quickly followed Seth, finding the bathroom due to the bustle of activity that had congregated around the room. They worked their way inside and peered down at the soaking chest.

"Simon, I sure hope whatever we need is in here. We weren't given a chance to look again." Seth explained about the room-service guy and then the demon attack.

"Three at once, eh?" Simon pondered. "Seems to me they are growing more agitated. They usually don't travel in groups like that. Now, let's see what's in this chest here. Surely there is a key hidden somewhere in this thing. Why don't we dump the contents into the tub? It will make it much easier to sift through everything."

As they upended the chest, trying to keep it submerged due to the noticeable rust starting to set in already just from the brief amount of time it was out of water, they turned the contents of the chest out onto the tub bottom. At the very bottom of the chest was an oddly shaped item which Simon believed to be the key. He picked it up, turning it over in his hands as he still held it underwater, not wishing for it to rust and be unusable with whichever of the books it went to.

"I believe this is it." Simon informed them.

"It certainly is unusual looking," Odessa remarked as she noted the odd shape of the key in Simon's hand. "Are you sure that's what it is, Simon?"

"I believe so. As a matter of fact, I believe I know which of the books this belongs to. I'll be right back." Simon laid the key back in the water, went back to the archival library, and began carefully examining the covers and locks of the five books.

"Ah, here you are." Simon smiled from ear to ear. He tucked the book beneath his arm and headed back into the bathroom.

He laid the book down on the step leading into the tub, took the key from the water, quickly dried it off, and placed it in the book's lock. A quick turn counterclockwise and the lock on the book clicked open and the hinge fell to the back. Simon quickly placed the key back in the tub for further restoration and returned to the library; Seth, Alec, Jason, and Odessa following closely behind him; all excited to see what information the book contained.

The rest of the Dragoman were already in the library, pouring over the archival books, still looking for answers to all the questions.

"Look here, Nuncio, Prisca, everyone, come and see! We've found the key for this book and have just opened it. Now let's see what it has to say, shall we?" Simon grinned cheekily at the group that had assembled around him. He opened the book and ran his hand gently across the first page, then lifted it and felt its edge. "The paper in the book appears to be made from papyrus, dating it back to ancient Egypt from anywhere between 4000 BC to 800 AD. The first page here looks to be a prophesy. Simon translated the ancient text.

"During a period of time, God shall choose champions from among the earth's inhabitants that shall fight the evil plaguing the worlds. Among these champions twelve will arise chosen by God to battle the beasts at the great and final battle. The names shall be written across the evil, tearing down walls, ending strife and pain. Should they fail, all will be lost, but should they succeed, they will rise above all mankind, to rule upon the thrones when the barrier shall fall and the worlds within worlds shall be connected. Each champion will sit as ruler over one realm, residing for the Most High, reigning and ruling over the lands. Some shall rule as one over the lands, and others shall rule at their own throne, in the mansions set forth for them by the Most High.

The Keepers shall overtake the beasts, ending the pain and strife, calming the evil that struggles with the good within. The Keepers shall rule the beasts and keep them, and peace shall be upon the worlds and all that is in them for many years to come. The beasts shall be at peace and learning good from the Keepers; strife shall end and plagues will cease. The torments of the lands shall be no longer for the worlds when the Keepers give peace to the beasts and the champions lay waste to the evil.

The Guides shall call out the names before the Lord, striking blow after blow upon the evil that plagues the lands. All the Chosen shall be avenged by their God as the names are called and the beasts shall lose the battle.

The champions shall be tried before the period of peace and must overcome that in which they are weak. And they shall seek to find the Armor of God, which must be acquired for the day of the great and final battle.

Call upon the dry bones, call upon the dead bones, an army shall rise to fight the good fight. A great battle for the lands and its people will be fought by the champions, the dry bones, the Keepers, the Guides. All shall fight for the good of mankind. Great evil shall perish at the hands of God's Chosen.

The earth shall sing the glories of the Most High and give thanks to the champions, the rulers of the lands below the Most High, and praises and great feasts shall be held in remembrance of what was done for the people, and all that was sacrificed for the people shall be remembered, as the scribes to the rulers shall make known all that transpired for the sake of the worlds.

I'm not sure what all this might mean," Simon said, unsure of what to make of some of what he read. "We'll have to do extensive studies to make sure that we know what to do with this information. Some of it is obvious, of course, but some I've never heard mention."

Simon continued telling them more about the book as they all gathered around to study the large twelve by twelve book. It held maps and locations where the Peregrines will have to search to find the missing pieces of armor, and in what order each piece was to be searched for.

"And so the search for the Armor of God begins. This is going to be a hard time for all of us. Considering where things are going and how quickly they seem to be escalating, we may have to move here to the island soon. It may not be safe much longer at our homes along Barrier's Edge. We Dragoman will have to keep close watch and read things correctly. We'll have to start talking to Ryan about leaving his charging station for permanent residency here. He won't like it, but he can no longer stay there alone."

Standing behind the Dragoman, Seth heard the front door open and then Shannon's voice as the head housekeeper greeted newcomers. Apparently more Peregrines had arrived. Hopefully they had a key for another of the books.

Prisca met with her team that had led the Jog Falls find. They had indeed returned with a key and also a message and bag of jewels. The interesting thing about the message was that it was in some sort of ancient text, which no one in the room had ever seen. Just one more piece of the puzzle the Dragoman would have to work tirelessly to put together. As the others studied the books to find the one that would fit the newly arrived key, Seth's thoughts returned to the very young girl, untrained and wandering the planes and the apparent dangers that she may not yet know exist.

"Simon, what about the search for Bridget Burke? If we need all twelve of the Peregrines for this final battle, shouldn't we be concentrating on finding her again?" Seth didn't want all the new information to overshadow one of the most important components for winning the great and final battle.

"Yes, my boy, we should. But until God decides to reveal her to us once more, there is nothing else we can do. Surely, in His own time, He will reveal all that we need to know. We just have to continue to trust Him."

Within the next four days all the Peregrine groups had returned to Reader's Island and all had the unique keys, each of which belonged to one book. Only one key remained to be found and one book still could not be opened. The computer databases were still unable to locate the last waterfall that Safra had drawn from Odessa's dream, and until the last key was found and the eleventh Peregrine located, the teams would all have to work on locating the armor pieces.

The Dragoman and Peregrines planned for the longest, hardest searches they would ever have to complete. The demons would surely be on the prowl more fiercely than ever before, trying to prevent them from locating the Armor of God. Once the last piece was found, the battle to save the world from utter and complete darkness for all eternity would ensue. And if the Peregrines failed to win the great and final battle, all would be lost.

From the end of the earth I will cry to You,
When my heart is overwhelmed;
Lead me to the rock that is higher than I.
For You have been a shelter for me,
A strong tower from the enemy.

Psalm 61:2-4 NKJV

Chapter 13

Bakrashan, Zanchier, Xantifal Mountains

Caroline and Bridget had been training with Oz on Xantifal Mountain for three weeks, and Oz was impressed at how quickly Caroline learned the skills needed to fight. Her speed, strength, and agility had progressed unbelievably. They attributed it to being a supernatural gift given to her by God. He was preparing her quickly, and Oz was a bit concerned as to why. In the thirty-seven years since Oz was called to the peregrination life-style, he had never seen anyone take to training this quickly. It usually took a new Peregrine who came with no discernible skills at all, at least a month or two to progress to a level far below Caroline's level of performance.

She had admitted that she had always been a book worm, never the athletic type. Seeing her now, Oz could almost believe she had been lying about that. She moved with an agility he had never before seen. He tried to think of all his past Peregrine friends and how they fought and moved in battle, and none of them, including himself, could do the things she could. Sometimes it appeared that she was almost flying the way she could leap through the air, landing very long distances below the lowest platforms onto the hard ground with no injury to her body. It had to be her supernatural, God-given gift.

Bridget on the other hand was still the same sweet, nonchalant, chattering teenage girl she was the day she arrived. Except now she could communicate with animals. She wasn't a bad shot, just not in any way a warrior. But since the local wildlife had taken such a shine to her, she didn't need a weapon. She had animals around her at all times.

The Pagorinx mother and the cub, whom Bridget had affectionately named Paxton, stopped by regularly to visit, and received a nice rub-down each time. The two Pagorinxes brought fresh meat and fruits when they came. With the offerings the giant cats brought to Bridget, the humans had no need to hunt, fish, or gather any food. Soon they had so much that they began drying the meat and fruit to make treats Bridget could give back to the animals when they cooperated well with her commands. Oz's life would have been a lot easier in the past if she'd been around back then.

While he and Caroline spent their days training, Bridget happily cooked and cleaned and visited with a slew of different animals daily. She worked with the animals to get them used to Oz and Caroline should they ever need the aid of any of them and Bridget wasn't nearby.

The visitor that had truly shocked Oz was a Kabihanxu. He gaped, open-mouthed, one day when he saw the massive bird-like creature sitting peacefully with Bridget. She had been up on one of the tree-house platforms for quite some time when Oz got a little worried and he and Caroline had gone to look for her. They wanted to make sure she hadn't fallen off. When they finally found her, she was on one of the highest ones in the tree house, hundreds of feet in the air, with the Kabihanxu lying beside her.

When Oz first saw her he panicked, afraid the giant bird would harm her. He went to pull his sword, but Caroline grabbed his arm and made him slow down and just watch.

There Bridget sat on the edge of the platform, the breeze blowing her hair ever so slightly. Her legs were crossed at the ankles, bare feet swinging below her in the open air as she gazed out over the Xantifal Mountains. The sunset blazed a golden yellow and orange across the sky, settling below the peaks in the far-off distance. She appeared to not have a care in the world. And lying directly beside her was the largest

Kabihanxu Oz had ever seen. Of course, he had never been this close to one and wondered if they were all this big. He had only ever seen them from a distance when they flew overhead, blazing fiery trails across the sky.

The four-legged creature lay beside Bridget, its thick front legs crossed as hers were, the rest of it stretched out behind her. It's long, slightly curved and pointed beak was also stretched out and relaxed on its front legs. The setting sun's rays bounced off the colors in the bird's feathers, making them appear to be glowing. As Oz drew so much closer than he had ever come to a Kabihanxu, he noticed for the first time that there were other colors visible in its plumage. There were hints of greens and blues mixed in among the varying shades of red, yellow, and orange, and this lavish display of colors tipped the long, pointed, golden tail feathers. Oz had to admit that they were magnificent looking creatures. He had always taken them for violent beasts, but this one appeared to be as docile as the pet dog he had as a young boy.

The sight before him was the prettiest thing he had ever seen. Every once in a while Bridget would reach up and stroke the bird's feathers back across its head, and it would lean into her hand as though it savored every touch of each finger, purring in a soft growl.

He and Caroline, as quietly as possible, had turned and walked back down the stairs, leaving her with her large beastly friend.

Shortly after returning from rescuing Caroline from the Scaithers, they began working on the additional bedroom for Caroline and Bridget. Oz was going to make two, but Caroline insisted that there was no need. One room would do them just fine. So, off the winding staircase on the right side of the tree house on one of the first platforms, Oz widened the walls and platform floor to accommodate the extra beds and furniture, using all the available wood from the felled forest trees surrounding his home. Since he was the only human inhabitant, there was no shortage of supply. Finding trees small enough to handle was the only real problem. He would at times have to trek the neighboring ridgelines to find workable wood, but not often.

He had dozens of soft, hairless, tanned animal skins from his years of trapping here in Zanchier that he had set aside in case he needed to make belts or weapon straps. The girls used these to make some extra changes of clothing. Caroline only had her pants and ripped shirt and the dress Riglan had put her in. Bridget had packed a few more items from home, but all her dresses were from the sixteenth century. So between Bridget's large bulky dresses, the skimpy dress from the Scaither camp, and the tanned leather hides, they were able to create some rather comfortable and better fitting items.

Oz had also instructed them in the making of leather boots. Caroline and Bridget each had a pair, which made walking in the jungle and climbing the trees much easier and safer.

Caroline's burn was healing well. The image of the ship with its open sails was quite evident now that the swelling had gone, and the skin was returning to its normal color, although still tinged with pinkish-red hues. At least the pain was gone, but the brand would forever serve as a reminder of how things could have gone had it not been for the might and power of God and His love for her.

As she stood in the newly finished bedroom peering out the large, opened window over the mountainside, Caroline's thoughts returned to Seth. Lord, how she missed him. She often prayed that he had survived the earthquake and was doing well. She also prayed that he wouldn't let anger at losing her keep him from giving his life over to Jesus.

"Caroline!" She heard Bridget calling her name from the kitchen below. "Dinner is almost ready. I'm certain you must be starving, as hard as you and Oz have been working."

She smiled at her chatty little friend as she entered the kitchen. "You would be correct. And thank you so much for taking the time to feed us several times daily." Caroline sat down at the table, smiling appreciatively at the young girl. Even though Bridget was sixteen and basically considered a woman of marrying age, she managed to keep a girlish quality—one of complete sweetness and innocence that Caroline didn't quite understand. Bridget had seen her share of evil and hatred and had lived with pain and loneliness most of her life, but she was in no way bitter or angry. Her natural acceptance and lack of judgment of everyone and everything she met confounded Caroline and Oz alike.

Caroline felt convinced that if it had been Bridget who was captured by the Scaithers instead of her, Bridget would have converted the entire camp by now. However, that wasn't something that Caroline was willing to entertain. She wasn't willing that Bridget should ever experience that kind of evil for fear that it would change her sweet countenance drastically, forever.

"Where's Oz this evening?" she asked Bridget, as they waited for him to make an appearance.

"I believe he went up toward the west ridge to look for some more wood to finish the wardrobe he was building for our room. Come to think of it, that was an awfully long time ago." Concern evident in her voice and expression.

"I think I'll go out and have a look." Caroline stood up and grabbed her bow and quiver.

"I'm coming too, and I think I'll call on Han to give us a ride. We will be able to see quite well from the sky."

Walking up to one of the higher platforms, Bridget cupped her hands around her mouth and gave a sing-song gurgle into the late afternoon sky. Soon after, the screeching call of the large Kabihanxu she now affectionately called 'Han' pierced the air, and he came soaring down to land on the platform next to them. The large, four-legged, bird knelt down, allowing Caroline and Bridget to climb up on its back just above its wings. Flapping its enormous wings a few times, it leapt into the air and effortlessly glided along the wind currents, sailing just above the tree line.

Bridget leaned forward and spoke to the bird. "West ridge please, Han. We need to find Oz."

Han turned slightly in the air and glided slowly and carefully, staying as close as possible to the ground so they could search for him. It only took them a matter of minutes to reach the west ridge of the mountain, and then it wasn't long before they found Oz, who appeared to be lying underneath a fallen tree.

Bridget nervously instructed the bird where to land. "Quickly, Han. Do you see him?" She pointed at an open area near where Oz lay.

They jumped from the back of the large bird and ran toward the motionless man.

"Oz…Oz, are you all right?" they asked the unconscious man as they searched the parts of his body they could see for injuries.

Bridget instructed Han to carefully lift the log off Oz's leg so they could get him home. The large bird grabbed the log with its front claws and easily lifted it, then deposited it off to the side. The women checked Oz for any major injuries, a bit afraid to move him but unable to leave him where he lay. It looked as though the weight of the small tree had fallen on his right leg, but that the rest of him had fortunately been lying in a small ditch, so that the majority of the tree just missed him and straddled the ditch where he fell.

"Han, once Caroline and I are seated on your back, I need you to *carefully* lift Oz with your front talons and carry him safely back to the tree house. Understand?" She instructed the bird in her best mother-hen voice.

Han dipped his head and raised it back up as though replying yes as it squawked softly at her.

When Bridget and Caroline were seated on the bird's back once more, Han did just as Bridget asked, lifting Oz in its massive claws, and flying them all back to the tree house. Caroline just hoped that Oz wouldn't become fully conscious until they were safely back on the platform. If he happened to wake up while in midair, he might put up enough of a fight to make the giant bird drop him. Fortunately he remained still. But that didn't bode well for them either.

Han laid Oz gently on the lowest platform he could safely land on. While Bridget thanked the bird and bid it farewell Caroline leaped from its back and ran to the lower-level storage room where Oz kept a gurney he had built to haul his kills back to the treehouse when he had to hunt for food. Caroline grabbed the gurney, then taking the steps two at a time, she rushed back up to the platform. She and Bridget managed to roll Oz onto the gurney so they could carefully drag him inside.

After Oz was settled on his bed, Bridget went to heat some water and gather some towels while Caroline checked his lower half for injuries, talking to him the whole time in an effort to get him to come around.

When Bridget returned, Caroline looked at her with questions written across her expression.

"The log was on his leg, why do you think he's unconscious?" Caroline asked Bridget.

"I wouldn't know, except perhaps when the log fell on him, he hit his head on the ground?" A speculative look crossed her face as she shrugged and moved to the bedside.

After placing a cool, damp, washcloth on his forehead, Bridget checked the back of Oz's head for any bumps. "I can't feel anything that would mean he's bumped his head."

"What about a concussion? It's something I read about in one of the newer medical journals my father ordered for the library."

"What is a concussion?"

"It happens when there is a severe blow to the skull and there is no visible damage to the head. The bump stays inside and can cause damage to the brain if not properly treated. All the pressure stays inside and can cause other damage as well. So, when he comes to we will need to see if there is any dizziness, blurred vision, or headaches. If he has any of these, he most likely is concussed, and we will need to keep him still for a while." Caroline tried to remember exactly what the medical journals had said. "I don't think he'll be going anywhere very quickly anyhow. He's broken the lower part of his right leg."

"Goodness. Poor Oz. I will try and find something to use as a splint." Bridget started to leave the room in search of some long wood pieces and something to use to bind them to his leg.

"I'll wait till you return before I try and set the leg. Besides, I may need you to sit on him to hold him down while I do it. The pain just might revive him." Caroline looked at Bridget with trepidation.

"I'll be quick." Bridget gave her a look of understanding, and left the room in a hurry, returning a few minutes later.

Caroline tied Oz's arms to the bedpost to secure his hands while Bridget, who was only about as big as a minute, put her full weight across Oz's lap in an attempt to keep him from jumping off the bed and injuring himself even more.

They both braced themselves as Caroline offered up a quick prayer. "Lord, help me do this correctly. Give me the necessary strength to get it right the first time. Please!" Then with all her strength she jerked his foot down so the bone was aligned.

Oz did indeed come out of his stupor, screaming in pain. He struggled frantically against the restraints and nearly knocked Bridget to the floor.

"Oz! Oz…calm down! You've broken your leg, and Caroline has had to set it back into place. If you don't stop thrashing around, you'll likely knock it out again!" Bridget yelled while trying to keep her balance upon his stomach.

"Why in tarnation do ya have my hands tied up!" he yelled in aggravation and pain.

"To prevent you from knocking both of us out when you came to! We knew it would hurt, and that was the best way to keep you still."

"Oh…well…you were right. It did hurt," he said morosely. "How'd ya find me, anyway?"

"Han found you. Caroline was worried when you hadn't returned for dinner, so we went looking for you. We rode on Han's back, which made short work of it. Found you right off. He even lifted the fallen tree off you, picked you up with his large front claws, and carried us all back here." Bridget untied his hands while Caroline splinted and wrapped his leg.

"Well, you'll have ta thank 'im for me next time ya see 'im," Oz said a bit hesitantly. He still couldn't bring himself to completely trust the creatures that Bridget had taken to, creatures that had viewed him as a meal before she came. But he couldn't hold a grudge any longer after this.

"I'll leave that to you as soon as you're well enough to walk." Bridget sweetly patted the burly man's hand with her smaller one, still keeping her vigil atop his lap until Caroline finished what she was doing.

Caroline simply smiled at the conversation, trying to hide her amusement at the relationship these two held. They were all like some odd little family. Oz the grumpy grandfather, Caroline the stubborn, headstrong, older daughter, and Bridget the beloved, innocent, younger daughter. *Anyone would swear we've all been together for as long as we've been alive.*

After tending to Oz's wounded leg, Caroline and Bridget fed him a hearty bowl of the soup and a large chunk of the bread Bridget had made for dinner. They gave him a draught for pain, instructing him not to move at least until tomorrow due to the concussion and the lack of a crutch, which they promised they would fashion for him tonight as he slept.

Caroline and Bridget gathered the necessary materials to make the crutch and went to sit in the cool night air on one of the covered platforms. A thunderstorm had rolled in earlier while they were eating dinner, but the branches of the trees were so large it was like being under a roof. As they sat listening to the thunder boom and watching the lightning streak across the sky, several of Bridget's forest friends gathered around her, snuggling into the layers of one of her old dresses she had chosen to wear today, which spread out around her on the platform.

The storm grew more intense, and Bridget and Caroline could see several portals opening across the open areas of the mountainside. Remembering what Oz had told them about the portals up here only bringing Peregrines in but not allowing them to leave, they just looked at each other and smiled, thinking about when they first arrived through just such a portal. The life they each had led before coming to Zanchier seemed but strange dreams they once had.

Bridget breathed deeply of the damp air around them. "I've never felt more alive than I do here, Caroline. I'm so glad that God brought you into my life when he did." Her expression softened when the look on her friend's face made her realize what she had said.

"I'm so sorry, Caroline, I didn't mean..." she started to apologize, but Caroline stopped her.

"It's all right, Bridget. I understand. I'm grateful for you as well; and Oz. I just wish that Seth could be here to share all this with me." Caroline wistfully looked out at the portals appearing and disappearing in the distance below them and changed the subject. "I know we've grown very comfortable here, but you do know that we can't stay, Bridget?"

"Yes." Bridget sighed. "I know that one day we will have to leave here. But with Oz injured the way he is, we can't leave just yet. The trip would be awfully hard on him."

"But as soon as he is well, we will need to discuss where to go and what to do next. I doubt we will have any trouble getting to the Dustbowl now. With all your influence with the local natives, I'm sure we could muster up a ride or two." Caroline smiled and motioned to all the unusual-looking sleeping woodland creatures curled up around Bridget.

Bridget giggled. "Yes, I dare say you are correct there. I will miss them all ever so much, Caroline. Whatever will I do without them? Especially Paxton and Han. They've become my closest friends, next to you, of course." She quickly added.

Caroline smiled. "Your gift is truly amazing Bridget. I'm a little jealous of the way you can communicate with all of them. I would love to be able to do that. Just know that no matter where God sends us next, I am sure your gift will go with you. I would think you would be able to communicate with animals of all kinds, everywhere."

They continued their task in relative silence as the rain poured down around them and the storm continued raging throughout the Xantifal Mountains. After a few hours Oz's crutch was finished. They only hoped it would support his weight, being the large man he was. They had measured his length to make sure it was long enough to fit his six-foot-three-inch frame and prayed the wood they had found was good and strong. As they stood up, all the animals disappeared back to their nests among the trees, and the two young women went inside, hoping that Oz would rest well and not be in too much pain throughout the night.

They took turns sitting up with him, not leaving his side for more than an hour at a time over the next several days until he could manage the crutch and the uneven floor of the tree house on his own. With Oz quickly on the mend, they would soon have to discuss leaving this enchanting place they had called home for the last month. They prayed fervently and asked God where and when he wished for them to go next.

And I have filled him with the Spirit of God, with wisdom,
with understanding, with knowledge and with all kinds of skills.

Exodus 31:3 NIV

Chapter 14

Reader's Island

The convergence of the Dragoman and the Peregrines on Reader's Island made for a very busy and somewhat chaotic week for the housekeepers, cooks, and groundskeepers. The sudden appearance of an extra twenty-five people meant more laundry, food, and supplies, and since most of the Peregrines had never been to the island the questions were limitless. Fortunately the thirty-bedroom mini-mansion had plenty of sleeping accommodations.

One of the great things about having the Portgens was how easy it made travel back and forth from Reader's Island to Simon's place at Garganthera, Prisca's at Grenoble, France, and the other Dragoman barrier-placed safe homes. It was especially comforting to Ryan, who was only a few punches of some coordinates away from his charging station in Scotland.

Simon or one of the groundskeepers would return to Garganthera daily to tend to the horses they now kept from the African rescue several months back. They had thought about selling them at the market in Garganthera, but the horses actually were a great deal of use to them, and they thought they may have need of them in the future. Now that they knew animals could traverse the space-time continuum, the Peregrine's would actually be able to acquire horses for their searches instead of walking everywhere. And since everyone may soon need to move to the island for protection, Nuncio had instructed the groundskeepers and all available Peregrines to begin the construction of a large stable to house the animals once it was no longer possible to stay at the Barrier's Edge safe houses.

With all the available help for the stable construction, it was coming along nicely. They were building enough stalls to house enough horses that each Peregrine would have one, and still have room for several extra animals for unforeseen needs.

When the Peregrines weren't helping to work on the stables, they took to the open fields to learn to work together in such a large group. Some of the more experienced Peregrines took the younger ones and showed them unique skills they each had acquired over the years to help them learn to fight well. With the probability of a demon war, they wanted everyone to be up to par on skills and honing their strengths.

Some of the Peregrines were beginning to exhibit supernatural gifts that they did not have before coming to the island. They wondered if they had these gifts because they were on the island and would be able to use them only when they were there. The Dragoman informed them that was not a probable conclusion, because they would have no need of their gifts due to the fact that demons could not come to the island. It was more than likely that the new gifts were a provision from God to aid them in the future.

The Dragoman were keeping busy with the hunt for the last waterfall and interpreting the ancient information in the recently found archive books. They hoped to find the answers to several new questions in the pages of the ancient texts. The only knowledge they had gleaned so far was that the guides mentioned in the prophecy were more than likely the Dragoman. The champions were the Peregrines of course. The texts also mentioned Keepers, and the Dragoman had no idea who the Keepers might be. They did have the approximate location of the first piece of armor and the order in which the pieces should be found.

Further reading into one of the texts did reveal that the Keepers would tend to the beasts. Since Wade seemed to have a special connection with animals, they began to believe that this was his calling.

It would explain why he was untrainable as a warrior and wasn't demonstrating any Dragoman characteristics. Of course, the role of Keeper was completely new to the Dragoman, and they had no idea how to train him. However, the young man seemed to get along fine without their instruction. They also wondered who else might turn up with the talents that would indicate a Keeper. The text made it clear that there would be more than one Keeper with every plural use of the word.

The animals on the island took to Wade like no other. They never showed fear toward anyone on the island, but they seemed to follow Wade at times. And several people had noticed him actually talking to them as though the animals could understand.

Seth had watched Wade on one such occasion as he told a fawn to find its mother. The fawn looked at Wade, turned to bound off into the woods; and sure enough, went straight to its mother where it stayed. This made Seth believe the boy really could speak to the animals.

"Does that happen often? The way you communicate with the animals?"

"Well, yeah, ever since I peregrinated to Prisca's, it's been happening more often." Wade blushed a little as if he didn't want to boast. "I've always felt close to animals of all kinds, like I can understand what they're thinking. I felt that even before I peregrinated, but I was never able to speak to them or understand them like I can now."

"That's a neat gift, Wade. I'm curious to see how that will play into our lifestyle here."

"Yeah, me too." Wade grinned.

The Dragoman hoped the next week would serve them well and they could at last begin sending the teams out to locate the armor pieces. No one seemed to know how long each of these peregrinations would take, but everyone agreed that these tasks would probably be much harder than the artifact finds of the past. The pieces they needed to locate were to enable them to win the battle against the evil plaguing the worlds. Satan and his followers did not want that to happen and would surely be planning many ways to hinder or stop them.

The Dragoman and Peregrines held nightly meetings and Bible studies to help encourage and enable their teams to withstand whatever

Satan threw their way. Seth learned that temptations, which seemed to be Satan's favored weapon of choice, would most likely be a grand factor. The Dragoman explained that the prophecy in the first book they opened spoke of mental and physical warfare that the Champions would have to endure and overcome to be allowed to hold the armor. It also mentioned that the fruit of the spirit would have to be obtained, which to the Dragoman implied the physical and mental warfare in which the Peregrines would be tested. Meaning they would be tested at their weakest points through whichever spirit fruit that was, and only God knew the answers to those questions.

The Dragoman ran across a particular problem one evening during study of the first book, which they dubbed *The Book of Armor*. The instructions in the ancient text stated that the Peregrines would have to work as one large group and find each piece together. The Dragoman took that to mean they could not split up into groups as before and have each team search for a certain piece, which would mean they could accumulate the armor faster. Every member of The Twelve had to be present to unlock the hiding place of each piece of armor.

This passage meant that the Peregrines would not be able to find even the first piece of armor without Bridget Burke. Simon decided they would have to ask Safra to beseech God once again for the location of the girl and whoever her traveling companion was. This companion must be important as well if she could also peregrinate. Perhaps she was one of the Keepers the book foretold? This one problem could hold everything up indefinitely.

This new information meant they would have to focus their efforts on the search for Bridget. They were at a standstill until she was found. The only other thing they could do was to work on deciphering and studying the *Book of the Keepers*, as they named it, to look for anything they could do to prepare Wade for his future as a Beast Keeper.

While Prisca, Malachai, and Vashti worked on deciphering the ancient text, Simon, Nuncio, and Safra concentrated on trying to find Bridget. Ryan continued to try to match the still elusive waterfall with the massive database that connected him to images all over the world. In a moment of frustration, the tech genius told Seth that nothing they had ever searched for before had taken this long to find. At the same time Ryan was trying to finish the last of four additional Portgens for the Peregrines, all the while complaining he could work faster at home in his charging station where all his technical equipment was located. However, the remaining Portgens would have to wait for a few more weeks until he could get home and bring all his equipment back to Reader's Island.

"Safra," Simon asked, "could we have made a mistake on the last waterfall image?"

"I do not believe so, Simon. All the other waterfalls have been found. Perhaps God has just not revealed this one to us yet. Certainly in this vast world of ours, there are places that we do not yet know exist?"

"Yes, but time is of the essence here. Surely He won't make us wait much longer. We truly need to begin the searching. Hopefully the Lord will reveal to you soon the location of young Bridget Burke, and we can get on with finding her and her companion and bringing them back here. She probably hasn't a clue of what she is actually called to do." A look of deep thought was planted on Simon's face.

"What has happened to your faith lately, Simon?" Safra scrutinized her friend.

"What do you mean, Safra?"

"You usually do not question God's timing in anything. Why do you do so now?"

Simon sighed. "You are right, of course. I just sense an urgency that I cannot explain. I know that God will reveal all when He chooses the time, but sitting here idly, waiting with every Peregrine here in camp with nothing to do, I just feel like I need to be doing more."

"First, the Peregrines are actively training here together. Building relationships they will need when out on the soon-to-come long journey to find the armor pieces. And they are also experiencing new supernatural gifts that God has blessed them with. Perhaps, if you are feeling useless, you should go to the training grounds and work with those who are not sure how to use or master their new abilities. You are, after all, a magus and surely could lend them some assistance." She smiled at the impatient man.

"Yes, you are right again, Safra. Perhaps it would do me some good to go out and help with training, especially with the younger, newer Peregrines. Thank you for your advice, and sternness with me." He smiled at the woman as he patted her hand and stood to leave. "I think I'll get on that right now."

"And I think I shall join you." She stood with him. "Until God reveals something new to me, I have some free time on my hands as well."

They walked together from the large house out across the lush green landscape surrounding them, in search of the large group of Peregrines who were training somewhere on the island. All they had to do was listen for the noise the group was making. Between the sparring, grunting, and sounds of metal on metal, they found them rather quickly.

The Peregrines had decided to make the most of the landscape afforded to them and travel out to the rocky part of the cliffs. There they had forest, rock, sand, water, and the lighthouse with which to train. It was perfect for the different types of terrain they often encountered on missions. Those who were exceptionally strong on certain types of ground helped to train the others who struggled in that area. They also decided to set up a few targets in which to practice using the gifts that had recently been revealed to almost everyone.

Seth was already a strong, large man, but his gift seemed to be Samson-like strength. Alec seemed to be able to teleport objects from one place to another but only if he could see them. He also found that if he was running fast, he could teleport himself several feet ahead—or behind if he was quick enough with his thoughts while in teleportation mode. Odessa, since her dream about the falls, had realized that she had the gift of premonition. If she concentrated on something or someone hard enough, she could see the possible future and sometimes even the past. The future she saw often happened within the next five minutes or so, but there were a few times she thought she had experienced déjà vu, only later to realize she must have dreamed it. Jason had shown no sign of any special gift yet.

Nicholas had discovered he could create fire from the palms of his hands and throw it like a ball. At first they were small and didn't travel very far, but he found that if he reared back, putting his whole shoulder into it, he could throw them quite a distance. His experiments caused a few problems at first, such as his catching things on fire. It was a good thing Sean was nearby and close to a water source at the time. And that was when Sean discovered he could manipulate water if he was near it. At first, he could only move it in small amounts, but his skills seemed to be progressing daily to where he was able to control larger quantities.

One day as Sean practiced moving water, Kristen happened to walk by. Sean called to her and then, grinning, doused her with water from the ocean. Kristen didn't think it was funny. With an angry shout she opened a sinkhole directly beneath him. Sean jumped back as Kristen's anger turned to amazement. "I just manipulated the earth!" she gasped.

Simon suggested that Kristen work on controlling her temper, especially around her teammates. He also suggested that Sean stop pulling childish pranks that might result in him finding himself in trouble.

Dinah discovered that with the wave of her hands and some concentration she could manipulate the wind. She could stir anything from light breezes to tornado-type storms, however small they still might be, but her skills were also increasing daily with practice.

Ezekial Davis, nicknamed Zeke by the others, discovered he could manipulate the weather to some extent. If there were clouds in the sky, he could turn them into a thunderstorm, which Uriah Mose found useful, since his gift was controlling lightning or energy. Uriah could use electrical devices of all kinds to create surges of power by collecting the energy in his hands and then pushing it out at whatever he wanted to hit.

Nadia Bonhomme also benefitted from the thunderstorms created by Zeke since her gift was snow and ice. She could turn the rain into hail and ice, and she could freeze water. She also could manipulate any type of moisture found in any living thing.

Gabrielle Bailey discovered she could produce an impenetrable, protective shield, and Zaccai Wekessa could control and manipulate plant life of any sort, making it do whatever she wished. Whether that was rapid growth, bending, warping, or wrapping around an object.

The Peregrines soon discovered that they all could work off each other's gifts while using their own. Storms generated lightning, electricity generated storms, water formed ice, water also created clouds, and earth and plants complimented each other. There were so many different ways in which to use their gifts that the possibilities were unfathomable. So they spent the next several weeks trying new things they thought might work together.

Timothy Johnson and Dominic Amando, like Jason, had yet to discover any such gifts or powers and were beginning to wonder if they were to be blessed with supernatural abilities. One day as Gabrielle and Dinah were sparring, another gift appeared. Gabrielle was trying to create a shield to use against Dinah's sword when her concentration was suddenly broken. A stray vine that had crept around her ankle pulled her to the ground at the moment Dinah swung her sword. Dinah's sword struck, and Gabrielle screamed in pain, grasping at the deep gash in her forearm.

"Oh, my goodness! I am so sorry, Gabby!" Dinah said in a panic, as she stared at the girl's injury. "I need help!" She frantically looked for something with which to bind the wound.

Peregrines stopped what they were doing and ran to them.

Zaccai knelt beside the young woman who was cringing in pain, tears welling up in her eyes. "Oh no, Gabrielle, I am sorry! It's my fault! I was trying to direct the vine somewhere else, and it wound its way around your leg. What have I done?"

Jason strode through the group kneeling beside Gabrielle. "Step back, ladies, and let me look at it. I do have some medical experience."

With one hand, Jason gently lifted her arm and scrutinized the deep gash.

"I need something to apply pressure to the wound with." Jason scanned the crowd of people who gathered around them. Sean quickly removed his t-shirt and handed it to Jason.

This is bad, he thought, as he applied pressure to the wound. *She's losing a lot of blood.* When his touch and thoughts lined up with the wound on her arm, Gabrielle's eyes opened wide in surprise. She pushed his compress away, and they watched, amazed, as the wound begin to heal before their eyes.

Jason was so shocked he dropped Gabrielle's arm. The moment Jason lost his concentration and let go of the wounded arm the wound stopped healing. *Could it be?* Jason lifted Gabrielle's arm again and gently touched the wound as he focused mentally on her arm being healed. Again the wound began to close as they watched.

"Well, Jason," Simon stated with a grin, "it appears you've found your spiritual gift. It is healing."

"That's really strange, but really cool at the same time," he said, wearily grinning up at Simon.

"That is something even my magic can't do. This is a great gift. It appears that God has given all of you amazing supernatural abilities." Simon turned to address the group of Peregrines standing around them. "Some of you are still searching for your gift, and I am sure God will reveal it to you in His own good time. But know this. These gifts are to be used *only* for the battle against evil. You are not to use them for your own gain. Heed this warning well. Use for your own gain will lead to ruin and destruction, not only for yourself but for those around you, as well. I have seen it before. Be very careful to keep yourselves and each other in check. Do not abuse these gifts."

Everyone chimed in, murmuring their understanding of Simon's warning.

"Sure thing, Simon, we understand." Jason stood and pulled Gabrielle up from the ground. "Are you all right, Gabby? Does it hurt at all?"

"No, it feels great! Like there was never anything wrong. There isn't even so much as a scar!" She stared at her arm in amazement.

On the following day during training, several of the Peregrines, including Timothy and Dominic, decided to go for a swim. They were playing around in the water when something clamped down on Timothy's leg and dragged him under the water's surface.

"Timothy!" Dominic yelled. Dominic, Seth, and Jason dove into the water and spotted Timothy fighting to free his leg from a shark. Seth rushed at the shark, preparing to put his strength behind a punch that would make the shark let go of Timothy. But it suddenly opened its mouth and just let him go. The shark looked at Dominic, then turned and swam away. Seth and Jason grabbed Timothy by the arms, pulled him to the surface, and dragged him onto the beach.

"Guys, guys," Timothy sputtered, "I'm fine! Look, not even a scratch." He pointed down at his leg while examining it.

"How is that even possible?" Seth asked amazed. "That was no small shark."

"It didn't even hurt. I was just hoping not to drown because I couldn't get away."

"How do you not even have a mark?" Jason asked shocked, checking the man's leg for an injury. "There isn't even so much as a tooth mark or scratch."

"Maybe I don't taste very good," Timothy said jokingly.

"But still, no one comes away from a shark attack without so much as a scratch." Seth's eyebrows furrowed in thought. "Tim, stand up. I want to try something."

Timothy complied and before he knew it, Seth was pulling back to punch him. Timothy gasped and threw his hands in front of himself to block Seth's blow as he stepped back in protest. He was just a little too late. Seth landed a blow that propelled Timothy backward onto the ground.

"What do you think you're doing, man!" Timothy shouted angrily. He jumped to his feet and took two quick steps to the huge man. "You could have killed me with your superman strength!"

"Yeah, but I didn't. It doesn't appear that I've even injured you in any way," Seth said amused.

Timothy stopped short, suddenly realizing that Seth was right.

"You know, except for being thrown to the ground, I really didn't even feel that." Astonished, Timothy asked, "What do you think that means?" His eyes roamed his arms and body like he was searching for something.

"I think we need to try a few more experiments to know for sure. But since that shark's teeth didn't so much as dent your skin, I wonder what a knife would do?" Seth asked.

He walked over to where he'd left his sword lying on the sand. He pulled his sword from the scabbard and walked back to Timothy.

"Fortunately, if this doesn't work, Jason is here and he can heal you right up. Let me see your hand." Seth looked at Timothy. Timothy hesitated, looked at the two men, then did as he was asked. Seth pulled the sharp edge of the sword across the palm of Timothy's hand, but when they looked at it, there was no blood, not even a mark. Seth then demonstrated how sharp the sword was by pulling it across his own palm. Blood welled up instantly and began to heavily drip onto the sand. Jason quickly healed Seth's hand before they addressed Timothy again. The other swimmers had gathered around Timothy, and they all stared at him. He appeared no different than usual but apparently his skin was very different,.

"It looks like you have skin like armor. You can still take blows and force but are uninjured by them," Seth explained. "You'll have to do more testing to see how much force you can take without injury, but I'd say God used that shark to reveal your gift."

Nadia and Zaccai, who had come along for the swim, had been looking at Dominic, to the experiment with Timothy, and then back to Dominic.

"Timothy is not the only person whose gift was revealed today," Nadia said in her thick German accent, as she pointed over the water to where Dominic stood.

Everyone turned to look at the fifteen-year-old boy who stood in water up to his waist, surrounded by all sorts of sea creatures. Dominic stroked the dolphins, sea turtles, and even a shark, possibly the very same one that bit Timothy.

"What the...," Seth exclaimed, stunned.

"It appears we have another Keeper in our midst," Jason told the stunned onlookers.

"Dominic!" Jason yelled and waved the boy to shore. When Dominic made it to the shoreline, Jason asked, "When did you first know you could communicate with animals?"

"Today," he answered stunned. "I usually hang around with Wade since we've been here on the island. You know, the both of us being close in age, we get along pretty well. He is always around animals, and they seemed to take to me too, but I thought it was just because I was with him. I never thought that I could talk to them myself. It wasn't until I told that shark to let go of Tim and it actually listened that I realized what I could do. That's why I stayed in the water, to test my theory." Dominic was astonished at his new ability.

"How did you know the shark listened to you instead of just realizing he couldn't bite down on Tim here?" Seth asked, backhanding Timothy lightly in the chest with a grin.

"Because when I yelled for it to stop in my head, it did; then it turned and looked at me and then swam away."

Zaccai spoke next. "I think we need to head back to the main house to inform the Dragoman of this new revelation. There must be some significance to there being two Keepers."

"What do you mean, Zaccai?" Jason asked her.

"We all have had special powers revealed to us, yes? But they are all different. Wade and Dominic have the same abilities, do they not? You do not find it curious that this is so?"

"Now that you mention it, yeah. It is a little odd that their powers are alike." A look of curiosity crossed Jason's features. "I agree. We need to get back and let the others know about it and about Tim here."

The group left the beach and headed eagerly back to the main house. Hopefully the Dragoman who were exploring the ancient texts which were found a month back in the sea cave, had gleaned some answers to some of the questions that still plagued them.

Seth and Jason held back a little from the others. Jason wanted to discuss privately with Seth some things that concerned him. After the others were far enough out of earshot, Jason began.

"Seth, don't you find it a little odd that all of a sudden we are gifted with these amazing powers?"

"A little, but I don't think odd is the word. More like frightening."

"Yeah. That's what I mean. Our strength and abilities have always been enough in the past to battle demons. Why would God give us these new powers now? I know everyone is excited about their new abilities, but it doesn't bode well with me."

"I know how you feel, Jason," Seth exhaled loudly. "I fear for what the future may hold when it comes to warring with the demons. There must be something really bad coming if God feels these gifts are necessary. I just pray that we learn to handle and control them before we actually have to put them to use."

"Me too, my friend." Jason patted Seth on the shoulder. "Me too."

They continued forward in silence, each wondering about the future. Not fearful, but wary of what was to come and how soon.

Knowing this first: that scoffers will come in the
last days, walking according to their own lusts.

2 Peter 3:3 NKJV

Chapter 15

Bakrashan, Zanchier, Oz's tree house

Oz's leg was healing in record time, whether from the clean break or
God's grace in the situation. At the end of three weeks, he was walking
on it with little pain and only a slight limp. Bridget and Caroline had
kept busy stockpiling firewood, fixing leaks in the areas where the tree
had split a few times in its ever-constant growth, and adding flooring on
the upper platforms where they had pulled away from the tree's massive
trunk.

The animals continued delivering food, and they continued to salt
and dry the meats and preserve the native fruits and vegetables in the
actual root system of the trees where it stayed dark and dry.

When not busy with food and repairs, Caroline continued her
training, discovering each day that her strength and ability seemed to
improve even more than she thought possible. She also discovered
completely by accident, that she was capable of mental telepathy. She
was thinking of something she needed to tell Bridget and Oz, and by the
time she arrived back at the tree house they already knew. They
informed her that they felt her mental connection and understood what
she was thinking, even if she had not felt them at the time.

Oz said that he too was telepathic, a supernatural gift given to him by God years back, and that he could teach her how to control whether or not she wished to share her thoughts. Bridget, who could already talk to the animals through her thoughts, figured adding people shouldn't be too difficult, and she was correct.

Caroline, Oz, and Bridget could communicate telepathically from some distance. They just weren't sure exactly how far the telepathic communication would reach.

Bridget, however, was still the only one who could communicate with the animals via telepathy. Oz and Caroline had formed a sort of relationship with them through their communications with Bridget. Even when Bridget was not around, the animals respected Oz and Caroline. The humans could tell that the animals knew what they wanted from them, whether by instinct or learned behavior. Oz and Caroline could work with the animals, but Bridget's bond ran much deeper. The animals seemed to seek her out, to draw some kind of comfort from her spirit. It was a beautiful relationship to behold.

By the end of the fourth week, Oz's leg was completely healed, and he was back to his old self, scaling the trees and mountainside as if it were nothing.

They decided to try an experiment one day to see just how far their telepathic abilities would allow them to communicate. Oz stayed at the tree house while Bridget rode Han, the large Kabihanxu, and Caroline rode Mother Pagorinx. Bridget and Han went in one direction while Caroline and the Pagorinx went in the opposite one, each taking some provisions with them just in case an emergency situation arose.

They would speak to each other occasionally, just to see if the line of communication was still open. When Bridget had traveled about seven miles by air to Caroline's four by ground, they found they could still communicate with each other and with Oz who was between them. Caroline and Bridget were now eleven or twelve miles apart and their thoughts were still connected. Caroline instructed Bridget to stay where she was at the seven-mile mark and let her continue on to see if the connection got broken. Caroline went another two miles still connected with Bridget telepathically.

There must not be a distance to this mental connection thing, Caroline thought. Just as she decided to turn back to the tree house, she heard people walking through the forest. She stopped to take a look, and it appeared that they were headed in the direction of Oz's tree house. Caroline recognized some of them as the Scaithers who had taken her. She reached out with her mind to tell Oz and Bridget about the troop headed in their direction. Caroline sat watching them trek noisily through the foliage below her and Mother, scanning them for their leader, Riglan, and his head crony, Marnor. There was no sign of Riglan, but she definitely recognized Marnor, Faigen, and Quenzie. She also caught a glimpse of the two women who were known to belong to Riglan. The one who had tended Caroline's wounds, Shraiva or Sofia, walked at the back of the troop carrying a heavily loaded basket atop her head. Her feet parted just enough to allow her to walk and barely keep pace with the others due to the chain attached at her ankles.

"I see someone who tended me when I was a prisoner in the Scaither camp. Caroline relayed her thoughts to Oz and Bridget. *She is as much a prisoner as I was, and I want to help her. There is only about a third of the Scaithers left after the animals attacked last month. I feel Mother and I can take them."*

Oz replied, *"You jus' stay right where ya are, girl, till me an' Bridget get there. I'm already headin' there ridin' Paxton."*

Caroline followed the Scaithers farther up the mountainside until Oz joined her in the treetops. The cub knew its mother's scent and headed straight for her. The large cats growled occasionally, which caused the Scaither's eyes to turn to the gigantic trees, scanning the upper branches warily. But the Pagorinxes were masters at hiding in the large, colorful, foliage, some of which bore the same colors that the Pagorinxes' coats did.

Paxton stopped next to his mother. "All right, girl, what's got ya so all fired up ta start another war with the Scaithers?" Oz was a bit frustrated with the situation.

Caroline pointed at the back of the troop's line to where one lone woman under the burden of her immense load was struggling to keep up.

Oz watched closely, trying to gauge who the woman might be. Her face was obscured by the large basket atop her head. Her clothing told him she was one of Riglan's concubines, and he didn't usually make his concubines do any of the work. Something was definitely different now.

"You reckon I killed Riglan when I shot 'im last month?" Oz questioned Caroline.

"I don't see him anywhere. Maybe so. Would that leave Marnor in charge then?"

"Not sure; pro'bly. But I guarantee there was a' all-out war fer that position. Most a them fellas down there envied Riglan an' wanted his power an' position. It all depends on who won, I s'pose. I just don't understand what they're doin' out this far with the whole camp."

"Do you think they're looking for us? They have to know we're in the Xantifal Mountains somewhere. Marnor did seem a little…keen on me." Caroline shuddered.

"Mos' likely. They don't take kindly ta people tryin' ta steal what they already stole. Even if the ones they stole it from are the rightful owners." He looked at her askance. "And you, well…yer already branded. Yer likely what they're up here a lookin' fer. 'Specially since Marnor new ya were a Per'grine."

Just then they heard the cry of the Kabihanxu alerting them of Bridget's arrival. As the large bird found a branch on which to light, Bridget climbed off Han's back and made her way through the treetops to climb on Mother's back with Caroline.

"So, what's all the ruckus about?" Bridget asked in her casual, unruffled manner.

"See that woman there on the end?" Caroline pointed again to the troop's end. "I wish to free her. She's a prisoner. Do you think we could snatch her from the back of the line where no one would see us?"

"We can send Han down to snatch her up. They'll think she's just become a meal for him and likely run and hide. Aren't Kabihanxu very hard to injure because of their thick, armor-like hide beneath their feathers?"

"Yeah, but they don' usu'lly come down onta the forest floor like that. Too many pickin's out on the open plains an' the treetops."

"Perhaps. But what would it matter why Han attacked here? As long as we get her out, there isn't anything they can do about it."

"You're right there. But I'm pretty sure a lot of 'em saw you ridin' Paxton here in camp that night. They'll prob'ly put two an' two together an' fig're it out."

"Even if they do, how in the world are they ever going to catch us on the backs of the animals?" Bridget gave a shrug of her shoulders and grinned.

"Well, I s'pose ya got a point there too." Oz grinned at her lopsidedly, with a shake of his head.

"Caroline, how d'ya know that's the gal that tended ya in camp that day? Ya can't see her face."

"There were only two of them, and the other one is riding up front in the basket carried by four large men. And she wasn't wearing an ankle chain like the other one. Even though I can't see her face, I'm betting that's Shraiva. There is a thin chain between the cuffs on her ankle. It's only long enough to allow normal girthed steps, nothing large and definitely no running." Caroline remembered not to use Shraiva's birth name without her permission.

The mountain began to rumble loudly around them, a signal that the terrain was about to change. The animals began to growl and pace, alerting them that the Shift could be very close, perhaps even underneath them. Sometimes the disappearing and reappearing terrain made for felled trees. Which is what gave Oz plenty of dried wood with which to construct his tree house.

Bridget jumped back onto Han's back and took to the sky and the Pagorinxes began their ascent into the treetops with Caroline and Oz on their backs, sprinting effortlessly through the branches in the direction in which they had come in an attempt to avoid the shifting lands.

Bridget and Caroline had never been this close to a Shift before. *Shift* wasn't a very technical term, but it was what Oz said the Scaithers had always called them when he overheard their conversations from above in the trees. They watched the Scaithers as best they could as they ran in separate directions, trying to devise a safe place to go to avoid being transported to the other side of the mountain, or falling off the side of whatever took the current terrain's place.

This gave Han and Bridget a golden opportunity to snatch the woman Caroline called Shraiva. If they could swoop down and snatch her before the terrain shift, no one would be the wiser.

"Let's go, Han, quickly, before we're noticed and before she disappears." Bridget patted the large bird's neck just above its breast.

Before Caroline and Oz knew what was happening, Han swooped down into the still dispersing crowd of people who were too terrified of the earth tremors, falling trees, and the dust it was creating, to even notice him. He picked up the already screaming and terrified woman, clutching her securely in his large talons, and carried her straight up into the air and away from the splitting ground.

Shraiva screamed and pounded her fists against the Kabihanxu's large feet, which she knew was useless. No one survived a firebird attack. At least she would be free from the life she had been forced to lead over the last ten years. She only hoped her death would be a quick one.

The bird flew a few miles before it descended to the earth in a small valley surrounded by trees and deposited her onto the ground. Shraiva lay still, afraid to move and waited for the bird to tear at her flesh. But nothing happened.

"Hello."

Hearing a human voice, Shraiva's back went stiff, and she pushed herself away from the hard, grassy, ground beneath her. She sat up looking around without seeing anyone.

"Up here," the voice said.

Was the bird talking to her, or was she delirious with fright?

Shraiva glanced up at the Kabihanxu which was standing against the sunlight, blinding her ability to see well. She adjusted her position as the large bird knelt to lie down in the grass. Sitting atop its back was a young girl.

Shraiva could only stare in disbelief, her mouth hanging open in shock.

"I'm sorry. I know this is all a bit irregular, but my name is Bridget. I believe your name is Shraiva?" the young girl asked her.

Shraiva began nodding her head yes when she found her voice, however shaky it was.

"Um…ye-yes. How-how did you…" She breathed heavily, unsure what to ask first, how she knew her name or how she was riding a firebird. She cleared her throat, looking between the bird and the girl called Bridget, and tried again.

"How do you know me?"

"Caroline told me of course." Bridget looked at her as though *she* were the oddball.

"Caroline?" Shraiva shook her head, trying to recall someone named Caroline. She stood, and her memory finally connected the dots.

"Do you mean the woman who escaped a month back?"

"Yes. She should be here shortly. The Pagorinxes, although fast, can't run nearly as quickly as Han here can fly." She patted the large bird affectionately as she slid off its back. Bridget noticed that Shraiva was standing stock still, apparently afraid to make any sudden movements.

Did she say Pagorinxes? Shraiva scanned the surrounding trees in fear.

"It's all right. You can relax. Han is harmless once he gets to know you." Bridget smiled brightly at the woman.

"How…?" She could only motion toward the large bird resting in the grass.

"Oh, that. Silly me. God has given me the supernatural ability to communicate with animals. I can speak with them just like I am speaking with you." She giggled at her remark then clarified. "They don't audibly speak, of course, but they understand me and I them."

Shraiva shrank back to the ground, feeling as though her legs wouldn't support her weight much longer.

"Why did you take me?" she asked, still confused and unsure of her fate.

"Caroline said you were a prisoner and wished to free you."

"Oh." Shraiva looked somewhat taken aback by the statement. No one had risked their own life for hers in a very long time. "Thank you. But what do I do now?"

"Well, do you have family somewhere we can return you to?"

"No. I've been with the Scaithers for so long that there surely isn't anyone left who would remember me."

Bridget's face softened with concern.

"Well, don't worry. You can stay with us. Surely Oz won't mind," Bridget said, turning at a noise in the trees.

Shraiva became fearful of the noise breaking through the underbrush on the other side of the clearing and began to crawl backward through the grass in an attempt to flee. Then she noticed people riding the Pagorinxes as well. She recognized the woman who escaped weeks before.

She stopped, amazed by what she saw. She was so focused on the animals trotting toward them across the field that she wasn't aware of standing until she found herself walking toward Bridget, who was standing in front of her, waiting for the approaching people.

Caroline and Oz stopped in front of the two women and Han and slid off the backs of the Pagorinxes onto the ground, watching the woman in front of them.

"Sofie?'" Oz exclaimed breathlessly as he scrutinized the rescued captive.

Caroline looked taken aback as she glanced between Oz and Shraiva. *I never told Oz the woman's real name.*

"Wendel?" the woman exclaimed in shock. "Is that you?"

"Yeah."

"I didn't recognize you underneath all that hair. But the voice is unmistakable." Sophia breathed in disbelief.

"I thought ever' one was dead. I thought *you* were dead," Oz exclaimed.

"And I you," she answered, still unable to look away from the man in front of her.

"You two know each other? How?" Caroline broke the silence. *So Oz must just be a nickname.*

"Sofie here is one a' us."

"You mean a Peregrine or Dragoman?" Bridget asked.

Sofia jerked around and glanced at the women in surprise. "You two are Peregrines?"

They both shook their heads in reply, carefully watching Sofia, who looked as though she might faint.

"How…how long have you been here?"

"Well, when I was captured by the Scaithers, we had only been here for two days."

Sofia looked at Oz. "Why do you think people are suddenly starting to reappear? It has been thirteen years since we first arrived here, and no one else ever came through the portals until now."

"I think it might be gettin' close. The final battle that is. Where have ya been all this time, Sofie?"

"Maybe we should continue this talk back at the tree house," Caroline interjected.

"That's a good idea," Oz replied. "Sofie, ya can ride with Bridget there atop Han. It's perfectly safe, I promise."

"I figured, since he hadn't eaten me yet, that I was safe." She gave a small smirk. Bridget climbed up first, and they realized quickly that Sofia couldn't straddle the bird's large back because of the manacles and chain still attached to her ankles.

"Oh my, we've forgotten something. We can fix that right up. Come stand here, Sofia, and don't worry, Han won't bite you." Bridget motioned her over to stand in front of Han.

Sofia stood as instructed in front of the large bird, closing her eyes, and preparing for the worst.

"Han, nip the chain in two please," she heard Bridget say. Sofia dared to peek out of one eye as she saw the large bird's head tip toward her, causing her to quickly close her eye and tense up even more. She could feel the large beak brushing the inside of her shins, and she turned her head and grimaced.

A moment later she heard Bridget say, "There. All done."

Sofia opened her eyes and looked down at her ankles. The chain that had been her constant companion for the last ten years had been bitten in two. She smiled and followed Bridget to climb upon the back of the Kabihanxu, swinging her now free legs across its silky feathers and clasping tightly to Bridget. She had never flown before, especially on the back of a firebird!

The foursome and their creatures headed back to the tree house. Sofia and Bridget soared high above the Xantifal Mountains trying to watch and make sure no one at ground level, save Oz and Caroline, could make out where they were headed. As high as they were and as wide as the Kabihanxu was, they doubted anyone could see them anyway. But since Sofia was the second trophy stolen from the Scaithers, they just might start to figure a few things out. Bridget decided they would take the long way home, circling the other side of the mountains just to be sure.

Sofia relished the feel of the warm breeze blowing against her skin with each powerful flap of the bird's wings. She could see the top of the ridge as the bird began its descent toward a grove of extremely large trees. Then she saw that there were wooden platforms among the massive branches nestled against the trunk of the tree.

The bird landed on the lowest platform that its large form could stand on and deposited its passengers. Bridget hugged the bird goodbye, and she and Sofia began making their way down the connecting platforms and steps until they were walking into what appeared to be the inside of the tree, making their way through a large gap that ran up the side of the tree from the ground, separating the bark and wood from itself.

By the time they made it to the lower-level Caroline and Oz had also made it back. Caroline set about finding Sofia something more suitable to put on, while Bridget made lunch and Oz and Sofia caught up on what each of them had been doing for the past thirteen years.

Sofia looked around the tree house and all the work that had been put into it. "How long have you lived here Wendal?"

"'Bout twelve years now, I reckon'."

"Where were you for the first year?"

"Slavers caught me an' worked me in the mines. I escaped an' made my way here. Found this holla' in the bottom a' this tree here an' started makin' it home. What about you? I thought fer sure ever'one else was dead."

"Yes, so did I." She half smiled at the man across the table from her. "Well, after we arrived, I managed to hide from the Scaithers for a while until the mountain switched and I ended up transplanted on the far side of Bakrashan, near Carpasmere on the edge of the Rhe Mountains. Fortunately, I hooked up with a band of travelers before the slavers found me and forced me to work in the mines like they did you. It was a decent living, moving from place to place, making wares to sell or trade for goods that we needed. Then one day, after three years traveling with them and making a new life and family for myself, we ran into a band of Scaithers. Riglan was with them. He took one look at me and slaughtered everyone, just because he wanted to. Caislan, the man I had taken up with, tried to stop him, so Riglan tortured him to death just to make a point. I tried to get away several times, only to be beaten by Riglan and then nursed back to health so he could have his way with me. That's why I had the manacles and chain attached to my ankles."

"We must a' both been transported by the same Shift. Only, I ended up gettin' caught by slavers. Still, seems like I got the better deal." Oz patted her hand sympathetically.

Caroline let them finish their conversation before interjecting.

"Here's a pair of pants and a shirt. You seem to be the same size as me. Maybe a bit taller, but they should fit just fine." Caroline handed Sofia the clothing.

"Thank you." She gratefully took the bundle offered to her.

"You can bunk in Bridget's bed. She and I will share mine. It's a little larger than hers so we will both be comfortable."

"And I'll see 'bout gettin' somethin' ta cut them manacles off yer ankles there."

"That would be wonderful. Thank you all so much for what you've done for me. I'm just going to go change." Sofia stood as Caroline pointed her in the direction of her room.

Oz found a tool to break the manacles apart where they connected. Sofia's ankles had calluses, bruises, and cuts where the constant contact of the manacles ate at her skin. Bridget made a poultice for both ankles, while Sofia and Caroline sat stitching Sofia a pair of boots that would protect her feet and skin against the perils of the forest.

Oz ventured out onto one of the higher platforms to beseech and pray to the God he had so long ignored, thinking he had been forgotten.

"Lord, I don' know what yer all about right now. Not sure why yer bringin' all these gals here all of a sudden. Show me what yer a wantin' me ta do. I need a clear answer. I fig're Caroline an' Bridget will be havin' ta move on soon. Do I stay, er do I go?" Oz sat on the platform for the next several hours waiting on God's answer.

That night, Caroline and Bridget sat praying as they had every night for the last several weeks, beseeching God for guidance. They wondered when they needed to leave and where they were to go. They both sensed that God was telling them it was time to leave. They only hoped that Oz was willing and ready to go as well. Sofia would surely wish to accompany them after years of imprisonment here in Zanchier. They would have a talk with Oz about it in the morning.

The next morning, after breakfast, Caroline called a meeting on the lower platform outside. The sun was breaking over the tops of the adjacent mountain peaks casting brilliant streams of light across the sky and the tree house. The breeze was light and cool, and the wildlife could be heard tending to their own morning rituals all around the ridgeline. The Kabihanxus soared across the sky, streaking it with beautiful trails of color as the sun's rays bounced off their colorful feathers. Bakrashan had found a special place in her and Bridget's hearts. If it weren't for the impending conversation that saddened them both, she would have thoroughly relished a morning like this, content with her current lifestyle.

"Oz, Bridget and I have been praying for God's direction for weeks now, and we feel He is leading us to leave Zanchier. Getting to the Dustbowl will be a breeze now with the animals, so there isn't anything holding us back. Except for the fact that we love this place, and we love you. We want you to come with us. Both of you." She glanced at Sofia. "Besides, you told me yourself that you are one of The Twelve that has to fight the final battle you told us about. We need you with us."

Oz sat looking between the two women. He had come to feel like they were the children that he had never had.

"I know it's time fer you two ta leave. Been feelin' it myself lately. But even though I'd go with ya in a minute, I feel God ain't done with what He wants me ta do here yet. There's somethin' I still have ta do. Not sure what yet, but He'll let me know when the time comes. Surely Sofie here'll go with the two a ya. There ain't no reason fer her ta stay here."

Tears began to glisten in Bridget's eyes. "Are you absolutely sure that you won't come with us, Oz?"

"Yeah, girlie, I'm sure. It pains me ta leave you gals, but we're doing what He called us to, after all, ain't we?" Oz grinned sadly, running his hand down the side of Bridget's hair to cup her cheek.

"Yes. I suppose we are." She sniffed, knowing the inevitable. Bridget turned to the woman who had arrived yesterday. "What about you Sofia? Will you come with us or stay here?"

"I'm not sure. I just got here. I wouldn't want to leave Oz behind. I think he's spent enough time all alone as it is. I think I'll stay and come with Oz when God calls him to leave. He did send me here too, after all, so maybe what I still need to do is here as well." Sofia grinned, satisfied with her decision to stay with her old friend.

"We must leave today," Caroline sighed. "I feel it very strongly. Bridget, call the animals to say your goodbyes. Instruct them to aid Oz and Sofia after we've gone also. And we'll need a ride from Han to the Dustbowl."

They spent the rest of the morning gathering much needed supplies to take with them on their peregrination. The mood was a somber one with everyone feeling the weight of yet another separation from loved ones.

Bridget called upon the Pagorinxes she had grown to love; she bid them farewell, and as Caroline asked, gave them firm instructions to keep an eye on Oz and Sofia. The Kabihanxu Han had arrived to transport them to the Dustbowl. Before Caroline and Bridget climbed on the giant bird's back for the last time, Bridget ran to Oz, wrapping her arms around the large man's waist. Her tearstained face peered up at the man in one last plea.

"Oz, are you sure you won't come with us? How will we ever find you again?" She choked back tears which now flowed freely.

"Aw…now, girl, ya know if it be God's will, we'll see each other again," Oz said, trying to talk around the lump in his throat. He hugged Bridget as hard as he could without hurting her and plucked her up off the platform to put her on Han's back. Caroline hugged Sofia goodbye, then turned to Oz.

"I don't know what we would have done without you these past two months, Oz. We'll miss you terribly, but I have faith that God will bring us back together." She flung her arms around his massive shoulders as tears stung her eyes. "Until we meet again." She pulled back and planted a kiss on his ruddy, hair-covered cheek.

Oz patted her on the back, his lip quivering as he cleared his throat. In a shaky voice he bid them farewell as Caroline climbed up behind Bridget.

"Now you two mind yer trainin', an' watch who ya trust. Not ever'body out there is like me. You know that. A-an' take care a' each other!" He yelled as the Kabihanxu took to the skies, flapping its massive wings, drying Oz's tears to his cheeks, as it flew off into the bright sun.

Bridget and Caroline took one last look at the place they had called home for the last two months. A longing stirred in their hearts as they waved goodbye to Oz and Sofia.

"Caroline," Bridget said suddenly, "what about your telepathy training?"

Don' ya worry 'bout that now, gal. Both a' ya are a quick study!

They both felt Oz's reassuring thoughts. Smiling at each other, they soared toward the place of constant tornadoes known as the Dustbowl, headed out to wherever God would lead them next. Hoping and praying that one day soon they would see Oz and Sofia again.

Marnor watched the firebird soar through the skies high above, trying to keep tabs on the direction from which it had come. He didn't know who these people were, but he was sure itching to find out. Anybody who could control Pagorinxes and Kabihanxus would be very valuable to him. He smiled wryly to himself as a plan began to form in his head.

Since Riglan's death last month, he had fought little to assume the position. The only person who had been stupid enough to really challenge him had been Faigen, and Marnor didn't figure he would try it again after the near-death beating Marnor had given him.

Riglan had been power hungry and stupid. Marnor would watch and figure out a way to get out of Zanchier, something Riglan never managed. He had been listening and learning all he could from anyone who was willing to tell him about these people called Peregrines and Dragoman. Apparently they were supposed to fight demons and save the world from its own destruction. Marnor would figure out how to capitalize on that and get out of Zanchier for good.

He also thought about the girl who had gotten away in all the chaos last month. Caroline. Now she was something. He would look for her in the process. She had to be one of those Peregrines, just like Shraiva was. Too bad that firebird had gotten Shraiva. He thought he was just starting to make a little headway with her.

He stopped for just a minute, realizing something. Those other two rescued Caroline, why not Shraiva too? Marnor wondered if that could have been what happened to her. Surely they didn't know that she was one of them. How could they have? However, he had heard the Pagorinxes in the treetops and the cry of the firebird just minutes before the Shifts started. If the land Shifts didn't get her, and the firebird didn't make a meal of her, maybe, just maybe, he'd find her up the mountain somewhere along with the others. He smiled again; this was proving to be an excellent day after all.

Now faith is confidence in what we hope for and assurance about what we do not see. This is what the ancients were commended for. By faith we understand that the universe was formed at God's command, so that what is seen was not made out of what was visible.

Hebrews 11:1-3 NIV

Chapter 16

Reader's Island

The island was still buzzing with activity as construction on the stables was nearly complete. With the discovery of their new gifts and how to use them came the added benefits of aiding the workers in the building of the stables. Seth's strength and Alec's telekinetic ability made transporting materials very easy, while Odessa's ability to predict the future aided in the avoidance of unnecessary accidents. Uriah used his gift of electricity to weld iron works as necessary, while Nick and Sean used their fire and water to heat and cool the iron for necessary horseshoes. Kristen took care of the dirt work with her earth powers, and Zaccai took care of transplanting plants to beautify the stable grounds.

Wade and Dominic, who could communicate with the animals, accompanied Simon and several available groundskeepers into town in search of good quality horses to purchase. They would need approximately twenty horses in addition to Simon's three to accommodate almost everyone, and since they couldn't simply have them delivered they needed all the help they could get to bring back that many horses.

While everyone was out taking care of business, training, or working on searching for the many still unanswered questions, Safra went once again to the temple to beseech God's grace on searching for the girl Bridget Burke and her companion. This time she received an answer. Safra quickly returned to her room and set about drawing the images God had revealed to her during her prayer time. This time He had given them a definite location where they could be found.

When she had finished with all her renderings, she went to the office on the first level and made copies for each of the Dragoman. They would decide who to send in the search and supply them with the necessary information. She then went in search of Simon and the others, hoping Simon had already returned from their journey to find horses.

She found him in the newly finished barns where everyone worked to secure the animals and place all the tack and feed in their rightful places.

"Simon." Safra waved the papers above her head in excitement. "God has spoken."

"Wonderful, Safra!" A large smile split Simon's lips. Simon took the papers she handed him and quickly scanned them, still smiling at the information in front of him. "This is truly wonderful, Safra. Thank you. The Dragoman will meet this evening to best determine which team we will send to find them. Would you take these and leave them in the office until later, please?" He handed the papers back to her and went back to work.

That evening, Simon, Safra, Nuncio, Malachai, Ryan, Prisca, and Vashti all met in one of the conference rooms to privately discuss the matter. They didn't want all the Peregrines involved in the meeting until they could decide who to send. Everyone was getting a little stir crazy and antsy, ready to go on a mission, and they didn't want to start an argument about it.

As Safra handed out the copies she made for them, Simon began the meeting.

"Safra is handing out the new location of Bridget Burke and the woman identified as her aunt. Now, we have all the teams here on the island, but I believe we should send the team with the most experience to try and convince these women to join us here. That would put my team as the ones to go. Do the rest of you agree with this?"

Malachai spoke, "What about my team? Zaccai has peregrinated for eighteen years and Uriah for fifteen."

"True," Nuncio answered, "but Dominic has only been at it for six months, and Gabrielle only two years. Plus, they are very young, Dominic is but fifteen years old and is now a Keeper, not a Peregrine as we first thought."

"Yes, you have a valid point there. But Seth has only been peregrinating for what, five months himself?" Malachai asked.

Simon replied this time. "That also is true, but Seth is twenty-seven years of age and a very capable and strong man who has already been in a battles with demons. The others on the team have been peregrinating together for a total of thirty-three years. If we are going to send out a team to search, I believe they are the right ones. Plus, they have already laid eyes on Bridget Burke and her companion once."

Everyone around the table agreed with what Simon was saying. He continued, "Safra's information puts the women in the year 2005, in Louisiana, in the United States of America. Hurricane Katrina hit the coastal area of Louisiana and Mississippi in 2005, then traveled up the Mississippi river, affecting many towns and cities on both sides. But New Orleans was completely flooded and destroyed. I'm not sure how easy it will be to find them in such a place, but this is God's will and He will guide the team in the right direction."

When they concluded the meeting, Simon and Nuncio summoned the team they were sending to search for the women to join them in the conference room, as the remainder of the Dragoman went back to their premeeting duties.

Jason, Seth, Alec, and Odessa all entered the room and took a seat at the table.

"Safra has had a new vision of the Burke girl and her companion. They are in New Orleans, Louisiana, in the year 2005. You need to make sure and get to them this time. We need time to train them and assess what they know. Surely they know something about peregrination or they wouldn't be storm-jumping."

Jason, who was team leader, spoke. "We can be ready to leave within the hour if you like."

"That is a very acceptable time, Jason, thank you," Simon replied.

"All right, everyone," Jason said standing, "let's get packed and get ready to go on another adventure. You know, I've always wanted to see the Louisiana coastline and experience the rich culture that exists there. I just never got a chance."

"Well I'm afraid you won't like what you see this time, Jason," Simon said regretfully. "New Orleans was completely devastated by flooding caused by a break in the levee system. It was, from what my research has revealed, a horrid sight to behold. This will not in any way be a pleasant trip. Most of the storms you have peregrinated through you have exited on the side of the least problematic results. This time you're walking into the aftermath of a major hurricane that did immeasurable and irreparable damage. Many people lost their lives. Prepare yourselves for the worst. You can set your coordinates to enter a couple of weeks after the storm hit. That should still make searching possible and not as troublesome."

"Sure thing, Simon. We'll find them this time. Come hell or high water," Jason replied.

"High water is exactly what you'll find there, Jason. Perhaps even a little of both."

The team of four packed necessary items for travel and set the Portgen for the appropriate coordinates and date. They decided they were less likely to be seen if they set the time for sunrise, hoping the glint of glaring light would possibly hide the portal opening. Being unsure of what was still standing and what might be underwater made it hard to set appropriate coordinates. They would just have to pray for God's grace to conceal them in this case.

New Orleans, Louisiana, September 15, 2005

They hadn't needed to worry about detection from the portal opening. New Orleans was all but a ghost town. The waters were still high in some areas, but the majority of the people who were out and about were volunteers and the national guard, still searching for people in need of rescuing. Seth had seen New Orleans back in 1891, and it was vastly different now. Especially with all the destruction from the storm surge and the flooding making it hardly recognizable as a city.

They had been roaming the city searching for any signs of Bridget and her companion for three days now with no luck. They asked anyone they came across to look at the photo of Bridget. Ryan had been able to take Safra's photo-like sketch, upload it to the computer, and get a colored, high-quality, photographic image.

It was getting late as they walked the northern docks area of Lake Pontchartrain, chatting with people and passing the photo, when they hit a bit of luck.

"Excuse me sir," Seth asked a gentleman who was tying up his boat in one of the dock slips, "have you by chance seen this young woman? We believe she and her companion may have been displaced due to the hurricane a few weeks back, and we are trying to find her."

Clovis Sebatier took the photo in hand, studying the picture as he rubbed the thick stubble of his graying beard. " I t'ink I jus' might member dat girl dere. She had a frien' wit' her and da two a dem needed a boat ride 'cross the flood waters several days back. Jus' 'bout ever'body 'round here don' evacuated someplace else. But I t'ink I 'member dem talkin' 'bout headin' west ta Lake Charles. Yes sir...strange pair dem two. Dressed like dey done come from some type a ren'ssance festiv'l or somet'n like dat. Perty lil gals dey were though."

Seth grinned to himself at the man's thick Cajun drawl. "Thank you so much, sir. And you're sure they talked about heading to...Lake Charles, was it?"

"Yes sir. Lot's a people here 'round went dat away. You be need'n a ride somewhere?"

"Thank you for the offer, sir, but I think we've got it under control. I just need to find my friends." Seth left the friendly man and went in search of the others.

He found them not far off talking to other fishermen who were staying in the area, trying to get back to their lives in some sort of normal fashion as the waters slowly receded.

"Hey guys, I just spoke with a fisherman a few slips down who said he actually gave them a ride a few days ago. Said he heard them talking about following the evacuees to Lake Charles. Apparently it's a city west of here. He also said they were dressed in renaissance type garb. So maybe, wherever they were prior to arriving here, was sometime during the renaissance period."

Alec answered Seth. "Maybe, but it seems like we must find a way to get to this Lake Charles."

"We could just use the Portgen. Besides, we already messed up by waiting too long to search here. We should have checked earlier," Seth replied.

"We could set the Portgen for two weeks earlier here and wait for them to appear," Alec answered.

Odessa spoke up at this suggestion. "I think I would rather head toward Lake Charles than go back here." She shuddered. "I've already seen too much of the effects of this storm. It makes me ill to think what lies in wait if we actually go back a week or two."

"I agree," Jason spoke. "I have no desire to see more unfound or forgotten corpses lying about."

Jason punched in some information on the Portgen's screen. "All right then, we head to Lake Charles. I would assume that they have already made it there. According to the GPS on the Portgen, it's only about a four-hour drive. So, since they left here a week ago, maybe they are still there. Let's at least pray that's the case. If we lose them again, Simon will have our hides," Jason said with a look of trepidation.

They set out in search of a remote location, which wasn't hard to find with all the deserted buildings, set the coordinates for what appeared to be a heavily wooded area just north of Lake Charles and opened the portal. Jason walked through first to make sure there was no one around and ushered the others through, then quickly closed the portal.

"So where do you think we are?" Seth asked as they trudged through the thick underbrush.

"I'm not sure. The GPS shows that we are in a state park called Sam Houston Jones, approximately five miles north of Lake Charles, so we need to hike out of these woods and see where it leads us."

"Too bad we don't have the horses," Alec said.

"It might look a little strange with four people riding horses out of the woods in 2005. They have a lot of automobiles in this time period. Horses are mainly used for recreational purposes these days," Jason answered.

"I suppose it's about the same as the year 2018 in the Hawaiian Islands?" Seth asked.

"Yes, pretty much. Except open carry laws aren't quite in effect as in 2018, so watch showing your weapons. We certainly don't need to draw any unusual attention to ourselves, especially with all the new people in town due to the evacuees arriving from New Orleans and all the other southern parishes hit by the storm. I'm sure the police will be on high alert."

Odessa spoke up. "Well at least we won't stick out with our packs strapped to our backs with everyone likely walking around doing the same. And it won't appear unusual with us asking questions about Bridget either. Surely everyone is looking for someone. Lots of people get displaced during things like this. Maybe we should tell people she's a relative. We may get further with the questioning."

Jason thought a minute. "I could tell people she's my daughter. I am the only one here who is old enough to have a daughter who looks her age."

They all agreed to that story, with Seth and Alec being uncles and Odessa being married to Alec since she knew him better than either of the others.

Alec secretly grinned at this since this was a dream of his anyway. He would relish playing this part as long as he could. This may be the only time he would be able to get this close to Dee.

They hiked out of the woods and followed highway 378, twisting and turning through the town of Westlake. As they stood assessing the I-10 bridge, a young man stopped and offered them a ride across it.

"Y'all lose your homes in the hurricane?" he asked.

"We just came over from New Orleans. We're looking for my daughter. We were separated in all the commotion. Do you know where the Lake Charles Civic Center is? That's where I was told she was taken."

"I sure do. It's just over the bridge here," he said pointing. "Hop in. I'll give y'all a ride over." Making small conversation for the two-minute ride across the bridge, they told him of a little of the destruction they had experienced while in New Orleans.

After the young man dropped them off in downtown Lake Charles, close to the civic center where the refugees were being housed, they immediately began asking after their "relatives." Volunteers showed them bunks and provided food and water, after which they each went in different directions in and around the large building located on the seawall of the city looking for the women. They hoped the women were still there as well and that they just hadn't stumbled upon them yet. There had to be tens of thousands of people in the place, making it very hard to search. They mainly asked questions of the people with volunteer labels or tags on their shirts or lanyards hanging around their necks. Surely someone had seen them.

They spent the next two days walking the Civic Center inside and out, searching and talking to everyone they could. They noticed many others also searching for loved ones. Some of these poor people had even been separated from young children and spouses somewhere along the way. With hundreds of thousands of people evacuating the lower parishes of Louisiana, things like that just tended to happen, however heartbreaking it was.

On the second day an elderly woman mentioned that she had spoken to the two women that they were searching for. She said they had mentioned heading toward the coastal cities just south of Lake Charles. She told them that the younger girl said she had never before seen a beach, and the two women struck off in search of one about five days ago. They thanked the woman for the information and set out in search of a place to rent a car.

Finding a rental company, but unable to rent a car due to the amount of extra people in the area, they managed to secure a ride to the coast. They asked the woman, who lived down that way, where was the best place to look for someone who wanted to visit the local beach. She informed them that there were four beaches on the coast. Rutherford, Holly, Constance, and Little Florida, all of which ran into the next and that the drive would take them about an hour and a half. Highway 27, she told them as they drove, ran most of the length of the beaches, before highway 82-Gulf Beach Highway branched off toward Little Florida Beach development toward Texas.

Once they reached the coast, they realized it was an unpopulated area for the most part, mainly due to the swamps and marshes that were strewn across most of the area. There were homes and camps scattered along the water's edge, some areas were more concentrated than others with dwellings, with long stretches of nothing but canals and grass for miles in between.

The driver dropped them at Holly beach at the local store.

After they said their thanks and goodbyes to the friendly woman.

"Guys, I think I just had another premonition on the ride here. I believe another storm is going to hit this area very soon."

Seth turned to look at her. "Why is that Odessa?"

"I just saw it very clearly. This entire area will be decimated," she said sadly.

Looking at their surroundings, they realized there were hundreds of camps in the area here and people were milling about hurriedly, packing up to head out.

Jason inquired of the clerk why people seemed in such a hurry.

"There's another hurricane coming," the young man told him. "It's supposed to hit here within the next day or so. People are gathering supplies for travelin'."

Jason looked at the others with concern. "That doesn't leave us much time to find them."

"Do you think that may be why they came this way? To pick up another storm for peregrinating out of here?" Seth asked.

"I have no idea. We didn't know about this storm either. But Simon had no reason to tell us about it since we were supposed to find them in New Orleans, and we no longer travel by storms."

Odessa said, "Perhaps it is just coincidental that they are here. Like the woman back at the shelter told us, maybe she just wanted to see a beach. The storm may just be a perk. And since they obviously travel by storms, they may be ready to catch this one out of here when it hits. We really need to find them, fast." Urgency was evident in her voice.

The four of them walked around the store and showed the picture of Bridget to anyone who would slow down long enough to look at the photo. Odessa stepped up to the counter to speak with the clerk.

"Excuse me, but you wouldn't have seen this young girl recently by any chance?" she asked the harried young man behind the counter.

"Uhh…yeah. Yeah, I think so. I remember the tall one. She was a real looker." That was all he said as he continued ringing up people's purchases and answering questions from others.

"Could you tell me when you last saw her and maybe where they could have gone?" she asked, a little frustrated.

"Um…let's see. Just a few days ago they asked about renting a place somewhere on the beach. I told them to check the bulletin board over there on the wall. It usually has listings for rentals." He pointed to a back wall.

"Thanks." She turned and wormed her way through the crowd of people toward the back wall, following the guys who had heard what the young man said and had already made their way toward the board.

They scanned all the ads for available rentals and took paper tabs off the ones that looked promising and offered an address.

Seth stepped back up to the counter to speak to the clerk one last time.

"Excuse me, but have you seen the young woman again since they asked about rooms for rent?"

"Nah, but McKenzie may have. She works the evening shift. She'll be here in about five hours, you might could catch her then, that is if she hasn't already evacuated. The owners will likely board everything up and close soon with the storm predicted to hit within the next few days."

Seth and the others stepped outside discussing what to do next. They decided to start at the lower end of the community and work their way west along the beach. The area was a few miles long, littered with small homes, campers, and trailers. Most of the homes were on stilts that lifted them about fifteen feet higher to allow for possible flooding. As they wandered between the homes, four rows deep along the beach, they noticed that most of the dwellings were already boarded up in preparation for the coming hurricane. Most people apparently had heeded the warning early on and had already left the area.

They decided to separate and each take a section of homes to knock on doors, trying to make quick work of it. They spent the better part of five hours with no luck. Finally, they decided to take a break and go in search of something to eat for dinner and a place to shelter for the night. When they went back to the little store to ask about food and lodging, they found it boarded up. No one was in sight.

"Well, looks like we'll just have to bed down somewhere outside. We could probably sleep beneath one of the raised homes, but we can't start a fire underneath it to cook on," Jason said.

"How about we just head down to the beach and camp there. We can gather driftwood for a fire, sleep beneath the star-filled sky, feel the salty breeze upon our skin, and listen to the breaking of the surf against the sand," Alec offered in his French, romanticized way.

"Alec, you can make anything sound good." Odessa giggled with a shake of her head.

"Life is an adventure, my friends. We should try to make the most of it." He smiled emphatically.

"If I didn't know any better, I'd say you had lived the life of a sailor and thoroughly enjoyed it." Seth chuckled.

"No, my friend, I never went to sea. But I did fantasize about it for a while in my latter teen years, but who could ask for more than this." Alec spread his arms wide to encompass all the vast natural beauty around them. "Most of the time, we traverse the known and unknown universe, seeing and experiencing things that very few others in this world ever will. Sure there are sacrifices we must make, but God has given us an amazing purpose and opportunity to view His creation without limits."

"Maybe you should be a preacher or motivational speaker when this is all over?" Jason joked with him.

"If that is what God wishes of me, then so be it." Alec smiled. "Let's head down the beach to where we stopped looking. Then in the morning we can pick up there."

The four of them headed out across the dunes and down to the beach once again. At the site of the last home they visited, they stopped to make camp. It was already well past dark, and the night air from the winds off the water began to chill their skin. They quickly found enough driftwood to build a fire and warm some of the food they had packed with them. After pulling out their easy-pack bedrolls, they unfurled them in the sand and hunkered down to rest, lying in a circle around the low burning fire. They would only rest for a few precious hours of sleep, knowing that time was not on their side.

Bridget stared out the small window that faced the water, watching as the ever-growing power of the waves pounded the beach. She sighed happily at the adventures that she and Caroline had shared in the past few weeks since leaving Zanchier. Even though the devastation they experienced in New Orleans would most likely haunt her for the rest of her days, she was still content with her present life situation. She glanced up and down the beach, trying to make out any signs of life in the darkness. She could spot what appeared to be a light on the beach a little distance to the east, possibly a fire from someone camping.

They must be crazy to sleep out in the open with the predicted storm looming over their heads.

"Caroline, I don't think I have ever seen anything so beautiful as the vastness of the ocean."

"Well, being from California, I've seen my fair share of the ocean. I do have to say though; this area is much less populated than the Pacific coastline. However, there is one thing that California has that Louisiana does not."

"Really, what's that?" Bridget asked, turning to look at her friend.

"Blue water," Caroline snickered. "I'm not sure why this water is so murky, but if you want to see some beautiful water, you really need to check out the California coastline."

"Perhaps God will be gracious enough to spit us out of the next storm into California then." Bridget smiled and jumped onto the small bed. "Caroline, do you think Oz is all right?" Her demeanor suddenly grew serious.

"I'm sure of it. He did survive for thirteen years there all by himself you know." She grinned slightly at her friend. "Besides, he isn't alone. Sofia is there with him."

"I know. I just miss him so. And Han and Pax. Well, *all* of them, if you must know. Xantifal will always hold a special place in my heart. It was where I first discovered who I am meant to be. Although, I'm still not sure what this ability is for. But I am certain God will reveal that to me whenever I need to know it."

Caroline grinned to herself at her young friend's mature understanding. "Bridget, you have to be the oldest sixteen-year-old I have ever met." She fondly smiled.

"I shall take that as a compliment." Bridget grinned back.

"We need to get some sleep. If my feelings are correct, and from what the weather is looking like outside, *and* if what people have been saying is true, we are in for a doozy of a storm. We should be able to peregrinate this one to somewhere, if it is going to be as strong as they are predicting."

"Caroline, how are we to stand in winds that are blowing full strength at a hundred miles an hour?"

"I've never peregrinated by hurricane before, but surely we will be gone by the time it gets that bad, Bridget. But if not, I am sure there is a way. Others must have traveled this way long before us."

They climbed into their beds and drifted off to sleep only to be awakened several hours later to the sound of the wind howling around the small camp. Large raindrops began pelting the outside roof and walls sporadically as the outer bands of the storm made their way inland.

"I think we might need to pack and get ready. Like I said, I've never traveled by way of a hurricane before, so I'm not sure when the portal will open. If a storm only needs to be a certain strength like Oz said, then maybe it will appear before the winds get unmanageable."

They packed up, waiting and watching from the safety of the dry camper as the storm's strength continued to grow in severity. It didn't take long for it to intensify enough for a portal to begin to open.

"All right, Bridget, there's a portal. I'm not sure if we can reach it in time since we have to run across the sand and against the force of the wind gusts. It will make it very difficult. But since there is a lot more intense weather to come, I'm pretty sure there will be other portals opening up. Like Storm Valley back in Zanchier where multiple portals would appear during the most intense and longer-lasting storms."

"I suppose we must be outside to be able to get to them. All right then, let's go." Bridget squared her shoulders as if preparing herself.

She grasped the handle to open the door and a gust of wind nearly knocked Bridget off the porch as it flung the door open with her still holding on to the handle. Caroline reached out to grab her and pull her back upright. They clung to each other as they carefully navigated the steps that led them down to the beach. Leaning into the wind and keeping a firm grasp on each other's hand, they hurried toward the portal. The wind was so forceful that it seemed they took one step back for every step forward. They could only watch as the portal closed before they reached it. Walking directly toward the storm's center and the water, the waves were now reaching a height of three feet. The rain, wind, and lightning intensified, and they huddled together, watching and waiting, praying that God would keep them safe until another portal opened.

The rain and gale force winds which were getting more intense by the minute, woke the four Peregrines sleeping on the beach under the now turbulent night sky. The winds howled around them and the surf pounded the beach, increasing in steadiness and strength. The small fire they had built just hours earlier had been snuffed out by the rain and wind. They picked up their packs and bedrolls and headed for shelter underneath one of the boarded-up and abandoned camps. They stood beneath the elevated floor, discussing their next move. They would have to find the girls quickly or risk losing them again. If the two women hadn't decided to leave here through this particular storm via portal, then the storm would surely wipe out the whole area, taking them with it.

They decided they had better escalate the search and begin pounding on every door that was left. They doubted very seriously that anyone remained in the camps. People here were used to this sort of thing and had grown wise over the years about listening when told to evacuate. Only having two Portgens, they decided to stay close as possible to each other so as to not get separated. With everyone pretty much gone, it shouldn't be too hard to find two people.

Seth had just walked up on a platform to knock on yet another door when a flash of lightning drew his attention toward the beach. Standing approximately a few hundred feet away were two figures huddled together as if waiting for something.

It has to be them, and they are waiting for a portal!

He waved and yelled to the others to get their attention as best he could before rushing in the direction of the women. As he bounded off the platform, he saw Jason and Alec wave. Seth pointed at the beach and took off running as fast as he could against the gale-force gusts.

Seth ran clumsily through the loose sand as the wind attempted to push him back. He yelled with all of his might, knowing that the gusts were stealing any sound that might escape his lips. He caught a glimpse of Jason, Alec, and Odessa coming up behind him as streaks of lightning electrified the air around them.

Seth continued to run as fast as possible, waving his arms in the air like a madman. He searched the dark for the figures before him, vowing not to let them out of his sight. At least each flash of lightning showed the two figures still standing, huddled together. Just then a portal begin to generate almost directly in front of the women.

Good Lord, no! He tried to run faster and screamed against the wind with all his might, trying to draw their attention. Just then the lightning lit the sky once more and the wind blew the tall one's hood from her head revealing her face. Seth froze in place, realizing who he had seen.

Caroline? Seth couldn't believe his eyes, but it was her.

Just as the two were about to step into the portal, Caroline turned for one last look over her shoulder.

It was definitely her!

"Caroline!" Seth screamed with all the force he could muster as he struggled harder against the wind and sand.

"Seth?" Caroline spun around, but she and Bridget had stepped into the portal, and it was too late to turn back. They were on the other side, not knowing where they were, and the portal was gone.

"Seth?" she breathed.

Dumbfounded, Caroline stood there, not quite certain of what she had seen. Then she fell to her knees as she began to cry for the first time since her strange new life began. Bridget, concerned for her friend, tried to encourage her to at least seek shelter from the rain and the storm they found themselves in on the other side.

"Nooo!!" Seth screamed, throwing himself forward, reaching out to grab her before she was gone as he stumbled into the portal just before it closed.

Jason, Alec, and Odessa fell to the earth, all of them out of breath from trying to run in the loose sand. Seth was gone and they had no idea where. So were the two figures that had disappeared into the portal. Maybe Seth had made it through with them. If not, he could be deposited anywhere, and they had no idea where that was.

"Alec," Jason yelled through the rain and gale-force winds, "did it sound to you like Seth was yelling Caroline's name?" he asked between gulps of air as the wind stole his breath.

"Yes, my friend! That is exactly what I believe he said!" Alec answered just as breathlessly, as they sat on the sand tired, wet, and praying for their now lost friend.

"We need to get back to Simon's and hope the trackers can find wherever it is he went. These things could be our only chance to find Seth!" Jason stated.

"Doesn't he have the Portgen?" Odessa yelled.

"No. Ryan only made enough for each team so far, and as team leaders you and I carry the only two we have between the four of us!"

"Fortunately," Alec yelled against the spindrifts hitting him, "Simon gave me some extra chips just in case. And I was telekinetically able to plant one of the chip devices onto the taller of the women. When the wind blew back her hood, I was able to get a glimpse of her and concentrate on a spot to send the chip. If they work, and the wind didn't prohibit my abilities, we'll be able to track not only Seth but Bridget and her friend as well!"

They all smiled at one another, then stood up, congratulating Alec on his quick thinking. Jason punched in the coordinates to return to Reader's Island and find out where they were to go next.

"*Aaahhh!*" Seth screamed at the top of his lungs from sheer anger and frustration, realizing he was alone as he fell to the ground on the other side of the portal. He had been so close and didn't even know she was there! For two hours of sleep, he had just missed Caroline! Two hours!

He lay on his back in the rain as his emotions got the better of him. He screamed into the sky once again as tears streamed down his cheeks, mixing with the water still pouring from the sky. Where could she have gone? And why wasn't he in the same place she was? He wasn't back on the beach, but there also was no sign of Caroline or Bridget.

"*Whyy!*" he screamed at the sky, angry at God. She had been so close. She was actually here in this world doing the very thing he was. Why was God doing this to him?

"Hey fella', ya need ta get out a' this rain, an' take shelter. This here be dangerous terr'tory, 'specially fer yer kind."

A strange drawling voice spoke to Seth from somewhere near.

Seth opened his eyes and jumped up from the ground, stumbling a bit before taking an offensive stance.

"Kid, if I wanted ta kill ya, I would a taken the opportunity when ya were flailin' 'round on the ground there. I sure wouldn' a' alerted ya ta my presence neither."

Standing before Seth was a man near as big as him covered in a sort of animal-skin coat, his arms hanging down by his side as he stood and looked at Seth.

Seth could only stare as he leaned forward, placing his hands on his knees to catch his breath, still breathing hard from the full-speed run into the portal against gale winds and loose sand.

"Well, if'n ya want ta stay out here in all this an' risk your neck ya go right on ahead. If not, ya can folla me." The large figure of a man turned and began walking away from Seth.

Seth straightened and looked around, unable to make out much about where he might be. He decided he'd better follow the man. He seemed to know what Seth was, so maybe he knew how to get him home. Maybe he could show him how to find Caroline. Seth followed the stranger into the dense, dark, forest, unable to think of anything else to do in his present situation. Rain still pelted him, as thunder boomed and lightning lit the dark sky.

The whole earth is filled with awe at your wonders;
where morning dawns, where evening fades,
you call forth songs of joy.

Psalm 65:8 NIV

Chapter 17

Bakrashan, Zanchier, Xantifal Mountains

Since the arrival of Bridget and Caroline almost three months back and finding Sofie again, Oz had taken to keeping watch over Storm Valley where God seemed to keep dumping new Peregrines for him to go and rescue.

Thirteen years and not a peep from another civilized human being. Now, all of a sudden, here God done went and dumped three new Peregrines right in his lap. And brought an old friend back. Oz figured God must be trying to tell him something, so he figured he better start listening a little more closely.

This new fella here though, seemed a bit strange, screaming at God like he was. But he reckoned he understood. The first time God dumped him here, he had felt like that too. Especially after what the Scaithers had done to all the others. At least he could be of some assistance to the people God kept sending here. Oz wasn't sure what there was about Zanchier that God found it necessary to keep sending them, but he'd do whatever part God needed him to. That is, now that he had found his way back to God's side again. Not that he had ever left, but he sure had felt like God had left him for the last thirteen years.

Oz still had no idea why God would have brought them all here years ago, except maybe to punish the guilty ones. But the rest of them hadn't done anything wrong. He guessed they all had to pay the price. The innocent suffer because of the guilty. Of course, it weren't God that betrayed all of them either. So he reckoned it weren't God's doin' after all.

They made their way up the mountainside through the torrential rains and the booming thunder to Oz's tree house. He could have called on one of the Kabihanxu or the Pagorinxes to pick them up, but the young fella behind him seemed as though he might need to cool off just a bit anyhoo, work out some of his frustrations. The walk might do him some good. Besides, he ain't likely never seen anything like the animals here on Zanchier before. Oz didn't want to scare him off right from the start.

They made it back to Oz's tree house within the hour. Good time considering it was still pouring rain outside. The Xantifal Mountains received vast amounts of rain. Probably the reason for the size of the trees and vegetation in these parts. Plus the oxygen levels here were also high, allowing for the growth of the animals. A lot of it was, of course, just God's design for Zanchier.

Seth followed the strange man up the mountainside to the bottom of a very large tree. They walked beneath its massive root system, which completely sheltered them from the rain. The large man pushed open a massive wooden door that immediately spilled light from the inside throughout the dark underbelly of the tree.

"Sofie, I brought company," the big man stated.

Seth followed the man inside, where a very pretty woman stood. Seth assumed she was Sofie.

"Really?" She turned to look at Seth. "Good grief, you're a large fellow, aren't you. I believe he's even bigger than you, Oz." She smiled at Seth. "Are you a Peregrine as well?" she asked, calming his nerves just a little.

Well, she knows what I am too.

"My name is Sofia. Oz here calls me Sofie." She extended her hand and Seth took it.

"Seth."

"Please, have a seat. Oz will go get you some dry clothes."

'Thanks, but there's no need…about the clothes, I mean. I have a dry set in my pack."

"Really. After all that rain you have dry clothing in that bag?" She pointed to his pack slung across his back.

"Yes, ma'am. The bag's a dry sack. Waterproof because of the weather traveling."

"Well, things have certainly changed. They didn't have anything that fancy back in the day when we were traveling," She smiled.

"You're Peregrines?" Seth asked, puzzled, as he sat down on one of the wooden chairs.

"Sure are. Oz and I both. Long story there. He can tell you about it later." Sofia pointed to the large, hairy, man who had shucked his rain gear.

"Names Oz." He turned, extending his hand to Seth. "Ya wouldn' by chance be Seth Jager would ya?" the man asked him, throwing Seth for a loop.

"Uh, yeah, I would. How do you know of me?" Seth looked back and forth between the two people who stood and stared in disbelief.

"Well now, that there is quite a story. Why don' ya go up that way ta my room an' get changed. We're gonna' be here a while. Yes, we are." The man rubbed the side of his hairy face and grinned at Seth.

Seth cautiously took the man's advice and went to change out of his drenched clothing. When he returned to the center of the tree house where the kitchen was located, Sofia had a steaming cup of coffee ready for him.

"Thanks," Seth said, taking the cup.

"I hoped coffee was to your liking. Never met a Peregrine who didn't live for the stuff." She chuckled. "The blend here in Zanchier is quite a bit different than what I'm sure you're used to. It can be quite strong. Do you need cream or sugar?"

He tasted the coffee before replying and nearly choked. "Yes, please, a little of both." He cleared the strong liquid from his throat. He gratefully took first one and then the other of the containers she placed on the table before him and added generous amounts of each to his large cup.

"I'll take your wet things and hang them outside to dry." She picked up his clothes. "But I will be back. I want to hear all about you too." She smiled and turned to Oz. "Oz, you wait just a minute now."

"So are you two married?" Seth watched Sofia climb a staircase leading up into the tree house.

"Goodness, no," Oz replied. "'Course, I suppose it might appear that way ta an outsider. I guess that's as good a place as any ta start our story. We're Per'grines from way back. We've been stranded here fer the better part of thirteen years now. Sofie there was a pris'ner a' the Scaithers fer the last ten years; they're some right nasty folk who roam this countryside. Anyhoo', me an' her just got reunited last month or so. We both were on teams that got trapped here after one a' our own betrayed the lot of us."

"Hiram Burke?" Seth asked, starting to piece things together a bit.

"Yep, sure 'nough. I see ya new fellas have heard the story."

"Only recently, and not really much. The name just came up and stirred up a bit of…emotions in some of the other Dragoman."

"As well it should!" Oz wondered about some of his old friends. "I have lots a' questions, but b'fore we get too far away from our story, we can save those fer later." Sofia had re-entered the small kitchen in the meantime. "Now, back then, all us Per'grines had special powers that enabled us ta fight the good fight. Some a' them decided to use theirs fer their own greed an' selfishness. One in partic'lar, Hiram Burke, betrayed us all. He wanted it all—the wife, family, Dragoman status, an' power. Decided he knew better 'an God, an' tried to per'grinate with his wife an' kid. Hiram fig'red that if Safra Driscoll was able ta do it, then his wife, Mary, could too. Problem was, she couldn' an' died in the process."

"I know Safra," Seth interjected.

"Still around, is she?" Oz smiled as the light of memories flashed through his eyes. "Now, Mary died when Hiram tried ta pull her inta a port'l. She could see the port'ls, but couldn' walk through 'em. That's why Hiram fig'red she could do it. She died, but his little girl survived the jump. Hiram was angry for a while. At God, at others who he thought could a preven'ed Mary from dyin'. We all thought he had event'lly come to terms with it, but after he got most a' the Per'grines slaughtered by an all-out demon war, an' stranded the rest a us here, we realized he was still angry. Only thing is, only people I know of that can see a port'l an' not make use of it's a Scaither. I of'en wonder if old Hiram knew 'bout this place, an' if Mary was a Scaither. See, no one ever met Mary. Frankly, Dragoman an' Per'grines knew better than ta get involved with a reg'lar person 'cause a' the life we lead. Hiram was amassin' quite a fortune back home. More so than the other Dragoman. No one knew how he was gettin' all his gold. I think it had somthin' ta do with this place."

"Wow, that's some story. I understand all the stigmatism attached to the Burke name now. Poor Bridget." Seth suddenly remembered losing Caroline again. "We've been tracking her for months now, trying to find her. Everyone thought she was number Eleven."

"Now that's a special girl, there," Oz said lovingly, catching Seth's attention again. "That's the next part a' my story. You asked how I knew yer name."

"I have to say I am very curious."

"Well, turns out after twelve years alone here in the Xanitfal Mount'ns, God decided ta bless me with the likes a one Bridget Burke an' one Caroline Jager."

"What? Caroline was here?" Stunned, Seth stood to pace the small room. "When? Do you know where she is now?"

"Now hold on there, fella. Calm yer nerves. Yeah, she was here. She an' Bridget appeared out there in Storm Valley one night, same as you. I weren't near as nice ta them two gals as I was ta you, but they sure wormed their way inta this ol' heart a mine anyhoo. They stayed here fer bout two months er so."

"Caroline was the one who decided to rescue me from the Scaithers," Sofia interjected. "I met her when they captured her. I tended to her wound after Riglan had her branded."

"*Branded!*" Seth yelled, standing so abruptly that he knocked over his chair. "*Who* branded my wife, and why?"

"Now jus' calm yerself, boy, an' sit down!" Oz boomed.

Seth looked at the two people in front of him knowing he was getting out of control and decided to do as asked.

"Now, as I was sayin', er as Sofie was sayin', I recognized young Bridget's last name, an' told the girls they had ta leave the next mornin'. I was angry still that God would send a Burke inta my house after what that traitor did. But I felt guilty an' followed 'em. We got sep'rated from Bridget in the Catamount Gorge, then one thing led ta another, an' that gal a' yers went an' got herself caught by the Scaithers. I tried rescuin' her, but Riglan took a fancy ta her real quick an' branded her as his own property." Oz held a hand up to Seth who looked about to explode again. "Let me finish, boy. Needless ta say, young Bridget has a special gift an' can commune with the animals. She showed up with a whole passel a' creatures in tow, rescued Caroline, an' me, before anythin' else could happen. We all came back here ta the tree house an' those two blossomed before my eyes. Caroline's skills are far beyond anythin' I've ever seen before. An' Bridget, she jus' talked an' cajoled the wildlife 'round here like a bunch a' little pups."

"What do you mean, 'Caroline's skills'?" Seth asked curiously.

"I don't know if ya know about The Twelve or not, but God allowin' her to get branded by Riglan was His way a markin' her as one of 'em."

"I do. I happen to be marked for Judah." Seth's mind continued piecing things together.

"Well, then, fella, yer in good comp'ny, cause I have the mark fer Issachar. An' Caroline has the mark fer Zebulun."

"So Caroline is number Eleven. But wait, something doesn't make any sense. Simon said that the only missing tribe was Zebulun. How can that be if you've been here all this time? He never mentioned you, so I am assuming no one knows that you're still alive."

"That would explain a lot. But unless things have changed, I'm pretty sure that I'm meant to be one a' The Twelve. But that is fer God ta decide. Not me."

"So you're telling me that Caroline spent the last two months here, in this very tree house, with you?" Seth asked, still trying to sort through all the information that Oz had just laid on him.

"Well, they've been gone from here fer almost a month now. I'm not sure where they are or if they're all right."

"I just saw them," Seth said numbly, "when you found me. That's why I was screaming in the rain after I fell out of the portal. I was so close to her; I could almost touch her. For the past five months I thought that she was gone forever, left back in 1906. That I would never lay eyes on her again. I now realize it was her who I saw run into the portal back in Dover. That must be when they ended up here." Seth sat still, in shock about everything that was beginning to come to light. "I need some air." He stood; his breathing intense as he tried to process everything.

"Folla me up the stairs here." Oz led Seth to the upper platforms of the tree house. The morning sun was just breaking over the adjacent mountain ranges, sending shades of yellow, orange, pink, and purple blazing across the sky. The Kabihanxu were taking their first flight of the day, screeching in the distance, drawing Seth's attention to the skyline.

"Seth, if it makes you feel any better, Caroline spent most of her time talking about you and how she hoped to one day find you. She feared you were dead, but hoped that you weren't," Sofia told him as she followed them out onto the platforms.

"I felt and wondered the same about her." He stood looking out over Storm Valley and breathing in deep lungfuls of the fragrant, cool air, trying to steady his nerves. "I have been so close to finding her twice now when I didn't even realize that I was looking for her. God only revealed Bridget to us, never Caroline."

"Surely that was for your own peace of mind. I know not knowing if she were alive or dead was torment for you, but at some point you would have made peace with it. Knowing that she was here somewhere would make you want to constantly search for her and your focus for missions may have been greatly affected," Sofia offered as a possible answer.

"You're right about that. I had made peace with it, but I still had hope."

"But now, surely you are destined to be together once more. You two must have a great destiny, Seth. I've never heard of God ever selecting both a husband and a wife for peregrination."

"Neither have I," Oz chimed in.

"So everyone keeps telling me." Seth turned and grinned at them.

"Now, ta figure out what God brought ya here fer."

"First, why don't I go fix us some breakfast while you two enjoy the morning. Besides, Oz, it looks like we may have more visitors, and introductions will be in order." Sofia pointed to the sky before turning to go back inside.

Seth looked up to where Sofia pointed to see a pair of very large, four-legged birds headed in their direction. Seth backed up toward the center of the tree to make room for the large birds. The pair flew down to land on the platform beside Oz, sticking their heads out for an affectionate rub from the burly man. Seth gaped in amazement.

"This here is Han. He's the male, and that one there is Cho. She's the female. Not real original names, but it's a sight better than callin' 'em Kabihanxus all the time. Slang term 'round these parts is *firebird*. Bridget named 'em when she lived here. These creatures used ta be the enemy. Now, since Bridget worked her magic, they take care a' us." Oz petted the birds, then walked over to a wire hanging on the left side of the platform underneath the tree's leaves, pulled what appeared to be large pieces of dried meat from the line and walked back toward the birds. "Come on over. I'll introduce ya."

Seth watched the birds, whose excitement seemed to grow the closer Oz got to them with the dried meats. He cautiously stepped forward as instructed, keeping his eyes on the birds in front of him. They could surely tear him limb from limb with little effort.

"You sure about this?" Seth slowly approached.

"Yep. You'd already been dead if'n they didn't like ya," Oz said, without so much as a smile. Seth suddenly felt the need to wipe his sweaty palms on his pants.

Oz handed Seth one of the dried meats to toss to the bird named Cho. She took the meat from his hands, swallowed it almost whole, then focused her attention on Seth. She turned her head to watch him with one large golden eye. After a minute of close scrutiny, she tipped her head down close to Seth's and pushed at him with her long beak, then rubbed her head feathers against his shoulder.

Seth reached his hands forward and rubbed beneath the bird's beak and down its long, thick neck. It made a noise almost mimicking purring. Seth grinned from ear to ear as the other bird, Han, came to him, wanting attention from the newcomer as well.

"Why are they so trusting?"

"Ain't got no reason not ta be. Bridget instructed 'em ta watch over us an' take care a' us before she left. It's really just learned behavior now. I can't speak with 'em. But they kinda know what we want from 'em an' we've learned what they want from us. They're jus' use ta us now, like part a' the family. You'll meet Paxton and Mother later as well. They're really big cats known as Pagorinx in these parts."

"This is amazing. I've never seen anything like them. Only thing I've ever seen this big is an elephant. And I think these birds are a little bigger." Seth couldn't help grinning as the birds pushed at his hands.

"The Pagorinx are jus' as large, so don't worry when ya see 'em." Oz turned toward the tree house. "How 'bout some breakfast?"

"Sounds good to me." Seth followed Oz inside with one quick look back at the beautifully colored, four-legged birds that were taking flight from the platform now that they were going back inside the tree house.

"Now, I heard ya mention Simon. Who else is still 'round? After we all got through the port'l an' realized the other side had been closed, we don't know what happened ta the others. Did anybody survive the demon war?" Oz and Seth sat down at the table, now laden with eggs, sausage, and bread.

"I'm not sure, Oz. I've only been at this for about five months myself and just recently met everyone. We've all been called to Reader's Island. The Dragoman believe it's unsafe for people to remain at the safehouses since demon attacks have been on the rise." Seth took a bite, chewed, then swallowed. "There's Nuncio, Simon, Malachai, Ryan, Vashti, and Prisca, as far as the Dragoman go."

Oz stopped chewing a minute and looked at Seth, almost lost in thought. He shook himself out of it before asking more questions.

Seth wondered if he had mentioned a name that may have had something to do with their exile here. Surely he would have mentioned it if that were the case. Maybe it had something to do with a relationship he had been in before ending up here? He said that he and Sofia were not a couple. Maybe one of the women back home held a special place in this burly man's heart? He remembered the soft look he had earlier when he mentioned Safra, but that was only a fond look of remembrance.

Seth filled him in on the current Peregrines, and Oz recognized Zaccai and Uriah. The rest apparently came after the war that had apparently killed all but Oz, Sofia, most of the retired people on the island serving in the great house, and those who had stayed at Prisca's safehouse to help her. Most of those who are now retired received injuries in that very war, including Nuncio. Oz told him that the Dragoman had taken up arms during that battle in an attempt to save them, but the hordes of demons that attacked that day were too many, and only a few got away with their lives.

Apparently there used to be many more Dragoman and Peregrines compared to what now existed. If they couldn't win against the demons then, having powers like the powers they had now, how were the new Peregrines supposed to win? Especially since some of them were young kids.

"We seem ta have a new breed a' Per'grine or Dragoman. Caroline, she learned ta fight, an' fight well. Bridget, not s'much. Not sure what she's supposed ta do with her abilities with the animals, but if'n they ain't 'round, she can't fight well enough to win in a fight with a demon."

"Well, we have discovered a new set of archive books that have specific information in them. One has a prophesy about the end battle, and it mentions the Keepers, referring to Beast Keepers. Back home we have two other young kids who can also converse with animals. One of them can even control sea life."

"Is that so?" Oz said curiously.

"I've never heard of such a power," Sofia added.

"These new books were found beneath Reader's Island in a hidden cavern. They each have a specific key, and the keys that open them were also hidden beneath five separate waterfalls spread out all over the world. All but one book has been opened. We haven't yet been able to find the last waterfall. They've been searching databases for months now and haven't had any luck. The other four were found pretty quickly."

"Does anyone know who may 'ave placed the books in the cave er who hid the keys 'neath the falls?" Oz asked, the wheels of his mind evidently turning.

"Not to my knowledge. The books had apparently been there for ages. Some of the keys were in some pretty strange places themselves. They may have all been beneath or behind waterfalls, but it wasn't like they were just lying around. One came wrapped in an undecipherable message found in a hidden cave behind the falls. That one is for the *Book of the Keepers*. And another was locked inside a pirate chest with lots of jewels and other artifacts. It was buried in the sand underwater at the base of a sea cave in the Hawaiian Islands. That one they call the *Book of Armor*, and it's the one that held the prophecy. I'm not sure they've gotten into the other two books yet. They've spent most of their time so far trying to find a way to decipher the *Book of the Keepers* which is written in the same language as the message found with the key."

"Hmm...there 're some falls here on Zanchier over a ways past Carpasmere on the other side of the Rhe Mountains. If Hiram had anythin' ta do with any of it, he could a' hid that other set a' keys somewhere here. That might explain why they ain't been able ta find it yet. If Hiram was as crooked as I think he was, then maybe he had a hand in tryin' to stop the final battle, 'specially since he was in league with the demons. If these books are that impor'ant, it may explain a lot. It could also explain why you're here. Do ya know what that waterfall looks like?"

"I sure do." Seth smiled at the people sitting across the table from him.

"Well then, let's pack up a few supplies 'cause it'll be an overnight trip, an' I'll call on our bird friends." Oz stood and grabbed a large, curved horn off the wall. They gathered whatever else they needed, such as bedrolls, clothing, and food, and headed up to the highest-level platform that was large enough to support the Kabihanxu. Oz had trained the birds to respond and come when he blew three short blasts on the Tarphamor horn. The Pagorinx, Oz told Seth, came when he blew one long blast. After signaling them with the horn, they only had to wait a few short minutes until Han and Cho arrived. Oz and Sofia climbed on the back of Han, him being the largest bird, and Seth apprehensively climbed onto the back of Cho, unsure of what to do or how to sit.

"Oz, am I sitting properly up here where I won't fall off?" Seth nervously yelled across the platform at him.

"Think so, didn't ever think 'bout it myself. Jus' climbed up." Oz patted Han, then yelled, "Away," and the large bird lifted off the platform with Cho close behind. Seth's stomach began to flip-flop and feel as though it were turning over. He clasped tightly to the bird's thick neck and felt the power of the magnificent bird within every fiber of his being. The exhilaration that he felt as they soared through the air high above the mountains brought a smile to his face that he couldn't get rid of. He imagined Caroline doing exactly the same thing that he was doing right now when she was here. This land was amazing, and he knew that they had to have been very sad to leave such a place. It may be a bit primitive in some ways, but that made the experience all the more enjoyable.

Since they had a several-hour trip by flight, Seth was able to see most of the countryside. He thought at first he had imagined it, but while flying over the Xantifal Mountains, he thought that he had seen the landscape change. Then it happened again, and he realized that it had actually moved. He also saw a long river that flowed from the top of the mountains down into the valley and into a small lake. The open plains beneath the mountain range were vast. He could see the high grasses, with shades of light purple and maroon, swaying in the breeze that played across them, ruffling the grass, and grasping seeds to deposit somewhere else. The leaves in the trees that graced the mountainside took on hues of yellow and green. Some also had shades of blue, purple, and aqua laced throughout.

It had taken them the better part of almost four hours to make the flight from Bakrashan to Carpasmere. As they flew above Everly Lake, Seth could see large communities on the water. One city looked to have at one point been a very beautiful place, but now appeared war torn. He could also tell that people seemed to be terrified of the Kabihanxus. As the noon-high sun cast the bird's shadows across the ground below, people began running for cover. If that was how the locals reacted to these birds just flying overhead, then he was very glad to be on friendly terms with them.

They continued on their flight over the peaks of the Carpasian Mountains until they came to a heavily forested land in a small valley. The tops of the falls were barely visible from his perch atop the airborne bird due to the thick foliage that covered the area below.

They began their descent toward the ground, unsure where these large birds were going to land. To Seth's surprise the trees here were almost as large as in Xantifal, making landing for the birds quite doable. The branches in some of the trees were very large and able to support the weight of the birds. It also made walking through the trees very easy since the branches were so large that the walking area was almost flat. They made their way toward the ground so Seth could get a good look at the falls from different angles. He concentrated on remembering what the picture of the last, unfound waterfall looked like. The Dragoman had asked all the Peregrines to commit the image to memory just in case they happened to stumble across it on a mission or God decided to lead one of them to it. Seth decided that the latter circumstance must be the case; the waterfall he was looking at was, indeed, the waterfall they had been searching for. Finding the falls here seemed to be more evidence that Hiram Burke definitely had his hand in way more than anyone had expected.

"Seems like what you suspected about Hiram and his double life may have been right after all, Oz. Why else would the last set of keys be hidden here beneath these falls, in a place that isn't visible from the fourth-dimension plane? No one there, I believe, knows about this place. How do you think that's possible?"

"Could be we ain't in the third er fourth dimension. Maybe we're in another one, like a fifth. I don't think we ever stepped out a' the other end a' the port'l way back when. I think we might be somewhere in between both sides."

"You know, come to think of it, if I had been able to walk out the other side of the portal after following Caroline and Bridget through, I should have exited with them. But somehow I ended up here. I do believe you may be right, Oz. This place must exist inside the portal, somewhere between the different planes. That would also explain why a search party hasn't come looking for me yet as well."

"How's that? How would they find ya if'n they decided ta do so?"

"Another device designed by one of the Dragoman. A brilliant young man by the name of Ryan Halloran designed these very tiny and almost un-seeable things known as chips. They attach to the skin below the ear here." Seth pointed to his.

"Huh, don't see a thing."

"Neither do I," Sofia confirmed.

"They work like tracking devices. The Dragoman can track us anywhere in the third or fourth dimensions. But apparently not here, or else someone would have shown up by now."

"Still ain't no storm here fer 'em ta come in on."

"Ryan also created a handheld device that creates a portal. We call them Portgens. We don't have to wait on storms anymore for traveling."

"Well, I'll be. Can't believe a person would be able ta do all that. But God creates us how He wants us, so I reckon He could make a fella with the smarts fer all that. You got one a' them Portgens?"

"Unfortunately, no. It is relatively new technology, and he hasn't been able to make one for each of us yet."

"Oh well, it'd be int'restin' ta see." Oz shrugged his shoulders "Now, what er we lookin' fer?"

"Well, I'm not really sure. Like I said before, each key was found in a different place and way. I just know that it is somewhere around this waterfall or in this basin here. The baseline here is maybe eighty to one hundred feet, so it isn't huge, but still a large area to cover. It may take a while to dive to find the key. Especially since I have no diving equipment."

"I fig're Hiram might a' just tossed 'em in the basin. I doubt he jumped inta the water ta hide 'em, 'specially since he didn't ever fig're on anyone ever lookin' here. Shouldn' be too hard a job."

"Except for the fact that they've been down there for at least thirteen or fourteen years." Sofia stated with raised eyebrows and a knowing look on her face. "That key, or keys, could quite possibly be buried underneath years of sediment or even washed farther out into the basin or even downstream. The river here is really only a small creek and trickles down to an even smaller stream farther down that empties into a lake several miles away. I know this because when I was traveling with the people I took up with when I first arrived here, we used to camp around this river and area quite often for the fresh water supply."

"Not to mention, with no light source beneath the water, I'm going to have a really hard time finding anything down there. Do you know how deep this basin is Sofia?" Seth began mulling over some sort of plan to achieve their goals.

"Maybe fifteen feet to the bottom. But as far as a light source goes, if you wait for nightfall, I think that problem will solve itself." She grinned, a slight curve to her lips.

"Why is that?" Seth was curious how darkness could make it easier to see.

"Well, luck would have it that this here particular falls and basin is known as Luminesce Falls, and it has a bioluminescent algae that grows beneath the surface of the water, and behind the basin of the falls where the rock has eroded and made an open area, like a cavernous archway. The darker it is outside the brighter the glow. And since there is a new moon tonight, we are in luck." She smiled brightly.

"Is that so? Never knew this place did that," Oz stated. "Last time I came through here was when I escaped from the Rhe mines. It was a full moon then though. I figur'd the water was just glowin' from the brightness of that big ol' moon that night. That moon was the only way I made it through here at night. Lit my path all the way 'cross the mount'nside. That was when I had learned ya could see better and were a bit safer the higher up in the trees ya went."

"Like I said, the only way to really see the bioluminescence is if it's really dark. The closer to the bottom you get the brighter it glows. We can all help search for it, just one word of caution though. There are also a few bioluminescent creatures that swim this basin as well. Some are harmless; others aren't."

"Which ones aren't?" Seth asked a bit worried.

"Not really sure. We never saw what it was that stung Bamerly, but he died a few days later. Horrible thing to watch. Many of us swam in these waters without mishap. Maybe he was just allergic to something. Either way, I'd try to avoid any of the natives down there if I were you."

"Too bad Bridget ain't here. She could just tell 'em to let us be. Ya did say one a' them fellas back home could talk ta the sea creatures, right?" Oz stared into the dark waters of the basin.

"Yeah, I did." Seth stared right along with Oz as they exchanged looks of apprehension about entering the water now.

Han and Cho had taken off a bit downstream to fish in the more shallow area of the river where the fish were easily seen swimming over the rocks headed to the lake below.

"Well, boys, I say we set up camp and wait till nightfall," Sofia said matter-of-factly.

They spent the rest of the afternoon planning how to divide up the search area to best utilize their time. Since searching could only be done at night and they only had a few nights before the moon began to form its waxing crescent, they decided to try to get some sleep until the sun would set low behind the mountain peaks.

Now to Him who is able to do far more abundantly
beyond all that we ask or think, according to
the power that works within us.

Ephesians 3:20 NASB

Chapter 18

Reader's Island

It was just after dawn when Jason, Alec, and Odessa made it back to the island and informed Simon of what had transpired just minutes before. Seth was gone to who knows where, and Bridget Burke and her companion had disappeared again as well, but not before Alec had a chance to use his teleport ability to plant a chip device on the companion.

"Are you sure it connected to her, Alec?" Simon asked apprehensively.

"No, I am not sure. But I think so. The winds were very forceful. I can only hope it went where I visualized."

They all walked through the house and into the computer room.

"Well, let's find out if we have a signal on her, shall we? And let's see if we can find Seth," Simon said. They were not surprised to find Ryan in the computer room. That's where he stayed, except to eat, sleep, and use the restroom.

"Ryan, we need to look for Seth's signal on the chipping program, and we need to see if a new signal is coming through."

"Okay, Simon. I'll check." Ryan slid his rolling chair down the long table, stopping at a large computer screen and turning on the monitor. After punching a few keys on the keyboard, he replied, "I see everyone except Seth. And there is a new one showing here." He pointed to an unnamed blip on the screen. Zooming in on locator beacon, they found the coordinates of where it was coming from and quickly punched them into the Portgen that Odessa had on her person.

"Odessa, you and Alec bring those two young women directly back here," Simon told them as they opened a portal right there in the computer room and went through. "Jason, I need to know exactly what happened when Seth disappeared. His chip is not showing a beacon anywhere."

Ryan kept doing searches for Seth's beacon throughout the regions, dimensions, planes, and time periods, but nothing was coming through.

"Just like we said, Simon. Seth went into the portal after Bridget and the other one, who Seth kept yelling after, calling her Caroline. At least that's what I think he was saying, and Alec concurred. It was kind of hard to tell with the wind gusting the way it was and that storm roaring louder by the minute."

"Is that so?" Simon rubbed his chin thoughtfully. "You don't think it could have been another demon, do you?"

"No, I don't believe so. Besides, I really think it was the same woman we saw back in Dover. We never saw her face before today, but she was the same height and build and wore the same cloak."

"How long was it before the portal closed after Seth went in?"

"Not long, barely a second. He kind of stumbled into it. The wind and sand both hindered our movements pretty well. I wasn't even sure he had made it until the lightning flashed and we realized he was gone."

"Hmm," Simon pondered. "That could mean he is stuck somewhere in between worlds. Inside the portal somewhere. Which is why his chip won't send out a beacon. They can't locate him because technically he is nowhere. It's only speculation, of course, just something I've always theorized about."

"How is that even possible?"

"How is any of this possible?" Simon said earnestly, looking at Jason. "I believe there is another plane or dimension that lies within the portal. Haven't you ever noticed the blurred images that whizz by when you're running through them?"

"Yeah, but I figured they were the periods between where we left and where we were going."

"Yes. So did I at first. But the more I think about it, the more I wonder. Years ago when Hiram Burke deceived everyone, many Peregrines disappeared never to be seen or heard from again. We have no idea where they went, but I do remember the day of the battle like it was yesterday. The demons who attacked seemed to be trying to prevent the Peregrines from entering the portal. The ones they didn't slaughter or leave for dead anyway. After the portal had been opened for quite some time already, the demons then pushed the Peregrines backward during battle and into the portal without following them through it." Simon sat down as he recalled that fateful time in history.

"The storm that generated the portals on that particular day was unlike anything I had ever seen before. I have seen storms where a portal would open and close, only to open another within close proximity to the last. But never like this day. This storm generated about ten portals all at once. They opened all around the battlefield and stayed open longer than any other portal I had ever seen. I'm certain that the storm was created by Hiram. He was a Magus, like I am; but he dabbled in the unnatural and the forbidden. There are things you just do not use your powers for or even speculate over. Hiram didn't like limitations or rules and therefore became drunk with power. Anyhow, apparently wherever it is that he met Mary, the people there can see the portals. They just can't traverse them."

"I thought regular people couldn't see the portals?"

"They can't. I suppose that is why he figured she could walk them. Hiram tried to bring Mary through from some unknown place. He never told us where she was from, but when they came through to the other side, Mary was dead. Bridget survived the crossover, but Mary did not. Hiram was furious! He was angry at God, me, Safra...everyone who could walk through the portals! We thought he had gotten over it, but it must have been eating at him for years. He had engineered the whole thing. He cleverly convinced every Dragoman that all the

Peregrines needed to go in search of something he called Rhenium and Ruthenium. Said it was of dire need to the cause and that God had given him a vision where to search for it. After the devastation caused by that day, some of us began putting the pieces together. We came to the conclusion that Hiram had been responsible for all of it. Because of his own selfish, petty anger, he wanted revenge for something which none of us were responsible. He somehow found out that we knew what he had done, and before we could find him, he had taken Bridget, who was about three at the time, and disappeared without a trace."

They heard someone clear his throat behind them, and Simon and Jason quickly turned. Standing just outside the doors to the computer room were Alec, Odessa, Bridget, and another woman. Bridget seemed transfixed with tears forming in her eyes. Suddenly she turned and ran from the house, followed closely by the other woman.

Simon sighed deeply knowing how much it must have hurt the young girl to hear about her father that way.

"How much did she hear?" He looked at Alec and Odessa over his spectacles.

"I'm not sure, but more than enough of it. All we had to do was mention Seth's name, and they came right with us," Odessa stated. "I tried to pull her away when I realized what you were talking about, but she wouldn't budge."

"Well, she was bound to hear it sooner or later. Especially once everyone knows she's here. I just wish I could have sat her down to talk with her first," Simon replied.

"I'll go and find them, Simon," Odessa offered closing her eyes to concentrate. " I see them headed toward the temple."

"No. It's all right, Odessa. I will go and speak with them. I knew her father and I think I need to explain a few things." Simon stood and left the room in search of the distraught young woman and her companion, who may or may not be one Caroline Jager.

The sun was completely hidden from view, and the small valley was enveloped in utter darkness except for the water beneath the falls.

The eerie, bioluminescent light emanating from the water illuminated everything around it in a light, greenish-white glow. As they peered down into the water, they could barely make out some fish darting back and forth beneath the surface. Seth picked up a rock from the edge of the basin and tossed it into the water, then watched the fish all scatter in different directions. Relieved that none of them attacked the unforeseen object, he pulled off his shirt and dove into the cold water; Sofia and Oz followed close behind him.

"All right, everyone knows what to do. See you both in a bit." Seth took a deep breath and dove to the bottom of the basin. The bioluminescent algae illuminated the bottom of the basin so well that Seth could see better than he could have using any flashlight. It made searching quite easy, if only he could hold his breath a lot longer than he was able to. The depth of the water was indeed at least fifteen feet, and the pressure on his chest from being at that depth made it hard to hold his breath for long.

Lord, I need your guidance right now. If we are to find this key, make it so.

He swam up to the surface to get another deep breath and descended into the deep water once again.

He felt around the bottom, looking for anything that appeared unusual. But as Sofia had pointed out, the key had been down there for roughly fourteen years. It could be covered by the very algae that was lighting up the water. As Seth skimmed his way along the basin floor, he moved his hands cautiously, trying not to stir the water too much and distort visibility. Suddenly a pocketknife that had worked its way out of his pants pocket fell to the basin floor. Seth was getting dizzy from lack of air, so he swam back to the surface, took another lungful of air, and swam back down. He reached out to grab his pocketknife, but a brightly colored creature darted out from a small crack in the rocks beneath the falls and pulled his knife into the hole. Seth peered into the crack as best he could, but the algae was only on the rocks and did not light the inside of the hole. Seth swam back up and waited a moment for Oz and Sofia to resurface. When they made an appearance, he captured their attention.

"I think I may know where the key might have gone," he said, breathing hard. "Apparently there is a scavenger down there that likes shiny or unusual things. My knife fell out of my pocket, and something grabbed it and pulled it back into a hole in the rocks. I might need your help pulling them apart to look."

"Let's go then." Oz and Sofia waited for Seth to dive down so they could follow.

Taking deep breaths of air, the three of them dove down to the rocky line of the waterfall basin. Seth showed them where the creature had pulled his knife into the rocks, and the three of them began pulling away the top layer of rocks, careful to remove only what was necessary to avoid losing the light of the bioluminescent algae. Between removing the rock and returning to the surface for air, it took them the better part of twenty minutes to be able to see where the creature had disappeared to. Removing all the rocks had stirred the sediment up so much that they had to resurface and give the water a little bit of time to clear so that visibility could be restored, only about ten minutes. They had disturbed the hiding place of the unknown creature living down there. When they pulled back the last few rocks, something glowing and electrified-looking swam by them so quickly in the murky water that they didn't get a chance to see what it was.

"We can't give the creature time to disappear with anything from his stash. Maybe it'll just stay away now that its nest isn't secure anymore." Seth stared anxiously into the pool.

They dove down into the now almost clear water and began searching the area where they had cleared away the rock. They found a variety of things tucked away in the corners of the small area. The creature apparently did like shiny objects and was hoarding all manner of things. Anything that got dropped into the river here near the waterfall basin apparently got claimed by the creature. The divers found jewelry, coins, shiny metal goblets and cups, even a silvery platter. They also found Seth's pocketknife, a set of military-issued dog tags, oddly enough, and the very thing for which they had been searching. An odd-shaped key that looked like it might fit the locked book back on Reader's Island.

They picked up only the items they wanted—the pocketknife and the key—and began the ascent to the water's surface. Seth had been carrying the key with him when something swam toward him, reached out with one long tentacled arm, and wrapped it around his left wrist and hand which held the key. The stinging sensation and electrical pulse that coursed up his arm was so sharp that he almost dropped it. He opened his knife in his other hand and sliced at the tentacle, cutting a deep gash into it and causing the creature to let go of him. When he broke through the surface, he let out a scream of pain.

"*Aahh!* Something stung me, and the pain is really bad!" he yelled, struggling to swim to the edge of the river. Oz and Sofia swam to him and helped him get to the side, then pulled him up onto the bank. Seth was clutching his arm to his stomach and holding it with the other. Sofia pulled his arm straight to inspect the damage. Seth still clutched the key in his swelling hand.

"Oh my, that looks like the same type of sting that Bamerly had. Only his was around his neck. I believe those dog tags down there were his. He had served in some type of military branch years ago when there was order here in Zanchier. At least that's what he told me years back. Apparently whatever stung him was what was living beneath that rock." Sofia spoke absently as she gently probed the site of the sting and the swelling in his hand.

"So this means what?" Seth asked through gritted teeth.

"That you are going to be very sick, my friend, or possibly worse. We need to get you medical attention, quickly," she answered him as honestly as possible.

"Well, we got what we came fer, now I think it's high time we get out a' this place." Concern filled Oz's eyes as he watched Seth writhe in pain. He looked at Sofia.

Sofie, how long did Bamerly last after that creature stung 'im?' Oz asked her telepathically so as not to frighten Seth any more than necessary.

Two days. A horrible two days.

"We best get 'im out a here," Oz said audibly.

"You have something at the tree house that can help him Oz?"

"Nope. But I bet they got somethin' back at Reader's Island. It's time we leave Zanchier."

Oz quickly called for Han and Cho. Working together, Sofia and Oz managed to get Seth up and onto Han's back. Oz climbed up behind Seth to keep him from falling off, while Sofia climbed atop Cho. They didn't even bother returning to the tree house. Oz instructed the firebirds to take them straight to the Dustbowl, which was an hour away. There they would catch a tornado to anywhere. Surely the Dragoman were looking for Seth. As soon as they returned to any dimension other than this one, they would see his chip transmitting once again and dispatch someone to find them. Oz only hoped it would be fast enough to save Seth's life.

Reader's Island

Simon found Bridget and Caroline right where Odessa said they would be. They were sitting on one of the benches in the middle of the prayer garden. Bridget was still sniffling while Caroline tried to console her young friend. Caroline turned to look at him as Simon slowly approached them.

"May I?" Simon asked, motioning to the open seat beside Bridget.

"If you'd like," Bridget sniffed, drying her eyes on her cloak.

"Bridget, I'm very sorry you had to hear all that. I never meant for that to happen."

"I'm sorry for what my father did to all of you, and I'll never be able to change your mind about him or make amends, but he was never that way around me." Bridget spoke between sniffles.

"Bridget, no one expects you to make amends for your father. And if there is anything that I am certain about when it came to your father, it's that he loved you and your mother very much. He may not have been a good friend to us, but I believe that when your mother died, it almost destroyed him. He was just so angry and so hurt that it changed him. He wasn't always like that, you know. There was a time when he and I were very close friends. But after Mary passed he pushed us all away and hid you away from all of us. We hardly ever saw you as a baby. Just know this, I will do everything in my power to see that you are treated with fairness and kindness by everyone here. If you have any problems with anyone, you come see me, understand?" Simon smiled at the girl.

"Yes sir," Bridget said with a half-smile. "It's just very hard to hear such horrible things about your father. Especially since he was always kind and caring to me. Except when it came to the whole Dragoman and Peregrine thing. He wouldn't discuss that with me at all. It made him very angry and upset when I asked him about it. Now I think I understand why at least."

"Yes, that makes sense. By the way, my name is Simon. Simon Lane." He held his hand out to shake Bridget's.

She grinned at him and giggled slightly, taking the offered hand.

"I suppose there is no reason to introduce myself, since you seem to know more about me than I do." She gave another slightly nervous giggle. "But this is my friend Caroline." She motioned to the woman beside her.

"Caroline Jager from California, say around 1906?" Simon asked with a quizzical brow.

"Yes," Caroline said a little shocked. "The people that brought us here said they knew Seth. Is it really my Seth? My eyes weren't playing tricks on me?" Caroline asked as hope began to make her voice shake.

"Yes, my dear, it is definitely your Seth." Simon grinned slightly.

"I knew I wasn't going crazy! I was certain it was him I saw. Where is he? Please, I need to see him."

"I'm afraid he isn't here. You see, when you two walked into that portal back in Louisiana, Seth stumbled into it as well. And since he didn't come out with you on the other side, he must be lost somewhere between worlds, and we have no idea where that is. Or how to find him," Simon said apologetically, his brow furrowed with worry. "But rest assured, we are doing everything within our powers to find him. Now, I am sure you two young ladies are starving. Breakfast should be well on the way to being finished by now. What do you say to heading back to the main house, and we will get the two of you fed and introduced? After which, one of the housekeepers will show you to your rooms and give you a tour of where everything is. Does that sound acceptable to you?"

Bridget nodded her approval and waited on Caroline to answer. Her friend sat transfixed and unmoving.

"Caroline? Are you all right?"

"Caroline, we will find him, rest assured," Simon interjected quickly, realizing the woman's stressed appearance at his revelation.

Caroline turned to them both and numbly nodded her reply, and the three of them got up and walked back to the main house. Simon suggested that Shannon show the girls where they could clean up. Taking the opportunity to avoid another awkward situation, Simon went to the kitchen to speak to everyone there briefly, explaining Bridget and Caroline's arrival and his recommendation that everyone be on their best behavior and act like the adults they all were.

When Bridget and Caroline entered the kitchen escorted by Shannon, they were received with a warm welcome. A few of the welcomes, mainly from the older Dragoman such as Prisca and Clancy the chef, were a bit curt, but welcomes, nonetheless. They ate breakfast with the others, most everyone asking Bridget and Caroline all sorts of questions. Bridget doing most of the answering for them both as Caroline had grown unusually quiet since they were told about Seth's disappearance. Only a few sat back and listened to the conversations flying around the table. Old hurts and unsettled feelings barred them from enjoying the new company as everyone else seemed to be doing.

After breakfast, Petra showed them to their bedrooms and where the restrooms were and how to work everything. Seeing as how Seth and Caroline were married, Simon had instructed Petra to put Caroline in Seth's room.

Caroline stepped into the room that had housed her husband for the last month. She walked around touching the things that obviously belonged to Seth. She took one of his shirts from the back of a chair and lay upon the bed, clinging to the shirt as she breathed deeply of his scent that still clung to it. She was so overcome that she burst into tears of mixed emotions. She was grateful for what God had done for both of them, saving them both from the earthquake and giving them this new life. But now he was lost somewhere, and they were separated again after being just a touch away. She lay on the bed, crying into the shirt as she silently prayed for Seth to be safe and return soon. She prayed through her tears until exhaustion claimed her and she slept.

When she awoke the height of the sun in the sky told her it must be well after noon. She decided to try out the bathroom's shower, trying to remember what Petra had shown her about working it. After showering, she put on the clothes that she had made in Bakrashan for training purposes, tied her hair into a tight bun behind her head, and then went in search of Bridget and the others.

Following a housekeeper's directions, she found most of the Peregrines out by the water's edge training. Most of the men turned to look at her as she approached the group. One in particular made his way toward her.

"So you're Caroline. My name is Jason Marshal." He extended his hand for hers. "Your husband, Seth, is my travel partner. I'm the one who found him when he first peregrinated."

"Hello, Jason." Caroline gave him a half-smile, not really in the mood to be friendly.

"Still worried about Seth?" Jason cocked his head and looked at her.

"Is it that obvious?" She did not make eye contact with the man.

"Look, Seth is a very capable man. He has learned a lot already and his gift is super strength. I'm sure he's fine wherever he is. Don't worry, we will find him. We found the two of you. Twice."

"Thanks for the words of encouragement, Jason. But the past five months have been a serious roller-coaster ride that hasn't ended yet. I don't mean to be rude, but until I can lay eyes on Seth again, I'm afraid you're stuck with a rather unpleasant person for now. No offense."

"None taken." He stepped away and brandished his blade. "I don't know what kind of training you've had, but if you want to work out some of your aggressions, I'd be willing to spar with you. I promise to take it easy, no insult intended."

"Sounds good to me." She stepped forward, pulled her blade as well, and the two began sparring. Everyone else wanted to see the newcomer take on one of the best fighters in the group and gathered around to watch. No one, especially Jason, expected Caroline to be as quick or as skilled as she was. She took him by surprise several times, landing some very good punches. She could also take a blow as well.

Soon onlookers were choosing sides and cheering on their favored competitor. Bridget, of course, cheered for Caroline. She bounced up and down as she called out suggestions about where to hit Jason and how to do it. The others seemed to enjoy both Caroline and Bridget, and they laughed heartily each time Bridget got excited by a punch or kick that Caroline landed. The entire group joined in the sparring match taking turns against each other. Jason, Odessa, Alec, Nicholas, Uriah, and Zaccai instructed the newer ones in fighting techniques. Zaccai and Caroline became fast friends as Zaccai gave her some crucial pointers on protecting her body from her opponent.

The training lasted until evening when one of the groundskeepers called the tired and sweaty group in for dinner. He informed them that it would be served outside on the patio beneath the pergola since the night was such a fine one. Everyone went in to clean up and then retired outside to eat. Sporadic conversation was friendly, but Caroline could see that she wasn't the only one worn out from the afternoon of heavy sparring. The Peregrines seemed to want to conserve their energy for eating. It was well past dark with the full moon sitting high in the sky when Ryan, who had taken his dinner in the computer room, came outside in search of Simon.

"Simon, excuse me, but Seth's chip is sending out a beacon," he said shyly among all the people.

Simon, Caroline, Bridget, Jason, Alec, and Odessa jumped up from their chairs and all but ran with Ryan to the computer room. There on the large computer screen was a signal that blinked "Seth Jager."

"Well, Jason, what are you waiting for. Go bring him home," Simon instructed.

"Yes sir." Jason grinned from ear to ear.

"I'm coming too!" Alec yelled after Jason's retreating back.

"Caroline," Simon quickly interjected, "they won't be but a few short minutes. No need for everyone to go." Simon offered an understanding grin as he peered at her over the top of his spectacles.

"You better be right, sir," was all she said as she looked at him without returning his smile. Then she watched the retreating backs of the two men who had run to get the Portgen to input the coordinates.

Simon and the three women went outside to fill the others in on the news while Caroline paced the grounds with bated breath. It seemed like hours to Caroline, but in truth it was only minutes before a portal opened just steps away from where they were all standing. Jason and Alec walked through with a very limp Seth supported between the two of them. Walking out after them were Sofia and Oz.

"Seth!" Caroline yelled in panic as she ran to them.

"Oz, Sofia!" Bridget yelled happily, running after Caroline.

Prisca Delacroix and the other older Dragoman and Peregrines watched in shock as two people followed Jason, Seth, and Alec out of the portal.

Did Bridget say Sofia and Oz? Prisca watched as they all approached the remainder of the group and the main house. She could only stare at them as they got closer.

"Wendal?" She asked, her voice shaking with disbelief.

"Hello there, Prisca," Oz said, a bit unsure how to respond.

Prisca fainted dead away as Oz quickly reached out to catch her and keep her from hitting the ground beneath them.

"I guess I'm a bit of a shock." He scooped Prisca up and carried her inside with everyone else following close behind.

Uriah Mose watched the scene before him play out, not sure what was going on. Where had Oz and Sofia been all this time? And what about all the other Peregrines that had disappeared all those years ago? He couldn't help but wonder how this might affect his future and that of the others here on Reader's Island

Be joyful in hope, patient in affliction, faithful in prayer.

Romans 12:12 NIV

Chapter 19

The entire main house was in an uproar. Shocked silence exploded into shouted questions, expressions of concern, and advice regarding Seth's unconscious condition, and the horrible looking wound on his left hand and arm. More opinions were voiced over Prisca's unconsciousness after the shock of seeing Oz and Sofia after thirteen years of presuming them dead. Everyone had questions, and the only people who would know the answers were Oz, Sofia, Caroline, and Bridget. In moments Oz, Sofia, and Bridget found themselves the center of attention as they were bombarded with question after question.

Jason and Alec hurriedly carried Seth to his bedroom with Caroline and Simon close behind. Safra had gone to retrieve her medicine bag before joining them. Half the group followed them upstairs while the other half, mainly the older ones who had personal interest in the history, followed Sofia and Oz as he took Prisca inside and placed her on a large, overstuffed sofa in one of the sitting rooms.

Shannon ran to get some water and smelling salt for Prisca, while Petra rushed upstairs to Seth's room with hot water and clean towels per Safra's instructions.

"All right, everyone except Caroline, out of the room and out of Safra's way," Simon barked, trying to make room for Safra and give Caroline privacy. "We will keep you all apprised of the situation." He closed the door on everyone. Jason, Alec, and Odessa unhappily walked downstairs with the others to await news of Seth.

Caroline sat holding Seth's right hand as Safra milled about the room tending to Seth, working quickly and quietly.

"Simon," Safra said, "do we know what caused the wound?"

"I will find out." He left the room. "Jason!" Simon yelled from the top of the stairs.

Jason ran to the foot of the staircase looking up at Simon. "Yeah?"

"Do we know what caused Seth's injury?"

"Oz!" Jason yelled to the large man in the other room whom he had just met moments earlier.

"I'm here." Oz appeared outside the sitting-room door.

"What stung Seth?" Jason asked.

"Not sure. Some kinda water creature back on Zanchier. Just know it can be deadly."

"How deadly?" Simon asked fearfully, overhearing his answer.

"Maybe a couple a' days. He got stung just over an hour ago." Oz looked at the people who were staring at him and hoping for answers.

Simon turned and reentered the bedroom with little information for Safra, noting that Caroline still sat holding Seth's hand, her eyes closed, her face tearstained and her lips moving silently as she prayed.

"Well?" Safra asked, looking at Simon.

"Some kind of unknown water creature in a place known as Zanchier." His monotoned voice relaying that the information would be of no help at all.

"Simon, what about Jason? He has healing powers. I don't know how to treat this. Perhaps he is our only hope." Safra turned hopeful eyes towards him.

Simon turned and quickly crossed the hall again. He summoned Jason and explained the situation as they walked to the bedroom.

Jason strode to Seth's side and immediately put his hands on Seth, praying that his gift of healing would save his friend's life. Simon and Safra silently watched, looking between Jason and Seth, who was still unconscious and shaking from the high fever. It took almost ten minutes for the swelling in Seth's arm and hand to go down, and another five for the tentacle marks to nearly disappear.

"I don't know what else to do," Jason said worriedly. "It looks to have healed, but he's still unconscious."

"Perhaps his body just needs rest. The poison could still be inside. His breathing is back to normal, and his fever seems to be going down," Safra said calmly.

"Let's leave him and Caroline to rest for a while," Simon said, knowing there was nothing else they could do for now.

"Can someone stay with me, please?" Caroline looked at them with pleading eyes.

"I will stay with them," Safra offered. She took the wet, cool washcloth and gently wiped Seth's forehead with it.

"Thank you, Safra." Caroline looked at the kind woman who only smiled and nodded her head in reply.

Simon and Jason left the room and walked into one of the upstairs studies to await news of Seth. Neither wanted to deal with all the questions they knew everyone would have once they went downstairs.

Soon Alec and Odessa slipped away from the group downstairs and found Simon and Jason sitting alone in the dark room with the door open, monitoring any activity coming from Seth's room. Simon quickly filled them in, and they all sat in the silence and darkness together, taking turns praying for their friend out loud.

Caroline, realizing that Seth's clothing was dirty and wet with sweat, undressed him with Safra's help and tucked him neatly beneath the sheets. She then curled up beside him pulling his right arm around her body, scooting in as close to him as she could get. She wrapped her arm around his large chest and began praying again as she drifted off to sleep, worry and exhaustion from the day taking its toll on her weary body and soul.

Safra sat ever watchful in the corner until sleep also claimed her.

The hour grew late, and Nuncio cut off everyone's questions for Oz, Sofia, and Bridget, claiming they would all have a chance tomorrow to ask more. With the excitement capped for the night, they held a prayer vigil for Seth before everyone retired to their rooms.

The house was quiet and dark when Seth stirred from his sleep. He wasn't quite sure where he was. The last thing he remembered was diving for the key. Oh yes, he remembered, some water creature had stung him. He lifted up his left arm, looking at his hand in the pale light of the full moon that filtered in through the window. His arm felt and looked fine now, except for some small, pinkish, circular, scars. Realizing someone was lying curled up beside him he panicked for a minute. *Who in the world could it be?* He tried sitting up slightly to get a look at whoever was lying across his chest when she began to stir and turned her face to look up at him. *Caroline?*

"Caroline?" Seth said in a disbelieving voice.

"Seth!" She squealed. Abruptly she sat up, grabbed his face with both hands, and planted kisses all over it.

Safra stirred awake and, smiling from ear to ear, left the room. As she walked down the dimly lit hallway, she noticed people asleep in the study. Simon, Jason, Alec, and Odessa were all curled up on the furniture.

"Simon," Safra said, waking them as they all stirred from their exhausted slumber. "Seth is awake, and he seems fine. I would leave them to their reunion for the night. You can all see him in the morning." She smiled and left to return to her own room.

They all smiled, praising God, and decided to retire to their own rooms for the remainder of the night, however long that was. Each of them vowing to sleep in extra-long.

"Caroline, is it really you, or am I dreaming?" Seth wasn't sure whether to believe his eyes.

"I'm as real as you are, handsome. I can't believe you're here. I can touch you, see you, feel you," she said through her tears.

"How in the world are you here right now? I don't understand. I'm not even sure how I got here," he asked, confused but happy.

"I'll explain everything in the morning." She planted another kiss on his lips.

Seth kissed her back with all the love and passion he had been holding onto since the last day he had held her in his arms. They held onto each other for the rest of the night, each one afraid to let go for fear the other might disappear forever.

Seth awoke with a start, afraid that last night was only a dream or a hallucination brought on by the creature's sting. But to his great relief Caroline was right there beside him. He lay still, thanking God for His amazing grace and gift. He and Caroline were together once more, and he would never let her out of his sight again.

He woke her, and they lay in each other's arms for a few more precious moments before deciding to share each other with everyone else. Seth still felt a little weak and lightheaded, but considering he should be on his deathbed, he was very grateful. Caroline explained everything that had happened to him while they dressed and then ventured down to the kitchen where only a handful of people were already gathered.

"Where is everyone this morning?" Seth asked.

Several people got up and came over to him, patting him on the shoulders or shaking his hands and telling him how glad they were he was all right. Malachai then informed him that most everyone had been up half the night, excited about Oz and Sofia's appearance and sick with worry over his condition.

Nuncio had declared that today would be a day of rest for everyone. With all the happenings, and all the training and strange new events, everyone was to take the day to just enjoy themselves and catch up with one another. Everyone heartily agreed, and most expressed a desire to sleep in as long as their bodies would allow.

"You two have any plans for the day?" Malachai asked as they sat down to eat.

"Well, since we just found out about our free day, we have yet to make any. We'll probably just walk the island and play catch-up on what has happened to both of us over the last four to five months." Seth looked at Caroline and grinned.

Malachai smiled back. "Sounds like a plan. Me, I am going fishing. I'm taking one of the long boats and venturing out past the barrier to just fish." He turned to the rest of the group. "What about you all?"

Kristen answered first. "I'm going to explore the upper part of the mountain peak here and then maybe go swimming. My dad used to take me camping all the time, and I miss hiking through the woods."

"You want some company?" Sean asked as a few others chimed in, anxious to explore the island as well.

"Sure. But you all better be able to keep up. I'm not slowing down for any of you." She playfully grinned. Several of the people threw their wadded-up napkins at her, laughing.

Seth was still surprised by the camaraderie of these people; many of whom were strangers just a few short weeks ago. He had never experienced the kind of friendship and trust he felt now, and he was grateful for what God had brought him through. The feeling of gratitude reminded him that he still had not had the chance to tell anyone about his salvation. *Who better to tell first than Caroline?* He smiled to himself and was quickly drawn into the conversations that were flying around the table. More people began appearing for breakfast, and everyone was happy just to sit and chat as they came in. No one was in a hurry to get anywhere or do anything. Today promised to be a great day for everyone on the island.

Prisca appeared in the kitchen only briefly, then went out to the veranda to have her breakfast in peace. She was still a bit shaken by the events of the night before. Seeing her old friends again had been a great shock. Especially Oz. She began remembering the old days, before all the Peregrines and Dragoman had been killed or had disappeared. She and Oz had been quite the item, strange as it was with their completely opposite backgrounds and upbringing. He was a rugged, rough, mountain man, and she had been a socialite, raised in France in the late 1700s by very wealthy parents who expected her to marry within her station. And that meant whomever her father chose for her.

Prisca had fought that decision so hard that her father gave her permission to choose for herself, but she was given limited nobility from which to choose, being of noblesse uterine blood herself. The men she knew were all dandies, and none of them would have made a good husband. At least not by Prisca's standards. She wanted a man who would be faithful to her forever, as she would be to him.

When she reached the age of twenty-five and still had not chosen a husband, her father tried putting his foot down and arranged several marriages for her over the next four years. She quickly refused them all. With her father vowing to disinherit her if she did not choose someone within the year, she was growing weary of her life and was planning to run away to some far-off place when fortune smiled upon her. That was when she had first peregrinated, during an excessively severe thunderstorm at sea. A large spindrift swept her overboard, and the huge waves and rough waters pushed her directly into a portal.

When she awoke, she discovered an enormously large and devilishly handsome man, tending to her every need. He was the kindest, gentlest man she had ever met. Wendal Ozer Osmond was the first man outside her high-society life she had ever been able to converse with. He had a very strange way of speaking with his semi-broken dialect, but that had only made him more attractive to Prisca. After she recovered from the PS symptoms, he tried training her and she fought him all the way. She never liked being told what to do and wasn't about to allow this man who was obviously beneath her station to do so, even if she was attracted to him. They fought like cats and dogs for months, for the amusement of all the others who shared their lifestyle and homes.

Samuel Thibault mentored both of them. Unfortunately, he perished during Hiram's coup all those years ago. He warned them to keep their tempers in check or they would end up falling in love with each other. They both laughed it off, exclaiming impossibilities and the reasons behind their beliefs. Within the first year neither of them could deny the irresistible draw they felt for one another. Prisca had learned about and accepted God her first year as a Dragoman in training, and she had learned that Oz was a very godly man. Their relationship blossomed even though they were both still pigheaded and argued frequently. Prisca had learned to throw off most of her spoiled-girl attitude, and Oz learned to deal with a woman who had a mind of her own. And so they learned to love and respect each other without fail. After three years of living this lifestyle, they married in secret, just the two of them before God Himself. She kept her last name so no one would know, and neither of them wore a ring. They didn't want the others to worry about their dedication to God's task at hand. The only person who had ever found out about their marriage was Simon, and he had kept their secret over the last twenty-five-years.

Now Wendal was back, after she had secretly mourned his death all those years ago. If he could return now, why had he not tried before? Had he been living with Sofia in a loving relationship all these years? That must be the case since they had shown up out of the blue together. Prisca fumed over what she believed to be the truth and yet felt as though her heart would break all over again at the loss of him. Never once had she been unfaithful to him, and she thought he held those same beliefs. Now she wasn't so sure.

Oz had spent the morning showering and shaving, which was something he hadn't bothered doing for the last ten or so years. The man staring back at him in the mirror was a long-forgotten memory. He wanted to look his best when he went to speak to Prisca. They hadn't exactly had a heartfelt, tearful, joyful reunion. She seemed to be very annoyed and upset. It wasn't as if he had a choice about where he'd been the last thirteen years. After finishing up shaving, he went in search of Shannon, who was a longtime friend. She was a beautician before her first peregrination, so it was natural that she would take on the task of cutting everyone's hair back in the day and he hoped she still did.

He found her in the linen closet of the upstairs hallway and asked her to cut his hair for him. It had grown so long that it was past his waist, and he had been forced to keep it tied back with string over the years. She happily obliged him feigning desperation to cut it off last night when he first returned.

They went out the back door to the side houses that the staff lived in. Shannon and Clancy's residence was quaint and perfect for the two of them. It was also where she kept her scissors and tools for trimming hair. Once she had him all cleaned up, they went back to the main house and into the kitchen, which was now full of people, all laughing, visiting, and making plans for the remainder of the day. When Oz stepped through the door, everyone stopped talking and stared, trying to identify the man standing in the doorway.

"Oh...my...word! Oz, is that really you?" Bridget's eyes were round with shock..

Suddenly people were whistling and catcalling.

"Surely, I don't look all that differ'nt do I?" He began turning a little red from all the attention.

Clancy the house chef called out from the other end of the room. "You look the same to me, old man! Just aged a few more years is all," he said with a wink.

"What a dashing big six you are, Oz!" Dinah called out across the table.

"I had no idea there was such a good-looking man beneath all those whiskers and dusty leather." Caroline laughed, standing to give him a hug. "I didn't get to say hello last night, I'm afraid. Thank you for taking care of Seth for me. Bridget and I sure have missed you for the last month." Her eyes were tearing up.

"Now, girlie, don' ya go an' get all emotional on me." He planted a kiss on the top of her head.

"So what's the occasion?" Caroline grinned with curiosity.

"Oh...nothin'. Just needed doin' is all." He cleared his throat. "Would anyone happen ta know where Prisca's got off to this mornin'?" he asked a little apprehensively. "We have some things ta clear up. It's been a long time since we saw each other."

Simon spoke up in response, trying to get in a reply as everyone took the opportunity to tease Oz a bit and make little knowing remarks to him.

"She took her breakfast to the veranda, Oz. Grab yourself a plate of food, and I will gladly show you the way," Simon said, trying to quiet some of the snickering and thwart some of the knowing glances.

"Thanks, Simon, 'ppreciate that." Oz took the full plate that Clancy handed to him and followed Simon out of the kitchen.

Everyone around the table began speculating about Oz and Prisca's relationship. Especially since Oz looked so different from the night before.

"Dinah, whatever is a big six?" Bridget asked confused.

"It's a term where I'm from that we use to describe a big, strongman," she said grinning. "Like Seth over there, or Jason and Nick. Even though they aren't quite as tall as Oz and Seth, they're still strong, handsome men."

"Oz, I'm glad to see you've returned. I've missed you, old friend," Simon said, patting him on the shoulder.

"Thanks, Simon, It's good ta be back. I jus' hope Priss will understand an' let me explain."

Simon chuckled at his friends remark, knowing Prisca's temper all too well himself. "Just be patient and give her some time. It was quite a shock to her last night. All of us, really."

"I know. Thanks, Simon." Oz stepped outside and walked toward Prisca.

Simon closed the doors leading outside to afford them privacy and to hopefully avoid everyone hearing the explosion that was sure to happen when things got heated between the two of them. He smiled to himself and headed back into the kitchen, making sure everyone knew to stay put at least for the next thirty minutes to give them privacy.

"Priss?" Oz questioned, "May I join ya?"

She didn't move or reply and stared straight out toward the ocean, watching the waves crash against the distant shore.

He took that as a yes since she didn't turn and throw anything at his head. He placed his plate on one of the smaller tables nearby, not really having much of an appetite anyhow, and pulled out a chair next to hers to sit down. They sat in silence for a few seconds as Oz thought about how he was going to start this conversation, praying not to say the wrong thing but not knowing what that was.

Just as he was about to speak, Prisca turned to look at him. Her gaze softened as she drank in his appearance.

"Where have you been, Oz?" she asked, trying to keep the tears at bay.

"A place called Zanchier. I'm not really sure where it is Priss."

"Why didn't you come back?" Aggravation became apparent in her demeanor as she turned away from him.

"I couldn' at first. For years I tried! The portal that took us all there was a one-way trip. It was years b'fore we knew of another place where we could escape. Ever'time a portal would open it would just spit us right back out where we started."

"By we, I assume you mean Sofia?" Her simmering anger beginning to boil, afraid of his answer yet still wanting to know the truth.

"Well, yeah, I s'ppose. Weren't too many of us left after the first few months."

"What do you mean by that?" She still had not really looked at him, averting her eyes to the ocean.

"There were lots a' really bad people there Priss. Killed most ever'body else off," he said sadly, remembering the past like it was yesterday.

"So, it's just been you and Sofia? All these years? Shacked up together like a couple of...of happy little honeymooners?" she spat, as she stood to pace, shaking with anger.

"Now why on earth would you say something like that, Priss!?"

"*Stop* calling me that," she yelled back, "I hate when you use that nickname."

By this time, everyone in the kitchen had grown quiet so they could hear what was going on. Oz and Prisca were so loud the sound carried all the way inside. Simon gave everyone a stern look, but that didn't dissuade them. Several people jumped up from the table, quickly followed by everyone else, and ran to watch out the large patio doors that lined the front side of the house and afforded a perfect view of the veranda.

"What in tarnation are ya goin' on 'bout, woman? What...ya think me an' Sofie's been livin' the good life er somethin' out there?"

"Well…haven't you?"

They all turned to look at Sofia, who waved it off. "She's a hothead. He'll line her out in a minute," she said with a smile. They all turned their attention back to the pair outside.

"What kind a' question is that? A course we ain't! You really think I'd do that to ya?"

"I didn't use to think you would be capable of it. But now I'm not so sure! What am I supposed to think, Oz? You show up after thirteen years with Sofia, and only Sofia, who happens to be a very attractive younger woman! And you expect me to believe that all these years have passed, and the two of you just happened to live together with nothing happening? Do I really look that stupid to you?"

"Yeah! Right now ya do!" His own anger began to boil.

She turned angrily at him. "How dare you…!"

"You said it!" he snapped. "Not me!"

"You insufferable man!" She seethed between clenched teeth as her arms went rigid beside her, her hands clenched in fists.

"Prisca Delacroix Osmond would ya jus' shut it fer jus' a minute an' let me explain?"

Everyone turned to look at Simon at the mention of her last name. He just looked at them and shrugged his shoulders, nodding his head yes.

"I never cheated on ya. Not once, an' believe me, I had opportunities! But I *love* ya!"

"I'm sure you did have opportunities. Plenty over the last *thirteen* years!"

"What about you, then? I reckon' ya had yer fair share a' opportunities as well!" He accused back.

"Why you, pigheaded, ornery, frustrating, stubborn…"

"You're right, Priss. I am stubborn!" He cut her off mid-sentence. He began slowly walking toward her as he spoke; Prisca stood her ground unflinchingly. "You're about the craziest French lady I ever did meet. Why God would burden me with feelins fer ya, I'll never know. This here ain't the kind a home comin' I was hopin' fer. I've spent the last thirteen years apart from the one thing in this world I love more 'an life itself. *You!* And I'll be hanged if I spend one more minute of it wastin' time arguin' with ya." He stopped right in front of her. Towering over her, he reached out, grabbed her, and planted a long-awaited kiss square on her lip. He didn't let go until she caved.

Prisca soon softened and threw her arms around Oz's neck. The entire house was in an uproar of screams, clapping, and 'Atta boy, Oz'! Oz finally let go of Prisca, and they both smiled and began to laugh, not only at themselves but at the commotion coming from inside the house.

"I think we've drawn a crowd." She giggled, jerking her head toward the house.

"Who could blame 'em with the ruckus we were makin'" he chuckled back at her.

"Oh, Oz! How I've missed you!" Tears trickled down her cheeks.

"Me too, love, ever' day. At first I had given up hope a' ever gettin' back ta ya. I figured God had jus' fergotten 'bout me. Then Bridget n Caroline showed up and hope sprung anew. I started dreamin' 'bout you again, an' us being together. We ain't hidin' our feelin's no more." He pulled two rings out of his shirt pocket. "I fashioned these here the last few weeks there in Zanchier, jus' waitin' fer when God would call me ta leave." He placed his band on his finger, then took her left hand in his and repeated his vows as he placed the beautiful, intricately carved, turquoise, red, yellow, and silver band upon her finger.

"Oz, it's beautiful! And it fits perfectly!"

"'Course it does, woman. I remember every part a' ya. Down ta the size a' yer tiny little hands." He raised her hand to his lips and brushed her knuckles with a kiss.

Several sets of the double French doors of the house burst open as everyone poured outside to congratulate the two lovebirds and tell them how much they enjoyed their little tryst. Simon looked at his old friends and just threw his hands in the air chuckling, looking at all the people milling about around them. They all three had a good laugh, thoroughly enjoying their new family of Peregrines and Dragoman.

244

"Observe my Sabbaths and have reverence
for my sanctuary. I am the Lord."

Leviticus 19:30 NIV

Chapter 20

After Oz and Prisca's tear-filled reunion, everyone quickly dispersed to spend their day however they chose. Seth and Caroline decided to walk the island for a while and catch up with each other. They promised Jason, Alec, and Odessa, along with several of the other older adults, that they would saddle up some horses and meet them all later on the other side of the island, that is if they were all still out riding by then.

All the older Dragoman and retired workers who knew Oz and Sofia before they disappeared gathered around Sofia as she told them about her life on Zanchier and what the place was like. She describe her rescue by Caroline, Bridget, and Oz. She also told them of Oz's place and what had happened since she had come to live with him there. Everyone was catching up on lost time—everyone except Prisca and Oz, who stole away somewhere to be alone and try to make up for thirteen years of lost time themselves.

All the younger Peregrines took to the mountainous part of the island on foot with backpacks of water and food, some like Kristen even announcing the decision to camp out for the night and not return until after dawn tomorrow.

Malachai found a fishing partner in Vashti, while Ryan decided to work on the Portgens again, claiming that creating things was his idea of relaxation. Because people decided to stay out all day, the cooks and housekeepers enjoyed a break as well. Everyone said that they would either pack a lunch or would make do on their own so that the staff could also spend the day catching up with their friends.

Seth and Caroline walked first to the temple, where Seth informed her of his decision to accept Jesus as his Savior. She was of course beyond thrilled, and they spent some time in prayer together, which was new for them both. They then walked the forest for a while watching the animals roam freely and without fear. They spotted the younger adults followed by the three youngest teenagers scaling the mountainside, Bridget right there with them. She had made quick friends with the other teens and seemed right at home.

They then found a secluded little stretch of beach where they swam and lounged for a while, then they took one of the rowboats out for a little cruise around part of the island.

Jason and Alec were becoming fast friends with Ezekiel and Nick, finding they had a lot in common. They were also fascinated by all that Nick could do with his prosthetic leg and questioned him incessantly, like schoolboys with a new toy.

Nadia, Dinah, and Odessa talked about girl stuff, something they hadn't done in years. They picked wildflowers as they sat and visited, and Nadia showed them how to make flower crowns like she used to do when she was a little girl.

As the afternoon stretched into evening, most everyone returned to the main house for refreshments and decided to get a game going out on the lawn. Nick suggested volleyball and quickly schooled everyone on the basics of the game. The chefs informed everyone that they would serve dinner around six out on the veranda so everyone who wasn't involved with the game could enjoy watching the others play. Even though they didn't have a volleyball just lying around, one was easily accessed from a modern time period through a Portgen. Once they gathered the necessary materials, they set everything up and commenced enjoying the remainder of their evening.

On the other side of the island about two miles away, as high up in the mountains as they could climb, were Kristen, Sean, Wade, Timothy, Dominic, Gabrielle, and Bridget. They had woven their way through the thick growth of tropical plants and trees, making their way up to the highest peak that they could reach. Wade, Dominic, and Bridget had attracted a flurry of animals of all different types. The animals either followed along with them or just watched them curiously as they passed by.

The breeze that high up was constant and smooth, cooling their perspiring skin and ruffling their hair. The scent of tropical flowers around them wafted through the air.

Kristen, who was leading the band of hikers, stopped as they had reached the highest point of the mountain with nowhere else to go. They all came one by one to stand beside her and gaze out over the beauty of the island that lay before them. They could see every side of it. From the height of the mountaintop, the barrier looked odd, as it was dimmed by the sunlight and the clouds that floated around them. They were so high up the clouds seemed almost touchable.

Turning north they faced a bit of jungle with some open valleys, all graced by beautiful flowers and trees bearing fruit of all sorts. There were many animals grazing in the valleys far below them. If they turned east they could see the thick jungle stretch out all the way to the shoreline where the rocks turned treacherous. Turning south they saw the path they had taken through the trees and brush toward the cliffs and the lighthouse. And westward were the main house, staff cottages, stables, and swimmable beach areas.

They all stood in silence for a brief pause, breathing deeply of the warm, moist air, and taking in the beauty that lay before them.

"Wow. Kristen, I can see why you like getting out in nature so much. This is amazing." Sean looked out over God's handiwork with great appreciation.

"Yeah, my dad and I loved camping and hiking. We went every chance we got."

"What about your mom? Did she ever go with you?"

"Oh yes. She went when she could, but she wasn't such an avid nature lover like dad and I were," she said smiling. "When I say we went every chance we got, I mean literally almost every weekend during my entire life at home." She chuckled at the memory.

Several others had been listening and joined in the conversation, relating their own tales of camping adventures or other stories from childhood as they made camp and ate an easy lunch of packed sandwiches and fruit. They laughed throughout the afternoon as they talked, getting to know each other better and forming friendships that they hoped would last a lifetime.

They also spent time exploring the area, looking at plant and animal life while Kristen taught them about most of it. Her knowledge of plants and animals gained through her father's teachings on those camping trips during her childhood and teen years was quite vast.

Sean's appreciation for Kristen seemed to grow daily. The more time he spent with her, the more he realized how wrong he had been about her. His first impression was that of a weak, pampered female. But Kristen was nothing of the sort. He sometimes still heard her cry out at night and often wondered why. Maybe he would ask her later, if he could find the nerve.

As the sun slipped lower in the sky, everyone grew quiet and watchful as it began its slow slide down as though it were sinking into the water. It shot out colors from every spectrum of the rainbow. The lighter colors such as pinks, oranges, and yellows were above the sun and faded into the bolder shades of reds, blues, and purples, which seemed to reflect off the surface of the water for what appeared to be miles on either side of the setting sun. The warm breeze began to still as the sun disappeared beneath the edge of the world.

Most of the group sat together chatting around the fire. Sean and Kristen sat silently at the edge of the mountain, observing the nightfall and the stars as they made their glorious appearance. With nothing to block their view of the night sky, it appeared to go on forever.

Sean gasped audibly at the beauty that stretched out as far as he could see and seemed to touch the water where the stars were reflected in the glistening still surface. He sat and leaned back against an obliging boulder, crossed his arms behind his head, and stared into the beauty of the night.

"Wow!!" he said almost as a whisper, catching Kristen's attention as she moved to sit beside him.

"Pretty amazing, isn't it?" she said with awe and appreciation.

"That may just be the biggest understatement ever." He gave her a lopsided grin.

She smiled back, laughing ever so slightly as he joined in.

They sat looking at each other in silence for a few brief moments before Timothy came over to sit on the other side of Kristen.

"Mind if I join you two?" he asked, sitting down. "I kind of feel a little out of place over there with the teenagers." He chuckled and smiled, pointing at the group of teens acting silly. He smiled down at them, mostly looking at Kristen.

"Sure," Sean said sitting up, a little perturbed at Timothy's untimely appearance, feeling oddly uneasy.

"How old are you, Timothy, if you don't mind my asking?" Kristen asked.

"No, not at all." He smiled at her. "And you can call me Tim. It's easier to say."

Sean's stomach began to feel like it was going to tie into knots. It was obvious that "Tim" was flirting with Kristen.

"I'm thirty years old. I'll be thirty-one in just a few days."

"Really? I would have never guessed you were that old. Uh…not that thirty is old," Kristen stammered.

Sean silently rolled his eyes at the conversation and Kristen's obvious reaction to Tim.

"You just seem much younger than that. That's all I meant," she said, feeling a little awkward. Tim was a very handsome guy. She had noticed before that he was good looking, but they had never seemed to really talk before now.

"Well, how about you two? Can I ask your ages?" Tim briefly looked at Sean, then smiled at Kristen again.

"Twenty-five," Sean said as he threw a rock out over the edge of the mountain, growing more and more agitated. He wasn't exactly sure why, but for some reason Tim got his hackles up. Especially when he flashed that million-dollar smile at Kristen.

Tim looked down at Kristen with raised eyebrows.

"I'm twenty-two." She shyly shrugged her shoulders.

Sean looked at her. He never thought about her age before.

"I thought you were a lot younger than that," Sean said without thinking.

"Why is that?" She asked confused.

"I don't know. I guess I thought you were still in your teens, maybe eighteen or nineteen." He chunked another rock out into the darkness.

"Really? I'm not sure how to take that. Do you mean I appear young or just immature?" she asked sharply.

"I don't know, Kristen. I just never really thought about it, I guess." He stammered, unsure what to say to soothe her temper. The last thing he wanted was to get into a fight with her. Especially with Tim lurking nearby.

"You mean to tell me that we have been partners for over a year now and you had no idea how old I am?"

"Well it's not like we ever really talked much until recently."

"You're right. It's not like we lived under the same roof and socialized with the same people for the last year," she said sarcastically, looking at him with raised eyebrows and tension growing in her shoulders.

Sean almost audibly groaned, growing more agitated. He stood up and held his hand out to Kristen, saying. "Well, it doesn't really matter now, does it? Why don't we go start a fire so we can cook some dinner?"

Kristen hesitated, unsure what to make of the offered hand.

"Sure." She looked at his hand questioningly but took it anyway as he pulled her up off the ground. She wasn't quite sure what to make of this new, nonargumentative Sean.

Sean was reluctant to release her hand, but she almost jerked it away. Tim stood also and followed them over to the center of camp to build a fire. Soon they were all pulled into the lighthearted banter of the teens across from them, laughing, joking, and playing with all manner of animals piled up around them.

Sean watched as Tim and Kristen continued their conversation. Kristen smiled and laughed at what Tim said, and Tim smiled and laughed at something she said. He had never seen Kristen this animated before. She seemed totally relaxed and unguarded. He knew surprisingly little about the woman he had spent the last year with. He just couldn't figure out why he cared all of a sudden. What changed and when?

He had to admit it, whether he liked it or not; he had real feelings for Kristen, and it appeared he wasn't the only one. Tim seemed to be enjoying himself quite a lot. If Sean wanted to pursue a relationship with her, he would have to bring his A game. With the search for the armor beginning soon, they would all be traveling together. Which meant that Sean would rarely, if ever, get Kristen to himself again. With this budding relationship between Tim and her starting, Sean would really have to watch what he said to her. It seemed that everything that came out of his mouth was wrong, and he couldn't afford that. Perhaps he would talk to Nick about it when they returned tomorrow. But for now he couldn't just sit and watch them. Sean got up and left the fireside without a word to anyone and walked to look out over the mountain edge once again.

As he walked past, Kristen glanced up at him out of the corner of her eye, still trying to listen to Tim. Sean seemed agitated for some reason but she couldn't for the life of her figure out what about. *Should I go check on him,* she wondered? *No, he is a big boy. Surely if he wanted to talk about something, he would.* But Sean could also be really immature and stubborn as well. As her attention turned back to Tim, she would occasionally glance at Sean's back, knowing something was bothering him. You didn't spend a year with someone without learning a thing or two about them. Well, apparently Sean could.

Sean stood at the edge of the mountain leaning against a large boulder and looking out over the land. All that was really visible were the lights that were on at the main house and the continually turning light of the lighthouse. With the discovery of new Peregrines, the Dragoman decided to keep the lighthouse running every night just in case more were to make an appearance.

Sean threw a silent prayer up to God to help him sort out his feelings and to guide him properly in them. If he was meant to pursue Kristen, then so be it, but if not, then he didn't want to lead her on only to hurt her later. He also wasn't too keen about putting his own feelings out there to be trampled on if she didn't feel the same way. But if he didn't try, then he may lose the chance forever now that Timothy seemed interested as well.

Sean decided he had better return to the party and get to know more about Timothy to better gauge what he was up against. He put on his best game face and went to sit down beside Kristen.

"So Timothy, what did you do before peregrination?" Sean asked him.

"I was just telling Kristen that I was a lawyer."

"A lawyer, really? Were you a trustworthy type of guy, or are you one of the deceitful types?" Sean asked with his best smile, playing it cool.

"Actually, I *was* a deceitful, conniving, underhanded kind of man. That is until peregrination. Funny story to my first peregrination; I was listening to Prince's song "1999" on the radio in my Jag when I rounded a curve in the road and an earthquake started. I took it as some kind of sign, thinking the world was really ending like in the song." Timothy laughed at the memory. "My car got swallowed up by a ravine. I remember falling for what seemed forever as my car bounced off boulder after boulder. I started praying to a God I didn't believe in yet to save me, promising to change my ways, and then I blacked out. I woke at Vashti's safe house, and my life hasn't been the same since. She really helped me to understand the Bible and what it meant to be a Christian." He finished, looking at Sean then settled his gaze on Kristen.

Great, so he is a believer already. "How long have you been peregrinating?"

"Oh, about three years now. I was twenty-eight when I first jumped. I had it all, money, and a successful career as a lawyer. I was fixing to be one of the youngest judges in our district. Then God saved me." He smiled.

Oh brother! This guy is pouring it on thick. Everything that comes out of his mouth only makes him look better. Sean decided to steer the questions in a different direction.

"So, were you married or involved with anyone?" He was hoping to find a flaw.

"No, actually, I wasn't. There was the occasional girl here and there but nothing serious. At the time I was only concerned about where my career was going. I really didn't have time to meet the right woman then. Things are a lot more relaxed now, though, and I'm waiting on God in that department. I figure He'll lead me in the right direction." He looked at Kristen and smiled even bigger.

Okay, enough of that! Sean stood up, getting everyone's attention, especially Kristen's, who was blushing from all the attention from Timothy.

"Why don't we play a game or something?"

"Great idea." Bridget beamed. "But I'm afraid my knowledge of group games is rather limited."

"What about charades?" Sean suggested. "Does everyone know how to play?"

"That sounds fun." Bridget clapped, as everyone except Bridget agreed that they knew the game.

"How are we dividing teams?" Wade asked.

"Well, how about me and Kristen, Dominic, and Wade, you two team with Gabrielle since you fellas will obviously need a smart female in your group, and Bridget you can team up with Tim. He seems like a smart guy, and he can help you with the rules." Sean hoped no one noticed the sarcastic emphasis he placed on the words *smart guy* in his last statement.

As they gathered together to plan out what they would act out, Kristen squinted at Sean curiously. "Sean, what is going on with you? You are acting a bit strange tonight. Especially around Tim."

"Nothing. I'm just not sure I trust that guy is all." Sean defensively looked back at her.

"Why? He seems to be a very nice and genuine type person."

"How do you know? You just met the guy a few weeks ago! Isn't this like the first conversation you've had with him?" Sean heatedly whispered.

"Sean, we literally just met everyone a few weeks ago. It's kind of the nature of our lives. You and I were strangers just over a year ago, you know. Apparently we still are since you know so little about me. And how do you know Tim and I have never talked before now?"

"We are not strangers. And…guys are just like that. You know we don't pay a lot of attention to things. And I don't know that you've never chatted before. I just assumed with everyone being busy training that no one really has time to practice social skills."

"There is still plenty of time to get to know people, Sean. You should try it sometime. Get out of your own little bubble and get to know some people other than Nick. Instead of always telling tall tales, why don't you try asking a few questions now and again. Now, are we going to play or what?" She crossed her arms across her chest and glared at him.

Sean was glad to turn the conversation back to the game. He wasn't ready to reveal his feelings just yet, thinking it wasn't really the proper time or place. They spent the next several hours playing charades until it got late and everyone grew tired. They all climbed into their bags, forming a circle around the low-burning fire, and fell asleep. All except Sean who lay awake, watching Kristen sleep, the fire dancing across the features on her face. When did she start to infiltrate his every thought? Every time he looked at her, he wanted to reach out and touch her hand, her hair, her face. And it seemed as though she was always on his mind lately. Especially since Tim seemed to be setting his sights on her too. He eventually drifted off to sleep as the hour grew later and the peaceful star-filled night sky hung glittering above him.

Sean awoke to find Kristen bending down over him, shaking him awake. He opened his eyes to see her leaning down whispering his name. It was still dark, and he thought he was having a very pleasant dream. He grinned up at her in a goofy sort of way, and without realizing it, reached up and put his arms around her, almost pulling her down beside him.

"Sean, what are you doing? Snap out of it!" she whispered threateningly, smacking him in the chest.

He shook himself out of his momentary stupor and asked, "What?" He cleared his froggy throat and tried again. "What's going on?" He sat up.

"Shh…keep still. Don't wake the others yet. I want to show you something. I woke up a little while ago. I'm not sure what woke me, but when I woke I was drawn to look out over the east ridge, you know, the side where no one ever really ventures to because it is so overgrown and the beach is rockier than it is by the lighthouse? Well, I saw something, and I want to see if you see it too or if my mind is playing tricks on me?"

She grabbed him by the arm and pulled him up to a standing position. They walked over to the boulder at the highest point, and she climbed on top, motioning Sean to follow her.

"Kristen are you crazy?" he loudly whispered. "You could fall and break your neck."

"Would you just come on. You can see it much better from up here. There's plenty of room for both of us," she loudly whispered back.

Sean apprehensively climbed the side of the rock, pushing against the neighboring boulders to aid him in joining Kristen at the top. He wasn't afraid of heights himself, so he wasn't at all sure why he was worried about Kristen climbing it. He reached the top by her side and looked down at the small space. There was room to stand, but not much. They would have to stand still and not move much if they didn't want to risk accidentally knocking each other off the ten-foot-high rock.

Kristen leaned close to his ear and pointed out in the water. Sean could smell her hair and the light scent of flowers that clung to her. He breathed in deeply before allowing his attention to drift to where she was pointing.

Out in the distance where the barrier disappeared into the surface of the ocean was a glowing light beneath the water's surface. Every few hundred feet or so it appeared that there was an area below the surface of the water that lit up ever so slightly. It looked bluish green in color but seemed to be stationary. As the ocean waves rolled through the barrier the glowing spots seemed to stay still.

"What do you think it is?" she softly asked, continuing to watch the water.

"It appears to be barrier gateways," he said, his attention caught by what he saw. "You know, the way entrances are a slight shade of yellow where we can safely cross. I always just assumed that the barrier stopped at the water's surface. That it didn't go beneath to the ocean floor. Why do you think there would be underwater gateways in Barriers Edge?" He looked at Kristen, who only shrugged her shoulders.

"This is very interesting, and I can't wait to find out what it means. We can ask the Dragoman tomorrow if they know about it and why the barrier would have that." He turned to look at her.

The moonlight played softly across her features illuminating half of her face. He took a slight step back to put a bit of distance between them, forgetting where he was, and almost slipped off the top edge of the rock. He would have fallen off if Kristen hadn't grabbed his shirt front and arm and pulled him to her so they ended nose to nose. They stood motionless, a bit rattled, breathing hard, and peering down over the edge. That's when Sean realized how close they were. They looked at each other nervously as they took a small step apart.

"Sean, are you crazy? You could fall and break your neck," she whispered teasingly, repeating what he had said to her earlier, grinning from ear to ear.

He looked at her and chuckled, as she joined in the silent laughter. After they silently giggled over the situation and nearly fell off the rock again, they realized they still held on to each other. Sean cleared his throat and unwillingly let her go, then slid down the rock. He knew Kristen didn't need help, but he offered her his hand anyway. She accepted his help down to the ground. Then, realizing that the sun was just about to rise, she decided to wake everyone else and fill them in on what they had seen. Timothy and everyone else wanted to have a look before the sun rose too high and diminished the glow of the underwater portals. They had some breakfast while they sat discussing possibilities, then packed up camp and headed down to the main house in search of answers.

Sean walked behind the others, thoroughly confused by the emotions wreaking havoc on his insides. Little did he know that Kristen too was feeling the emotional battle inside as well.

Kristen thought about the events that had transpired just within the last couple of months. How Sean had acted toward her back in Shimoga and then just in the last, what, twelve hours or so. She and Sean had barely tolerated each other for the first thirteen months. What was happening now? Sean seemed different somehow, ever since the trip to India to search for the key. Especially in the way he acted toward her, and he almost seemed jealous of the attention Tim was giving her last night. Maybe he was just learning to pay more attention to his peregrination partner, personally growing up a little and learning to think of others rather than himself all the time. Surely that was it. He couldn't possibly have feelings for her. Could he? And could she be having feelings for him? And what about Tim? He really seemed interested in her, and he was definitely good looking and easy to talk to. She would just have to wait and see where, and to whom, God led her.

It was nearly nine when the camping group returned from the mountain. Most everyone at the main house was up milling about the kitchen or working out in the stables tending to the needs of the horses. The hike down had only taken a few hours since coming down was quicker than going up. Sean and Kristen went in search of Prisca or Simon to inform them of what they had seen. They didn't find their mentor, Prisca, anywhere, but they stumbled upon Simon in the archival library with the *Book of the Keepers,* looking at the odd language with Malachai and Vashti.

"Simon, may Kristen and I have a word?" Sean asked, approaching the three Dragoman.

"Certainly. Malachai, Vashti, please excuse me a moment," Simon said.

"No, with all of you," Sean corrected. "See, Kristen discovered something last night up on the mountain." Sean looked at her to finish.

After she filled them in on what she discovered, with Sean throwing in what he believed it to be, they asked if the Dragoman knew what it was and if it could be gateways.

Simon answered first. "I've never heard of underwater gateways before. We've always known the barrier extended underwater because of submarines that have disappeared through the Bermuda Triangle over the years, but I never knew about the gateways."

"Nor have I, Simon," Malachai chimed in as Vashti nodded in agreement.

"Can we take a boat and go check it out?" Sean asked hopefully.

"No. I don't think that would be a good idea just yet. Perhaps one of the other books reveals something about it. Until we have a chance to search the books first, I don't want anyone going near that area of the barrier. Do you both understand me?" Simon looked at them over his spectacles, eyebrows raised in sternness like he so often did.

"Yes sir," Sean said, saluting playfully.

"I mean it, Sean Doran," Simon admonished. "We don't know where it leads. It could be very dangerous. It could be an area where your trackers don't work, like Zanchier where Oz and Sofia were trapped for thirteen years and Seth disappeared to for a while."

"I understand, sir," Sean said more seriously. "I'll make sure and tell the others."

"Now, if we could just find that other missing waterfall and key, we may be able to find some answers to these ever-increasing questions in the last unopened book." Simon pondered the problem. Just then Oz and Prisca walked by the library doors on the way to the kitchen.

"Did I hear mention of a key?" Oz asked.

"Yes, Wendal. We are still looking for a lost key for one of the recently discovered archive books." Simon ran his hand through his hair in frustration.

"Well, in all the commotion a us comin' back an' Seth bein' injured, I guess we all jus' plumb fergot. But we found a key back on Zanchier at the base of a waterfall. That's how Seth got stung. Divin' fer the key." Oz had captured everyone's interest.

"My word! Well, where is it?" Simon asked excitedly.

"Well, I don't right recall." Oz scratched his head. "When we pulled Seth out a' the water after he got stung, I think maybe Sofie put it away somewhere. We was jus' in a hurry to get ta the Dustbowl an' get Seth some medical attention."

"Let's go find Sofia, everyone!" Simon and the others walked out of the library in separate directions in search of Sofia. Sean and Kristen, per Simon's instructions, went in search of the others to inform them of Simon's orders about that side of the island and the underwater lights at the barrier.

Simon ran into Seth and Caroline out by the stables and asked Seth about the key. Seth admitted that he couldn't remember what happened to it after he passed out but that he did remember having it in his hand when Oz and Sofia pulled him out of the water. Simon then asked them if they knew where Sofia was, but they both answered no.

"Would you like us to help look for her, Simon?" Seth asked.

"No, it's fine, my boy. I'll find her somewhere. She couldn't have gotten far, could she?" He smiled, walking off toward the prayer gardens. He found her sitting quietly on one of the benches, deep in prayer. He was turning to leave so as not to disturb her when she looked up and turned to him.

"Simon, did you need something?" She stood up to meet him.

"I'm sorry. I wasn't going to disturb you."

"It's quite all right. I was just finishing up anyhow." They both began walking back to the house.

"I understand that Seth found a key in Zanchier. Do you happen to know where it is?"

"Yes! We completely forgot all about it in all the excitement. I have it in my room. I pulled it out of Seth's hand when he was stung and stowed it away in my pack for safe keeping."

"Great! Now let's go get that key, shall we?" Simon smiled happily.

They hurried to the main house and upstairs to Sofia's room. Sofia stepped to a small writing desk, pulled a drawer open, and stared blankly at it.

"I know I placed it right here in this drawer." She rummaged through the writing desk.

"Are you absolutely sure this is where you left it?"

"Yes, I cleaned out my pack the morning after we arrived, and I placed the key in this drawer." Confusion written in her expression.

"Did anyone know you had the key? Did you tell anyone?"

"No. Like I said, I had forgotten about it until now. What do you think this means, Simon? I mean, who would take the key?"

"It means, we may have another traitor in our midst." Worry and trepidation filled his words.

You will hear of wars and rumors of wars, but see to it
that you are not alarmed. Such things must happen,
but the end is still to come.

Matthew 24:6 NIV

Chapter 21

Sofia and Simon turned her room upside down just to make sure Sofia hadn't absentmindedly moved the key elsewhere or left it out to be put away by the housekeepers. Simon also called on Shannon, who was the head housekeeper and whom he knew he could trust. When he asked her if she had seen the key, she said she had not and knew of no one else who had mentioned it. She said she would inquire of the staff if anyone had found a key matching the description Sofia gave her.

Simon instructed the women to keep it quiet. He didn't want an all-out suspicion war happening among everyone on the island. When people think there is a traitor among them, all manner of things begin happening. None of which are in any way pleasant. He wanted the camaraderie and relationships that were being formed here to continue. These people all had to learn to depend on one another during a demon war and even quite possibly during their own trials. Thinking that anyone could be the traitor could very well destroy it all.

He also informed Shannon to quietly call a brief meeting of the Dragoman, including Oz, in fifteen minutes. While all the Peregrines were out training and unlikely to ask questions about the meeting, he wanted to discuss the missing key and the necessity of keeping its disappearance quiet. He and the other Dragoman would come up with a viable story to tell anyone who asked about it and the book.

Simon asked Shannon to bring a pot of coffee and cakes into the smaller meeting room located at the back of the house. No one ever used this room or ventured this way since there was nothing to draw anyone back here. This area of the house only had the meeting room, a restroom, the laundry room, extra storage closets, and a door that led outside the back of the house to where the staff cottages were located. They could meet without fear of being overheard and alerting anyone unknowingly to the problem at hand.

When the Dragoman had gathered, Simon said, "I called everyone here this morning secretively because the last key to the last archive book has been found."

"That is great news!" Malachai exclaimed.

"How wonderful! Now we can see what is inside its pages." Vashti excitedly stated.

"However"—Simon interrupted the excited responses—"someone has taken the key."

"What? No, not again!" Prisca exclaimed, worried because she knew another traitor was in their midst.

Nuncio spoke up. "Simon, perhaps it has just been misplaced."

"No. Sofia and I looked through her entire room. She had placed it inside the writing desk drawer, but when we returned to get it, it was gone. She knows for certain she put it in there."

"Oz, you and Sofia are the only two Peregrines who know about the key's disappearance and only a handful more knew of it being found. So if anyone should ask about the contents of the last book and the key, we will simply tell them that the key would not open the book. That it was the wrong key." Simon instructed everyone as to the story. "I also suggest that we each include only one of our most entrusted Peregrines to keep an eye on everyone and everything. If we have another betrayer in our midst, we could have another incident like the one we had thirteen years ago. We *cannot* allow that to happen again."

"Why do we not inform more of our trusted people, to help keep a better eye on things?" Vashti asked.

"We thought we could trust Hiram, remember?" Simon said sorrowfully. "Plus, we don't want a lot of people walking around suspecting everyone to whom they speak. It could be disastrous for the missions and their safety. The Peregrines must trust one another to be successful."

Everyone nodded and mumbled their agreement.

"So whom shall we bring into the circle?" Malachai asked.

"Well, Seth is the only one who knows of the key's existence from my group. Prisca, Sean and Kristen both know that Seth found a key because they were speaking to us when Oz informed us that they had found it. However, Kristen is too inexperienced to be burdened, and Sean, perhaps a bit too immature. Seth already knows and also knows what the key looks like, so we will have him be watchful, and I would like to include Jason in this because he has military experience that I believe would be beneficial in this. Oz," he gestured to him, "of course, will be another set of eyes, as well as Sofia."

Malachai spoke next. "Zaccai would be my choice from my group. Everyone trusts her and looks to her for help with their problems. So I believe she would be the one to figure out if it is anyone from my group."

Vashti looked a bit concerned. "Everyone from my group is a relatively new Peregrine. The most experienced that I have is Ezekiel Davis, and he has only been at this for four years. Having said that, I do trust him."

"Simon, what about the others that know of the key?" Nuncio asked thoughtfully.

"We'll simply tell them to not mention it to anyone else so as not to get their hopes up. We also need to take the books and keys and hide them or lock them up to make sure nothing else goes missing."

"Good idea." Malachai stated appreciatively.

"All right then, next order of business. We need to consult the *Book of Armor* and get these people out searching for the pieces."

"Agreed," Nuncio stated. "However, we have a new problem there, Simon, that we've never had before."

"What is that, Nuncio?" he asked confused.

"We have three very young people who are neither Dragoman nor Peregrine. What are we to do with them? Surely we can't send them on these missions with the others?" Nuncio said, a bit concerned as to the solution. "Not to mention that they must be a necessary element to the end battle to have an archive book written expressly for them. Do we really want to risk their injury or quite possibly their deaths?"

"He has a very good point," Vashti stated.

"Prisca forcefully stated, "Yes, but what if part of what they are to do is out on the missions with the others? We would then be hindering Gods work by keeping them here."

"True, but if they are killed, what then?" Nuncio exclaimed. "Wade cannot fight to save his own life, Dominic has some skills but hasn't even grown a whisker yet, and Bridget is about as sweet and innocent as they come."

"Then God will surely raise another. He always has in the past," Malachai defended. "None of us are guaranteed another day; we are all replaceable."

Oz stepped up and cleared his throat. "Now, I don' know 'bout them other fellas ya mentioned, but I'll tell ya this. Bridget ain't afraid a nothin'. I've seen her charge a whole camp a' Scaithers back in Zanchier. Jus' her an' a passel a creatures. If it weren't fer Bridget, Caroline, me, an' Sofie wouldn't be standin' here today. She may be tiny, but her trust in God rivals that a King David himself as a boy. I guarantee that. God himself put these younguns here fer a reason. Keepin' 'em stuck here on the island ain't gonna' get 'em no experience against the evil they'll surely have ta face eventually."

"Very well said, Oz," Simon stated. "You're right of course. The others may have to protect these new Keepers on occasion, but we can't expect them to learn or reach their potential if we hide them away because of their age or lack of fighting abilities. Like Oz said, they are God's chosen. It's our job to figure out what for and guide them in that direction. And to do that we need to decipher the *Book of the Keepers* and that message that came with the key.

"All right, everyone, you know what needs doing. Discreetly pull aside your Peregrine leaders and explain the situation to them. Prisca, search for Sean and Kristen to explain about the key. I'll go in search of Sofia and Seth and explain as well. Unless there is anything else we need to discuss, then the meeting is adjourned." Simon looked questioningly around the room.

Everyone was satisfied with what was decided and filed out of the room in search of those they needed to speak with. Most of the Peregrines were at the training area down by the beach while the Keepers were wading in the ocean as Dominic instructed them to try out their abilities on the sea creatures. Bridget was leery of some of the more odd-looking creatures, and the fact that she hadn't learned to swim yet. So the boys spent the better part of the morning teaching her that as well.

Simon instructed Shannon to nonchalantly send for Jason, Seth, and Sofia to report to the archival library so that he could speak to them in private. He knew that if Alec or Odessa spotted him speaking with them, they would be curious and know something was up. He hated keeping secrets from his Peregrines—he completely trusted them all— but he had no choice.

Simon waited in the archival library at one of the tables in the back of the room to afford them privacy.

"Hey Simon, what's up?" Jason asked, walking into the room. Simon motioned for him to have a seat. Soon Seth, and then Sofia, appeared in the door, and Simon motioned them over to join them.

"We have a very real problem. Seth, the key you found has disappeared again. Sofia had placed it in a drawer in her room for safe keeping, and it's gone. This means someone purposefully took it, and we haven't a clue who it could be. So if anyone asks about the key or book, you are to simply inform them that it was the wrong key. That it didn't work when we tried to open the book. Do you all understand?"

"How do we explain that? Every other key from every other waterfall worked," Jason asked.

"Simply say that perhaps there was another key beneath the falls where it was found, with all the shiny objects the creature had stockpiled, it was simply overlooked because we assumed that we had the correct one. We'll say that some of us Dragoman will return to Zanchier to search for it."

They nodded in agreement.

"Now, I also need you to keep your promise to *not* tell anyone else about the possibility of there being a traitor in our midst. We need to keep everyone's spirits up and the camaraderie going here. This is crucial to the missions ahead of us all. However, that being said, I also need you to keep your eyes and ears open. We need to find out who the traitor is before we have another episode like we did thirteen years ago. There are other Peregrines from the other Dragoman who will be informed of the situation as well. Oz, because he already knew of the key, and Nicholas, Zaccai, and Ezekiel since they are the leaders of the other groups. You all need to work together without making it obvious that you know something the others do not. Please, this is crucial. And if you happen to find the traitor, you'll have to make it appear coincidental, not like you were searching for them. Do you understand these instructions?" Simon asked them, making certain they got the importance of it all.

"Yes, but Simon, why am I included in this?" Seth asked. "I'm relatively new to all this."

"Simply because you already knew of the key's existence and what it looks like. However, you cannot tell Caroline, Seth."

"Simon, I'm positive she has nothing to do with this," Seth said defensively.

"I understand that, but as I said the fewer people who know the better, because it will decrease the suspicious glances flying around. We need to keep the trust circle going."

"Yes sir. I understand. I just don't like keeping secrets from her."

"I understand, Seth. I don't like it either. I don't want people to think we don't trust them. But this is the only way to not alert the betrayer that we are on to them. If the betrayer thinks it is the wrong key, perhaps it will be returned. Hopefully it won't be tossed away. Just so you know, we will be calling a meeting of everyone tonight to discuss the need to search for the armor pieces, so when you hear it later, you'll understand. Now, off with you three. Back to whatever it was you were doing." Simon stood as the other three followed his lead and left the library.

Simon found Nuncio in another part of the library, and with his help took the new archive books and keys to hide them in a safe place away from prying eyes and potential thieves. Only the Dragoman would know where they were hidden so they could continue their work on them. And if the books or keys somehow ended up missing, then they would know it was one of the Dragoman who couldn't be trusted.

At lunch, Nuncio informed everyone that they would have a meeting out on the veranda that evening after dinner and before Scripture study to discuss the soon-to-come missions, and that everyone needed to be present for the briefing.

It was just past five when everyone started returning from wherever they had been that day. With the house having only ten bathrooms for the forty-two people in the house, everyone had to make quick work of showering and cleaning up. The staff, which consisted of thirteen people plus three more from Prisca's place, was gracious enough to allow people to use their bathrooms in the staffing cottages out back, which helped. But only the three married couples had their own cottages. The rest used bunkhouse-type dwellings with one bathroom each. All in all, everyone seemed to manage nicely.

Clancy, the head chef, announced that dinner would be at six-thirty out on the veranda, which gave people more time to clean up.

Simon sat looking at the huge table before him with its long bench-style seats on both sides and the two shorter ones on the ends, which would soon sit twenty people whom he had to send out to risk their very lives within a day's time. Yes, they would all be traveling together, but he was afraid they faced many a savage battle ahead, both mentally and physically. His heart was heavy for their safety, and he and the others who remained on the island would hold nightly prayer vigils for their safe return.

He was soon stirred from his musing as people began filing out of the house, freshly bathed, laughing, and joking with each other. Many bonds had been formed here on Reader's Island over the last month or so, and he hoped those friendships held fast through the trials. Satan was a cunning foe, a trickster who would stop at nothing to tear each and every one of these people apart. Simon only hoped that where one person was weak, a stronger one would bear the burden with, or for, the other.

With the main table full and the surrounding smaller tables holding the staff and everyone else, dinner was served. They spent that time laughing, telling stories, and enjoying their time together for the last evening, although the Peregrines didn't know yet that they were leaving tomorrow.

Clancy, the head chef, had made a very large cake for an after-dinner celebration. As the cake was cut and passed down the table to everyone, Nuncio stood from his seated place beside Simon and the other Dragoman, took his glass in hand, and waited for the chatter to grow silent as people noticed him standing.

"As you've all noticed, Clancy and the others have been gracious enough to make a large confection to celebrate many things." Everyone clapped and offered a thank-you to the staff. When things quieted down again, Nuncio continued. "Such as the finding of one's true love," he said looking at Seth and Caroline and Oz and Prisca. Alec glanced at Odessa with longing in his heart.

"The finding of the books and keys, the making of new friendships, and the reinforcing of old ones." As Nuncio talked the people around the table looked at one another with smiles or gestures. "Amazing new technology created by our young technical wizard, Ryan Halloran." Everyone clapped and cheered, thanking Ryan for all he does for them. Ryan actually smiled ever so slightly amidst all the praise. "And newfound gifts, which I believe you have all mastered quite well over the last month. Oh, and one more thing, I believe we have a birthday tomorrow. Timothy will be thirty-one." Nuncio smiled and raised his glass to Tim as everyone wished him a happy birthday. "And that goes for anyone else whom we may have forgotten or not known about. Remember these days, people. Here's to each and every one of you." He raised his glass once more as others were raised around the table in toasts to one another.

Nuncio sat down while Simon stood to speak to the group.

"Thank you, Nuncio, for your kind words. My words, however, take a different turn. Nothing negative, mind you." He cleared his throat and began again. "Tomorrow you will all set out on your new missions to begin the search for the Armor of God. Now, in the first-dimension world where we are all from, the Bible talks about these pieces as being figurative. They represent the things of God, such as His Word. Here, however, for the chosen Twelve, they are literally pieces of armor that you will need during the final battle. Now, only The Twelve will need this armor, and so it will likely be revealed only to them. But the rest of you will take the journey to help search for the armor. I believe the rest of you will be of great use to The Twelve during the trials. However, I'm not sure if only The Twelve will be tried. You all may have things that you need to deal with and work out. Whether or not you are tried is entirely up to God Himself."

"Do you have any idea as to what the trials might entail, Simon?" Alec asked.

"I'm afraid I don't. Only that they are mainly focused on the Fruit of the Spirit. On top of these trials, you will most likely encounter run-ins with demons as well. Remember these times here at the island, the joyful times, times of bonding, friendships, and love. They may very well get you through some very dark days that lay ahead of each of you. Remember to trust and rely on each other without doubt. But also remember the God who goes before you. Laying your path ahead of you. If you keep your faith and trust in Him, all will be as it should. Those of you who are newer and have yet to be in battle, trust in yourselves and your gifts and the God who created you for such times as these."

"Do we know where we are headed first, Simon?" Jason questioned.

"Well, we know the first piece of armor to be somewhere around Timna Valley in southern Israel. There are mines there that were considered for years to be Egyptian. Then in the year 2012 it was discovered that they were actually Solomon's copper mines. The *Book of Armor* tells us that at one point all the pieces of armor may have been forged there and hidden among King Solomon's treasures. These twelve suits of armor were embedded with jewels and precious stones that corresponded to each of the tribes, with capes that mark the colors of each of the twelve tribes' flags. However it is very likely they have all been scattered across the earth."

"So, once we retrieve the first piece the next will be revealed to us somehow?" Odessa questioned.

"Yes. I'm not sure how, but God will reveal your next location," Simon answered.

"Do we have a search order for the pieces?" Ezekial asked.

"Yes, the first piece is the Belt of Truth. Now, I'm not certain that you will find the belt hidden in the mines somewhere in Timna Valley. The mines are only a starting point. You will certainly have to use your wits and powers of deduction to locate the pieces. I will give you an order in which to search for them, based upon what the book tells us, but keep an open mind. God may have very different plans."

"Simon," Ryan Halloran interrupted, "the new people need to be fitted with a chip, so that we can keep tabs on them."

"Oh yes! Thank you for that reminder, Ryan. We certainly don't need anyone else disappearing, do we?" Simon grinned at everyone seated at the table. "After dinner, Oz, Sofia, and Bridget will need to be chipped. Caroline already has one. That's how we found you two." Simon motioned to her and Bridget.

"When did that happen?" Caroline asked surprised.

"Back on the beach in Louisiana," Alec explained. "I was able to telekinetically plant one on your neck before you both walked into the portal."

"Really? I can't even feel it!" Caroline felt her neck for the chip. "I guess I was so excited, and then worried about Seth, that I never even thought to ask how you found us."

"I believe that Ryan has already labeled your chip on the computer system. Of course we should probably check it to make sure it is in the correct spot for optimal transmitting." Simon looked at Ryan who nodded his head yes in agreement.

"I wish to read something for you from the Bible," Simon said, picking up the book to hold while he read. "Deuteronomy 31:8 says,

'The LORD himself goes before you and will be with you; he will never leave you nor forsake you. Do not be afraid; do not be discouraged.'" Simon closed the Bible. "Remember these words; hold them in your hearts. Your Peregrine leaders are, of course, each group's leader. Everyone will report and take orders from your group leaders, who will in turn communicate and decide among one another the best course of action to take in every situation. Now unless anyone else has any more questions, I suggest you all take the evening to prepare and pack for the long journey ahead." Simon looked around the table. Since no one spoke up, he continued. "All right then, enjoy your cake, and everyone report to the library at eight for our evening study time."

After dessert, Oz, Sofia, Caroline, and Bridget reported to the computer room where Ryan took care of their chipping devices, running them through a few tests to make sure everything worked as expected.

After the half-hour-long Bible study in the library, everyone disappeared to their rooms to pack for their next mission, while the groundskeepers and a few of the other staff members went to the stables to check and make sure all the horses were ready for the peregrination in the morning.

Oz and Prisca disappeared once more to be alone, knowing that tomorrow they would be separated again for an unknown amount of time. Seth and Caroline, too, knew this would be their last evening to truly be alone, and they also disappeared.

The main house was relatively quiet with the Dragoman sitting in the archive library sifting through the information in the *Book of Armor* and making notes to give to the Peregrines in the morning before they left.

Ryan had found sufficient time to make enough Portgens for every Peregrine to receive one. He also programmed a home button into each one. With one push of the button, the coordinates for Reader's Island would appear and bring them back. One of the older, retired Peregrines had also been a leather worker made each Peregrine a pouch in which to carry the Portgens. These pouches could be hooked to their belt strap or wherever they wished and would fit snuggly to whatever they were clipped to.

The next morning the activity in the house was almost chaotic with everyone running in different directions, getting breakfast, seeing to last minute laundry needs, speaking with their mentors, and acquiring important mission information. It was ten o'clock in the morning by the time everyone had been fed and packed up and the staff had all the horses saddled, packed, and ready to go.

Prisca and Oz stood in one last embrace, as she looked up at him to speak. "Now, Wendal, you better take care of yourself and return to me. I don't think I could handle losing you again," Prisca said tearfully.

"Don't ya worry 'bout me Priss. If I can spend twelve years alone takin' care a myself, I'm sure I'll make it all right with this motley crew." He smiled as he gestured at the group behind him. His tone softened just a bit as he wiped her tearstained face once more with his thumbs before planting a kiss on her cheek and then hugging her goodbye. "I'll be back, Priss. Don't ya worry 'bout that."

As everyone began mounting their horses, Simon pulled Jason and Seth to the side.

"Now remember your mission, boys," Simon said as confidentially as possible. "And also remember to watch out for the younger and inexperienced ones. As I said before, most have never been in any kind of battle before, much less a demon battle."

"We will, Simon. And we'll be sure to keep our eyes and ears open as well," Seth reassured the older man.

They mounted their horses as the rest of the leaders trotted to the front of the line to join them. All the other mounts filed in behind with some of the more experienced Peregrines spacing out along the line to cover all points. Jason yelled for everyone to follow as his Portgen opened a portal, and they were off to southern Israel in the year 1840 to search for the first piece of armor. Everyone was either a little anxious, nervous, or excited with no one really knowing what to expect. They all knew that they would have to experience some sort of trial or test, and they prayed to God as they went along that He would grant them strength and grace to face whatever trials He chose for them or allowed them to go through.

The Dragoman and staff all stood watching and waving goodbye as each Peregrine passed before them.

"May God keep each and every one of them safe," Simon said as they watched the last of the Peregrines disappear into the portal before it closed.

The End.

If you've enjoyed reading this second book in the Peregrination Series, please help me out by leaving a book review on whatever venue you choose or where you purchased the book. For more information on future titles visit:

www.sgboudreaux.com   or   www.zanchierpublications.com

Book 3

Solomon's copper mines were a vast underground system of tunnels and caverns that ran beneath the desert floor of Timna Valley. These mines were once a buzz of constant activity during the reigns of King David and King Solomon in the tenth and ninth centuries BC. The tunnels were extensive, and Zaccai had no idea how they were going to find anything down in the dark, dusty caves. Not to mention it could take them years to explore every one of the tunnels. The leaders would have to take a look more closely at the information the Dragoman had sent along with them concerning the area and the history of the valley and the copper mines. Perhaps something from the copies of the *Book of Armor* would give them more insight into where to look for the first piece of armor.

The Dragoman did tell them that this journey to find all the pieces of the Armor of God would be extensive. They said it was a journey that would require stamina, patience, and skill and would put them through physical, mental, and emotional trials.

The Peregrines didn't know when they would return to Reader's Island. They had no idea when or where the trials would begin or when the first piece, the Belt of Truth, would be revealed. Then, after finding that piece, they would move on to the next, which according to the *Book of Armor* should be the Breastplate of Righteousness. That is *if* they were to search for the pieces in the order in which they were written in the Bible.

The archive books were just books transcribed by early Dragoman. They were not written by God as the Bible had been. But without the information written in the archive books by all the previous Dragoman, their jobs would be much harder. The books were left as instructions, guides, geographical maps, storm histories, and Peregrine and Dragoman history. However, the recently found, five, unique-looking, and locked books, appeared to be somewhat different. They seemed to be more than just useful recorded history. They appeared to be instructions from a higher power, perhaps from God Himself, but no one really knew the answer to that question.

They would have to wait and see what else the books revealed about certain unanswered questions still plaguing the Dragoman, and if the other two books that they had yet to look through thoroughly held any answers. Then there was the last book, still locked because someone among them had stolen the recently found key. Why? What could that book hold that someone would want to stop them from learning?

Not only would they have to battle trials and temptations, and quite possibly demons as well, while searching for the armor, but they also had to search for a betrayer who obviously was one of their very own.

Zaccai prayed that God would lead them to this person, before another slaughter of God's chosen warriors could take place and mankind was lost forever.

Other Book in the Series

Book 1:   Earth

Book 3: Fire

Book 4: Water

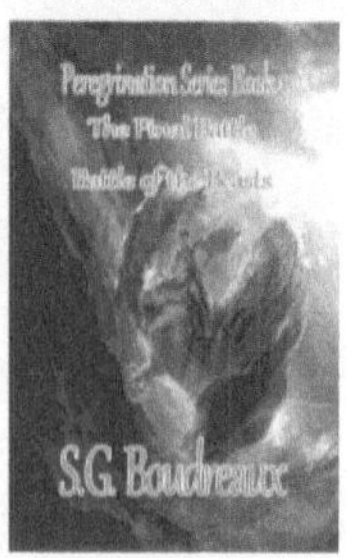

Book 5: The Final Battle; Battle of the Beasts

ABOUT THE AUTHOR

S.G. Boudreaux began writing clean fantasy, fiction, and time-travel in 2017. She felt people needed a clean alternative when reading these genres and believes that what she writes may influence someone else. Because of this, she puts her faith and beliefs into everything she writes. Her love of these genres began with Star Wars when she was young, and her inspiration for clean writing stems from other authors such as C.S Lewis, and J.R.R. Tolkien. She enjoys music, especially playing the drums for church or for special events, writing, creating new creatures for her books, learning new things, gardening, animals, and all things beach related. She and her special needs daughter, youngest of three children, reside in Louisiana.

For more on her life and current events that she is involved in, visit her website at www.sgboudreaux.com or her amazon authors page at amazon.com/author/sgboudreaux

www.ingramcontent.com/pod-product-compliance
Lightning Source LLC
Chambersburg PA
CBHW020721310726
48979CB00004B/1018